Sophie Draper won the Bath Novel Award 2017 with her debut novel *The Stranger in Our Home*. She has also won the Friday Night Live competition at the York Festival of Writing 2017. She lives in Derbyshire, where both *The Stranger in Our Home* and *The House of Secrets* are set, and under the name Sophie Snell she works as a traditional oral storyteller.

www.sophiedraper.co.uk
@sophiedraper9
facebook.com/SophieDraperAuthor

By the same author:

The Stranger in Our Home

THE
HOUSE
OF
SECRETS

SOPHIE DRAPER

avon.

Published by AVON
A division of HarperCollins*Publishers* Ltd
1 London Bridge Street
London SE1 9GF

www.harpercollins.co.uk

This paperback edition 2020

First published as 'Magpie' in Great Britain by HarperCollins*Publishers* 2019

A catalogue copy of this book is available from the British Library.

ISBN: 978-0-00-840339-3

20 21 22 LSC 10 9 8 7 6 5 4 3 2 1

This novel is entirely a work of fiction. The names, characters
and incidents portrayed in it are the work of the author's
imagination. Any resemblance to actual persons, living or dead,
events or localities is entirely coincidental.

Typeset in Minion by Palimpsest Book Production Limited,
Falkirk, Stirlingshire

Printed and bound in the United States of America by LSC Communications

For more information visit: www.harpercollins.co.uk/green

For my boys.

One for sorrow,
Two for joy,
Three for a girl,
Four for a boy,
Five for silver,
Six for gold,
Seven for a secret,
Never to be told.

CHAPTER 1

CLAIRE – BEFORE

There's a dog protesting from one of the cages on the ward. Pain, the animal's in pain. Its cries cut across my thoughts and I turn away from Duncan's consulting room, past Sally on reception and through the doors to the back of the building.

Imogen, the animal care assistant, is already there, doing her rounds. Her body is bent as she checks each animal. She reads the clipboards pegged to every cage and tops up food and water.

'Is it the Great Dane again?' I ask.

She nods, gesturing to the biggest enclosure. It's out of sight by the stockroom and I turn the corner. The dog is on its feet, swaying from side to side, one back leg visibly shorter than the other. It lifts its head, jowls wet with saliva, pressing its cheek against the bars. Large brown eyes roll as it recognises a human face and it howls again, a long two-toned cry, setting off another sequence of barks and whimpers in the room.

I unhook the door, dropping to my knees. The Great Dane hobbles cautiously towards me. It easily matches me for height in this position, pushing against my body. I take the animal's head into my arms.

'Hey, there, big fella, how're you doing?'

I shift my feet, holding one hand to the side of the dog's head, the animal panting. Its eyes are dilated, its tongue hanging out, tasting the very smell of me. The dog tugs away, distrusting even the comfort of my body, yet drawn to me. Its oversized legs are partially splayed, its tail tight and stiff. I run my hands along the underside of its stomach, pausing in the middle before slowly rising up and along the back, approaching one hip. The animal lets out a moan and throws its head like a horse.

'It's okay, sweetheart, I know.'

I press with care, eyes watching the dog closely, pressing just enough to determine the exact spot and no more. The dog moans again and I let my hand drop.

'Imogen.' I raise my voice. 'Can you come and help me here a moment?'

'Coming!'

I hear the clatter of a metal bowl being set on the floor and Imogen appears, slightly out of breath.

'What is it?'

'How long has she been like this?'

'Since I came in this morning.'

I frown. My hand reaches up to turn a page on the clipboard.

'Has she eaten at all?' I nod to the full bowl of dried food pellets.

'She had some of the wet food last night, but none of the dried.'

'But she's drinking?'

The water bowl is full too, I note.

'Claire – I'm not sure . . .' Imogen looks at me uncertainly. Then: 'Yes – I filled it only a few moments ago.'

'Okay. It's happened again – she's dislocated her hip . . .'

'Claire!' It's Duncan, my husband, striding round the corner. He stops in front of us, lifting one hand to his smooth round head. He towers over me as I crouch on the floor and glares at me with barely concealed annoyance.

'Claire. Sally said you were looking for me.'

His voice is clipped and professional. He smiles at Imogen. 'Would you give us a moment?'

She throws me an anxious glance.

'Sure,' she says. 'Lovely to see you, Claire.'

Duncan's arms are toned, his neck bare against his dark blue tunic. His name is embroidered on the front pocket: Duncan Henderson, Clinical Director. He waits until Imogen has gone, then turns on me.

'What are you doing, Claire? I really don't appreciate you coming onto the ward like this. It confuses the hell out of the staff and undermines my authority. We've talked about this before.'

He steps between me and the Great Dane, gently pushing the dog back into its crate.

'Come on, now,' he says to the dog. 'I know, I'm sorry. But you're next, I promise.' He pats the dog.

I feel the heat rising up my neck. The Great Dane moves slowly around in the confined space, claws tangling in the blanket at its feet. Water spills from the bowl. I feel clumsy and embarrassed as Duncan slips the door catch back into position. He turns to me, but I speak before he does.

3

'She's got a dislocated hip and I noticed the femoral head on the x-ray—'

'Have you been going through my notes?' He's openly angry now.

'You left them on the kitchen table,' I say. 'It's the second time this month, isn't it? Dislocation. Manipulation isn't going to work this time, there's a—'

'You need to go, Claire. And leave me to do my job. Why did you come here?'

'I . . .'

I don't know what to say. *I came to say hello?* He's not going to believe that. I thought . . . I don't know what I thought – that there was still a way for us to connect? When we were newly married, we always discussed difficult cases. As I look at his face now, I know he doesn't even remember that, or doesn't want to. And he certainly doesn't want to hear what I have to say about the Great Dane. Well, screw you, Duncan, you can work it out for yourself, then.

'Nothing. I was in town and I was dropping off the notes you left behind.'

I rummage in my bag and produce a folder. He takes it, our fingers not even touching.

But that's a lie. The file is just an excuse. I know there's no point in trying anymore.

I came for a look, to check out the staff. To work out if . . . which one of them, this time, it might be.

CHAPTER 2

CLAIRE – BEFORE

I was never quite sure about this house. It's not a house, it's a barn. A great, vast tomb of a place, all gleaming sleek lines and huge panes of glass. Very beautiful, very impressive, but not a home. Not at first, not to me.

Duncan said I'd get used to it. All that space, the mod cons, the view – that amazing aspect over the valley. It's Derbyshire at its best, lush and verdant with the reservoir glittering at the bottom of the fields. And the privacy. There's not another house for at least a mile in each direction, who wouldn't want that? And even I had to admit, I did appreciate the privacy.

But home to me is smaller. Shoes by the back door, coffee stains on the table, dog hairs on the sofa, knick-knacks, photographs and postcards cluttering the mantelpiece. A proper mantelpiece, not one of those engineered slabs of wood buried in the wall.

If he clears my stuff away, I discreetly put it back. And if

Joe, our son, or Arthur, the dog, leave muddy footprints on the tiles, I cheer. That first scratch on the polished work surface in the kitchen was uniquely satisfying. Always striving for perfection is not much fun.

The front door glides shut with a soft clunk. Duncan has gone to work. I hear the smooth hum of his car and the measured crunch of wheels on gravel. I stretch out the fingers of my hand and roll my shoulders. Then I gather my long hair at the back of my head and twist it into a loose bun. Strands of brown hair fall on either side of my face; I never was much good at grooming.

The wind gusts across the walls of the house and a sweep of rain splatters against the full-height window in the sitting room. I see my own shape reflected back; it makes me look taller, larger than I am, at least that's what I tell myself. Strong. The sky is green, not grey, coloured by the triple-layered tinted glass so that even the view is tainted by Duncan's choice of architecture.

Everything about this place was his choice, not mine.

I turn back to the sink. The deep-set window behind it was the only thing left unsullied by the builders. At my insistence. One last remnant of the building that was before, the old cottage that stood beside the barn. I would have kept it whole, perhaps linked by a glass atrium, but Duncan wanted it gone, to focus on the barn itself, stripped and open to the roof. There's not much sense that this was all once a busy working farm.

As I plunge the mug into the hot water, I see my son, Joe, crossing the lawn from the top field. His head is bent against the weather, his dark hair damp and curling against his neck.

Moments later, the utility room door flies open and dead leaves bluster across the floor. Arthur, our black Labrador, scampers inside. His jaws are slack, drooling with saliva, and he shakes the rain from his coat so that water sprays on to the cupboard doors. He heads for his metal drinking bowl and I hear the sound of his tongue pushing it across the floor.

Joe hops on one foot and then the other, slinging each boot into the corner by the ironing board.

'For heaven's sake, Joe, take some care!'

He ignores me. He doesn't even look up as his awkward frame passes into the kitchen.

'Where have you been?'

It's a stupid question, I know the answer. It's almost eight o'clock in the morning and he's been out all night. Not clubbing or drinking like most teenagers – I should be so lucky – but out there, in the fields.

Joe doesn't reply and I see that 'thing' he always takes with him, the metal detector. He's left it against the wall, looping the headphones and cable over the handle. He crosses the kitchen to find the biscuit tin, fishing out a handful of digestives. He shoves one in his mouth and the rest stick out from between his fingers like the roof of the Sydney Opera House.

'Joe!'

I raise my voice, trying to break into his thoughts, but he simply gestures to his full mouth with his biscuit knuckle-duster and leaves the room. I swear I love my son very much, but his lack of eye contact cuts right through me sometimes, even now after all these years.

Today, he seems more than usually distracted.

He takes the stairs two at a time. A door bangs and the music starts. Thump, thump. Rude and raucous and irreverent. Very satisfying. The volume blasts up a notch, a heavy tune-less beat that reverberates through the ceiling. There's the surge of hot water from the shower in the bathroom. The sound carries across the open roof spaces in the barn. You can hear everything, despite the distance. I let it wash over me. It's the silence of the house that gets to me, when he isn't here. Like a cathedral with no worshippers, a grand theatrical production that no one comes to watch. But when he is here, the noise of him annoys me, too. Eventually. There's no pleasing me. My mouth twists into a smile.

At least he's looking after himself. Not like before.

I dry my hands, leaving the towel dumped untidily on the kitchen island. I pour hot water from the kettle into a new mug. My fingers reach around to comfort myself and I breathe in the warm steam. The familiar smell of coffee tickles my throat. Familiar is good: a hot drink, a slab of bread thick with butter. It grounds me.

At least this time my son has come home.

'There was this man ten years ago who discovered a hoard in Somerset.'

I'm prepping tea and Joe is sat at the kitchen island with a long glass of milk in his hand. He fidgets on his seat, as if he can't stop himself from moving.

'It was in a field next to an old Roman road. He'd found a couple of coins and ended up discovering a clay pot of some kind, sunk into the ground. It was crammed full of coins – can you imagine that?'

He doesn't wait for me to answer.

'And so heavy you couldn't possibly lift the whole thing out. The sides of the pot were broken and he had to leave it in place, carefully removing the coins under cover of night. He did that so that no one else knew what he'd found.'

I have an image in my head of an old man in his cardigan pulling out green coins with his bare fingers by the light of the moon. I have to smile.

'Layer by layer, coin by coin, over several nights, until the whole thing was extracted. He didn't report the find till after that. There were more than fifty thousand coins in total!'

Joe loves telling me these stories, when he finds his voice. It's his dream, finding a hoard. When Duncan's not around he talks about it endlessly, the different coin types, how to date them, how to clean them, the different patterns on each side.

'The rules are complicated,' he says. 'And the coroner has to be told.'

Joe's told me this so many times. I'd always thought coroners only dealt with the dead, but they deal with treasure too, apparently.

'They have to estimate the level of precious metal content – that's important when it comes to what happens next and how much the find is worth . . . Mum, are you listening?'

'Course I am, Joe. You were telling me about the coroner.'

'No, I was telling you about metal content.'

He flashes a look of frustration at me. Then he's off again, detailing different measurements, his hands animated, his body leaning over the kitchen island, gulping down his milk in between long, rambling fact-filled sentences.

It's a boy thing, I tell myself, all that data and statistics, the kind of information overload that makes me want to walk away but sets Joe on fire. All I can think is, at least he's doing something constructive, active, and he's communicating with me. I feel the guilt of my disinterest wash over me. It's nice to see him on fire.

'Come on, Joe, that's enough for now, tea's ready. If you drink too much of that milk you won't be hungry. Help me take this through to the table.'

I shouldn't begrudge him the milk. As a teenager, he guzzles the stuff. Listen to me, I sound so much like the mother that I am. Joe goes to the fridge for more milk and I text Duncan upstairs to say that tea is ready.

We eat in silence. Duncan pushes the pasta into neat piles before scooping it into his mouth and Joe shovels it like a farmhand clearing out the stables. I glance between the two of them, the one with too little hair, the other with too much, and then Duncan's mobile beeps.

His fingers tap twice and inch towards the phone, then he pulls back.

It beeps again. He looks at me. I refuse to look at him and Joe keeps on eating. After a few minutes, I push my plate away, all pretence at hunger gone.

Then the stupid thing beeps again.

'Can't you switch it off?' I say.

My voice is quiet but sharp and the pulse at my neck is racing. Duncan's eyes meet mine then slide away. He carries on eating as if I haven't spoken.

Lo and behold, the phone beeps again. I feel my cheeks suck in and taste the blood on my tongue. I reach for his phone and he grabs it just in time.

'No phones at the table, we said. Remember?' I let my voice twist into a sneer.

'I'm on call,' he says.

'Like hell.'

Joe stops in mid-forkful.

'It's only work, Claire. You know that.' Duncan's tone is smooth and appeasing.

I hate him when he's like this. As if I'm a child, playing up, or a fool, easily deluded.

'No, it's not,' I say. 'We both know it's not.'

'That's nonsense, Claire, you're being paranoid.'

He arranges another pile of pasta.

'Oh, really?'

Joe is watching us both, eyes wide and unblinking. It reminds me of when he was little, still trying to make sense of the world. Like when we shared a bedtime story, his gaze glued to me as I read, not the book. He'd follow the cadence of each word on my face. I drop my eyes, curling my fingers and breathing long and slow, trying hard to keep it in. But my eyes are drawn back to the phone and then Duncan. He's actually smiling, like it's a game.

'How can you sit there and pretend?' I say. 'Day in, day out. How can you do this?'

He doesn't answer. His fingers tap again and he stands. He picks up his plate and turns round, his back stiff and unyielding. He moves into the kitchen. I hear the click of the automatic bin and the clunk of the dishwasher. A few minutes later there's the swoosh of the front door. He's gone. And Joe goes back to eating.

I think of the papers hidden in the folds of the magazine by my bed. The appointment I've made for tomorrow. Duncan thinks that nothing's changed. That I'll stay, like I always have. But our son is eighteen now; he left school months ago. He's all grown up, a legally independent, responsible adult.

And I'm the one in control here, not Duncan.

CHAPTER 3

DUNCAN – SIX WEEKS AFTER

Duncan's gloved hands were stained with blood. The dog's skin was peeled back, revealing the bloodied bone and yellow subcutaneous fat. The radio played softly in the background and the monitors beeped with a reassuring regularity as he dabbed at the opening with a swab.

There were three of them: Duncan and Paula, the newest vet at the practice, and Frances, the senior nurse. Their legs and hips were pressed against the operating table and the light blazed a harsh white over their heads, picking up a glint of red hair from beneath Paula's surgical cap.

'Okay,' said Duncan. 'Let's get this little chap put together again.'

He tugged gently on the flaps of skin, pulling them towards each other. It was a struggle; the dog was barely a year old and the metal pins holding the leg bones left little space for the original skin to meet. Duncan shifted the skin a little higher.

'Frances – can you hold it there?'

She took the clamps into her hands.

'Left a bit. Hold it . . . wait . . .'

Duncan pursed his lips and pulled again, reaching in with a suture needle, feeding the thread between his gloved fingers to make the first stitch.

'Excellent,' he said. 'And another. Paula, can you clean around here?'

They worked together in silence. Ten minutes later, the opening had been closed. Frances gave a relieved smile and Duncan took a step back.

'That's it. Thank you, both. I'm glad to see that one done.'

'She's looking good,' Frances replied. 'You should go and ring the owner. You've earned that. We'll finish off and resuscitate. I'll see this one to the ward.'

Frances smiled again. She was older than Duncan, her darker skin and years of experience warming her features, the lines around her eyes creasing above her mask.

Duncan pulled the gloves from his hands, dropping them into the refuse bucket. He tugged the mask from his face and left the room, pushing the door with his shoulder and reaching up to rub his neck. Three hours on one dog – the smaller animals were often the most difficult. But it had been a success. He headed for his consulting room to make the call.

'Duncan!'

It was Sally on reception. Her usually straight blonde hair was falling unkempt about her shoulders. A collection of dirty coffee mugs stood by the phone and the printer was spewing out blank sheets of paper. As ever, the room was busy with people and animals. Duncan nodded briskly at the man who lifted one hand in greeting.

'Yes?' Duncan responded to Sally.

'Call for you – urgent, they said. I'll put it through.'

He mouthed a question and Sally shrugged her shoulders. Her lips said *police*. He glared at her and she jabbed one finger towards his consulting room.

'Okay,' he said, biting down his emotions.

'Duncan Henderson, here.'

He sank into his chair and swung round to face the window.

'Duncan, it's Martin. Very sorry to disturb you at work. I'm afraid I have to ask you to come back to your house.'

One phone call, that's all it took to hijack all those appointments. Duncan turned his car up the drive to his house. The constant slash of rain against the windscreen had left him with a painful furrow of concentration on his forehead and a thick spray of black mud on the paintwork of his car. The vehicle slowed on the deep gravel, cruising between the pink cherry trees that lined the drive. Spring had been interrupted by a blast of cold, stormy weather, and wet leaves and translucent blossom clung like damp butterflies to the big sheet window. The barn glowed a peachy flushed red.

Duncan felt his heart contract, his jaw tighten. There were cars and vans slewed every which way they could, blocking his usual turning circle. Beyond the perimeter fencing, where the fields tipped towards the silver bowl of the reservoir, already a double line of blue-and-white plastic tape rippled down the slope.

He squeezed his car into a gap, in the corner where Claire used to park. He got out. The grumbling blast of a generator assailed his ears. A pair of uniformed officers stood by the top gate, stiff and upright like tin soldiers. By the garage, a tent had been pitched up, and in the distance, at the bottom, were more tents, slick with wet. Grey sheets of rain blustered across the valley and figures in white hooded overalls ran across the scrub. The whole scene had the surreal air of an alien landing site.

Duncan approached his front door.

'Excuse me, sir. Can I see some ID?' An officer appeared at his shoulder.

Duncan swung round to face him.

'I live here,' he snapped.

'Even so, if you don't mind.'

Duncan scowled and fished out his driving licence. There was an awkward pause as the officer scanned the photograph.

'Mr Henderson, thank you. The boss said to have a word with you as soon as you arrived.' The man gestured towards the first tent. 'If you don't mind.'

The boss. DCI Martin White. They'd known each other since their first day at school.

'This way, please, sir.'

The tent opening thrashed in the wind. Inside a huddle of officers stood around a table with several computers, and their papers scattered upwards as the flap fell back into place.

'Duncan?'

A man looked up, his hands holding down the papers. He wore a green waxed jacket, his grey suit loosely buttoned underneath. His hair was cut close to his head, black peppered with white, and a broad platinum wedding ring glinted from the back of his hand.

'Martin.'

Duncan wiped the rain from his forehead. The police team

15

wasn't huge for the area, it was inevitable that Martin would be in charge. Duncan had a brief image of Martin standing by his side in the registry office at Claire and Duncan's wedding, leaning forwards in his shoes, discreetly scanning the room like some kind of security officer.

'Thank you for coming back,' said Martin. Their eyes met. 'I expect this is a shock.'

Duncan didn't reply and Martin dipped his head in acknowledgement.

'I'm sorry to be here in these circumstances. And I apologise for the disruption. But I'm sure you understand why this is necessary.'

Duncan's eyes were drawn to the table. There was a shallow crate covered in a cloth.

He felt his body sway, unaccountably off balance. He clenched his hands and pushed them down his side, forcing himself to stay upright.

'Cup of tea, sir?' A younger man stepped forwards, offering Duncan a mug.

'Do you think I want a fucking cup of tea?' Duncan turned on the man, eyes flaring.

A blue light flickered from one of the computer screens and the wind sucked at the canvas over their heads. Silence had fallen on the tent.

'I'm sorry. I . . .' Duncan pushed his hand across his head, rubbing the bare skin, then smoothing down to the closely cropped hair at the back of his neck. His jaw moved and his eyes closed momentarily.

'It's alright, Duncan.' Martin followed his friend's gaze. He gestured to a chair. 'Everyone here understands. Why don't we sit down?'

Duncan shook his head. He stood still, his arms held stiffly by his side.

'No,' he said. 'I don't want . . .' Duncan's breath heaved in and out and his eyes were pulled once again to that crate.

Martin took a step closer.

'Duncan, look at me. It's okay. Look at me!'

Duncan lifted his eyes to Martin. It seemed to him there were just the two of them then, in that tent, all sense of the outside, the weather, the people, the cars on his drive, banished to the edges of his mind.

Then he took control of himself, responding to Martin's unspoken signal.

'What exactly have you found?' He pushed the words out between his lips.

'Human remains. A body has been found by the shore at the bottom of your land.'

Martin paused, as if unwilling to broach what came next.

'What kind of body?' Duncan said.

There was another pause.

'Come on, man, you can't not tell me!'

'We're not sure yet. I'm sorry, Duncan, that's all I can tell you right now.'

Duncan made himself move, reaching out one hand to clutch the table, forcing himself to stay focused.

'I don't understand . . . I . . .' His body swayed.

'Duncan, are you alright?'

Martin took a step forwards.

'*Duncan*—'

CHAPTER 4

CLAIRE – BEFORE

'Hey, Becky. How are you this morning?'

I can hear a voice in the background, the clunk of crockery and a tray being set down on a table.

'Are you up to a visitor around twelve?' I ask.

'Yes, please,' says Becky.

She sounds happy. One of the things I've always loved about Becky is her cheeriness. Upbeat and optimistic, despite her circumstances.

'Great. I'm in town anyway this morning to do some jobs. I'll bring us some lunch, shall I? Fish from the chippie sound okay?'

'Sounds perfect,' she says. 'It'll just be me. See you then.'

The phone clicks and she's gone.

Town is busy. It's market day and the car park on the small square has been taken over by stalls and vans. Every street is filled with parked cars and the cobbles judder under my wheels then disappear as I turn into the customer car park of the veterinary surgery. I ease the car into a spot furthest away from the front door. One of the advantages of being the boss's wife is I get to park for free whenever I need to. Through the glass doors I can see the reception desk, the familiar head of Sally bent over the screen. I walk out of the car park, dodging the bus shelter to head towards the main precinct and the estate agents behind the town hall.

'Hi,' I say to the young man leaning back on his chair behind the desk nearest to the door. 'I have an appointment. Claire Henderson.'

My head swings over my shoulder, scanning the street outside. I will the man to speed up and he senses my agitation.

'Sure. Hold on a minute,' he says.

He tips forwards and pushes away, standing up to disappear into a conference room. When he comes back, I think how he doesn't look much older than my Joe, a narrow blue tie swinging against his crisp white shirt. Except these days you'd never catch Joe in a white shirt, let alone a tie.

'This way,' he says.

I move too fast into the conference room.

'Hello, there. Do sit down.'

This agent is older than the lad by the front door. Hungry-looking, like one of those midsized birds of prey hovering over a small animal by the roadside. He's assessing me.

'Mrs Henderson, how are you?' He doesn't stand up but reaches out a cold hand.

It's one of those questions you're not supposed to answer. I contemplate actually telling him. *Do you really want to know?* says the voice in my head.

'I think I've found the perfect place for you,' he says. 'Not too far, like you asked. Though perhaps a little closer than you wanted, but there's not a lot out there on the market at the moment. It's near the reservoir with a bit of character and a fantastic view.'

He pulls out a one-page leaflet with a small flourish, pushing it under my nose. My eyes scan the paper and I have a brief impression of a rambling old cottage with a defunct hanging basket blocking the back door and a roof that sags in the middle. Character – that's one way of putting it. Agent-speak for a house that's small and run-down and probably expensive to heat. He taps on the rent.

'It's four hundred pounds a month.'

That is cheap for round here. The location is doable. It's on the other side of the dam, so there would be a wall of concrete between me and Duncan. *How appropriate*, I think. I glance up at the agent's face.

'Can I view it?'

'Of course you can.' He smiles. 'Let me check the diary.'

He snaps back to his PC, scrolling down the screen.

'How about on Thursday, eleven am? My colleague, John Hardcastle, will show you around.'

I nod. He starts to type.

'Can you remind me of your current address, Mrs Henderson?'

'Brereton Barn, Hob Lane.'

'Ah! Yes, of course, lovely spot.'

He doesn't ask why I'm looking for a place to rent. Or why I don't want to buy. And he doesn't ask about my financial circumstances. He knows of my husband, the town supervet, with his shiny new practice and growing reputation, living in one of the poshest houses in the district. Why else would his wife be searching for a new home? Instead, the agent looks me briefly up and down, as if speculating if Duncan knows yet. Everyone knows everything about your business in this town. It won't be long before the gossip spreads.

Which means, now I've started this, I'm already running out of time.

'Ooh, that smells amazing!'

Becky pokes her face into the greasy papers and takes a good long whiff. Her short hair is fluffed up and she gives me one of her big open smiles, freckles creasing on her cheeks. I've always envied her that smile – it lights up the room. Duncan has the same smile, when he chooses to use it, it's one of the things I loved about him when we first met, but that's where their sibling likeness stops.

'Sinful, but who cares!' she says. She grins again and places the package on the table.

'Where's Alex?' I ask, referring to her son.

Becky swings back to the cupboard to pluck out a cheap carton of salt and some vinegar.

'He's at the day care centre. Dropped him off earlier. We've got a couple of hours.' She turns back with a plate in each hand and slides onto a chair. 'Grab us some cutlery, will you?'

I rummage in the drawer behind me and Becky tips the food onto our plates. There's a moment of silence as we both dive in with the same hungry enthusiasm as Arthur after a long walk.

'Mmm, this is good. So . . .' Becky catches my eye. 'How was your appointment?'

Appointment? I feel a prickle of alarm; I hadn't told her I

had an appointment. I haven't told her anything yet. How can I? She's Duncan's sister for all she's my best friend and I don't know where to begin to explain that I'm about to leave her brother. Besides, I need to finalise things and tell Joe before I tell anyone else. Let alone Duncan. I owe him that at least.

'It was okay.' I force myself to relax. Becky's just interpreting the 'jobs' I mentioned on the phone. 'Boring stuff with the bank.' I scatter salt on my chips. 'I had to sign accounts and stuff, what with technically being a director of the business.'

How easily the lie slips from my tongue. Not that my story means very much. Yes, I'm listed as a director of the surgery, but Duncan's always been fiercely protective of his business. He doesn't let me see anything.

'You should make him let you work there. Alongside him as a partner.'

'Oh, God, no. I mean, I like the medical stuff, and the research especially, but the business side of things? We'd only argue. We have quite different ideas about how to manage things. No, I could never work alongside him. Besides, it's been such a long time since I was in the profession . . .'

'Come on, Claire. Joe's eighteen now. You'd pick it up again. I know you, you've kept up to date with all the science and I bet you've been hankering to go back to work for years. And you're darn clever, every bit as much as Duncan. I know you've had Joe to deal with, but he's settling down a bit, isn't he? Not like before.'

Not like before. All those years of Joe screaming at the teachers. Joe digging his heels in and refusing to go to school. Joe disappearing for days on end and driving me frantic. I bite my lip. The last time Joe went missing for over a week, it was just before his A-level exam results. Perfect timing. But who am I to complain about my son? Becky has far more to deal with than I. She puts me to shame. My son is hale and hearty. Her son, Alex, is confined to a wheelchair, profoundly physically disabled.

'It's true,' I say. 'I'd like to go back to work. I have thought about it, but I'm not sure.'

It's half a truth, isn't it? I have every intention of going back to work. I'm going to have to, we'll need the money, Joe and I. But not with Duncan, and probably not even here in Belston. Derby, perhaps – or further afield, if I have to go that far to find the right thing.

Whether or not Joe will stomach it. After.

CHAPTER 5

CLAIRE – AFTER

The horse moves with a fast, rhythmic pace, its broad back swaying beneath its rider's legs. I watch them pass the giant shrubs of rhododendron that block out the light. Their buds are almost pink and the leaves are almost black, gleaming in the cold, steady rain.

They ride on, beyond the gardens. Into the woods. The mist hangs low over the canopy of trees, lingering with the reluctance of the newly deceased floating over a still warm bed.

The reservoir is visible now. Not far. I hear the water lapping and the ducks calling to each other in the reeds. A pheasant hurtles from the banks, a flash of red, shrieking, guttering, the sound bouncing along the shore like stones skipping across the water.

The young man's head scrapes across the ground, the weight of it dragging on his neck. I can almost feel the pain that must be spreading across his body, his shoulder blades and back.

Each thump and drag of his head erupting like fireworks behind his eyes. I feel it as he feels it, as the rider slows the horse to a walk. The lad tries to lift his head, only for it to fall. His body lurches into movement as the horse moves on, pulling upon the rope.

He is like a stick floating on a stream, stones and earth, the lumps in the ground forcing his skull up and down, buffeting him this way and that. Black mud is smeared on his face and his wet clothes cling to his body, sucked in against his frame so that the bones are clearly visible. I see him try to lift one arm – his arms are free, but not his legs. They are tied. The rope red around his bare ankles. The rider shifts his grip, nudging the horse with the heels of his boots again, urging her to move faster along the path beside the reservoir.

The view opens up. The full expanse of water is revealed. A glint of metal pierces the surface not far from the shore. The slender shape is half tipped, draped with soft black weed, as if poised between two realms. It hasn't appeared for a hundred years, not since the summer of 1918. The last year of the Great War. One cross in a field of crosses, marking the growing dead. That's what they'd said in the village then, as the women grieved for their men.

The cross is taller than before. A spindle, sharp enough to prick a finger.

My gaze returns to the boy. I see the debris brushing against his cheek, how the clagging scent of the forest makes him want to retch. He tries to cough but the angle is all wrong. His chest must be burning from the effort to breathe, his tongue swollen, his airways blocked, his flesh bloated like rehydrated seaweed. They're right on the shore, riding over stony mud, and it drags against his flesh. The speed at which they're moving and the

grogginess of his brain means that all he can do is flap his arms
uselessly like a drunken swimmer until they fall back above his
head and the ground beats and pounds his skull and he's near
faint with the pain of it.

I am consumed by nausea. I feel it as he feels it, everything
blackness and confusion. His brain – my brain – stuck inside
my skull like the tiny building in a glass globe. Snowflakes, I see
thousands of snowflakes fluttering into life, my head fixed but
everything else loose and drifting.

The horse's hooves sink into the mud. Water swirls about the
rider's boots and the boy floats. The rider tugs on the rope and
his hair blows across his face and the metal cross shines, dazzling
his eyes as he waits for the geese to pass, for the mist to draw
breath. For the spire to sink from sight and the sun to rise unseen
and the breeze and the birds to settle.

There's a voice in my head. 'It shouldn't have been like this,'
it says. 'If only the boy had accepted his fate and stayed upon
the island. They wouldn't have had to do this.'

The rain has turned to snow, the snow has turned to hail
and stones of ice pitch down against the water. The rider spurs
his horse again and again, and she plunges forwards into the
lake, deeper. As their bodies begin to disappear, the rider's face
turns back towards the shore. His lips move and I hear his voice,
even though he does not speak.

'Hasn't it always been like this, Claire? Especially with the
young ones.'

Our eyes meet.

'They just don't want to die.'

I let out a soft moan and my head rolls to one side. The
mattress heaves beneath my body and beads of damp trickle

down my skin. The air in the room sweeps cool across my face and I slowly open my eyes, blinking once.

Then I remember.

Joe, my son, has gone.

CHAPTER 6

CLAIRE – BEFORE

I've met the agent, Hardcastle, at a gate marked *Private*. He's standing by his car, waiting for me. A man in his later years, short and round, he wears a loud pin-striped suit and he looks like he doesn't quite belong, here, in rural Derbyshire.

I press the button to lower the window. He leans down to speak to me.

'Mrs Henderson. Delighted to meet you.' His voice has the strangled tones of an independent education. 'Oh, you don't need to worry about that,' he adds.

He dismisses the weatherworn sign with one hand. Rust obscures the top half of each letter and it swings in the wind, back and forth, with the inevitable regularity of a metronome.

I follow Hardcastle's Mercedes in my functional estate. We could have afforded better, but I like my car; I don't have to worry about every scratch, unlike Duncan, obsessing about his smart Lexus SUV. He has the more reliable vehicle, since he has to go in and out in all weathers to get to work. Hardcastle and I drive one behind the other, bumping along the road parallel to the edge of the reservoir until we turn up into the old village.

I know the village well. I know the whole valley. I've lived in the area for so many years. On my right is the dilapidated farmhouse skirted by a straggle of barns. On my left, a sequence of run-down cottages. Some of them face each other like partners in a dance, each house wearing its abandonment with an air of genteel humility – lichen-dusted walls, plants peeping from the gutters, window frames faded and stripped by the sun. The windows all have the same delicate white leaded inserts and the doors, the same peeling blue paint. Even the brickwork is all a matching shade of Georgian herringbone red, warm and welcoming but for its neglect. Gorgeous in the crisp morning sunlight.

It should have lifted my spirits, all this. The evident decay of the village simply adds to its charm. And yet there is no sign of life. Never has been. No washing on the line, no pot plants in the windows. Not even a bowl of water for a cat or a dog. Most houses in the country at least have a cat to keep down the rodents.

I see a ramshackle pair of iron gates with a drive leading into the shadows. There are no cars, not one by a single house, except for us, of course. I'm not sure I like it. The whole village is resolutely derelict. I've avoided it before. I hadn't realised the property would be so close to *here*. It's on the far side of the reservoir away from the Barn.

We pass the last house and turn off again, climbing the hill. Hardcastle takes a left, off the lane onto a dead-end track where the tarmac has melted in the heat of last year's summer. I follow and the grass verge is so overgrown you can't see past each bend. The trees and hedges grow so tall and dense that the fields above are hidden. Daylight has morphed into dark shadows, bathing the track with the shifting patterns of moving branches, and I jam on the brakes as a squirrel bounds across the lane right in front of me. I have one of those unsettling moments of déjà vu, like I've done this before. But I don't think I've been up this way, why would I? *That's good then*, I think.

Then we're there, at last. The cottage.

I feel my heart skip a beat. It's a wreck. I expected it to be, but I still love it.

To be fair, they did warn me of the state of it: *In need of some development. Landlord happy for tenant to make the place their own.* Translate that as damp and cold from years of neglect and in need of total renovation. If not tearing down and starting all over again. Not that that's an option.

It must have been standing empty for several years.

The building sits sideways from the track, with red bricks and white painted windows like all the other houses in the valley. It wears its slouch like a tired old man. I cast my eyes down the slope. You can see the reservoir in the distance, exactly like they'd said. My heart gives another leap. Not too close, but close enough.

I'd promised myself it had to be something located near the Barn, ish, painful though that is. I don't want Joe to have any excuse to refuse to come with me. He won't give up his metal detecting and I won't take him too far from his father, despite all the conflict. I want to reassure him about that. They still need to see each other and I won't have the money for expensive train and bus fares. Besides, there are so many secluded corners in this valley, old farm buildings and shepherd huts slowly degrading beneath the weight of their own walls, I think it might just work hiding from Duncan in plain sight. I have faith in Joe, he won't let on if I ask him not to. If I need to. I suck my bottom lip between my teeth.

I park my car beside the estate agent's and get out. As I follow him up the short, overgrown path, he reminds me of the rent. I lift my head and he smiles at me with the wide-eyed confidence of a salesman who knows he's already got the deal. We come to a stop and he looks away, restless, like now we're here, he's already thinking of the next appointment.

'Why are they renting and not selling?' I ask.

Not that I can afford to buy until the divorce comes through. This is only temporary, I tell myself.

'It's part of an old estate. The family aren't prepared to sell. They don't want to break up the estate.'

I nod. I know about the family. Everybody does. There are a few stories about them, none of them particularly salutary, mostly around unreasonable rules and wilful neglect.

The agent gestures to the view beyond the cottage, over the fields and down the hill. He launches into his spiel.

'Lovely, isn't it? The whole valley is subject to a ninety-year-long restrictive covenant, so nothing's been built, not even a shed, since the Second World War. People pay over a million for those few houses further up the hills . . .'

His voice trails away. He knows I must be aware of this. He'll have seen my name and address on the contact form. Wife of, mother of, Mrs *Henderson* – is that all I am to other people? Even in this day and age, defined by my relationship to men. That's what you get if you choose to be a full-time mother. Certainly, in this part of the county. Though *choose* isn't quite how I'd put it.

Hardcastle steps ahead of me and unlocks the back door, shoving it hard to get it to open. It grinds in a painful way due to the loose stones caught under the bottom of the door.

'You'll be hard-pressed to find anything prettier in all of Derbyshire.'

I look up – he's right, the cottage is very pretty, in a down-at-heel, scruffy kind of way. Shabby chic, that's how I imagine it could be, picturing it with whimsical fairy lights and vintage candles. But the view down to the reservoir still pulls my eyes. A thin trail of mist slithers out low across the surface and a large bird breaks through. Another and another, a line of geese rising up. Beating wings, open beaks, their gulping cries breaking the peace of the countryside. Their wings pull with a steady rhythm as the mist parts and coils out of place, and the yellow light from a weak sun dances briefly across the water.

The agent smooths his hands down his tie – silk, so much classier than the young man who greeted me at the office. That super-confident smile of his is making my stomach curl.

'It's a project, like I said.' He croons like a jazz singer. 'It means you've got the freedom to decorate exactly as you please. The view is particularly striking from the master bedroom.'

Master bedroom. As if. Judging from the floor plan on the details there's barely enough space for one double bed and a small cabinet. I contemplate the flaking wooden windows. There's a second bedroom under the eaves. I might have to take that one, given how tall Joe is. A 'doer-upper', cloistered in a long-forgotten valley, the lush slopes the select preserve of one family, a couple of farmers and a handful of rich, obsolete businessmen.

I squeeze past the buddleia bush leaning out across the doorway and duck underneath a hanging basket that trails dead leaves over my head. I eye the drunken shape of the roof, its missing tiles and the grime-encrusted, cracked panes of glass in the door. As I step inside, I see peeling wallpaper and a mustard-yellow 1950s kitchen. This place, I realise, hasn't been touched for decades. I feel my excitement bubble.

I move into the room and then I spot the ancient red enamelled range. It's been pushed into an old inglenook fireplace with a blackened beam above, pitted and scorched with age. I run my fingers over the grooves in the wood, peering more closely. There are markings that seem familiar, circles within circles and letters too, a *W* and *AM*, carved with a crisp precision that have nothing to do with the natural cracks from the heat. I feel myself falling even deeper in love.

'What are these?' I say, fingering the marks.

I know the answer, but it's something to say. The agent leans forwards.

'Oh, those are witches' marks, carvings from long ago, probably from when the house was first built. People did that stuff then to ward off evil spirits. It's quite common in this part of the county. So you'll be quite safe here.'

He grins in a rather wolfish way for an older man. *Creep*, I think. Then he turns towards the back door, pulling out his mobile phone.

'I'll let you look around on your own.'

He's already lost interest, swiping at the screen.

I scan the ceiling. The brochure hadn't mentioned that the roof leaked or that there was no central heating. I can see pipes running from the side of the range to the sink, then along the wall again and up into the corner through the ceiling. I'm guessing the fire heats the hot water. I daydream of waking early in the morning, heading down the stairs in the freezing cold to stoke the ashes from the night before, piling on the logs to relight the fire in the range and generate some heat. I could put an armchair right in front of it, with that old rag rug Duncan thought I'd thrown away. It would be perfect there under my feet. Flagstones, I see proper giant slabs of flagstone. I've always loved the idea of having those.

I wonder if I might even be able to buy the place if and when the family decide to let it go and my divorce comes through.

I feel my anticipation grow. A new routine to take over from the old routines of my life as it was before. I've been with Duncan for so long, ever since we were students together at the veterinary school in Nottingham. It's hard to conceive of a life on my own.

Though, not quite on my own.

Joe has to come with me. I can't go without Joe.

And Arthur, of course.

It'll be Duncan left on his own.

CHAPTER 7

CLAIRE – AFTER

I wake. The bedroom is deathly quiet. The kind of silence that plucks the air from your lungs, eyes wide open listening for a creak in the walls, the flutter of birds in the trees, the switch of illicit shoes climbing the stairs.

It's dark, the air cold upon my skin. I lie on the bed frozen to the mattress, legs bent, one arm under my head, eyelashes brushing against the pillow. I listen, hardly realising that I'm holding my breath until I let it go. My ribs move and I force myself to wriggle my fingers and pull one leg free from under the covers.

I have woken too early, too tense, the nightmare still filling my head. Fear pumps through my veins like a drug. It's as if the bed, the whole room will implode, swallowing me up, dragging me down into a narrow chimney of thick stone and earth, falling, falling, scrabbling for roots and clumps of soil but unable to grab hold, water gushing through the gaps. I am Alice in her Wonderland, too big for the space, too small to fight back, too disbelieving of my fate, as I'm sucked down into a vortex of my own making.

I gasp and sit up, pulling myself out but into yet another new nightmare.

Joe?

I'm panting, dragging great lungfuls of air into my chest. I reach for the bedside lamp, pick up the clock and cast my eyes around the room. I see the spill of daylight growing through the gap in the curtains. For a moment it all seems strange, an alien place I've never seen before. The clock has a new face, the curtains a different pattern. Even the fragile dawn is a strange colour, sharper, cleaner, more luminescent than before.

I exhale and place the clock back on its table. I let the brightness bring me slowly back to life. That's when the memory taunts me. The memory of my son.

I remember the sweaty, musky scent of him that clings to his unwashed clothes, the way his hair falls in lush waves across his cheeks. I hear his music, the thudding beat asserting his presence in the Barn. I smell the cold air on his coat, the dead leaves under his feet, the ice upon his skin. And something else – a damp, earthy, rotting kind of smell, like mushrooms spawning in the dirt.

I am awake. I must let it go, whatever it is that still pulls me to that dream. I will myself not to think of Joe like that. Instead, I think of the scent of him when he was newborn. That sweet Joe smell, my Joe – no one else's Joe – nestled in the crook of my arm. His fingernails are soft and peeling at their tips, his knees folded to his chest. His skin is pink and white and blue, the strands of black hair on his skull slick with the soft grease of birthing. That smell.

I squeeze my eyes shut and push the memories away. Are they memories or dreams? I'm not sure. I have a fierce headache that won't go away. They told me I will have to get used to it, that it's to be expected after what's happened. But as I lie here, I can't even remember who said that or where it was. Only that he's gone. My Joe.

He didn't come with me.

I open my eyes, listening for his footsteps just in case.

I betrayed him. I left him behind. It overwhelms me, how I could do that. I can't let myself think about it, my head hurts trying.

But now I hear something. There *are* footsteps, after all. I'm sure it must be him. I've been texting him all this time, making sure he knows where to go. At last, he's come home! To our new home. The cottage. I hear a steady, cautious creak upon the stairs. My bedroom door swings open and a shadow reaches out across the floor.

It's Arthur. The dog. His black head is up, sniffing the air. He pauses as if to check that it's okay to come in.

He moves again, his three good legs bearing the bulk of his weight as he limps uncertainly towards my bed.

CHAPTER 8

DUNCAN – AFTER

A hand lightly touched his shoulder. Duncan started and the hot coffee burnt his fingers. It was Martin, his face grey and strained, the elasticated plastic hood of his forensic suit pulled down from his head.

'I'm sorry,' said Martin. 'I didn't mean to make you jump, but you didn't answer the front doorbell.'

'I . . . It's okay, what did you want?'

'I wanted to see how you are.' Martin gestured through the window.

Down by the water, someone had drawn back the door of the main tent. Even at this distance, in the fading light, Duncan could see a glimpse of bare earth, cut away into different layers and trenches. It was a pitted labyrinth of mud and water, flags and poles numbered and labelled to match the records in the control tent.

'Thank you for your patience with all this, especially in the circumstances.'

Especially in the circumstances. As if Duncan had any choice other than to tolerate the noise and disruption, the complete invasion of his privacy. In a bizarre way, he was almost grateful for that. The Barn felt empty without his family in it. His eyes slid back to the window, to the scene at the bottom of the field laid out like the trenches of the Somme. He nodded, only half aware of what he was doing.

'Have you eaten?' Martin said.

Duncan swung back to his friend's face. With the hood down, he could see Martin's damp wiry hair, speckled white at the temples, and his eyes, sharp and observant. Even with his obvious fatigue, Martin had the edginess of intellect and experience. Duncan had always respected that, but it also made him wary.

'No,' Duncan replied, his stomach rumbling.

Martin produced a couple of plump brown paper bags.

'From the mess van,' he said, nodding to the white van outside, with a generator of its own and a stench of fried chips. 'They do a mean bacon cob.'

Already, Martin was pulling back the flaps of brown paper, tearing open a catering sachet of brown sauce and squeezing it over his food.

Bacon – there was something so vibrant about bacon. The smell of it, the taste of it, the sizzling as it cooks. Claire had been vegetarian. Duncan, too, when they were students. To Claire's fury, it had been bacon that had broken his resolve, despite all his scruples.

'Sure,' said Duncan, giving in to his hunger and moving to

join Martin. The two of them sat side by side on the kitchen sofa.

'I never thanked you properly for looking after our cat,' said Martin. 'He's doing well.'

Martin's cat had been run over two months ago. Duncan had managed to save it, after wiring the jaw and removing one eye.

'You're welcome,' he said. 'He was lucky.'

The density of cat casualties never failed to enrage him – a quarter of a million of them each year in the UK, mostly people driving too fast, not caring at all.

'Well, the wife was hugely relieved. He stays inside now.'

The one eye didn't leave them with much choice. Duncan didn't hold with keeping cats inside, but in this case, he'd had to make it absolutely clear.

'Good,' he said. The monosyllabic answer was all that he could manage. He took a bite of his cob.

Martin cast his eyes around the room. The heavy swathes of curtain fabric at the full-length windows by the sofa, the matching oversized lamps on the side tables on either end. The designer scented candles had not yet been burnt. It was Claire who was into burning candles. Duncan could see Martin assessing his taste, his wealth. Martin's family still lived in a three-bed semi on a modern estate the other side of Derby. Some vets earned more than doctors, which spoke volumes for how people valued their pets.

'You didn't say much, yesterday.' It was a question, not a statement. Martin squinted over his roll. 'I know it was a lot to take in. Bit of a shock, especially . . . there's not a huge amount I can tell you at this point, but is there anything you wanted to ask?'

Duncan folded the paper round his roll, tucking it neatly underneath. His eyes half-closed as he thought about it.

'How was it found?' he said.

'Bob Shardlow found the remains, or rather his dog did. They were walking along the shore. It was half-submerged in the mud.'

'What was Bob doing there? That's my land on either side of the road, right up to the water. He's got no business walking his dog there.'

Duncan knew that his annoyance might be seen as unreasonable in the circumstances, but he didn't care. It seemed to him as if he shouldn't care. About anything. That way was so much easier.

'The path on the south side of the reservoir dam is blocked at the moment because of the high water levels and Shardlow had to find an alternative route.'

Duncan didn't respond. He carried on eating, not looking up. Until:

'Can you tell me anything about it?'

The body – they were talking about the body.

'I can't tell you that, I'm sorry, mate.' Martin let his words fade away, using the excuse of the food to fall silent.

Duncan nodded – they both ate. For a moment, it was no different to the two of them sitting on the wall outside the school, or lying back against the grass on the slopes behind the swimming baths. It had been six weeks – he still felt numb. This new development was surreal. Duncan let it flow over him. He was aware of Martin watching him from the corner of his eye.

'I'm okay, really I am.'

Duncan pushed the last of his bacon roll into his mouth

and scrunched the paper bag in his fist. He kept his face studiously indifferent.

'They're good at their jobs, you know.' Martin spoke gently. 'We'll do our best to keep this as quick and efficient as possible. But we don't have much choice.'

'I know.' Duncan sat with the paper bag still in his fist.

'I'll keep an eye on things, I promise.'

'Thanks.' Duncan stood up to place the bag in the kitchen bin. His voice lifted. 'I appreciate that. When do you think you'll know more?'

'Hard to tell at this stage. I'll get an initial report from Forensics tomorrow. We'll talk to you as soon as we can.'

There was another silence. Duncan moved to the sink. The cold-water tap gushed as he filled a glass, water frothing up and spilling out over the rim.

'Right, I'm off now.' Martin slapped Duncan on the back. 'But I'll be here again in the morning. You need anything, Duncan, anything at all, or anyone bothers you, you let me know, eh?'

'Thank you, mate. I appreciate it. And thanks for the food. Have a good evening.'

Duncan turned to lean back against the sink, watching and sipping his drink as Martin left the house. When Martin had gone, he cast his eyes around the room, everything put away in its place, not a speck or a crumb in sight. He'd even had the granite work surfaces repolished. Already. He smoothed his hand across the top of the kitchen island. Claire would have hated it like this, too clinical – like a room at the surgery, that's what she'd once said. But Duncan could do what he liked now, couldn't he?

Now that she had gone.

CHAPTER 9

CLAIRE – BEFORE

I've been sorting through my clothes all day today. One pile for the bin, another to give to charity. My arms ache from lugging stuff up and down the stairs, making the most of the time that Duncan's out. He's working late today, operating on the spine of a big dog. It could be a very late night, he'd said, don't bother to cook for me. My head throbs. I've been fighting it all day, resisting the need for painkillers. I give in and head to the kitchen, rifling through a drawer for some pills.

I hear a bang. It's a door upstairs. There's the thunder of feet running down the stairs and Joe appears in the kitchen. He's changed into jeans and a khaki-green jumper – the one his dad bought for his last birthday. The sleeves are already too short, but Joe still wears it, the sleeves rolled up irrespective of the cold so that no one will notice. He slams his body down on a chair, folding one leg over his knee so that he can put his trainers on.

'Where are you going?' I say. As if I didn't know.

He lifts his head, defiance pulling his lips tight.

'Out.'

He nods towards the metal detector leaning by the back door.

'Please, Joe, not tonight. It'll be dark soon. Why do you have to do this at night, for goodness' sake?'

He stands up. My hand reaches across my chest for the soft spot in the hollow of my shoulder. I rub it as if it hurts. Joe balances on one foot and lifts his other leg, jamming the second trainer on, struggling to get his big fingers round the laces.

'I told you – if the other guys see me, they'll get there first, take whatever there is – we can't let them do that.'

The 'other guys' – he means the metal detectorists. Treasure hunters. There's a whole community of them, apparently; though I gather most of them are a lot older than Joe. It worries me, because it seems to me that my son doesn't belong in such a group, not at this stage in his life. He should be out with people the same age as him, clubbing, drinking, meeting girls and boys and having fun. Not glued to online chat sites, poring over photographs of ancient treasure, participating in endless conversations about gold and silver coins, artefacts of the long dead, chasing stuff – *stuff*. It's just a vain dream.

He stands upright and walks down the kitchen, opening and closing cupboard doors as he looks for food he can take with him.

'No,' I say, my voice firmer. 'Not today, not tonight. I don't want you going tonight.'

I stand with my legs apart, willing myself to look taller.

'You listen to your mother, Joe. You're not going out tonight.'

I swing round. It's Duncan.

44

He's come in from the hall and I stare at him in surprise. He's home early. The operation either went really well or really badly. Or his latest girlfriend has blown him out and cancelled their plans for tonight. Our eyes meet briefly. It's like this game between us – the texting and calls, all those late nights and excuses. He must realise I know he's having a full-blown affair by now, even if I don't know who. He's been very careful about that.

He likes hurting me, letting me know in subtle ways how little he thinks of me, how meaningless our marriage has become. But never anything in public. He expects me to carry on, always has, because of Joe. He doesn't know that I'm planning to leave, that I've been carefully saving, waiting, biding my time . . .

'Joe! Did you hear me?' repeats Duncan.

He's in a foul mood. I can hear it in his voice. I flinch in spite of myself. He doesn't care about Joe going out, he's looking for another argument.

Joe acts as if he hasn't heard either of us, still banging the cupboard doors like a drummer crashing on cymbals.

'Joe! Stop that!' Duncan's voice fills the kitchen.

Joe stops and turns to face his father.

'Why?' he says. 'Why shouldn't I go out?'

'You heard what your mother said. It's almost night. It's not sensible to go out in the fields at night. How can you possibly even see properly? Never mind this fantasy you've got of finding some kind of treasure hoard.' Duncan stresses the word *fantasy*. 'Enough's enough, boy.' Duncan's voice deepens. 'Your mother said no.'

Blaming me. As always, Duncan somehow makes me out to be the bad guy.

Joe riles at the word *boy*.

'Fuck you!' he shouts, stepping forwards to push past Duncan into the utility room.

'Don't you swear at me!' says Duncan, bristling.

He moves to block Joe's way, filling the door frame, holding one arm against the architrave. I see Joe's eyes move to the metal detector propped up in the corner by the back door and my hand moves to my throat.

'Please, Joe, let's not do this tonight.' I throw a warning look at Duncan. 'Why . . . why don't we go out for a meal instead? The three of us – pizza in Belston. You'd like that.'

He used to, when he was little. It's been a long time since I went out for a meal with Duncan, let alone with Joe as well. Duncan looks at me, surprised at the suggestion, and Joe looks from one to the other of us, disbelieving.

'What and watch the two of you fighting?' he says.

I see the bitterness in his eyes. He bends down to duck under Duncan's arm, but Duncan moves again, stepping forwards to meet him, one hand pushing against Joe's chest. Suddenly, this whole thing has escalated to a physical confrontation. Joe bats his father's arm away and I can see the indecision fly across Duncan's face. Fight or let him go. There's no winning that.

Instead, Duncan spins round and strides across the utility room to grab the metal detector before our son can get there. He snatches the battery pack that powers the thing.

'I've had enough of all this. There'll be no metal detecting for you tonight, Joe. It's time you lived in the real world.'

Joe stands there, his face pale and stark. Like he can't believe his father just said that, undermining the very thing that means so much to him.

Duncan marches into the hall. He exits the front door and it swings shut with a muted clunk. I hear the car door slam and the engine fire up. Joe is galvanised into action, growling almost like an animal.

'Joe! He didn't mean it!'

He ignores me. He takes the stairs two at a time. Moments later he comes down again, another battery pack in his hands. My eyes widen. I'd laugh if it wasn't so upsetting.

'Joe! You can't!'

But it's too late. He loops past me in the kitchen and grabs hold of the metal detector, fixing the new battery pack into place. He snatches at the back door. Arthur slips through the open gap to follow Joe. And this door slams with a proper satisfying *thunk*.

Joe has gone. Duncan, too. And I'm left standing on my own in the kitchen.

CHAPTER 10

CLAIRE – BEFORE

I'm done with my sorting for a while. It's frustrating, because I can't pack properly till the very last day. Dusk has fallen early, the way it does in winter, and there's a chill to the Barn despite our expensive underfloor heating. I decide to have a long, warm bath.

I head for the master en suite – it's my bathroom now. There's a freestanding contemporary bathtub in Apollo Arctic White that Duncan had placed right in front of the low window to make the most of the view. I run the tap for a while, strip off and lower myself into the water until it reaches my chin. The water is hot, turning my skin pink. Steam rises from my body, making me feel like one of those snow monkeys bathing in the hot springs of Japan.

The bath is huge. I slip further into it, until my head disappears beneath the water and I lie there, hair drifting to the surface, eyes wide open, staring up at the ceiling. I feel the warm clean bathwater lap against my knees. The future, Joe, my new home, that has to be my priority now. The thought of it rolls around in my head.

I let the heat seep into my bones, until my blood sings and my teeth part and I open and close my mouth, rising slowly up and down like a fish to breathe. Relax, Claire, relax. I finally let my thoughts drift.

Joe *will* come with me, I know he will – if he's forced to choose, he'd rather be with me than Duncan. I hate that he'll have to choose, but we're not going far. I won't deprive Duncan of his son, or Joe his father. Joe needs him, now more than ever. I'm hoping that afterwards, Duncan will make more of an effort, find a way to reach out and understand his son. A little distance can be a good thing, making you work harder.

It hasn't always been like this – between Joe and Duncan and me. I remember Joe when he was about seven. He was just coming out of that baby stage, when all he really wanted was to be with his mum. Suddenly, he was discovering there was a world beyond my domain and asserting himself as a little boy. I'd felt an odd mixture of grateful relief and regret as he began following his dad around instead, like a mini helper.

There was a day when Duncan was chopping logs up from a fallen tree. We'd not long moved into the Barn and there were still piles of builders' rubble scattered across the drive with a skip taking up the corner by the stone walls. There had been a big storm the night before. Leaves and branches littered the turf. The old oak tree in the top field had finally keeled over and Duncan had set up a workstation beside it and lit a small bonfire.

Curls of blue smoke drifted over our heads. I was breaking

up twigs for kindling for the house and I thought Joe could help – boys and sticks are made to go together like bread and jam. But Joe was far more interested in what Duncan was doing. He was fascinated by the blade of the axe. Duncan stood there, sleeves rolled up, lean and fit. He'd swing the axe high over his head and then down to split the log end on. My heart was in my mouth. I was torn between admiration for my husband and a fear that Joe would step forwards into the blade at exactly the wrong moment. But Joe held back, re-enacting the arc of Duncan's arms with his own as the pair of them swung in unison, Duncan with his real axe and Joe with his imaginary. It seemed to be one of those gentle outdoorsy afternoons, all of us in our own way working at the same task.

Until I realised that Duncan was in a world of his own, quite unaware of his son behind him. There was a grim expression of determination on Duncan's face and each log was being split with ever more physical exertion, as if Duncan were taking out some inner fury on the wood. The last log bounced apart with such energy that one half exploded into narrow shards that almost flew up against Joe's face.

I dropped my bundle of twigs and leapt forwards to pull Joe back.

'Careful, Duncan – he's right behind you!'

Duncan turned round to look, scowling at my interruption.

'Then keep him out of the way. You need to look after him, Claire!'

Like it was my fault. I stared at him, willing him to understand. For once he seemed to realise. He lowered his axe, filled with remorse. He reached out to sweep Joe into his arms. Joe folded his limbs about his father's body, one hand trying to grab at the axe.

Duncan set him down again, this time by the log. He pulled out one of the smaller pieces of wood and balanced it end up on the block. Finding a lighter splitting axe, he held it up to Joe's hands and grasped the handle with him. He demonstrated the lift and blow, then stood back and let Joe take it. Joe pursed his lips, straddled his feet just like his father and raised his arms. Down came the axe. To his amazement, and I think Duncan's too, it split perfectly in two. The grin on Joe's face was one of those family moments.

I grieve for them both – Duncan, the husband, and Duncan, the father – it was always a bit hit and miss. He never quite got the hang of being a father. It was as if he was holding something back, like he didn't quite believe he could be any good at it. Those were the good days, relatively speaking. It's not like that now. I think of Duncan's attitude earlier in the kitchen. It hasn't been for a very long time.

I come up for air. The water swishes over the side of the bath, flooding the tiles beneath, soaking the pile of dirty clothes on the bath mat. I want to cry. But I won't. Instead, I close my eyes and will it all to be over. For me to be already at the new house, Joe beside me, all my stuff moved without any arguments or upsets. Except I know it won't be like that. It's not like Duncan wants me, loves me anymore. God knows, he's made that clear. But there will be consequences to our split. Financial consequences. The mortgage, the Barn, the pension – Duncan's – *our* investment in the business, all of it will be at stake. Duncan's reaction will be . . . The weight of all that fills me with trepidation and I feel the tension in me increase.

I push back into the water. I need to chill out, to calm down and get everything in perspective. I have to face it, unless

I'm going to give up now and stay like this, trapped for the rest of my life. This move is for me. I've waited long enough. I'm not giving up or running away, I'm making a fresh start.

I sit upright, smoothing my hands over my wet hair. I reach out for the taps to top up with hot water. I feel the energy washing through my torso, my fingers buzzing, my toes wriggling, the skin on my face clean and bright. No tears, not today. *Come on, Claire.* I feel better, rational, in control. It's a good feeling. And I should stop worrying about my son. He's not a little boy anymore; he has to stand on his own two feet. I should trust him to be the adult he now is. I need to live in the present.

Can't I do that?

I suck the steam into my lungs and relish in my vitality. I don't want to let the negative thoughts crush me. I'm going to push them from my head. I want to be the person I was before Duncan, before everything that followed meeting him. The person I should have been. I'm not going to let any of it get to me. Not Duncan, not our past, not his girlfriend, whoever she may be . . . My buoyant mood falters.

It shouldn't matter, but it does. I still want to know who she is, his girlfriend, the woman who's sleeping with my husband.

CHAPTER 11

DUNCAN – AFTER

The surgery was full again, dogs barking, cats yowling, owners shuffling on their seats. An elderly man was berating Sally on reception and Duncan could see she was struggling to keep a pleasant expression on her face. He clocked her beseeching glance.

'Mr Garfield,' he said. 'I do believe you and Betsy are next?'

Duncan reached out a hand and nodded briskly towards his consulting room door.

The man gave an impatient tug on his dog's lead. A long-suffering greyhound followed them into the room, its thin, stiff tail tucked firmly between its legs. The man sat down and Duncan crouched on his heels and ran his hand over the dog's head.

'So, what can we do for this old girl?'

His voice was light, but his jaw was set. The dog looked back at him, its eyes deep pools of warm brown.

'Lost control of her bladder, 'asn't she. Keeps pissing on the floor all times of day. Can't be 'aving that. Reckon it's time to say goodbye.'

Duncan felt his fingers clench, then he smoothed his hand over the dog's ears and down its neck. The animal wriggled its haunches and turned its head away, skittering on its rear legs. It seemed to have understood what was being said.

'I don't think we should jump to any conclusion about that. Let's have a look at her.'

Duncan drew his hand down the dog's body, feeling her underside, reaching for the area over her bladder, then moving on to inspect under her tail. The area looked raw and uncomfortable, the effect of urine scorching her skin. A pungent, dark-coloured puddle had already appeared at her feet.

'See what I mean?' The old man gave the dog a rough tug.

'There's no need for that!' Duncan said, unable to contain the sharpness in his voice.

It was the kind of appointment he abhorred. When a client had had enough of his animal's problems and wanted the cheap, easy way out. The man wasn't worthy of owning a dog. He eyed the colour of that puddle on the floor.

'There's nothing here we can't fix. Incontinence is not unusual in an elderly female dog. Is she relieving herself normally outside?'

There was a hesitation, then the man nodded.

'Aye. Tak' her out most days.'

Duncan frowned. The dog was panting and she'd dipped her head as if it were too heavy to hold up. Duncan gritted his teeth. What had Garfield been doing to her this time?

'Is she drinking plenty?'

Another hesitation. Duncan's suspicion increased.

'You *are* giving her plenty of water?'

The man still didn't answer.

'Jesus Christ, man – if you don't give her enough water, you'll make things even worse. Is that what you'd do to yourself?'

The man dropped his eyes. Duncan took the dog's head gently in his hands, observing her face and nose, then carefully pushing on each side of her mouth to inspect the gums.

'She's clearly dehydrated. What are you playing at, eh? Did you think reducing her water would mean less mess? You need to give her plenty!'

It could be an infection, Duncan mused. The water would help flush it out. Or it could be loss of control of the sphincter muscle. That wasn't uncommon for a dog her age.

'The more concentrated the urine, the more uncomfortable it's going to be.' Duncan leaned back and the man grunted. 'See that rawness under the tail? How would you feel if that were you?'

Garfield didn't reply.

'How long have you had her?' Duncan stroked the dog's head.

He already knew the answer; Garfield had been coming to the practice for years. The question was more to make a point.

'Since she were a puppy,' said Garfield reluctantly.

'So you *do* care about her, don't you?'

'Course I do!' The man ground his teeth.

'Well, she's definitely not ready to meet her Maker.' Duncan's tone hardened. 'I suggest you make sure there's plenty of padding in her bed, that she has a clean, *full* bowl of water every morning. Take her for walks, *every* day. Especially first and last thing – and as many extra ones as you can both manage. You need to wash her backside with clean, warm water on a regular basis and we'll start her on this.'

Duncan tapped out a prescription on his PC and the printer began to chug.

'Quite often, it's the result of a hormonal imbalance, so I'm hoping this will help. There's lots we can do, Mr Garfield, before . . .'

Duncan snorted. He couldn't bring himself to say the words. He turned his back on the man, reaching out to grasp the prescription from the printer tray.

'*Humph.*' Garfield took the piece of paper and stood up.

The dog was still looking at Duncan, as if to say: *Don't make me go with him.*

'If it's causing you a problem, keep her in the kitchen – and remember that absorbent padding on her bed.'

Another grunt.

'I want to see her again in a week's time.'

You'd better bloody turn up, thought Duncan.

The man and his dog left.

CHAPTER 12

DUNCAN – AFTER

The emergency exit door of the veterinary stockroom slammed open, bouncing against the brick wall. Duncan stepped out into the cold air. His fists were closed tight and a fierce expression creased his face.

The door pushed open again and Paula appeared in the doorway.

'Fucking idiot!' said Duncan.

He pushed a hand into his trouser pocket, searching for a new stick of chewing gum. He knew Paula was there but didn't turn round.

'How can anyone claim to love their animal,' he said. 'Then demand it be put down just because it's incontinent!'

But this was Garfield, so he wasn't that surprised. Paula didn't reply, standing on the doorstep as if waiting for him to vent his fury. She was still relatively new to the practice, but she already seemed to have the measure of Duncan.

'He wanted me to put the dog down!' he carried on. 'Garfield doesn't deserve any animal! It's all very well when they're cute and cuddly and doing what they're told, but when they grow elderly and actually need a bit of time and attention, funny how the love dries up!'

'It's not as simple as that. It never is,' said Paula. She stepped away from the door.

'Isn't it? Then how should it be?' Duncan swung round.

He was caught up again by her red hair; it had been hard to ignore it when he'd interviewed her – a bright, lustrous natural red. Her academic credentials had been impeccable.

'It's hard looking after a dog when you get to Garfield's age,' she said.

'So why have one?' he snapped back.

'Company, affection – he clearly lives on his own.'

'Then he should be more loving towards his animal. Don't be fooled by Garfield's doddery old man routine! That man's been coming here for years. He knows exactly what he's doing.'

Garfield had always liked to play a part. Just because you were old and apparently fragile, thought Duncan, didn't make you a nice person.

'Jeez – you've really got it in for him, haven't you?'

'Aye, and I've good reason to. He couldn't care tuppence for his dog!'

'He must do or he wouldn't come down here like he does – particularly given how you treat him!'

'And how would you know, Paula?'

Duncan's fingers closed into a fist. Paula's eyes dropped to his hands and then back to his face and there was an imperceptible tightening of her expression. Duncan felt a twinge of guilt. She didn't know Garfield came here because the treatment was free, how could she? She'd barely been at the practice six months. Duncan had kept it quiet. It wouldn't do if everyone thought he was a soft touch. Not that it was an act of generosity, but the whole story was complicated, and only Sally and Frances knew. The man still pressed his buttons, though – now even more so.

'Don't take it out on me!' said Paula. 'I deal with these people every day, remember!' She was flushed with anger.

Duncan let out a deep breath. Paula was right to push back. Perhaps he should tell her.

'I'm sorry, Paula; really I am. He comes here because we give him free treatment – I don't normally do that and it's a long story. And I'd be grateful if you didn't say anything to the others. Trust me, the man's a dick.'

He let his fingers relax, reaching up to push them over his head.

'I just can't stand it some days.'

Today, he meant. And yesterday. And the day before that. What was he doing? This wasn't about Garfield, was it? He couldn't say *her* name. Claire's name. He couldn't put it into words. The feelings that simmered each day. Battened down, as if nothing had happened.

He rummaged in his pocket. He couldn't find his chewing gum and he was desperate for a smoke, despite having given up years ago. Or maybe what he really needed was a drink. He took another long breath, trying to will the blood pumping through his body to slow. His hands opened and closed, thinking of the club he'd gone to in Derby the other night. He refused to look at Paula now. No, what he really wanted was a shag, a quick, sharp shag like when he and Claire had first got together – the thrill of fumbling, youthful, irresponsible student sex . . . A million miles and years ago from now.

He could never actually put it into words, but he missed her.

'Duncan . . .'

It was Frances. She was standing behind Paula, looking anxiously at her boss. She gave a small gesture to Paula, who nodded and left.

Frances waited until Paula had gone.

'You need to be careful, Duncan,' she said. 'I know you have every reason to be upset, we all do, but . . . are you sure you should be here? Why don't you take a few days off? We'll cope. It's—'

'No!' he said. 'I'm not taking a fucking holiday.'

He could see Frances wince at the language. He turned to face her.

'I can't, not now, there's too much going on. There are operations lined up, procedures that Tim and Paula aren't qualified to do. I can't take time out like that.'

Tim was the other vet, more senior than Paula. Duncan scowled. Did he sound arrogant? Probably, but it was true, they didn't have the knowledge yet that he had and the whole business was predicated on his expertise. Work, the surgery, it had been his life's ambition, opening up his own practice. Claire had done a lot to help make that possible. No, he wasn't having it. Frances had said enough, hadn't she? She thought she had the right.

He pushed away from the wall and walked towards the road. Frances sighed and turned back to the door to leave. Then at the last minute she swung round.

'Claire's gone!'

Her voice carried across the staff car park, louder but sympathetic. Frances had a knack of getting to the crux of a matter regardless of what was being said.

'She's not coming back,' she continued. 'You need to accept it and let go.'

Duncan didn't know how to reply. To anyone else, her words would have seemed harsh. Only Frances could get away with saying that. Older and wiser, she'd always been direct. It was one of the reasons Duncan liked working with her.

'It's not like that . . .' He paused mid-stride. He wasn't sure that he believed his own words. 'She's . . . *she* . . . is still my wife.' He pushed his hands into his pockets, scrabbling again for the gum.

'Not anymore,' she said. There was a bitterness in her words. 'And then there's Joe . . .'

Duncan's head jerked up. Frances had her hand on the back door again in readiness to leave. Her eyes held his gaze. He didn't reply. It was the one bone of contention between them. Him and Claire and Joe and . . . Frances had always taken him to task over Claire and Joe. And he'd let her, hadn't he? But she didn't know all of it.

Once more the stockroom door bounced back against the brick wall, the sound reverberating across the car park.

CHAPTER 13

CLAIRE – BEFORE

I have often seen them in the fields, further along the valley, slowly pacing the ground. Sometimes one of them drags a spade behind him whilst another holds a spade over one shoulder. Always there are at least two or three of them at a time, leaning forwards over the turf. They hold out their detectors, silhouetted against the trees or frost-blue sky or the morning fog, stalking the field together like a pack of black crows.

Joe discovered metal detecting online. Whilst most boys were either obsessed with football or hunched over their computers playing games, at fifteen, Joe was bashing away at his keyboard discussing early Roman coin types on the metal detecting chat sites.

When he was fourteen, I took him for a long weekend to Northumbria. It was a treat, just for him and me, to make up for the trouble he'd been having in class. I had this idea that if I could tap into his historical curiosity, he'd *want* to study instead of always feeling forced to comply with school.

Joe hated secondary school, at least in the last few years; the whole uniform and rules thing, the stink of the boys' toilets, the getting up too early in the morning and forcing himself either to go in with me or catch the bus – he was always half asleep. The studying, exams and books and teachers on his back, day in, day out, essays, extracts, questions, long feet stuck out from under his desk, long enough to trip up a teacher. And the girls gossiping in the corridors with skirts that skimmed their thighs and sugar-pink lipstick, tapping on their phones to slag Joe off on Facebook. At least if you believe Joe, that's what it was like.

They always laughed at him, he'd been convinced of that. Too tall like a stick man, they'd said. Stick Man. Stick *Boy*. Anything to get a reaction. When he wasn't sleeping, all he wanted to do was go outside metal detecting, the fresh air banishing his thoughts, the absorbed concentration drowning out his emotions. I'd hated school too, for different reasons, so what could I say?

He'd loved Roman mythology as a small boy, gods and monsters battling for the heavens, or Roman armies marching into war. I thought, what if I took him to Vindolanda, one of the best-preserved Roman forts in the country? It was right on Hadrian's Wall near the border with Scotland.

It was a huge success. It filled his head with stories of the Roman infantry, military tactics and soldiers guarding against the Picts on the northern reaches of the empire. He pored over the cabinet displays and dragged me from one object to another, fascinated by the layout of the buildings, the sculptures and tablets, the scraps of preserved leather, pottery and metal brooches. Clues to another time, another life.

But it was the coins that had him transfixed. There was a whole wall dedicated to the various coins found on the site. Gold and silver glittering on a white background, lit up by a row of narrow spotlights. He was full of it on the way home, the patterns and designs, the different metal components, the names of the emperors whose heads were engraved on the back.

'There's this one coin type, Mum, an aureus. It's a gold coin from the time of Emperor Nero. He went mad – did you know that? He became emperor when he was only sixteen.'

I laughed at that. 'Fancy yourself as an emperor, do you, Joe?'

'Course not,' he said. He always took me seriously. Then he looked at me. 'I'm not mad, you know, Mum.'

'I know that, Joe,' I said, my gaze turning briefly from my focus on the road.

I flashed a smile at him. He seemed satisfied.

'He was a treasure hunter. He sent his men into Africa looking for gold. He killed people, though. Murdered Britannicus, his stepbrother, and then his own mother, Agrippina.' Joe frowned. 'And his wife. She was called P-p . . . Pop . . . Poppaea Sabina.' He'd hardly paused to catch his breath.

All those names tumbling from his lips. The museum had really captured his interest. I was euphoric. Finally, he was motivated. Finally, you could see how bright he was. I could never remember all that stuff. Back home, even his teachers commented on his sudden interest in ancient history. Trouble was, not much of it actually featured on the school curriculum.

That's when he started researching online, devouring data and statistics about coins. He must have stumbled on the metal detecting websites and begun asking and answering questions. Before long he was pretty knowledgeable, with a host of new internet friends. Ironically, he used StickMan as his online name.

By fifteen he'd bought his first metal detector. There was a local group near Matlock and he joined up, spending his weekends tagging along, learning from them. I was glad. I'd decided it was good for him. He thrived on their acceptance, being part of a group. That was important to him. He'd never found acceptance at school. Or home.

The morning doesn't come. At least that's how it feels. I look out of the big window and there's fog right up against the glass. I can't see a thing.

I stand on my tiptoes, as if that would help. It's like the Barn is suspended in the air, travelling at more than thirty thousand feet. I feel disorientated, Dorothy in her tiny shack, spinning through the sky towards the Land of Oz. The glass is cold beneath my fingers, and the swirls of fog float and curl like blooms of white ink in water. I'm not sure that white ink is even a thing.

I'm tired from the night before. I've hardly slept a wink. Duncan hasn't come back, not that it surprises me. Joe hasn't come home either. Must be the fog – he'd easily get spooked in that. I hate to think of him out there, in the cold. If he's got any sense, he'll have taken refuge somewhere, waiting it out. The fog moves again, drifting apart and back again, heaving like a giant's breath. Duncan will have gone to work by now, rolling out of whatever or whoever's bed he's slept in.

I fantasise about Duncan never coming back. How much easier that would be, if he suddenly disappeared from the face of the earth. Walked out and never came back. No messy divorce, no emotional meltdown, no arguments over money. He won't like being forced to sell the Barn. I smile at that, sweet revenge for all those years of neglect.

What if he died? The thought comes to me from nowhere. I'd inherit everything. I could sell up and do whatever I liked.

The very idea, however, fills me with horror. I think of his body mangled in the mud, his legs bent the wrong way, his head twisted to one side, eyes wide and staring. Her too, whilst we're at it. Whoever she is, her long hair splayed on a dashboard – it's got to be long hair, it's far more visual, crimson blood trickling down her head. Oh, God, what am I thinking?

I don't want that. How could I want that? This was never what I wanted. For a moment I ask myself if I can really do it, leave Duncan, leave everything we've built up between us. The comforts of our life, the home we have, even if I don't particularly like it. I know I'm damned lucky compared to most people – ungrateful, that's what my mother would have said. Just as well she's no longer here to see me. She died five years ago, my father two years before that. Mum always approved of Duncan – she thought he could do no wrong. A handsome man with his sleeves rolled up, saving doggy lives . . . what's not to like?

Duncan and I have been together for ever, since we were both eighteen – the same age that Joe is now. I've hardly known anything else. Have I really stopped loving him? I think of Duncan when we were newly married. His warm body pressing down on mine, his breath teasing at my ear. His energy and wit. I adored him then. If I didn't love him still, then it wouldn't hurt like this, would it?

I sigh and the fog sighs with me, rolling back to reveal a glimpse of the outside. There must be a breeze, there always is, up here on the hill. But the trees are unmoving. I see the horizontal lines of the five-bar gate, the darker shapes of the hedgerow in the fields, the uneven turf. Under all that grass, there are dips and hollows and holes dug out by rabbits and moles and foxes . . . I feel the touch of cool air on the back of my neck, almost as if I'm out there not inside. Then the fog lifts, uncertainly, like a grey sheet flapping in the wind. I can see through to the far slopes of the valley on the other side of the water. There are figures. Dark, black figures. People.

I lean in. There are four of them, I think.

Moments later, the fog sinks down again and I can't see them anymore. Then the fog rolls back and now there are only two. I'm not sure if what I'm seeing are real people, wearing coats and hats and earphones, holding those stupid sticks. Or if they're animals, cows or even sheep in the distance. It plays tricks on you, the fog, especially here in the valley, something about the light being distorted by the shadow of the hills. Or maybe I need a pair of glasses. I watch as the fog closes in again, thick and solid against the window, like the safety curtain on a stage. I can't see them anymore. I can't see a thing. I wait and watch and moments later, when the fog shifts and the view opens up, the men, or whatever I saw, are gone.

A short while later, there's the scrabble of a hand on the back door and the sound of Arthur's wet paws clattering on the tiles. A cold draught gusts across the kitchen.

'*Mum?*'

It's Joe. He's back.

'Mum – are you there? You won't believe what I've found!'

CHAPTER 14

CLAIRE – BEFORE

'Look, Mum! Did you ever see anything so beautiful?'

I look at the tiny disc in his hand. It seems little more than a clump of dirt to me. But I can make out that it's a coin. Albeit of the chewed, dull and damaged sort.

The edges aren't quite circular and the disc is slightly bent from its years under the ground. Perhaps it's got crushed by farming equipment, or simply warped through the process of time. The metal is heavily tarnished, soil still clinging to the surface. Joe turns it over in his hand and there's definitely some kind of pattern on each side. One is more obscured than the other, but the reverse has the clear shape of a head, crowned with a laurel wreath.

'It needs cleaning,' Joe says. 'But wow! Look at it!'

'That's amazing, Joe. Very nice.'

I'm not sure what else to say. Nice – what an awful word

that is, but so convenient. I lean forwards, trying to show more interest.

'Where did you find it?' I ask.

'In the bottom field. I've been working that rough ground beside the reservoir near the road. On my own. I've not told any of the other guys what I'm doing as it's our land. They're out there today, further up the valley, so I had to come in. I found this last night only a few inches down in the earth. I've not found a coin as old as this before!'

His fingers hold the coin as if it's the most precious thing in the world. He folds his fingers around it and I can't see it anymore. He kicks off his shoes, leaving them abandoned on the floor. Then he reaches up into one of the cupboards, grabs a bowl with his free hand and exits the kitchen, climbing the stairs. I hear the usual bang of his bedroom door and then silence. No music, not this time.

That coin, I guess, will keep him occupied for hours.

I pick up the shoes, tucking them out of sight, and unlatch the power pack from the metal detector – Duncan will have a fit if he knows Joe has a second one. I take it up to Joe's room and knock on the door. He doesn't answer.

I nudge open the door and it swings back on its hinge.

'Joe?'

He's not there. The door to his en suite is closed. I hear the sound of the shower running on the other side. His bed is strewn with dirty clothes, and a week's worth of socks and pants lie scattered on the floor. There are deconstructed bits of bike and a deflated inner bicycle tube curling like an abandoned snake skin on the carpet. His desk isn't much better: littered with half-eaten crisp packets and an empty bottle of Coke. I hate that – I've had a running battle with him about fizzy drinks ever since he was old enough to spend his own pocket money.

The bowl he took up is there on his bedside cabinet. My eyes flicker across to the coin that rests inside. I place the power pack on Joe's bed, scoop up some dirty laundry and back out before Joe's even aware that I've come in.

He's been in his room for hours. I wonder if he's fallen asleep. By lunchtime, I make a sandwich and climb the stairs again to knock on his door. Any excuse to see what he's up to. I hear music, ambient high-tech, sci-fi kind of music. Duncan would approve.

'Come in,' calls Joe.

He sounds tired but happy.

'How's it going?' I ask, smiling.

I perch on his bed. He's sat at the desk. The bowl is there now with a shallow layer of sudsy water and a toothbrush balanced on the rim. He's loaded his laptop and I can see he's been searching pictures of different coins. They fill the screen with profiled Roman noses of various degrees of imperious pointedness.

He swivels round on his seat. His hair is too long, hanging in loose black curls that any girl would die for. His face is pale and waxy from lack of sleep, but his eyes shine big and bright.

'Come and see,' he says.

I stand up and walk across to his desk. I don't normally get invited to look. The coin itself is lying on a flat pile of neatly folded toilet paper. Some of the dirt is gone – not all, but enough to see the pattern more clearly. I lean forwards, not really paying attention.

71

'Oh, wow, Joe. That's amazing. You've done a good job of cleaning it up.'

Joe frowns.

'Yeah,' he says, 'but you have to be careful. Too much cleaning and it might get damaged. Still, it's better than it was.'

He gingerly picks up the coin and holds it end on between finger and thumb. Then lays it back down on the paper.

'Take a closer look.'

I peer over his shoulder, guilty at my own disinterest. He needs me to take more interest. I squeeze my eyes and give a little gasp.

The figurehead is clearer. He looks Roman, or some version of that, with that wreath about his head. There's the usual long, straight nose and a stylised beard with elaborate curls that match the individual leaves on the wreath. But there, where you'd expect an eye to be, is what looks like an arrow-head poking down through the man's eye socket.

I stare at it, silent.

Eventually, I feel compelled to speak.

'What is that?' I say.

My voice is quiet. This isn't just another coin. It's like none of the coins we saw in Vindolanda, or anything that Joe has found before. That arrowhead in the socket is cruel. And unique. He doesn't know – how could he know?

I've seen it before.

'I'm not sure,' says Joe. 'I've never come across anything like this.' He slowly touches the arrowhead. Joe's hands are surprisingly long and elegant. 'You don't get that on normal Roman coins. Or anything medieval. Weird, isn't it?'

The fingers of his other hand move to tap the surface of the desk. He's impatient to get back to his PC.

'It's even more interesting on the other side.'

He tips the coin over gently, setting it back on the tissue so I can look.

On this side is a man riding a horse. The figure looks almost comical, cartoonlike. The arms of the man and the legs of the horse are exactly the same, straight and narrow and knobbly. Bones, not flesh. Underneath the horse is another shape, three adjoining swirls, a kind of spinning skeletal disc. Like the symbol for the Isle of Man. I glance up at the screen on Joe's laptop. He's been googling it: *Isle of Man flag*. Yes, there it is, similar but different – three spiralling armour-clad legs bent at the knee, the *triskele* or *triskelion*.

He follows my gaze.

'I've been trying to work it out. I knew the shape was familiar. I've found this story about the Celtic god of the sea, Manannan. He was a wizard and the first ruler of the Isle of Man. He cloaked the island in mist whenever his enemies approached and turned himself into a spinning wheel of legs to roll down the mountain.'

Very handy, I think. Joe loves this stuff. I'm still unable to quite take it in.

'He had a horse, too – Enbarr of the Flowing Mane – who rode on water. I was thinking maybe the rider on this side of the coin is Manannan.'

'You think the coin is from the Isle of Man?' I find myself wanting to ask questions, to distract Joe from my reaction.

'I *did*. I wasn't sure.'

He goes back to the coin, pointing to it.

'But I don't think that now. Look at the rest of it – there are more shapes both above and below the horse.'

He's right – above the rider are seven dots, linked together by more lines. Stylistically, they're exactly like the joints of the rider's arms.

'They're star constellations,' says Joe. 'I'm sure of it. See that one? It's the shape of the Plough, it's unmistakable – the constellation of Ursa Major.'

It's not the star constellation that draws my eye. It's the rider's hand – it doesn't look human with the usual four fingers and a thumb. Instead, it's like a lobster claw, one half thicker than the other. It's surreal, like the arrow pointing down from the eye socket on the head on the other side. The coin feels foreign now, not in a geographical way, but in an alien, not-of-this-earth kind of way. It doesn't belong. Not here. I feel the weight of my own head, wooziness making me reach out for the edge of Joe's desk.

'I see what you mean. How intriguing.' My voice fades away. There's a noise rushing in my ears.

Joe wriggles in his seat.

'I think I've figured out what it is,' he says suddenly.

I stare at him blankly.

'Look!'

He moves the mouse on his laptop, jumping to another screen. The website is headed *Journal of Archaeological Studies in Eastern Europe and Asia Minor*. An article is highlighted in pale grey:

This particular coin is one of the most enigmatic of the late Iron Age coinage, dating back to the early third century BC. *It shows a male laureate head on the obverse, his eye replaced by an arrowhead.*

'See?'

Joe flips the coin again, pointing out the arrow jutting from the emperor's eye. Then he turns it back over and slowly scrolls down the page on his screen so that I can read:

> *The reverse side of the coin shows a rider astride his horse, but only the upper body of the horseman is depicted. The triskele is shown below, a symbol common to Celtic culture. Most coin finds featuring these images are centred in the area around Hungary, Austria, Serbia and Croatia, which is consistent with the distribution of Eastern European Celtic tribes at that time.*

Joe is virtually bouncing on his seat.

'It's called a *puppetrider!*'

The name has a ring to it. And it's appropriate. I look at the man on the horse again and yes, he is a puppet rider. His body is cut off at the waist with no legs, no feet, and he has the bony body parts of a skeleton. Even the horse's head and limbs look like the bony arms of the man, this time pointing downwards. There's no attempt at realism. The rider is a half skeleton astride his horse, a living corpse that floats on the animal's back as if held in balance by some invisible force. A celestial puppet with no strings.

'And look here!' Joe dabs at the screen again with his fingers.

> *The puppetrider is one of the rarest, most distinctive of a range of early Eastern European coins. Only a handful have ever been found in the UK. In every case, they have been part of significantly valuable coin hoards.*

He doesn't know. How could he know? It's part of a secret that's been buried since before he was born. I close my eyes. *Oh, God,* I think. *Has he found any other items?*

He can't have, since he's not mentioned anything else. I try to imagine the coin frozen in a line of cement, or buried in the mud. Or drifting free in a current of water. It can't be possible. Of all the things to turn up out of the blue, for Joe, my own son, to find . . .

That coin belongs underground. Deep beneath where no one can find her.

It belongs to something that Duncan and I haven't spoken of once, not since before Joe was born.

It belongs to *her.*

Evangeline.

CHAPTER 15

CLAIRE – AFTER

I can't face the morning. Nor do I like the night. It's when the cottage feels too small and empty. The roof contracts and the walls flex and the windows shiver in their frames as the wind sweeps over the brow of the hill.

It's not the silence that gets to me – there is no silence, there's always some kind of low-grade noise somewhere in the cottage – it's the lack of human company. I go downstairs, padding across the kitchen in my pyjamas. Arthur is stretched out in front of the range and I'm grateful for his presence. I kneel on the floor and stroke him in that soft spot he likes under his chin.

From here I can see all the spiderwebs in the room, glistening in the low light. There are bits of dreck that fill the cracks between the floorboards and dead flies that line up along the skirting board under the window. So much dust and dirt has accumulated whilst the cottage was empty, and

I'm not sure how long there's been between the previous tenant and me. I didn't think to ask the estate agent; it must have been a fair length of time. I'm going to be busy cleaning, if I can bring myself to do anything at all.

I stand up and sit in the armchair. Arthur picks himself up awkwardly and moves a little closer, depositing his warm body on my feet. I retrieve the remote control for the TV from the gap between the cushion and the armrest and press the button.

Light and noise fill the room. Faces I don't recognise flash across the screen, voices jangling one over the other, so many I can't hear the words, louder and louder . . . I jab at the remote, banging the thing against the side of my chair until the volume rises even more rapidly. Arthur lifts his ears. The button must have got jammed. I panic and punch the thing again. Silence. I let a sigh shudder from between my lips. The screen still fizzes with tiny white fireworks darting in all directions. I clench my teeth – doesn't anything work in this house?

Nothing ever goes to plan. Not Duncan, not Joe, not even my move to this cottage.

Joe was supposed to come with me. But he didn't.

Instead, he went AWOL again. I was afraid of this. The last time he did that – went off and didn't come back – was in August, just before his A-level results were due. He must have been worried about it all summer. He was gone for over two weeks. I was frantic then. It had always been no more than a few days before; though his absences had been getting longer. I'm frantic now – it's been way longer than that. As each day goes by, I've grown more and more anxious. It doesn't help that Duncan and I aren't speaking. Not even for Joe's sake.

I've not had one phone call from Duncan, not one. But then, I haven't rung him, either. How could I? Instead, I've blocked his number.

Those early days were a blur. My nights have been full of nightmares, my days are . . . I don't know, unreal. I've been in shock, I guess. It didn't exactly go to plan. *Duncan?* My hands clutch the arms of my chair.

I got here a physical and emotional mess, and to find myself here at the cottage after all my careful planning, in the state I was – am – in . . . I wake up each day gasping for breath. Everything hurts – my head, my body, my brain . . . even now.

I had to go without Joe. It hurts just thinking about it. That I left Joe behind.

I'm almost glad he's gone AWOL. It means he's not with Duncan. My first thought was that Joe had gone back to the Barn, after I'd gone. But I know he wouldn't do that. He was so upset with his father that last day. I was almost on the verge of calling the police, then I got one text:

Mum – I'm okay. Don't come looking for me. Goodbye.

I texted him back. *Ring me*, I said. He never rang. I rang him, again and again, but he didn't pick up. Still doesn't pick up. And that text just sits there, blazing from my screen. *Don't come looking for me*. He hasn't texted me again. As if that's it, that's your lot, Mum. I don't need you anymore.

Oh, God, it hurts so much. I'm stuck here on my own and I can't bear it. I hang on thinking, just one more day and I'll get another message. I've even told him exactly where I am. He'll come to me, of his own accord, I know he will. If I wait here long enough.

I bitterly regret choosing this cottage. It's too close to the

Barn. *Why on earth did I think this was a good idea?* I convinced myself it was in Joe's best interests, that we could do this like adults, Duncan and me. And now I'm terrified. Hiding, almost. I can't go anywhere near the Barn, or the north side of the reservoir, the other side of the dam. Or anywhere else. Not Belston, not Derby – not anywhere I might be seen. I can't bear for anyone I know to see me like this, to ask questions.

And Joe is still missing. It's been over six weeks and Joe is still missing.

I've worried about Joe ever since he was born. I knew something was wrong right from the start. I could never quite put my finger on it. He cried and cried and cried as a baby. Nothing settled him unless I held him close. I was exhausted, terrified, tired all the time. I needed to put him down, to look after myself, to do basic stuff like go to the bathroom, eat, sleep. Then one day, I threw him down – he literally bounced in his cot. He screamed like hell then.

I was full of remorse – what if I'd hurt him? What if I'd thrown him against a hard surface and not his soft bed? I was a monster! Why wouldn't anyone help me? Couldn't they see the state I was in? Didn't Duncan, my brother, Ian, even his wife, Moira, understand?

No, apparently, they did not. Duncan assumed looking after Joe was my job and everyone else assumed that Duncan was looking after me. Such a great guy, my brother had said – *You've done well, Claire.* If only he knew.

Secrets, shame, families are full of them.

Every time Joe screamed, I was sure it was my fault – something I'd done or not done in the pregnancy, brain damage or something he'd inherited. I've alternated between fear and pain and guilt. And anger. In those last few days, it was anger.

That Joe would choose to go missing again right then, right when I was finally leaving Duncan. I'd waited eighteen years, putting my whole life on hold for him, banking on the fact that once he was an adult, he'd be sorted, that I could step back from looking after him and take my turn. Well, he must have decided that he's old enough, too. He's upped and gone.

But what if he hasn't? I look at Arthur. Joe should be here. With me. With Arthur.

I feel the fear wash over me. I jump up from my chair. I can't think like this, it does my head in. He's fine. He must be. He said he was. And I'd *know* if he wasn't. Arthur watches me uncertainly, struggling to his feet, wondering if I'm about to take him for a walk. I shake my head.

'No, Arthur, I'm sorry.'

He collapses back to the ground.

I think of that coin Joe found, right before I left. My fingers mentally trace the pattern and I feel such sadness. I would have brought it with me if I could, but Joe must have had it with him – it wasn't in his room when I was packing all of his other things. I remember it clearly. I've held it that many times before it ever passed into Joe's hands, albeit a long time ago. I shake my head. I can't bear to think of that coin anymore.

I think of Joe's excitement. Maybe he's out there searching for more. Maybe he's given up on all that metal detecting stuff and moved in with one of his mates and not bothered to tell me. Part of me almost believes he would do that. Communication was never his strong point. Perhaps the shock of what happened and me leaving has jolted him out of his obsessions. Is he angry with me?

I hold my head as if it'll stop my thoughts from spinning. Maybe something *has* happened. Perhaps he's banged his head and forgotten about his family. You hear stories like that, where amnesia means the person can't remember the life they had before. I have to remind myself, he did send me that one text.

But it's torture not knowing where he is. I have to believe that he's okay, that someone has taken him in and perhaps even now he's crashed out on their floor, stirring only to drink another can of lager and shovel cornflakes down his throat. Someone else's cornflakes.

I pace the room, moving to the hall. I tear at the peeling wallpaper, even though I'm still in my pyjamas. I pull at the wall, arm over arm, fingernails filling up with bits of paper and old glue. Anyone looking in from outside would think that I'm mad, trashing my own home. Anything to block out the one thought I don't want to voice in my head.

That this time, maybe, Joe's not coming back.

CHAPTER 16

DUNCAN – AFTER

'Duncan, is that you?' It was Martin on the phone.

'Hi, Martin, yes, it's me. Any news?'

There was a hesitation.

'Yes and no. The body we found is historic.'

'What? I don't understand,' said Duncan. 'What do you mean?'

'Forensics reckon it's at least a hundred and fifty years old.'

'A hundred and fifty . . .' Duncan fell silent.

'Duncan, are you still there?'

'Yes, I'm here. My goodness. How can that be so?'

'Well, we've yet to verify exactly under what circumstances. But it looks like there's more than one.'

'*What?* Did you say more than one body?'

'That's right. We believe we've found the remains of several skeletons. All of them old. In fact, it looks like we've hit upon a possible burial ground.'

Duncan fell silent again, taking it all in.

'Duncan—'

'But that doesn't make sense,' Duncan interrupted. 'Why would there be a burial ground in that spot? Where there's no church and it's more than a mile to the nearest village.'

Brereton Edge. He was talking about Brereton Edge, the old estate village not far from his property, albeit long since abandoned.

'I know. It is a bit strange. But the proximity of the reservoir is probably no coincidence. I've been doing some research and there was a church in the valley before it was flooded to make way for the reservoir. It's quite possible the graves in the cemetery were exhumed and relocated to dry land. We think that's what we've found.'

Duncan looked it up later when he got in. He was gazing out over to the big window of the sitting room from his desk on the mezzanine. He could see a woman was talking to one of the officers on the drive outside, too tall, too thin, not his type, at least. But her hands were animated, her face alive with whatever she was saying – not one of the usual police CSI types. Someone from the university?

His computer beeped with an incoming email and Duncan turned back to the screen. He stared at it blankly, unable to concentrate. It said something about medical supplies for the surgery. He clicked out of his emails and typed smartly into the search box: *Belston Reservoir*. A mix of images and headings popped up. Duncan chose what looked like the most sensible one:

Belston Reservoir is the eighth largest reservoir in England
with a capacity of 31,869 megalitres. Located five miles
south of the market town of Belston, it was formed by
flooding the valley between Belston Heights and Brereton
Hill. A relatively deep stretch of water and once the site
of extensive waterworks, the reservoir is long and narrow,
known for its variety of wildlife and . . .

It carried on, listing native species and technical statistics.
Duncan's eyes scanned the screen then he reverted to the
search page, adding the word 'church'. *Belston Reservoir*
Church. There it was. A grainy black-and-white photograph
of a church steeple half risen from the water. It looked a bit
weird like that, as if it had been flooded.

Several buildings were submerged in the creation of the
reservoir, most notably the church of St Bertram's. It caused
a considerable stir when it reappeared in 1918 as the result
of an unusually severe drought. The whole project had
taken over fifteen years to complete at the turn of the
century, and was later redesigned to serve the growing
populations of Manchester, Derby and Nottingham. When
the drought hit, the church temporarily re-emerged. A host
of visitors were attracted to the site, marvelling at the
building, which had remained intact all that time under
the water.

There was no mention of a graveyard, but he supposed
Martin's theory made sense. He leaned back in his chair,
contemplating the photograph. Then googled a photographic
map of the surrounding area. He could see the long kidney

shape of the reservoir and the main road at one end that ran between Belston and Derby. He zoomed in, tracking the pattern of fields, including those on the slope down from his house. A smaller road led all around the edge of the water, past his land, past the dam and back around the far side of the reservoir, where eventually it popped out again further along the main road. It was almost a full circle.

Beyond the dam, another lane turned up into the hills, leading to a cluster of buildings denoting the old estate village of Brereton Edge and the Hall. A few minor tracks disappeared in odd directions, but all of them were dead ends. The valley was to all intents and purposes cut off, owned entirely by the estate, the family who had once lived in the Hall. Except for the reservoir itself and the few fields attached to the Barn. The land attached to the Barn, Duncan knew, had been an historical anomaly. A son-in-law had been allocated a small-holding in the nineteenth century, apparently to keep a favourite daughter close to her family. Around the edges of the reservoir, several streams leached out across the valley, shining like blue capillaries under a green, earthly skin.

Duncan let his fingers hover on the mouse, then zoomed again, clicking between the map and aerial photography, scanning the woods and paths and the open fields at the bottom of his land. Then his fingers snapped on the mouse and the screen went blank.

He pushed his chair away from the desk and spun round to face the window. He stared sightlessly at the view of the fields and the silver-blue expanse of water in the distance.

CHAPTER 17

CLAIRE – BEFORE

Things got slightly better with Joe as a small child, once he could walk and explore. Before he went to school. After being a screaming, restless baby, he was a quiet toddler, utterly absorbed in whatever caught his attention. He'd play at my feet for hours without much fuss, as long as he could see me. He'd kick off if he couldn't see me. At the preschool where I helped out, he occupied himself well, finding a corner with bricks or digging in the soil in the garden – never the sandpit, that would have been too sociable. Bit of a loner, they said, that's all. I didn't let on he couldn't bear to lose me from his sight.

Starting proper school, however, was tough. That first day, he stood beside me at the school gate. He was reluctant to walk away but unwilling to speak or even look at me. We stood there, the pair of us, on the edge of the playground watching everyone else. Him, the other kids, me, the other new mothers, both of us assessing the staff. His hand stayed in mine, his tiny fingers warm in my palm, until eventually a teacher tugged him free.

'Come on, Joe, it's time to be a big boy, like the others,' she'd said.

With his face screwed up tight, he'd screamed.

He screamed and screamed that first week, and the next, and the next one after that. Eventually, he calmed down. A bit intense, they said. Very focused on his tasks. That was a good thing, wasn't it? But it was only in play, the stuff he *chose* to do. He wasn't so focused on his learning. And he wasn't much cop with the teachers who didn't like questions – backchat, they called it. You'd think they'd appreciate his questions. At least he was trying.

By the time he got to secondary school, it was another story. He hated all the rules, the vast size of the place and all those different people. They had expectations of him. He was truanting every week. I'd drop him off at one gate and he'd go in only to scoot round the other side and out from another. I spent half my time searching the streets for him then bringing him back to school. It ruined any chance of me going to work.

As he grew up, I was told he was bright but antisocial, physically a young man but immature. 'Unable to focus.' That phrase kept coming back at me. That's a laugh! I never knew a boy who could focus half as much as Joe. It just had to be something on *his* terms. When he found a project he really liked, he was obsessed. Like the metal detecting.

Since he's officially left school, he's been out there metal detecting almost every night. He started work somewhere in the bottom field near the scrubland by the water. He's said there are bumps in the ground that aren't normal and he's absolutely convinced there's something there. When he gets his teeth into something, that's it, he's off. That's my Joe.

Joe's always been different, solitary, intense – even slightly paranoid. I've had my suspicions. ADHD, autistic, Asperger's? Somewhere on a sliding scale. Every child is different. We never got a diagnosis. Perhaps because he wasn't quite far enough on the professionals' charts. Or perhaps a diagnosis would have meant staffing, funding, and neither the school nor the council wanted that. Too many pressures already competing for too few resources. Borderline, they said. Or maybe something else, medical, even a birth defect.

'Is there a family history of genetic abnormality, Mrs Henderson?' the headteacher once said.

I could have punched her.

Perhaps I didn't push hard enough because I was afraid of what the consequences of a diagnosis might be. Who's going to give an autistic boy a job? What girl is even going to look at him if he has a label like that?

They all saw Joe as a problem, but not one they were prepared to solve. I saw Joe as my son. Special. Talented in his own way. I would never have changed a thing about him. When he was sixteen and first in love, he would drench himself in body spray after a shower so that the whole house stank of Black Temptation. When he was twelve and breaking out in spots, I felt the same distress that he'd felt each morning when a new batch of pimples had spread across his forehead. When he was eight, I would sit on the floor and help him, the two of us a mean Lego machine, building endless futuristic moon bases that sprouted up across the carpet like lily pads on a garden pond. When he was four and still a baby, the two of us would snuggle up in bed with a picture book, and he'd beg for the same story again and again until I could recite every word of it off by heart.

I see me in Joe. Not Duncan. I refuse to see anything of Duncan. My boy is now a young man, with my eyes and my hair and my strength and determination. Isn't that what life is about? Giving birth to the next generation? The selfish gene – such an ugly phrase, but apt. Otherwise, sooner or later everything would come to a stop. I chose to be a mother. I know it's not the trendy thing, not these days, the feminist, independent, self-reliant thing, but for me, with my child, it was the right thing to do.

If I could change the past, I wouldn't hesitate – things would be different for sure. But not Joe, never Joe. To say that I wouldn't have married my husband, that I would never have had my son? No, I couldn't say that. Never to have known Joe is unthinkable.

Joe has made me promise not to tell anyone about the puppetrider. Least of all Duncan.

'You don't understand, Mum. If anyone in the group finds out,' he says, 'they'll be all over our land.'

His metal detector friends, that's what he means. It seems they aren't really his friends, after all.

'Promise me, Mum!'

For once I'm happy to agree. I have my own reasons for that. I bite my top lip.

'Don't you want to share your discovery?' I ask. And then, just to be sure, 'And aren't there rules about treasure finds? You said there were.'

Joe goes suspiciously quiet.

'Joe? I can look it up myself if you don't tell me.'

Somehow, I don't think he has any intention of contacting the authorities.

'There are rules,' he says. 'Depending on the number of coins and metal content. But I've only found one coin so far. We have to be really careful the night hawkers don't find out.'

'Night hawkers? What's that?' I almost laugh.

'You need to take it seriously, Mum – they're metal detectors who illegally search on land for which they don't have permission. Or raid legitimate archaeological sites. I found this on *our* land. We need to keep it quiet, till I've had time to search further. If anyone gets wind of this, our fields will get targeted.'

'You're kidding me, Joe!'

'Please, Mum, I've been working for this for so long – you won't tell Dad, will you? He won't understand. He . . .'

Joe lowers his head and his voice tails off. My heart goes out to him – Duncan really doesn't understand. He still clings to the idea that Joe should be into football or rugby, something more like sport – the sort of thing Duncan enjoys, not Joe. It's always been a frustration between them that Joe and Duncan never connected with something they both liked, as father and son. It's been Joe's dream, this whole hoard thing, and now he's actually found something . . .

But *that*? I have to handle this carefully.

'It's okay, Joe. I won't tell anyone. But I don't like the sound of this. If that coin is so significant, perhaps it would be better if you let me look after it for you, whilst we figure out what's the right thing to do. How to deal with it.'

I hesitate to use the word *properly*. That would be an insult to Joe. My hand hovers anxiously over the coin. He snatches it away, folding it between the sheets of tissue paper.

'Do you want them digging on our land?' he says.

'Well, I . . .'

It had never occurred to me that Joe's metal detecting could result in this. He thinks he's found something of real archaeological significance.

I feel a wave of emotion sweep over me. Nausea and shame. Fear. I push it back. My mouth gives a bitter twist. Perhaps I should tell him that I've heard tales of landowners and property developers being bogged down in archaeological digs for years, unable to build on or sell their property. That if Duncan and I are parting ways, I need for the Barn to sell quickly and easily when the time comes. Except Joe doesn't know about all that yet.

I can't tell him the truth.

Gently – I need to deal with this gently, or I will push Joe the other way.

'Okay, Joe. I'll leave it for now. But you've got to promise me not to get into any trouble over this. Maybe stop the digging for a bit, hmm? So people don't realise what you're doing, eh? And no telling anyone on the internet.'

Now I'm telling *him* to keep quiet.

He nods.

'Promise?' I say.

He nods again and I heave a temporary sigh of relief.

It's only later, when I'm chewing it over, worrying about what he's found, that I realise his nod was in response to my second request. That the likelihood of Joe not digging anymore, just when he's found something of interest, is about as likely as our dog, Arthur, landing on the moon.

CHAPTER 18

CLAIRE – BEFORE

Duncan hasn't come back. After the argument with Joe, and Duncan walking out last night, I didn't expect him to. He could have bunked down at the surgery, on the sofa in the waiting room – that's what he's told me before. Too tired to come home after a late-night emergency. Yeah, right, Duncan. He could have found himself a hotel, too pissed off with Joe or me to come home. Maybe. But I know it's most likely he was sleeping in that other woman's bed.

Surely, he'll come home after work today. If only to get a change of clothes. Joe's still in his room, glued to his PC, and I settle to cooking in the kitchen.

Food, to me, is my one comfort, the act of preparing a dish, the unity of a shared meal. Maybe it's a peace offering, an attempt to reach out. To Duncan, to Joe, for Becky and her son, anyone who deigns to keep me company.

My grandmother loved her food. In a very real way. She'd

lived through the Second World War and knew what it was like to struggle for sustenance on a day-to-day basis. I remember visiting her as a child. Her old fridge rumbled like a car revving outside the front door and if you looked carefully, you could see it move, edging slowly out of position as the day wore on. My big brother, Ian, and I laughed about it when we got home, as if it were a living thing trying to escape her kitchen.

Granny kept it cram-packed with food. Cheeses that were over three months old, milk that had gone sour, bacon that had gone grey, let alone the permanent presence of an open tin of Bentos steak and kidney pie. She was obsessed with Bentos steak and kidney pie. There was always a cut half of a raw onion sitting on the bottom shelf, usually white with mould – it tainted everything else. She wouldn't throw anything away unless it was actually growing real live fur. Mum said it was because food was so hard to come by after the war. It was a national pastime, collecting and hoarding food. Or cultivating the neighbours because they grew vegetables in their back garden. Or trading a kiss with the village butcher in lieu of ration coupons. It should make me smile, the thought of Granny sneaking off for a side of beef. So to speak. Except it doesn't.

Once, when I was little, Ian told me that after Grandpa died, Granny kept it quiet for weeks, just so she could use up the last of his coupons. It haunted me, that image of Grandpa's body decaying in an armchair whilst my grandmother baked cakes in the kitchen. It didn't occur to me that Ian was pulling my leg. That groaning fridge made me absolutely believe him.

Ian lives in Australia now, with his wife, Moira, and the kids, where the food is exotic and abundant, and the kids burn it all off with endless rounds of cricket and rounders on the beach. They moved a few years ago. Duncan approved. He said it was a good thing for Ian and Moira to start a new life the other side of the planet, to make their own mark on the world. I think he likes the fact that they're too far away to observe or interfere in our relationship.

It was after Ian moved away that I really started to put on weight. My fault entirely. But then, look at Joe – he can eat anything he likes and he still burns it off. Too scrawny, a weakling, Duncan used to say, when Joe was younger, on the days when he was too frustrated with Joe's behaviour even to consider the impact of those comments on his son. I could have kicked him.

It's little wonder Joe chooses to escape the house the moment Duncan gets back. And only stays with me when Duncan is away.

When Duncan's father died, Duncan took it very badly. He'd always looked up to his dad, even though his father never seemed to notice. His father had died of cancer and, suddenly, Duncan became very food aware. He started to fret about approaching middle age, that the same would happen to him; not that he ever voiced the words, but I knew that that was on his mind. He had a renewed interest in sport, bought trainers and smart clothes. He even joined a gym, somewhere in Derby. None of this surprised me, he'd always loved his sport. But now he was rigid about his routine, disappearing for hours every evening, only to come home flushed from exercise and sweet-smelling after a shower.

I hated this new regime. Duncan had also begun eating his main meal in the middle of the day, which meant he ate at work. I'd treasured our evening meals. It was a time to unwind, for us to catch up and talk. Now, it was a rare event. Joe and me on our own, struggling to find something to talk about other than metal detecting.

Food, to me, is one of life's pleasures, for so many reasons. When I was pregnant, I could eat what I liked. When Joe was little and I was still feeding him myself, it was the same. Even after Joe was weaned and later when he started school, I ate well. Comfort eating, I guess. This whole thing started long before Duncan's new gym routine. The weight crept on. An inch around the waist, cheeks fuller than before, breasts that filled my clothes in a way that pleased me – and Duncan. Or so I believed. I never really thought much about it. I knew I should be doing the same, upping my fitness levels, but I was tired, always tired, and Duncan didn't really want the company. Not my company.

Those stints at the gym were his time away from things, from me, I got that. What with sport and the Barn project taking up all his spare time, I didn't have a chance. But I've known, I think I've always known. Derby is an implausibly long way to travel for a gym, a strange choice for someone who works in Belston.

I just didn't want to face up to it.

It was a few days before Christmas when I found out. *Happy Christmas, Claire.* I was at the supermarket in Belston, queuing for a turkey. I was recognised by a couple of women in the queue behind me – two of the other mothers from those days at the school gate.

'Hello, Claire,' said Alicia.

She was dressed in an impractical white tightly waisted trench coat.

'Planning a family roast? We're having a whole salmon this year – so much healthier, don't you think?' Mandy added.

Her skinny jeans and high-heeled boots gave me all the more reason to dislike her.

'And how's Duncan, Claire?' Alicia said. 'I hear he's so clever and he works so *hard*.'

This, followed by a light, girlish giggle.

'We saw him only last night, grabbing a quick drink with one of the girls from the practice. I'm sure I recognised her from when I took my dog in. Must have been the office Christmas do. Nice place, Moretti's – if only my husband's works do was somewhere so posh.'

Moretti's was a restaurant, not a bar, and he'd told me that the night before he'd gone to the gym. I felt a blush of humiliation and anger sweeping up my neck.

I'd been living in a bubble of my own making, which Mandy and Alicia had cheerfully burst. It had taken me too long to acknowledge what I'd long suspected. I tried to push it from my mind; I didn't want to assume the worst. But this time it wasn't some faceless woman in Derby, a one-night stand or a drunken aberration, however I tried to justify it in my mind. No, this time it was someone from his work. One of the girls from the surgery.

I dismissed it from my thoughts. He wouldn't be so foolish; you couldn't keep a thing like that a secret for long. But who? I couldn't keep the question from nagging at my mind. Who was it? One of the veterinary nurses or care assistants on the ward? Frances, Madelaine or Imogen? Or was it Paula, the new junior vet? Or Sally, the receptionist? A picture of each of the women he worked with passed through my head: their hair, their faces, the size of their bust or waist. Which one would he be most likely to go for? But I couldn't imagine it – Imogen's married, Frances is too old, Sally too young, Madelaine . . . could it be Madelaine? Oh God . . . it probably didn't matter if one of them was married or had a boyfriend. After all, it didn't matter to Duncan.

I think back to the years gone by, how Duncan has grown more and more distant. Staying out late, or not coming home at all. The lies. How many lies? We don't even sleep together anymore – separate rooms on either side of the upstairs gallery. We told Joe that it was because Duncan has to get up early for work, to do the morning round on the wards before the first client appointment. It was partially true, wasn't it? That's the way to lie, bury it in a half-truth that you can then persuade yourself to believe.

Duncan stopped caring a long time ago, long before I began to suspect he was sleeping around. Maybe I hate that even more than the fact of the affairs. The total lack of concern for my feelings and the way it shames *me*, not him. A man gets a slap on the back for sowing his seeds, but a woman is shamed for not holding on to her man. Even now in this day and age.

Duncan does care about his reputation, though, his professional reputation. An affair at work is way too close to home. No, he wouldn't be that stupid, surely.

I guess for a long time, I was simply in denial.

After Evangeline, I was always in denial.

CHAPTER 19

CLAIRE – AFTER

I've worked myself up into such a state that my heart races with each new sound, straining to hear outside. It's as if I'm looking down from above, in one of those out-of-body experiences, watching myself pacing the room, stopping to search from one window and then the next, pacing again, getting more and more agitated.

It's been too long. Joe's never been gone for more than those two weeks last summer. Okay, he's over eighteen and left school, but that doesn't make me feel any better.

I call him on his mobile, as I have done every day since I got here. It rings out. I can almost imagine it, playing some heavy metal riff from a song by the band Rammstein, until my call kicks over to his answer machine.

'Hi, I'm Joe. If you can be bothered, leave me a message, and if I can be bothered, I might call you back.'

Very funny, Joe. Not. I chew my finger. What next?

I ring Callum. Again. I've tried a few times. I don't like him. He and Joe were friends at primary school, but not as Joe grew older. Then suddenly, this last year, Callum was on the scene again. It was like Joe wanted to be 'grown-up', that Callum was his way into adult life. Callum's already got his own tiny flat on the east side of Derby. I went there last summer, when I was looking for Joe. I was that desperate. It stank of weed and stale alcohol. I thought, this isn't Joe's scene, is it? This kind of guy? The tone rings and the call still goes unanswered.

I hesitate, then with a burst of determination, on the off-chance, I ring the number again. This time, to my surprise, Callum actually picks up.

'Hello?' he says.

His voice is deep and alarmingly masculine. I remember him as a high-pitched, whiny twelve-year-old. I school my voice to keep it steady, but it comes out a rushed, husky whisper.

'Hello, Callum – I'm looking for Joe.'

I hear Callum sigh. *Oh God*, he's thinking, *not Joe's mother again*. My voice strengthens, gathering in a rush.

'He hasn't come home for . . .' Six weeks and how many days? I hate this, it's shameful admitting I've lost my son. 'I wouldn't ring except he's got a dentist appointment.' There's no appointment, but it's plausible enough. 'I wondered if he's bunked down with you and just forgot?'

'Hello?' Callum's voice sounds confused and sleepy.

I wait and he speaks again.

'Hello?'

The phone clicks – there's static on the line, nothing new about that, not up here, especially when it's windy. He can't hear me. Or maybe he's pretending, that wouldn't be a first. I feel myself tense.

'Callum! It's Joe's mum. Callum, can you hear me?'

Another pause. The crackling worsens.

'Fuck off!' comes the reply.

I hold the phone from my ear. How dare he! The phone line's dead. I feel tears pricking at the back of my eyes. Bloody teenagers.

Callum hadn't heard me. It *was* a problem with the line. Or more likely, Callum recognised my number and chose to ignore me. Maybe he didn't recognise the number and thought I was a crank caller, about to hassle him about a non-existent insurance policy.

It's humiliating making these calls. The desperation must have been evident in my voice. Joe's mother. *She's always ringing me, chasing after him. She needs help . . .* I can just hear him moaning to his mates, then laughing and swigging another beer. I don't feel comfortable with the idea that Joe has reignited his friendship with Callum, especially since the guy kept his distance at secondary school for so long. Something doesn't quite stack up.

I'm sat down, my hands flat on the kitchen table to keep them still, pressing my fingers down one by one until the joints bend the wrong way and my fingernails turn white. Should I call the police? Is *now* the time to call the police? When I rang them last summer, they were very clear about it – if he's over eighteen and left school, has no registered health problems and there are no specific suspicious circumstances, then there's nothing they can do.

Do you know how many young men go 'missing', luv?

101

A person can *choose* to go missing.

Martin said pretty much the same – he knew Joe's history, but that they'd keep an eye out. And Joe did come back. I thought this move would change things, yet here I am playing out the same routine, chasing after my son. Except this time, I can't call Duncan. There's no way I'm going to speak to Duncan. Besides, I know he won't want to speak to me. And Martin? I'm not sure . . . I've had that text from Joe. Martin will tell me there's nothing they can do. That unless there's clear evidence of foul play . . .

I could ring Becky, though, couldn't I?

I pick up the phone then throw it down again. No, I can't call Becky. She'd ask too many questions. Every time I think of it, I know that I can't call her. She won't understand. She's my best friend but she's Duncan's sister, too. She's never going to forgive me for leaving her brother. How can I explain to her the truth behind my marriage? The way things really are between Duncan and me. How can I accuse her brother of all those one-night stands, the affairs? Let alone tell her about Evangeline.

Oh, God. I swallow painfully. It might come to that eventually. No, it can't. Never.

A darkness descends on me.

I can't tell her. It's too much to expect of her, family or no. The longer I wait to pick up the phone, the harder it seems to become.

I think of my other friends, but there's been no one as close as Becky. I've been so focused on Joe, I guess I've pushed other people away. Becky was family and the only one who understood or cared, given her own experience with Alex. It's amazing how quickly people walk away once they realise you come encumbered with problems.

I think of the women I've met at school. The staff who look down on you for birthing a difficult child, or blame all of his problems on bad parenting. The stay-at-home mother types who've made a career out of looking smart for their men, cleaning their homes and being seen at the right coffee mornings – they wouldn't touch anyone like me, who's over-weight and more interested in books than make-up. The busy working-mum types, dashing from childcare to work to school runs, too harassed to have time to chat or have sympathy for any problems other than their own – *Oh, Claire, my boy adores your Joe. It's so sweet, why don't we set up a playdate? Yes? Fabulous – I'll bring him round to yours for a few hours on Saturday – will nine to five do? Perfect.* Bloody hell, the number of times I fell for that one. And the grandmothers besotted with their grandchildren, standing in for parents who never have time to do a school run at all, other than turn up once a year for parents' evening.

I don't fit in, never did fit in. Thanks to Joe. No, thanks to Duncan. No – that's not fair. I can't blame it on anyone but myself – my fault, my decisions, my failures . . . it's just how I choose to rationalise it, isn't it? When I'm feeling low.

I'm tired, my eyes drooping in spite of myself. Nothing seems to matter anymore; I only want to sleep. I lay my head against my arms, feeling the cold, hard wood of the table against my skin, a counterpoint to the headache pounding behind my eyes.

There's Frances. Duncan and I have known her a long time, she's been at the practice since the start. She's a few years older than me, no kids, never got married, yet wise. Wise because she never got married. Wisdom grows when you work with animals. I've always liked Frances; though we've never been close. I wonder if she has an idea of what Duncan's really like but doesn't want to say. It's hard, breaking that unspoken code of keeping your nose out of other people's business.

She's pretty forthright, though. I've seen her give a few of the staff a dressing-down when they've made a mistake. She tore a strip off Tim once, when he gave a dog the wrong dosage. Fortunately, the dog was okay, but Tim was mortified. He never made the same mistake again. She can even keep Duncan in line when she chooses to. Which is probably why I like her. But she's fond of him, always has been. Is it her, his affair? I can't bring myself to believe it. She's too nice, too . . . I don't know. No, I can't talk to her, either.

I feel my body sinking into a half-slumber. It's started to rain outside. I hear it drumming on the garden path. It should be soothing, but I hate it. I can't bear the cold sound of drops pattering against the glass, the steady chink of water flowing in the drains, getting louder and louder. The old cottage window frames creak, adjusting to the damp, like the water is pushing on them from the outside, trying to get in.

I drag myself awake. New life pulses in the rain, the fresh, metallic scent of it seeping through the gaps. I gaze at the lush greenery in the garden, the leaves bent vertical by the rain. I search the brooding clouds. Rain is good, it cleanses the air, replenishes a thirsty ground. It brings everything back to life – healing, that's how I should think of it. But it's no good, it only makes me feel bleak.

A male blackbird scoots across the lawn despite the rain – scoot and stop, scoot and stop, lifting his yellow beak, shaking the droplets from his head. He turns to one side, searching, checking each time he gets a little closer to his goal. Whatever that is. He clucks – a sharp, repetitive sound, like a fire alarm on a low battery. Then I see the cause of his anxiety – a magpie is rooted to the tree above. Its blue-and-white plumage shines in the rain and one beady eye swivels down to the ground. I'm witnessing a magpie–blackbird stand-off, the one hungry for blackbird chick pie, the other desperate to protect his family.

Sing a song of sixpence,
A pocket full of rye,
Four and twenty blackbirds,
Baked in a pie.

The blackbird hops again, scoot and stop, daring the magpie to get any closer as it chatters overhead. Eventually, the magpie gives an angry flutter of its wings and flies away. The blackbird clucks one last warning before disappearing into the hedge beneath, swallowed up by its tightly woven branches.

Someone came to visit me yesterday. I'm not sure who. I think maybe someone from the estate. Checking on me. There was a knock at the door. I didn't answer it. Something made me hang back and I'm sure I saw him walking away. It was a *him.* But every time I try to picture the man in my head, my brain veers away. I have this constant feeling of dread, terror almost, and the nausea returns. It's as if, since I left Duncan, I've become paranoid: about Joe, strangers, living here on my own – I never used to be like that. It never bothered me at all living out here in the countryside, miles from my nearest neighbour.

I don't want to go to a doctor. I'm not depressed. I don't want to tell them how I feel. I don't want them to put me on medication, or tell Duncan – would they tell Duncan? He's still my next of kin. I feel the anxiety in me twist even tighter, like strips of willow in a log basket. Nothing seems quite real.

Until I hear the sound of hooves outside on the lane. That's real. I perk up. A rider. I thought there was no one living around here, the village empty, the cottage on its own dead-end track where there's nowhere else to go.

The horse gives a soft whinny and the hooves seem to stop and start, as if the animal is restless or won't go on. It can't go on. It must be turning round. Then the sound picks up, increases and fades away until the horse and rider are gone.

Something's wrong with me. I'm not the same as I was before. I don't seem to be able to cope now that I'm living on my own. I rub my eyes, kneading at the middle of my forehead. Joe, Becky, living here on my own. I didn't think it would be like this.

CHAPTER 20

DUNCAN – AFTER

This morning, the surgery was already stupidly busy. Duncan was going to have to consider expanding operations again. Tim was always fully booked and recruiting Paula might not be enough. It was exciting but daunting, too, and finding more money might be a problem. Duncan was fast becoming a victim of his own success. Animal baskets blocked the floor and the reception area resonated with barks and yowling cats, and there was a long queue at the desk.

Duncan ignored them all as he strode through the waiting room to his office. He was an hour late. He was never late. When he sat down, he was surprised to see Sally there, drawing the door shut behind her with a soft click.

He shrugged out of his jacket and tugged at the V-neck of his short-sleeved surgical top, then spun round to his PC under the window, tapping into the screen to log on.

'Now's not a good time,' he said, his voice brisk and businesslike.

'I need to tell you something.'

Not *speak* to you, but *tell* you something. Duncan gave a sigh and turned to face his colleague. She stood with her back to the door, her hands still clutching the handle, her face taut but oddly purposeful.

'Let me guess, you're pregnant!'

Sally flushed. 'That's hardly funny!'

No, it wasn't. Cheap shot, thought Duncan, in very poor taste, marvelling at his own bad mood. Just as well he was his own boss. Sally looked petite and young against the door, her skirt a little too short, her green practice T-shirt flattering her shape. She lifted her chin. He didn't apologise.

'Well, didn't you hear me?' he said. 'Haven't you noticed the queue out there? We've got Mr Garfield and Betsy next, I think.'

The elderly, incontinent greyhound, on her return appointment.

'That's what I need to speak to you about.' Sally bit her lip. 'Garfield's not coming.'

'So?' Duncan gave a puff of annoyance. 'Make him another appointment and send me whoever's next.'

Duncan swung back to his screen.

'I can't. I mean, I tried to. He *did* come, he was at the front desk a few minutes ago, but only to say that he's not bringing her back in.'

Duncan turned back to Sally again, scowling.

'What's his excuse this time? You know I want to keep an eye on that one.'

'Duncan . . . I . . .'

'Spit it out, Sally, what is it? I'm already running late.'

'Betsy, the dog, that is . . . she's . . .'

Sally looked suddenly tearful. She lifted her chin and released the door handle.

'He's had her put down.'

'What!' Duncan's voice reverberated around the room.

Outside, the reception area had gone quiet. Sally cast an agonised look over her shoulder at the door.

'He came in,' she said, 'to say that because you wouldn't do it, he had to find someone who would, a different vet. To put her down.'

Duncan pushed himself from his chair, swearing bluntly.

'For fuck's sake, what kind of vet would do that?'

'I don't—' Sally started.

'Where is he? You said he's just been in, is he still here?'

'He left a few minutes ago . . .'

'Out of the way, Sally!'

She jumped aside as Duncan grabbed the door and sprinted into the reception area. Carving a path through the crowd, he burst out of the main door and into the front car park. Sally followed, gesturing helplessly to Madelaine on the desk. Duncan stopped to scan the car park and the pavement beyond.

Garfield was still there, waiting at the bus stop on the far side of the street. Leaning on a stick, with his gaberdine mac and cloth cap, he was the very picture of elderly innocence. A red bus approached, indicators flashing. It screeched to a halt and Garfield made to climb on board. But Duncan was already there, blocking his path, almost dragging the man back towards the bus shelter.

'You murdering fool!' cried Duncan.

There was a screech of alarm from the old man. His stick fell clattering to the ground and he tottered on his feet. Duncan was vaguely aware that the bus driver looked visibly shocked.

'You killed your dog! After I specifically told you how to treat her!'

A sea of faces in the bus ogled through the windows. A schoolboy pressed his nose against the glass with the kind of expression of one watching a horror movie for the first time. Duncan shoved Garfield in the chest and the man staggered backwards into the bus shelter as Duncan snarled again.

'Are you seriously telling me you had Betsy put down? A perfectly healthy dog!'

'She were too old, she 'ad no bladder control. She were clearly struggling.'

'Only because you denied her water!'

'I had 'er checked out by another vet. They agreed with me. That she were suffering and should be put down.'

'Who? Which bloody vet said that!'

There were only two other vets in the area – Duncan knew them both. He couldn't imagine either one of them agreeing to euthanise a frail but otherwise healthy dog.

'That's none of yer business . . .'

'Oh, yes it is!' Duncan felt his fists clench. 'Have you done it yourself? God help me, Garfield, I'll . . .'

'Excuse me.'

A young man had stepped off the bus.

'Stay out of this,' Duncan snapped.

'I'm sorry, but I can't. You're threatening this man and I think he needs my help.'

The lad looked no more than sixteen but confident in

himself for all that. His voice was calm and frustratingly reasonable. Duncan eyed him speculatively. He was younger even than Joe. Duncan's expression changed. Would Joe have come to a stranger's rescue like that?

'You've got no idea what's going on,' he said, his voice tightly controlled. He turned back to Garfield.

Garfield had retrieved his stick. He wobbled on it, milking the situation. The bus driver was speaking urgently into his radio. The engine throbbed in neutral and the stench of diesel filled the air. Duncan felt sick with fury and disgust as he looked from the young man to the bus driver and back to Garfield.

'I'll report you this time. Both you and your *vet* to the RSPCA. There was no justification whatsoever for killing that dog.'

'Duncan, please . . .'

A voice came from behind him. It was Sally. Her hand tugged at Duncan's arm.

'I'm sorry,' she addressed the bus driver. 'This man' – she nodded at Garfield – 'has had his dog put down against Duncan's professional advice. We're all very upset.'

'Why don't you come on board, Mr . . .' The student held his arm out to Garfield, ignoring both Sally and Duncan.

Duncan rocked on his heels, clenching both hands. The muscles on his bare arms bounced into profile. Garfield took the student's arm and shuffled with surprising agility onto the bus. The driver flung his radio down and eagerly revved up the engine. Sally held onto Duncan.

'Get off me!' he growled.

He pulled away, moving towards the bus as if to mount it. Then he thought better of it and stepped back. The bus doors slid shut and the vehicle lurched into motion. Sally was still holding onto him with the tenacity of a lioness.

Duncan jerked his arm free with such force that this time Sally lost her balance and stumbled backwards. He raised his face to the rear of the bus, noting its passengers were still staring wide-eyed from the windows. He lifted up one fist, middle finger up.

'Fucking wanker!'

CHAPTER 21

CLAIRE – AFTER

MISSING, JOE HENDERSON

Age 18, brown hair, blue eyes, height 6 foot 2

Las%t se££en . . .

My head hurts like hell today. I can't even count my own fingers. I hit backspace and keep the key pressed down until those last two words disappear, then type again. Thinking about Joe has left me even more unsettled. It's been long enough. I need to *do* something. I print off a batch of posters, pushing them into thin plastic wallets. I decide to spend the day pinning them to trees around the immediate area.

Where the lane drops over the hill, the view opens out to reveal a close network of gently sloping fields, enfolding the smooth waters of the reservoir. I can see the grey concrete expanse of the dam, the rooflines of the houses in the old village and in the distance, on the other side of the valley, the familiar shape of the folds of the hill, beyond which I know lies the Barn. It's a long way away, but for me, today, not far enough.

The landscape here is different to the rest of Derbyshire. Or so it seems to me. The fields are an extra degree of lush green, populated with an unlikely variety of trees. Their shapes and colours ornament the hedgerows, each tree having reached its full height unhindered, the way that old estate trees do. A few sheep drift across the upper fields with the laziness of domestic animals and the birds on the water seem to have no fear of predators.

The rain stopped hours ago and the roads glisten. Every now and again, water bursts through the hedges, draining from the slopes above. I slow the car and open the window to feel the tentative warmth of an early spring day. The dappled verges are filled with sunshine daffodils and the first stitchwort are scattered under the trees like tiny white star-shaped sequins. It seems a pointless exercise, these posters, for I haven't seen another soul in the valley all day. But I have to try. Eventually, I turn the car towards Brereton Edge. I have two posters left.

The start of the village is marked by a handful of red brick buildings. It's more of a hamlet really, a cluster of houses, with one defunct farm and the old Hall. The trees lean close where the perimeter walls of the Hall undulate beside the lane, and a plethora of chimneys boast of the size of the building and the wealth of the family who built it. I stop the car at the entrance. The gates are locked. The brickwork of the wall shines an extra level of red. Here, I think. On the gate itself. It's as good a place as any.

I switch the engine off, resting my arm on the open window. Arthur's wet nose nudges me from behind and I hear his tail thumping against the back seat. My eyes are drawn to the reservoir, visible between the trees. Before Joe was born, long before we came to live here, Duncan and I would drive here often. It was our secret place. Duncan had an old Renault Clio then and we'd park it on a verge of the main road, clamber through the fencing and walk paths that were long overgrown and hidden. In summer, we'd bring a picnic and a blanket. We'd walk, then find a spot sheltered from the wind, have sex and eat, then have sex again. The air over the bowl of the valley would heat up and the paths would turn to dust that clung to our trousers and arms and mixed with the sweat on our bodies.

The tree beside me flutters with grey. The branches shake and I see pigeons, at least three of them. They're excited, flying up and down in turn as if jostling for position. They must be feasting on something in the tree. Berries maybe, but not yet, not at this time of year; insects then, do pigeons eat insects? Probably.

The sound of their wings and the stir of wind on the young leaves holds my gaze a little longer. A cool breeze flows across my cheeks. I close my eyes and listen. To the voices in my head. Duncan shouting in the house. The sound of feet running down the stairs, the slam of car doors outside and the revving of an engine. My own voice rising above the weather. I open my eyes and shake my head. I reach for the car door and get out.

I tie my poster to the gate and turn to go back. But I'm

115

curious about the houses – they're so pretty, so full of character, yet empty. I can't understand why they are empty, why they haven't been sold off and renovated. Who wouldn't want to live here? I've no real intention to pry, but as none of the houses are occupied, what harm can it do?

I leave Arthur in the car with the window still open and walk to the first cottage. It's no bigger than mine. A path leads to the side. There's a porch with enough space for one person to shelter from the rain and take their boots off. Cobwebs fill the window sills, coating my fingers with grey strands of silk. I push on the door. It doesn't budge. I try the handle, but that doesn't work, either. I bend down to peer through the letterbox. There's a single room with a fireplace at one end and kitchen units on the other. On the opposite wall is another outside door. I head around the back. The grass is overlong and last year's apples lie rotting on the lawn. That second door opens. For some reason, it doesn't occur to me not to go in, that it being unlocked means someone might be home.

The room is empty but for a single frayed armchair. The carpet is a dirty green with lighter patches where bigger furniture once stood. A soggy puddle of water shimmers under the bay window and the glass is broken where the rain has come in. The wooden cabinets of the kitchen stand with their doors hanging open like the wings of the pigeons on the tree by my car. A space has been left with exposed pipes for a gas cooker, as if such a thing had even existed when the house was last inhabited. I stand uncertainly, contemplating whether or not to take a look upstairs. I think I've heard a car. And was that Arthur barking?

I spin on my heels to look through the window, but there's

116

nothing. The wind has dropped, the sun has gone and the road winds up and out of sight, empty.

I hear the creak of a floorboard. Is there someone upstairs? 'Hello?' My voice reverberates against the bare walls.

Trespasser – the word hisses in my head. An apology is already forming on my tongue. There's no reply.

The late afternoon sun has broken through again and a faint square of amber light reaches across the carpet. It trembles as it gathers strength, forming a new pattern at my feet, light and shadow from the leaves of a moving branch. I stride across the room. The back door is open, exactly as I left it. A half-dead bluebottle struggles on the floor, its wings rattling in the draught from outside, its tiny legs scrabbling to find purchase. I listen but there's nothing else to hear. I feel the guilt of my presence thudding in my chest.

I duck through the back door, glad to be outside again. I pull it shut behind me quietly as if there's someone to listen. My pulse is racing and I feel foolish. What excuse would I have come up with if someone *had* arrived to challenge me?

I fling my head up and he's standing right in front of me on the garden path. A man.

My heart hammers. My feet take a stumbling step backwards.

He's wearing a tweed jacket, double-pocketed and closely fitted around the chest. It's like some kind of old-fashioned riding jacket. His legs are encased in black boots and pale breeches, and his hair curls under a Derbyshire cloth cap. He can't be much older than me but he has that distant, detached look of someone from the aristocratic hunting fraternity. For a second, our eyes meet. I drop my gaze and his mouth pulls into an amused sneer.

'I'm so sorry!' I say. I feel my hackles rise, but I'm the one in the wrong here. 'I was looking for my son. I thought the house was empty, that maybe he'd bunked down in here for the night.'

I feel myself blushing.

'The house isn't empty, as you can see.'

He should be annoyed, but the man's voice is level and quiet. Too quiet. I glance over my shoulder, through the window. The room is empty but for its armchair. My eyes slide back to him as if to say: *Really?*

'You'll be the new tenant,' he says. 'How are you settling in?'

'Fine, thank you.'

I search his face. He might be the man who tried to visit me the other day.

'Good,' he says. 'I'm sure you'll find everyone is welcoming.'

Who's he on about? I wonder. He's the first person I've seen. He smiles then, all white, even teeth like something from a 1980s soap opera. I think *Dallas* or Jilly Cooper or . . . I'm embarrassed by the turn of my own thoughts.

'Everyone? I don't understand. No one lives here, at least . . . the village is abandoned, isn't it?'

'Whatever makes you think that?' he says, smiling still.

'Well, I thought it was.'

'Some of the houses are empty, but not all. People come and go.'

He doesn't elaborate. Holiday cottages, I think. Of course – that makes sense. I look doubtfully back through the window. Perhaps it's a work in progress. Or he just wants me to think this place is occupied.

'My son is missing, like I said.' I pull out the last poster. 'Can I give you this?'

Joe's face stares blankly from the paper, pixelated in black and white. The man takes the poster from my hand and makes a show of examining the photo.

'Your son?' he says.

'Yes, he's eighteen. He's been gone too long.'

I bite my lip. I sound like a foolish mother again, unable to let go. But I'm hardly going to tell this stranger the whole story. He looks up. His eyes are surprisingly probing.

'You must love him very much.'

That seems an odd thing to say. Of course I love my son.

'Sure,' he says next. 'I'll keep an eye out for him. Well, it's been nice meeting you, Mrs Henderson.'

He folds the poster into one neatly gloved fist. Like a magician with a playing card.

I gasp, shocked that he knows my name. Knew my name, all along. Then it dawns on me, he called me 'the new tenant' – is he part of the family who own the estate? Up from London, perhaps, playing at country living. Is he my landlord, or someone from the family's representatives? He hasn't introduced himself.

'You drive carefully, now,' he says. 'And take it easy.'

I walk back to my car and he to his, a functional-looking Range Rover parked neatly on the verge. It's not a city car. As I look around the village again, I wonder how many other people are hidden in these run-down but beautiful houses. It seems different now, more welcoming. I should put my posters through all of their doors, except I gave that man my last one. I'll have to make some more.

Then I notice the trees. There's a smattering of wild ash.

They sprout up everywhere in this valley, up and down the lane and all around my cottage. I'd spent an afternoon the other day pulling out ash tree seedlings from the front garden. If you don't get them when they're young, they root in and they're the devil to get out. Last year's keys hang in dry, brittle clusters, silhouetted against the still-bare branches over the man's head. They rustle in the wind. It makes me think of severed hands, some 1960s block colour horror movie where the blood drips beneath their fingers and old bones rattle above like Spanish castanets. I almost smile at the idea, but as the man ducks beneath them to reach out and open his car door, there's an expression of real annoyance on his face. He must be cross with me after all. I'm sure I've read somewhere that pagans believe the ash has special protective properties.

When I reach my own car, there's a patch of water on the front seat. The wind has blown it through the open window from the trees above. I frown and look up. The man is inside his car now and I'm unsure whether he meant *he* lives in that cottage or not. I should have asked him. I can see my poster in his hand. He's unfolded it and is lifting it to the light. He grasps it between finger and thumb as if in distaste.

Then he scrunches it up and throws it onto the back seat.

CHAPTER 22

DUNCAN – AFTER

Duncan crouched forwards on his chair. His elbows rested on his knees and he stared at the screen. An x-ray of a dog's chest cavity shimmered in front of him. He searched the ghostly greys of the rib bones and the butterfly white of each segment of spine, toggling between the two images on the screen. He tucked himself closer under the desk and with his fingers on the mouse switched between each photograph again and again as if there was some logic to the comparison, even though there was not.

Then he let the mouse go. He checked the door was closed, picked up his mobile phone and swung round to the window. He dialled a number and held the phone to his ear, one hand resting behind his head. He tilted his chair back.

'Hi,' he spoke into the phone. 'Are you free for a run tonight?' There was a pause. 'Seven o'clock by the canal?

Perfect. I'll look forward to it.' He let his voice soften with his next words. 'Oh, and why don't you bring a change of clothing?' he added.

When he turned to place the phone back on his desk, the door was open and Frances was standing in the doorway.

Shit, he thought.

At closing time, she followed him into the car park. Duncan held out his key fob to unlock the car, the hazard lights beeping and flashing on and off once as she let the stockroom door bounce open and shut behind her.

'It hasn't taken you very long!' she said.

He frowned. 'I'm only going for a run, Frances.'

He had his tracksuit on and a holdall thumped to the ground as he let it drop from his fingers. Frances cast her head across her shoulder, making certain that the other staff had all gone, that it was only them in the car park.

'You promised me this would stop. I'm not an idiot, Duncan. Did you think I hadn't realised?'

'Realised what, exactly?' he said.

'Who is it this time, hmm?' she said, ignoring his question. 'What is it with you, Duncan. Are you so heartless?'

'I don't know what you're talking about.'

He was being deliberately obtuse. But they both knew what she was referring to. Duncan reached out to open the car door. He retrieved his bag and tossed it on the back seat. Frances took a visibly deep breath, holding her hand to her chest as if she could barely contain her anger. Her voice was precise and calm when she spoke.

'Why do you play these games? Even now. I won't stand by and watch you do this again, Duncan. And we had a deal:

I would keep quiet if you stopped. For *her* sake, not yours, I might add!'

Duncan steeled himself. He turned his head away so she couldn't see his face. She was the only one who walked into his consulting room like that without waiting to knock. He should have been far more careful. He'd not been himself – this wouldn't have happened seven weeks ago. *Shit, shit, shit.*

He decided to brazen it out.

'We've known each other for a long time, Frances. I respect your knowledge and experience and value your . . . friendship. But I'm only going for a run. God knows I need it right now. And who or what I do in my spare time is none of your damn business.'

'Yes, it *is* my damn business. I'm making it my business. I won't stand by and watch you hurt her. Everyone at this office respects and admires you. Are you going to wreck that, too?'

'Well, that's good to hear,' said Duncan, again ignoring the bits he didn't like.

'Don't you get smart with me, Duncan Henderson. I didn't want Claire to be hurt. I never said anything *then* because I didn't want anyone to get hurt. But she found out anyway, didn't she? What did you do? And now she's gone! Claire is *gone.* What does it take to make you stop? Are you going to carry on like nothing's happened? It's not normal!'

'I'm a free man. I'm entitled to do whatever I choose. Things were over with Claire a long time ago, we both knew that. And life carries on. I've never made any promises.'

'So, this whole "let's go for a run" thing is you starting another affair? Really? Who is it this time? And how do you think she's going to feel when she finds out?'

Affair – such an old-fashioned word, it sounded like

something bored businessmen did at three-star conference hotels near the M1. It was a word loaded with deceit and vanity and intransigence. That wasn't him, was it?

Frances turned on her heel to leave, but Duncan sprang forwards and caught up. He flung out a hand to catch her arm.

'Jealous, Frances?' he asked cruelly. Attack, it was the best form of defence.

She stared at him.

'She's a grown woman, Frances,' he said. 'And it takes two, as I recall.'

'No, it takes one,' she said. 'In your case, it's just one!'

She jerked her arm free but didn't move.

'What if I tell them, Duncan?' Her voice lowered to an angry drawl. 'What if I tell the whole practice the truth? What do you think they'd all think of you then?'

She scanned his face.

'And what if I tell Martin?'

Martin, his old schoolfriend. The policeman. His best mate. Duncan tightened his fist then let his hand fall loose by his side. He wasn't going to bite. He wasn't going to let on that any of it mattered or that he had any feelings at all. The best way to deal with a threat was to call her bluff.

'You go ahead, Frances – I'm a free agent,' he said. 'I can do what I want. I've made no promises and I make none now. It's your choice what happens next.'

Frances lifted her chin and held his gaze. Looking at her, it seemed to Duncan that she'd made a decision. And that perhaps he'd made a mistake.

'No,' she said. 'Not this time. It's *her* choice what happens next.'

CHAPTER 23

CLAIRE – BEFORE

Last night Joe went out again. I knew he would – after finding that coin he was bound to want to get out there and look for more. A few hours after our talk, he was back downstairs with his illicit battery pack. He made no attempt to lie, to pretend he was doing something else. He didn't say a word. I saw him walking across the hall and ten minutes later, when I went into the kitchen, his gear and Arthur were gone.

At least he's taken Arthur – I feel so much better when I know he has his phone and Arthur.

Joe and lies never did mix. I don't mean only the straight lies, but those little things we all say and do to tactfully misdirect from the truth – white lies, omissions, even the polite expressions like 'How are you?' that we say, never expecting an actual reply. Try that on Joe and you'll get an honest response. 'I feel crap,' he'll say, if he's feeling bad, even if it's to a shop assistant or the driver on the school bus. Never did go down well in school.

It's part of who he is. He's as bright as a button in so many respects, he remembers way more than I do, but when it comes to emotional intelligence – understanding people, reading people, knowing what not to say or how to lie – it just isn't him. Joe never could fathom what's going on in other people's heads. It wouldn't even occur to him that what you say isn't necessarily what you mean and the concept of tact or discretion is quite alien. It's one of the reasons why he and Duncan clash so badly. Duncan always expects his son to concede in any argument, and Joe can't back down and apologise unless he really means it.

For Joe, everything is black and white. Principles count. You have to admire that.

This morning, I stand at the kitchen sink, wiping a pan again and again, watching through the small window in front of me as the leaves swirl across the grass. I'm playing my plans over and over in my head to be sure I get it right. It's making me jittery; I hate having to orchestrate leaving Duncan like this without him or Becky knowing until I've gone. Let alone managing things so that Joe comes with me and doesn't get upset.

'*Where is he?*'

I jump. It's Duncan, standing in the doorway with an angry expression on his face. He clocks the empty dog basket and strides across the kitchen to glare at me. I lean back.

'Where the fuck is he?' he shouts, even though we're in the same room.

'He said something about going to one of his friends,' I reply.

I can't look him in the eye. The lie slips out with the ease of years of protecting my son. I'm in my light polyester pyjamas and a matching dressing gown. I put the pan on the draining board and reach to pull the belt tighter around my waist, knotting it twice as if that's some sort of defence against Duncan.

'Which friend? That idiot, Callum what's-his-name, who wastes all his days shooting up behind the supermarket in Belston?'

'What?' I take a step towards Duncan. 'What do you mean by that?'

'Haven't you realised? Jesus, Claire, you're so naïve sometimes!'

'Are you saying Joe's into drugs? That's bollocks. I've never seen any sign of that and I don't believe Callum would do that either!'

I totally believe Joe wouldn't touch drugs, he couldn't cope with the mind-bending messing up of his head. But I'm not so sure about Callum. I feel a seed of doubt squirming in my brain.

'And how would you know, Claire? When did you last go calling on Joe's friends? You sit here in this ivory tower and spend all your days cleaning the house!'

'Oh, really, is that what you think?' I smart at the glorified *you're just a housewife* quip. 'How dare you! I've given up everything to look after Joe, and you for that matter. My career, my freedom, my time – do you think you could have built your business without *me*?'

'You chose to have children, nobody forced you! Look what a disaster that's been!'

I take a sharp intake of breath, my face flush with heat.

Tears threaten to spill over, but I won't let them. I won't let him see how much that hurts. He knows it's unfair; he's saying it because he likes to rattle me. I struggle with myself and let the anger win, grinding my teeth.

'You don't know the first thing about Joe's friends,' I say. 'You're too busy carving out an empire in progressive limb surgery for dogs, or cruising the streets of Derby for a shag to bother to learn what actually interests your son!'

His eyes flash but he refuses to be drawn.

'Take a look around the back of Tesco's on Alcott Street on a Friday night, then, Claire. You might be surprised by what you see.'

I don't reply. No, I won't believe it. This is Duncan trying to hurt me. He knows my soft spots. But that seed of doubt is growing. I knew I didn't like Callum. And how well do I really know my son? What does he really get up to when he stays out all night? Is he tripping out at Callum's flat when all the time I thought he was metal detecting? I feel my body sway.

Duncan apparently relents.

'I don't think he's doing drugs, Claire.' He gives a staggered sigh. 'Just his friends.'

My face is pale and I'm feeling sick.

'Maybe,' he says. He's smiling, making it clear how much he's enjoying my discomfort.

I wish to God I had the courage to tell Duncan now. That I'm leaving him. That our life together is over and he can go fuck himself. But I don't know how he'll react. He could make things really difficult for me, with money, with Joe. He might even call the estate agents; try to stop them from giving me the lease. There is only one estate agency in Belston.

And he's too close. I can feel the fast rhythm of his breath. His eyes flit across my body, taking in the thin pyjamas and dressing gown, my feet bare against the cold tiles, my breasts cool against the fabric. Suddenly, I am all too conscious of my nakedness beneath.

He takes a step towards me, one arm reaching out to grasp mine.

'Claire . . .'

His grip is hard and painful. How long has it been since we last made love? *Made love.* What an old-fashioned, meaningless phrase that is, belonging to the days when women had to 'love, honour and obey'. He hasn't loved or honoured me for years. I pull back.

'Piss off, Duncan!'

His hand tightens and I try in vain to shake it free.

'You're a cold bitch, do you know that, Claire?' His voice is low and threatening. 'All these years and you've never really responded to me.'

We both know that's not true. I use my free hand to slap his. A sharp, hard slap that means business. He swears. His hand releases me with a jerk. He casts around with his eyes then storms into the utility room. My heart gives a leap – he's noticed that the metal detector is gone. He flings open the back door.

'Joe!' he yells. 'Joe!'

It's completely pointless. I hug myself as the cold air whistles around the bottom of my pyjama trousers and I hear Duncan swearing again as he rages through the stuff leaning up in the corner of the utility room. He throws the ironing board down on its side for the sheer hell of it, then he sprints out into the hall and up the stairs. I hear the slam of Joe's bedroom door, once, twice, and he comes back down again. I eye the empty dog bed on the far side of the kitchen island, glad that Arthur, too, can't see this.

'Claire?' Duncan says. His voice is calmer, fiercer.

I don't reply. I'm back to my washing-up, like the good little wifey I am, like none of this is happening.

'Has he gone metal detecting again? How did he manage to do that? I've got his battery pack. I took it with me to work. Has he gone to meet up with his metal detecting friends?'

'I don't know,' I lie again. My voice has dropped. I know I'm the one in trouble here, not Joe.

'For fuck's sake, Claire – I thought you didn't want him to do this? I was trying to support *you* the other night!'

'You call that support?' I round on him. 'You practically attacked him! And then you walked out and stayed out, all night!'

It hangs in the air between us: Where were *you*, Duncan Henderson? The blood is roaring in my ears. I tighten my hold on the plate in my hand and stiffen my back.

'I barely touched him!' he says. He makes it look like he has no idea.

I ignore that. Just as he's ignored my reference to his own activities.

'You tried to take away the one thing he adores,' I say. 'His metal detector. How would you like it if someone nicked the keys to your car?'

'That's hardly the same, is it, Claire? And I only took the battery. I was trying to stop him from disappearing again.'

'Well, he's gone anyway, thanks very much.' Bitterness creeps into my voice. I feel my defiance surge: 'He had a spare pack!'

I regret the words as soon as I've spoken them. It's a betrayal of my son. But it feels so satisfying to tell Duncan all the same. To tell him how Joe has got one over on his father.

Duncan takes another step towards me. I start as he slams his fist down on the granite worktop and the plate slips from my hands, crashing onto the floor between the sink and me.

'I'll bloody murder him when he gets back!'

I wince. That kind of statement scares Joe because he takes it so literally. But Duncan is scaring me too, now. His voice has changed again. I don't turn round. Instead, I see our reflections in the window in front of me. The way he towers above me and the curved fist of his hand. I feel a delayed stab of pain from the broken plate at my feet and the warm ooze of blood on my toes. But I don't move. I stand at the sink and hold his gaze.

Duncan growls at me, like he barely comprehends what's going through my head. Then he opens his fist, swings round and leaves the room.

CHAPTER 24

CLAIRE – BEFORE

Duncan has gone. Left for work. Stepping away from the broken plate, I have moved to stand at the big patio window in the kitchen and I cry. Slow tears that well from the bottom of my eyes and sit warm on the mound of my cheeks. I can't stop myself. I brush them away with the back of my hand, but they keep on coming until the tears become audible sobs. Most days I cry. When no one else is around. Until I shake my head and wash my face and tell myself to grow up. Button it. Don't give him the satisfaction, Claire. I don't like to admit to myself that this is what I do. What he's reduced me to.

This isn't what I want, it's never been what I want. I loved Duncan so much in those early days. I remember how he used to come home from his first job as a vet, tired and stressed but bearing some small treat – a takeaway to eat on the patio, or a bunch of flowers – not expensive designer bouquets, we couldn't afford it, but a bunch of daffodils from the supermarket or roses cut from the front garden. I loved those daffodils, bright and yellow and full of cheer. All I ever wished for was for us to have a family of our own, a place where I belonged, to use my brain and build a home and leave something good behind me when the time comes.

My brother, Ian, wanted that too. He couldn't hack it in the UK, not after Mum died. He said he hated how things were going in this country, the way everyone treats foreigners, each other, the politics. He said there was nothing to keep Moira and him in the country anymore. It didn't seem to occur to him that *I* might be a reason to stay. I guess he thought I was all sorted, happy with Duncan.

Maybe I'm better at lying than I think.

I turn away from the window, bending to touch the petals of an orchid plant positioned on the table by the sofa. It probably needs watering. A thing of beauty needs nurturing, I should know that. Just as well orchids are pretty robust. The only reason that I keep them is because they somehow survive my lack of care.

I want to think of good things, not bad, the small sensual pleasures of the life I have. The scent of mown grass drifting through an open door, the feel of summer rain lightly dousing my skin, or the rains in November thundering on the roof, running down the tiles into the gutters, filling them to the brim, glistening as each drop teeters on the edge, waiting until it's big enough to fall.

Each image holds me, feeds me, helping me forget.

Maybe Ian knew the truth of how things were between Duncan and me but decided to go anyway. It's hard to forgive him for that. He must have seen the change in me. He's the only person still alive who's known me all these years. But we were never close and I know he has his own life to live. We all of us make our choices.

No, I don't want to forget. I think of Duncan the night Joe was conceived. How, later, Duncan lay face down on the sheets of our bed beside me. He sighed as I leaned forwards, my breasts full against his back, his skin naked to my touch. My fingers ran down his spine, counting each vertebra, naming them one by one, cervical, C1, C2 . . . thoracic, T3, T4 . . . following their individual knobbly shape. I circled and trailed, naming each new bone until I found the small hollow on the base of his back, above the coccyx. I was determined to show him how much I loved him, in spite of our growing distance. My hand flattened out. I pressed into his skin. I reached down to kiss him, there where my hands had been. He rolled over and my hand drifted lower and he sighed, like the wind through an open window. I felt the smooth pressure of my own legs against his and my hand moved again.

Me and Duncan having Joe was an act of love.

I can't bear to think of Duncan sharing all that with someone else. It's not the physical act of sex that I'm jealous of – it's what comes with it, the intimacy, the shared pleasure, the soft words of passion that slip between lips and skin.

I saw an item that had been posted on Facebook once. It showed a watercolour painting of a cavalcade of fairies. The colours flashed up on the screen, lush greens and dark browns, but it was the story that caught my eye. How the queen of the faeries abducts a young woman's husband.

The queen bewitches him so that he only has eyes for her. When his wife begs for her husband to be set free, the queen says yes, if the wife can hold onto him long enough. The wife waits until the faerie court is riding through the forest at midnight. She steps out and pulls her husband from his horse. She holds on even though he tells her to let go. She holds on even when he kicks and swears and tries to shake her off. The queen turns him into a dog that bites, a bull that kicks, a snake that writhes and twists and whips from side to side, even a lion that threatens to consume her . . . until the wife can take no more. Still she holds on. Next, the queen turns him into a fire-breathing dragon. The husband and wife are consumed by flames. Through it all, the wife holds on until finally the faerie queen gives in. Thus, the wife wins back her husband.

There was something about that story that made me think. I held on. Far too long. I think about all those years we've had, Duncan and I, the sacrifices we've made, our hopes and aspirations, the business, this house, us – how things have changed over time and how I have weathered it all. Wasted years. Years when both of us could have been happy elsewhere. Joe, too. If he'd been happy and secure, even with his problems, he wouldn't keep going missing like he does, would he?

Why hadn't I realised that?

But no more. I can't hold on anymore. They've sent me the rental paperwork for the cottage by email and I've signed it. I get to collect the keys in a few days' time.

My new home is waiting for me.

CHAPTER 25

CLAIRE – AFTER

I try to sleep. I drift off for a while, but it doesn't last. I wake again and the air bites. The top blankets have fallen from my bed and I turn onto my side, not wanting to open my eyes. A pulse beats on the side of my neck and my body begins to shake. I'm frozen. I draw my legs up to my chin as I always do and it comes back to me, my new nightmare.

I'm in the bath. My body is naked and the water is too cold. The bathroom window is set low into the eaves and my gaze is caught by the view. I squint at the reservoir. I can't quite make it out, but it looks like there's something sticking out of the water. It could be a piece of metal, cross-shaped and tilted to one side.

Small waves tug at the weeds that trail from each arm, the strands and strings of black weeping across slowly shifting liquid. It's like one of those skinny makeshift scarecrows planted in the soil. Or a sword, Excalibur held aloft by the Lady of the Lake. It's none of that – I think it's the cross at the top of a church steeple.

It can't be. More like it's an unwanted piece of junk. There could be all sorts of debris in the reservoir. People dumping stuff when they shouldn't. Perhaps with this amount of rain, some-thing's been dragged up by the currents. Reservoirs do have currents, especially this one, the flow of water deep beneath the surface, pulling in and out as and when the water inlets and outlets surge.

I feel the cold engulf me, yet I don't want to leave the bath. Nor does my hand reach out to top up the hot water. I can't. It's like I'm trapped in a punishment of my own making. Something darkens the water of the reservoir around the cross. The shape wavers in the distance. It's too far. And yet I can see.

The water breaks, white and silver churning up the surface. The shadow moves again and it's like a living thing, more than one of them, a writhing coil of creatures in the water, mad for something unseen. The weeds on the cross pull and stretch as if something's trying to suck them underneath, and the crea-tures twist and turn with a frenzied fluttering like a pool of flesh-eating piranhas. Then I feel his hands around my neck. Duncan's breath against my skin. He pulls me back against the bath and I watch the distant fish with my tongue rolled back and my body locked in ice with Duncan's fingers crushing my windpipe . . .

I force myself to sit up. I press my hand against my neck, the other against my chest, blocking the images that fill my brain with a visceral reality. My heartbeat races and my breath comes in short, sharp gasps as if I really can't breathe.

The endless rain has stopped. The cottage inside and out is unnaturally quiet. Arthur with his dicky leg is comatose in the kitchen.

It was just a dream, wasn't it? Not a memory.

CHAPTER 26

CLAIRE – AFTER

Things got worse after Duncan set up his own practice. He'd worked for several years for a chain of vets in Derby before deciding he wanted to be his own boss. His ambition was to specialise in small animal surgery. He chose Belston, a town not far from the city, because it had a thriving community. It looked good on paper. That was when money was really tight. We lived in a run-down Victorian semi on the edge of Matlock. The main road was a nightmare until they built the bypass, a constant stream of traffic at the weekend as people trailed through towards Chatsworth and the wilder country-side of the Peak District.

Within a couple of years, the business exploded. Duncan's reputation and referrals had grown. He was clever and hard-working. He had a stern, direct manner that seemed to inspire confidence in his clients – the owners, that is. The animals too. Dogs in particular adored him, always eager to obey his command. Duncan had a particular thing for dogs. The feeling, evidently, was mutual.

Joe was about five years old then. He'd started school. Duncan was talking about hiring a second vet and I said why not me? I didn't have to be a stay-at-home mum anymore, we could get a childminder for those hours before and after school and I could pick up my career and make a real contribution. But Duncan said he wasn't sure. Joe was already playing up and a third childminder had rejected him. I was torn between pushing for my professional freedom and looking after Joe. It hurt that Duncan didn't want me. It was always as if he didn't want me.

He hired Tim, who was brilliant. Younger than us but full of ideas and energy. And Tim was a local lad, the son of a farmer. A sleeves rolled-up kind of guy. All his friends and family spread the word about the new business, it was a smart move by Duncan. They all worked hard and I watched my husband and his growing team drive the practice forwards.

Suddenly money wasn't a problem anymore. Duncan began to talk about moving house. He'd always hankered after a modern property, with a big drive and a triple garage – something to impress. Me, I loved the older, more characterful houses. What I fancied was one of those old Derbyshire stone farmhouses with a walled garden and a vegetable plot. We talked endlessly about it. I say talked, argued is a better way of putting it. The only thing we could agree on was something that was detached and in the country.

He came to me one day and pushed a brochure across the table.

'Take a look,' he said. 'I've found the perfect solution.'

The words encouraged me. He was listening after all. I took the glossy pages into my hand and eyed the cover – there was a photograph of a green field with views over the valley and water in the distance. On the far left was a tumbledown pile of stones that might once have been the corner of a building. I squinted.

'I don't understand, that isn't a house.'

'No, but it could be – don't you see?'

'What, you want to *build* a house? Are you serious? That would cost a fortune and where would we live in the meantime?'

'We'd carry on living here. I've worked it all out. We can get one of those self-build mortgages; they loan you the money in stages as the build progresses. It's a stunning location, overlooking Belston Reservoir. You love the reservoir. Commuting will be really easy. There *is* a house but it's unliveable, a complete wreck. What really caught my eye is the barn. It's even more of a wreck, but that means we can do whatever we want with it. It could be absolutely stunning. There's already planning permission for a three-bedroomed bungalow, so the precedent for a domestic development is set.'

'I don't know, Duncan, it sounds like an awful lot to take on . . .'

'Nonsense,' he said. 'It'll be fine. I've had a chat with the planning office and they're open to a bigger project, with all the right considerations.'

Eco-friendly stuff, that's what he meant, as it turned out. If we installed a water recycling system, generated our own electricity with solar panels or a wind turbine, and used all the appropriate materials, then they'd consider a more

141

substantial reconstruction of what the original barn might once have looked like.

'We'd have the best of both worlds, a character building with all the mod cons and space we could dream of. I've already put in an offer on the site.'

'*What?*' My voice squeaked. I couldn't believe he'd made such a big move without discussing it with me first.

'And it's been accepted!'

He whipped out a bottle of champagne and set it on the table between us. I stared at it, wanting to knock the bloody thing over. He seemed to cotton on then, his face creasing to a frown.

'It's a chance to start afresh, Claire. Think about it. You and me. And Joe would love it in the countryside proper. It's the perfect compromise between old and new, isn't it?'

I felt hope surge. He was right, I did love the reservoir – it was our special place, where Duncan and I had fallen in love. Once it began to sink in, once he'd convinced me the finances would work, I realised he might be right. He couldn't have chosen a better spot. And he was like a man obsessed, as if this would fix everything. Fix us.

It's no good, I can't relax. The cottage is cold and damp and in spite of myself, right now I really miss the easy comforts of the Barn. I can't believe that Joe is sleeping rough, not for more than a night or two. He'd want a roof over his head and food. I think again of Joe's supposed friend, Callum. Who else does Callum know? I torment myself with visions of drug dealers and city gangs.

I reach for my phone on the bedside cabinet and I press the button to bring it back to life. I dab on the icon to make a call and then the one with Joe's photo. His picture fills the top half of the screen. His head is tilted to one side and he's pulling a face. The tone gives a rhythmic buzz.

I wait. But it kicks over to Joe's answer machine, exactly like it did before.

'Hi, I'm Joe. If you can be bothered, leave me a message, and if I can be bothered, I might call you back.'

Where *is* he? Why doesn't he answer my calls? I'm angry with him now – how could he put me through this?

I throw the phone back onto the cabinet and sit up in the bed. A gale rumbles around the house, battering at the windows. The trouble with a view is that it comes from being high up. That means you catch the wind, too. I hear a slate sliding off the roof over my head and crashing to the ground below. And another one. I look up towards the ceiling and my anxiety levels shoot.

Now all I can think of is *why* Joe might not be able to answer the phone. I can only imagine the worst. That he's been walking on the lane and the wind has blown a tree over, crashing on his head. Or he's been run over by a car, his body left lying in a ditch twitching in the muddy water. Perhaps he's gone up onto the moors, some remote corner of the Peak District where not even the walkers want to go. I see the tangled mess of his arms and legs, like the mangled tyres and broken spokes of a bike, crushed at the bottom of a cliff. A body could lie up there for months and never be found. Or maybe he *did* go and see Callum, and got punched by some maniac in a back alleyway behind the supermarket in Belston, kicking Joe's exposed belly, blows raining down on his nodding head, swearing, cursing, leaving him to bleed out. His body prostrate amongst the yellow skips. Black plastic bin bags spilling their contents out along the tarmac like guts.

Does he even have any ID on him? He could have been wheeled into an A & E department weeks ago, or worse, and I'd never know.

The walls of the cottage tremble again and something bangs about on the ground in the garden outside. A flower pot or a bag of rubbish or . . . I don't know, something else.

I was trying so hard to forget.

CHAPTER 27

CLAIRE – BEFORE

It's a new morning, bright and cold and windswept. Outside the kitchen window, the bare trees whip sideways in the gale and twigs and branches roll across the grass to rest like broken mannequins.

'Mum!'

Joe – he's back. Hurrah!

I hear the harsh rasp of his breath and the kick of his shoes against the floor. Arthur's legs are covered in mud and he sits down with his tail swishing slowly against the floor tiles.

'I saw them,' says Joe, struggling to drag his arms from his coat.

'Who?'

'The guys, they've been out there. I think they're following me. I think they know.'

I realise then that Joe's face is damp with beads of sweat and his eyes dart from the door to me to the door again.

'Joe, you're not making any sense.'

'I was on the chat site yesterday, on my phone, and someone began talking about puppetriders. Right out of the blue. Asking questions about where they've been found, how many and when. Then he started on about Tutbury.'

'Tutbury?' *Here we go*, I think.

'I think someone may have hacked into my account and seen my search history. They can do that, you know.'

I roll my eyes. He's unaware of my expression, twisting his body one way and then the other, pulling off the rest of his coat one-handed. It's oddly endearing, his paranoia, indicative of how much this means to Joe. He lifts his head, mentally catching up with my question.

'The Tutbury *Hoard*,' he says.

He stops there as if I should know all about the Tutbury Hoard, whatever it is. He pushes the fingers of one hand through his limp hair, dangling his backpack from the other.

'Joe, I've no idea what—'

'Fucking shit!'

He stares at me like I've landed from Mars, then dumps his bag in the middle of the kitchen floor. He ignores me and races out into the hall. He mounts the stairs at full pelt and the door slams overhead. There's even a waft of dust drifting down from the structural beams that support the mezzanine.

I sigh and Arthur sighs with me, dropping onto the ground and resting his head on his front paws. I look down at him.

'Is he like this with you, too?' I say.

His lifts his big brown eyes towards mine, in what I can

only describe as the canine equivalent of a philosophical shrug.

Joe won't come down. I've called him for tea and even knocked on the door. All I can hear is manic typing on the keyboard and the squeak of his office chair tipping back and forth. I eat on my own, then clear away and pour hot water onto a teabag in a mug, warming my hands against the heat of it. I breathe in its sweet peppermint smell. It clears the pathways of my nostrils, filling my mouth and lungs with the astringent taste of home.

I fetch my tablet and sit down again at the dining room table. It blinks into life and I nurse my tea and shuffle forwards to tap into the search line: *Tutbury Hoard*.

I scan down the search results. There it is – there are loads of entries. 'The Biggest Find in the UK,' one headline boasts. 'Three hundred and sixty thousand coins discovered in 1831 right on the Derbyshire border with Staffordshire, near Tutbury.'

Wow! That's a lot of coins and from the sound of it, dramatic stuff. Especially in those days. When you consider that one gold coin can be worth several thousand pounds now, depending on its history, of course. I tap on another likely looking article, reading quickly through and tapping on another.

The first coins turned up in a clump, found by workmen in the millrace of the River Dove. Then more appeared in ones and twos, lying on the riverbed. The news triggered a mini gold rush. So many opportunists gathered in the area to dig in or near the banks, up and down the river, that all the local boarding houses filled up. There were arguments with the locals, brawling in the pubs – even, apparently, a murder.

I read on. There's a story about the Earl of Lancaster and Derby who in the fourteenth century rebelled against the king. The Earl retreats to Tutbury Castle, there to await his Scottish allies, but they fail to turn up. So he flees across the River Dove. But he's caught and not long after executed. The Tutbury Hoard was thought to be part of the funds he planned to use to pay his armies.

There's a description of some of the coin types that comprised the discovery. One word jumps out at me: *puppetrider*. Amongst the coins found scattered across the river was an unusual pair of puppetriders.

I lean back in my chair, pondering this fact. Puppetrider coins are much older than the fourteenth century. I'm not sure they've got anything to do with the story about the Earl of Lancaster and Derby. Perhaps there was a second hoard that got confused with the first. Could there be more than one hoard?

I lean forwards again, peering at the screen. I can't stop myself from checking on that murder. I'm no better in that respect than anyone else – intrigued by lascivious tales of true-life crime and death. I tap onto the screen again: *Tutbury Hoard murder*.

In 1852, more than twenty years after the first coins emerged, a reclusive farmer and his wife were killed. John and Jane Blackburn. They had an isolated farmstead on the gentle slopes overlooking the River Dove. Their house had been found burning. People did their best to put out the fire, but given the limited resources of the time, without much success. When they were eventually able to enter the house, they found the couple's charred bodies slumped one over the other in the kitchen and a single ancient coin clutched in one of their hands.

That was when the rumours started: of a second stash of coins further up the river. The two grown-up sons of the couple said their parents had once mentioned finding their own hoard on a patch of land near the riverbank. Instead of handing it over to the authorities, they'd kept it hidden all those years on their farm. This hoard, if it existed, was never recovered, but four men were accused of the farmer and his wife's murder.

One of them, their own son.

I feel the tension in me abate then ratchet up again. I'm sharply aware of the reality of what Joe has found. His coin could be connected, that's what he'll be thinking. The River Dove flows down past Ashbourne, just a few miles from here. It's one of several waterways that help to feed the reservoir. He'll be thinking maybe his coin belongs to a second hoard left undisturbed further upstream. And if so then he'll know that if word got out, the whole metal detecting community would arrive here in force looking for it. One coin, especially a rare one, could be worth quite a bit, but a whole pile of them? We're talking life-changing sums of money here. No wonder he rushed upstairs like that.

I search the term *night hawkers* – that was the word he used. Finding a hoard is the Holy Grail of metal detecting and whilst clearly most metal detectorists are completely legit, I still find loads of stuff about thefts from archaeological sites and landowners waking up to find their fields dug over. Earlier, it had all seemed a bit far-fetched. But with so much potentially at stake, Joe must be worried about stirring up the interest of illegal treasure hunters.

I lean back, letting my eyes drift over to the window with its view out over the valley. He'll go digging again, I know that for sure, despite what we agreed. Though, he didn't actually agree, did he? And how could he resist?

I can't let him go digging anymore. I can't bear to think of the lengths to which he might go, what he might find. When he first got into metal detecting it never occurred to me for one moment that it might lead to this.

CHAPTER 28

CLAIRE – AFTER

The nightmares are getting worse. Not just at night but by day too. My whole body clock is out of sync and I doze off by day and lie awake at night. I'm not well, it's clear to me now. The headaches, the anxiety, the sense of confusion. Some days drift by without me having the will to do a thing. I'm all tied up in knots in my head and I'm crying every day. Maybe this is what they call a breakdown, triggered by the stress of leaving Duncan and losing Joe at the same time.

The sun lowers in the sky and I feel the tension in me increase until I can't stand to stay indoors anymore. I jump in the car, crash the gears and speed along the lanes.

Burnished copper sweeps down the slopes on the far side of the valley. Above the darkening trees, a cloud of rooks caw and clatter, swirling like giant bees. I slow down through the old village. There's no sign of life, no curtains closed at the windows nor lights on by the front door. No Range Rover, no cars at all. I accelerate along the straight flat road beside the reservoir hardly aware of the colours spreading like an iridescent oil slick across the smooth water.

I reach the cattle grid at the far end of the road, the one that marks the juncture with the main road. In one direction it goes to Belston, in the other Derby. The gate is wide open. Pausing only long enough to shift gears, I trundle over the grid too fast. A lorry gusts past, headlamps blazing, horns blasting. I jam on the brakes and the car lurches to a halt. I roll the car backwards and stop to catch my breath. The lorry has gone, hurtling round the corner in a rush of dead leaves and broken twigs. I look left and right and left again, and pull out onto the road. I gather speed – thirty, forty, fifty miles per hour – leaning into each bend as if I'm on a motorbike.

The quiet patchwork of fields and lanes soon give way to the lurid flare of suburban Derby. Traffic lights, house lights, upstairs windows lit up from within by the flashing colours of a TV. A garage forecourt zooms past my eyes with its red-and-yellow fluorescent strips. Streetlamps alternate with the huge trees that line the boulevard, punctuating the pavement with pools of amber light. It reminds me of all that Duncan and I sought to escape.

I pick up the ring road, traversing the city to the eastern side, where the police station is situated at Chester Green. By now, I'm in such a state I don't even know what I'm going to do or say. I imagine myself pushing through the main door, storming over to the desk and thrusting one of my posters at the receptionist.

'Here!' I'll say. 'Take it! My son's missing!' I'll scarcely pause to draw breath. 'I don't care how old he is or how busy you are – I want help!'

Please, somebody, help me find my son.

Nothing makes any sense to me anymore. I'm not driving on the road to Derby. I'm not at the police station. I've got no further than the cattle grid. The tyres of my car are only inches from the steel frame and the engine purrs quietly, hiccuping every once in a while. I'm convinced of it now – I must be going mad.

There's a magpie on the road – two of them. Their bodies bob up and down as they strut around in a circle a few feet from the car. I sit there in a daze, my hands locked onto the steering wheel. My eyes are caught by their strange little dance. They seem more interested in each other, but every now and again one of them throws me a curious sideways glance.

They're not like other birds, magpies, they're far more intelligent. I did a study of birds once, as part of my university course. I was looking at brain size and levels of intelligence. The magpie is one of the few birds with a nidopallium (a part of the brain that determines higher cognitive tasks) the same size as chimpanzees and humans. Magpies can recognise themselves in the mirror and they demonstrate elaborate social rituals. They've even been known to express grief. These two seem to be a couple, the male flashing his wings in a high-speed fanning movement every few seconds. She looks impressed. Sometimes the couples stay together from one season to the next. Sometimes they don't.

My fingers flex against the steering wheel, debating what to do. There's no one in the valley. The hills on the far side are a dark mass of black. The surface of the reservoir is now pitted by falling drops, constantly moving. It makes me feel sick just looking at it. The rain pings against the bonnet and steam rises from the metal carcass of my car. Still the male magpie does his dance. As the light fades, it's getting colder. On the main road, another car flies past, oblivious to my presence, swishing round the bend until it's gone. The birds suddenly, too, are both gone.

I don't know what I'm doing here. That headache's back, pounding in my skull. On the opposite side of the road, through the gaps in the hedging, there's movement – a herd of cows seeking the warmth of their fellows. The metal grid buried in the road is like an electric fence – tangible but almost invisible, a barrier that holds me back.

My hands shake as I push the gear lever into reverse. I do a clumsy three-point turn until the car points back the way I've come. The dashboard is lit up red and I turn on the radio to calm myself. Music floods the cabin, a folk song from the 1970s. It's a woman's voice, soft and sweet and pure.

The tune worms its way into my brain. It pulls me in, haunting and familiar. It's like the deceptively simple soundtrack of a horror movie. Like Britt Ekland in *The Wicker Man*, slapping her hands against the policeman's bedroom wall. It fills my head with images of a moonlit countryside, the Derbyshire moorlands further north, windswept hills and standing stones, satanic rituals performed under cover of night.

I picture the blood of beauty and youth and innocence seeping into the damp and fragrant earth. My son's blood. I think I see Joe, drifting in the water, his body bloated and wet. His skin is plump and swollen, a long shape sinking down into the murk. His legs are encircled by weeds like a chain, tugging him, pulling him, unknown hands grasping his ankles as he's slowly dragged beneath. It's my nightmare again but worse.

I turn the radio off, put my foot down and accelerate. This time turning up towards the village of Brereton Edge. It's raining, always raining as it does in early spring, and the wipers on my front screen bend and turn, bend and turn, echoing the rhythm of my heart. I drive past the first house, towards the old Hall, willing the car to climb up the hill, then push my foot down hard and slam on the brakes.

The car hums restlessly in the middle of the road.

Someone has taken them down. All of my posters. I've only just realised. The one here at the Hall gates, the ones along the road. Every single one around the southern perimeter of the reservoir is gone. It's like I never put them up. Except I clearly see the drawing pins and broken lengths of string.

I feel a growing flush of heat that makes my cheeks burn. It's like someone has systematically removed each one.

Who? That man I met at the village? I saw him crush my poster in his hand. Or someone else? I can't understand why anyone would do that. I swallow. Maybe it was Joe himself, not wanting to be found. I feel tears pricking at my eyes again. Are things so bad with Joe that he doesn't want to be found?

Then another thought hits me. My mind has been casting around like a ball in a pinball machine until it stops. Not the man in the village, or some stranger with no reason to hate Joe. Nor even Joe himself.

What if it was Duncan?

CHAPTER 29

DUNCAN – AFTER

The door swung to behind him. Duncan slapped his gloves into the bin, pulling off his cap and smoothing what short length of his hair there was as he dropped onto his office chair. It had been hard keeping himself focused. Maybe that was why the operation hadn't worked out. Anger fuelled his frustration – anger at himself. His own stupid fault. Now he had to ring the dog's owner. Shit.

'I'm sorry. It's bad news,' he started, his old north-country accent slipping through.

The silence was always heartbreaking.

'Why? I don't understand why.' The woman's voice was trembling. 'He was doing so well after the first op. You said the operation would fix him.'

'He was, it did, but sometimes the body can't adjust. It was always fifty-fifty – and there are bugs in the body that sometimes we can't deal with; we talked about that.'

Silence, always there was that silence whilst people processed what they'd been told.

'I'm so sorry, really I am,' he said. 'We did everything we could. In the end, he passed away as comfortable as we could make him. I can honestly say there would have been no pain. And you gave him every chance at life that you could.'

That he was sure of, at least. What else could he say?

For Duncan, it was more than just the loss of an animal. The dog had been his patient. When the call was done, he leafed through his notes. A photograph of the spaniel had been pinned to the file, he insisted on that. Big eyes, round and trusting, a soft toffee-coloured brown-and-white coat, a typical mad-capped spaniel. Everyone had loved him on the ward.

'You okay, mate?' It was Tim, poking his head round the door. 'It was bad luck, you know that?'

'Maybe.' Duncan gripped a pen between his fingers.

'Don't stay too late, hmm?' Tim hesitated, then: 'Goodnight, Duncan.'

'Night.'

Duncan scanned the medication charts and took another look at the x-rays on his screen. He stayed an hour, bleary-eyed, sipping coffee under the narrow beam of his angled desk light. Then he stood up and walked through to the operating room.

He contemplated the body of the animal still lying on the table. You could drive yourself mad, trying to figure out what could or could not have been done differently. Already, the warmth of the dog's blood had faded, the eyes glazed over, the life in him gone. Duncan lifted up the surgical sheets around the body, tucking them in on either side. It was a useless gesture. He dropped his shoulders and turned away, unable to look anymore. He wasn't seeing the dog. Then he was aware that Sally was in the doorway.

'What is it?' he snapped.

'I need you to approve these invoices, before I can go.'

She couldn't look him in the eye. Somehow that made him feel even more irritated.

'For fuck's sake, not now!'

He stood up and walked over to the door, slamming it right in her face. He was only vaguely aware of the alarmed expression on her features and Frances walking by.

That evening, Duncan didn't go home. He drove to Derby and sat on his own in a restaurant. He ordered Dover sole and potato dauphinoise and smothered the whole thing in vinegar. Claire would have been horrified to see him treat a delicate dish like that.

Why did his thoughts keep coming back to Claire? He was trying so hard to block her out.

He downed a pint of lager and then ordered another one, watching the other diners. They were couples mostly. An older couple sat nearest to him, eating in comfortable, communal silence. A younger pair sat the other side. It was a corner table with a plush two-way built-in padded seat. She wore far too much make-up; he looked like the cat that had got the cream. Their arms and legs were entangled like the misplaced tentacles of an octopus. Poor sods – too young, the pair of them, just like he and Claire had once been.

His first sight of Claire had been her riding a bicycle. It had been one of those old-fashioned sit-up-and-beg things with a basket that shook as the bike bounced across the wet cobbles in front of Nottingham Castle. It had been their first term as students, late October, and a soft, mild southerly wind had blown wet red and yellow sycamore leaves like painted hands across the street.

She'd worn tight jeans and a loose wide-necked T-shirt. He still remembered how it had shrugged off one shoulder, revealing an expanse of smooth, soft skin. Her whole body juddered as the bicycle rumbled over the gleaming stones. Her brakes squealed to a stop and her feet hit the ground and she tipped and hopped, leaning over to one side to prevent the bike from careering right into him.

'I'm so sorry!' she said, her voice gasping, out of breath, her cheeks pleasantly pink from effort.

Duncan had reached out to catch the handlebars, holding the bike before it rolled further towards his body. It also brought him closer. Her long hair swung in a ponytail down her back, glistening in the autumnal sun.

'It's alright,' he said. 'I'll live.'

He laughed, softening the impact of his words, watching with poorly concealed pleasure as her slim legs swung over the saddle. She stood in front of him, shoulders straight, taking back full control of the bike. Her eyes searched his face uncertainly, as if deciding if he was merely being polite or rude. Then she smiled.

'You're at vet school, aren't you?' she said.

'How'd you know that?'

'Seen you in class.'

How could she have been in the same class and he'd not noticed?

It was as simple as that. A chance meeting outside the castle in Nottingham. He'd asked her out for a drink and that evening they pushed through the after-work crowds on the street into the Olde Salutation. He found a nook where a narrow wooden monk's bench meant they had to sit thigh pressed against thigh. Duncan had to resist the temptation to push one hand across the fashionably ripped fabric of her jeans. Within a week, they were dating.

They were seen everywhere together, locked in physical contact whatever the excuse. It was one of those uni romances that everybody envied. They sat together in class, ate together at the student union café. They got drunk together, did all the concerts and festivals together and camped out under the stars. He didn't date anyone else and Claire and he were married scarcely a month after graduation.

His eyes were drawn back to the couple in the corner. Octopus girl and octopus man were now bonded in multi-limbed unity. Duncan nodded to the waitress, ordering yet another lager, even though he knew he had to drive home. The pair were kissing now, all lips and nose and tongue, and her hands had disappeared under the table. Duncan swivelled to face the other direction. He couldn't stop himself from thinking about Claire. Already, he could feel the heat in his own body.

That summer they moved into a crappy rented flat over an antique shop in Beeston, the trendy student end of Nottingham. On Saturdays, the front doorbell of the shop below would ring like the servant bells of one of those grand aristocratic houses and in the evenings, the smell of pizza and Chinese takeaway would drift across from the busy end of the high street.

He still remembered his first bitch spay, the animal's organs sliding between his fingers, panicking as he tried to figure out what was what and make sure he'd tied up all the relevant bits. It was Claire who went through it all with him when he got home, despite her being ill. She'd got the textbooks and calmly talked him through each stage, each image, bolstering his confidence for the next one. You wouldn't think it now, with his growing reputation for technical expertise and his smart, shiny new practice.

He owed a lot to Claire.

Duncan took another sip of his beer, downing the remaining liquid in the glass. She'd been there right from the start, encouraging him, helping him, loving him. In spite of everything. He hadn't deserved Claire and she hadn't deserved him.

Duncan paid the bill. Afterwards, he went on to a club. The strobe lights and sound levels were enough to drown his thoughts, for a while. Men and women staggered on their feet, bodies writhed, and the whole place stank of sweat and tequila. Duncan watched from the bar, feeling too old, slowly drinking another lager.

'Hey, gorgeous. Haven't seen you in here in a while.'

A woman draped her arm across his shoulder. Her hair was jet black. Too black, apart from a little fading at the roots. Her lips were bright red and a heavily beaded dress slid across her hips. Her breath smelt of red wine and she let her hand play against Duncan's neck, long painted finger-nails smoothing over the base of his neatly trimmed hair. Duncan turned towards her as she whispered something in his ear.

He and Claire had been mated for life, that was what all of their uni friends had said. Bonded for ever, like swans or wolves or turtle doves. Or so it appeared to everyone who knew them. If only that had been true. His anger returned. She'd gone. Left him behind.

'Fuck you, Claire,' he muttered under his breath.

Then he stood up and led the woman with black hair down the corridor.

Student life was one thing, real life another. That summer they graduated – the summer he first saw Evangeline – had changed everything.

CHAPTER 30

CLAIRE – AFTER

I slept a lot when I was married to Duncan, in those later years when Joe would allow me. It was my only escape from reality. As Joe grew older, I gradually gave up all hope of a career.

They say depression makes you sleepy. It used to make me angry reading that, like being depressed was lazy, or a medical condition with no basis in reality. I raised it once with my GP, naïvely thinking he'd understand. Depression, he implied, can be the result of chemical emotions that have no meaning, no cause, a bodily response that can be fixed, given the right set of pills. Mothers, he said, can be particularly prone to the level of their hormones. I felt my anger grow. It seemed that my aspiration to be an intelligent, career-minded woman had been completely superseded by my bodily functions. Like one of those Victorian theories about women and their 'humours'. He launched into this questionnaire:

Claire, do you feel like hurting yourself?

Claire, have you ever had thoughts of suicide?

Mrs Henderson (I wasn't *Claire* anymore), *have you ever thought of hurting your son?*

Each time he said my name like that, it sent shivers down my back. I was no longer a person. I was a patient, a liability, a potential lunatic. It was so humiliating being asked all that just because I was tired and low, because I was a mother, a woman, stuck at home with her challenging son. What was I supposed to say – *yes*?

The consequences overwhelmed me – what if they took my son away? What if they incarcerated me in some institution and no one ever believed me after that? What if they put me on drugs so that my brain turned to mush and I couldn't even look after myself? Even if any of those questionnaire answers *were* yes, sometimes – how could I possibly admit to that and set hares running over which I had no control? Did they really expect me to answer those questions honestly?

And besides, even if I actually had any of those thoughts, it didn't mean I'd act upon them. I doubted myself after that, even more. If only Duncan had had to go through all that, had *his* confidence undermined by prodding and poking both physically and mentally. Try answering those questions yourself, *Duncan*.

I suppose the GP was only doing his job. Following up on statistical risks, ticking boxes just in case. But I felt reduced to nothing. Another mother who couldn't cope. It felt like a denial of me as a mature adult person. I wasn't depressed, not like that. I was sad for good reason. My resentment grew. Sad and miserable for lack of love. Sad and miserable from the stress of it all. Sad and miserable because no one cared.

Certainly not Duncan, or Joe, or the staff at the school – not my doctor, or Ian, my closest family. Nor any of the other people I met.

Except Becky. Becky cared. She understood what it was like. She's been through it all herself and then some.

I feel the guilt of not telling her the truth, the whole truth. The way I've kept my plans from her, then left my husband, her brother, with no warning. She's not answered my texts, or my phone calls – I *have* rung and she answered once, but I hung up before I could say anything.

All those years of friendship. She wasn't just my sister-in-law. We shared our pain about our sons, but I never told her how things were with Duncan, it was too private. Too personal. She didn't know about his affairs, or if she did, she never said. Perhaps she was waiting for me to speak first.

And I've never, ever told her about Evangeline. Nor did Duncan. There's no way either of us could tell her about Evangeline. I still remember that smell – a smell like disinfectant. The sickly-sweet metallic smell of too much blood. The woozy, hazy stench of the drugs that filled my head. The soft music that pumped into my ears, each note more perfect than the last, exaggerated by my intoxicated state, like nectar drip-fed into my arm. And all the time the pressure of Duncan's hands, his wide, strong hands too hard against my skin. And white against *her* skin. I can't breathe, I can't hear, I can't, *won't* look . . .

CHAPTER 31

CLAIRE – BEFORE

I'm flitting from one task to another without settling properly to any. I've just been told I can have the keys to my new cottage tomorrow. That's a few days sooner than I expected and it's thrown me into a spin. It's all suddenly very real and it feels like I have to do everything in the next hour.

I pause to look outside. The weather's turned. From bright and windy, now it won't stop raining. The news is filled with pictures of heavy snow on the Continent, ski resorts closed by the risk of avalanche and German motorways brought to a standstill. The rain slides down the big sheet window of the Barn and I think, thank God! At least it's kept Joe indoors.

The home phone goes. I almost jump. I didn't give that number to the estate agents and it hardly ever rings since we each have our mobiles. But there it is, trilling from the side of the sofa. I kneel on the seat cushions to lean over the arm and pluck the phone awkwardly from its rest.

'Hello?'

There's no reply.

'Hello?' I say again, louder.

I feel guilty as if it's Duncan, already aware of what I've got planned. But that's nonsense of course, never mind he always rings me on my mobile.

I hear a scuffling and the sound of breathing, not the creepy, heavy breathing sound that women dread, but the uneven rasp of air caught against the microphone. And crackling. Then the phone line goes dead.

The phone goes again, a different sound. It's my mobile this time. I make a dash for the kitchen, where it's buzzing against the granite worktop. Must be the estate agents.

'Hello?'

'Hey, love, thought I'd see how you're doing.'

It's Becky. I feel my hands tighten around the phone.

'Hi!' I try to keep my voice light and carefree. 'Did you just try to ring me on the landline?'

'Now when have I ever rung you on the landline?'

'Oh, I thought . . . never mind, it must have been someone else.'

A wrong number, I think.

'Is Joe with you today?' says Becky.

'Yeah. He's upstairs.'

I look up at the rain outside and Arthur bedded down on his big cushion by the sofa. He's snuffling in his sleep, the covetous wobbles of his nostrils giving way to little wistful sniffs.

'Got anything planned?' says Becky.

'Not exactly,' I lie.

Like hell – more sorting, packing, girding myself even for

that conversation with Joe. I'm dreading it – what if he refuses to come with me? I simply don't know how he'll react to the idea of leaving his home, especially now when he's so excited about a possible hoard. Oh, Lord, that coin business couldn't have happened at a worse time. He might not believe me when I say we're not going far.

'Then how about a day trip somewhere, with Alex and me?' Becky breaks into my thoughts. 'I was thinking, in this weather, a trip to Nottingham, maybe a look at the shops and some lunch?'

'Oh . . . I . . .' I try not to let my voice sound wary.

I picture myself telling Joe about my plans. Tonight – no, I can't do that. Tomorrow morning, then. Or only once I have the keys? How late can I leave it? I can't do this – go out with Becky, never mind the stuff I have to do. If she sees me today, the state I'm in, she's very quickly going to figure out that something's up. I wrack my brains. I promised Duncan I'd go with him to an event tonight. Bloody hell. I have to keep up this façade of our life just a little longer. That is if he remembers and actually comes home.

'I'm sorry, Becks, but I don't think I can. Duncan and I are going to an exhibition in Belston tonight and Joe's not really himself right now . . . I'm not sure I can fit it all in. It's just not a good day.'

I feel my eyes scrunch up with pain, cringing at my shame. It's as well Becky can't see my face. It's a half-truth, but I can't think of what else to say.

'I'm so sorry, Becky,' I add. 'That's a lovely suggestion. Thank you, anyway.'

There's a slight hesitation.

'That's okay, love. I understand.' And then, more warmly, 'Hope he cheers up.'

'Thanks, me too – speak soon.'

I give a nervous laugh and end the call quickly after that before I say anything else that will give me away. I keep the phone clutched in my hand as if somehow that redeems me.

I move to stand at the patio doors, staring outside. It's sleeting now, clumps of soft ice landing in splats against the glass. All the windows were triple glazed by a Norwegian firm, giving insulation worthy of a Scandinavian winter. It was ferociously expensive, but Duncan said the architect insisted. More like *he* did. Inside, the glass is warm to the touch. Outside, it must be almost freezing. The sleet is driven onto the glass at a slant, slowly melting as it converges to a point. All things, I think, must come to the same point. Joe and Duncan and me.

Becky has always had broad shoulders as far as Joe is concerned, listening to me pouring out my heart about his behaviour and problems. She'd listen as willingly about anything else and it's not that I don't trust her because she's Duncan's sister. Maybe I don't trust myself. My feelings run too deep for me to trust myself. Once the doors are open, I don't think I could stop.

That's what I tell myself as I brood by the window.

Poor Alex, with all his complicated medical problems. He was born with a genetic condition – Angelman, it's called. His back was bent and his head too small. Becky and her then husband knew that something was wrong. Alex was over a year old when they finally got a clear diagnosis. He had seizures, he couldn't talk, his arms flapped like wings and the twisted back was the result of severe scoliosis. By the time he was old enough to go to school he was in a wheelchair.

When I think of all the battles that Becky has had to fight

on her son's behalf, to get the support they both needed . . . It had been a nightmare trying to navigate schools, hospitals, social workers, funding, let alone the practical aspects of caring for a growing disabled boy. All without a partner. Becky's husband had left her by the time Alex was two. Couldn't hack it, Becky once said. She seems philosophical about it now. I suppose I should be grateful that at least Duncan didn't do that to me. I grit my teeth – I'm not grateful at all.

I've seen Becky's ups and downs, the impact it's had on her health, her wellbeing – we're none of us saints. When Alex got to ten years old, she almost gave up. The daily grind of caring for him was too much. I'd come round to help after dropping Joe off at school to find her in a heap at the kitchen table, sobbing as if her whole world had collapsed. She'd been told that her regular social worker was being replaced by a new one.

In the greater scheme of things, it wasn't such a big deal, but she got on really well with the old one and it pushed her over the edge, the idea of having to start again, building up a new relationship of trust and understanding. Suddenly, she'd come to realise she couldn't carry on as she had been, juggling caring for Alex with work and school and appointments and weekends and . . . I helped as and when I could, but she'd had to concede that she needed some time to herself, a few days when he could be elsewhere on a regular basis. Respite care, they called it.

Care for the carer, that's the first rule of looking after someone, she later told me. You have to be well yourself to look after someone else. It took us both a while to realise that.

She's shared with me all the joy of her son too – his quirky big-faced smiles, his first broken, tortured speech, the way his painful body kept on growing, from small child to young adult, folded into his wheelchair ever more like a broken bird. The day his hand squeezed hers, a small, rare gesture of affection, had meant everything to Becky. It was Alex's way of telling her, in a manner that his damaged voice could not, how very much he loved and appreciated her. She was in floods of tears after that.

AngelMan and my boy, StickMan. They were a pair, Alex and Joe, our superheroes. Becky and I were too. If she could do it, against such obstacles, then surely so could I. Her strength, her love inspired me to carry on.

CHAPTER 32

CLAIRE – AFTER

I sleep from sheer exhaustion. A deep, embalming sleep that blocks out daylight, moonlight, all thoughts, all pain . . . but it's only a temporary reprieve. I wake too early and now that I'm awake, it's all coming back. Joe's excitement about the coin, Joe's fear of his metal detecting friends, that story he'd told me about the Tutbury Hoard rolling around and around in my head – has he found something more? And is it them, those other metal detectorists? Have they hurt Joe in some way, to get at what he's found? I bury my head in the pillow, trying to understand.

I should go and see where Joe was digging. Maybe that will help. But I haven't gone in that direction before, across the dam to the north side of the reservoir. What if Duncan sees me? The thought consumes me as I get dressed. It's still dark. He'll be in his bed. It'll be difficult to see properly, but then that's why it will be okay. Now I see the irony of it – me doing exactly as Joe did, scouring the valley under cover of darkness. I'm filled with doubt – the same doubt that Joe had: what if there are night hawkers, what if I give the game away, what if I inadvertently show them exactly what Joe has been seeking to hide?

I drive slowly down the hill. It's the quiet hour before the countryside wakes, with that half-light that marks the cusp between night and day. A faint blush of rose pink stains the clouds and the crescent moon lingers low in the sky. I descend into the village and take the road that follows the reservoir the other way, towards the dam and the road on the Barn side of the water. I've left Arthur behind because that way I can be more discreet. Through the open car window, the air is sweetly damp and a stretch of white mist floats across the central span of the reservoir, hugging the bottom of the valley.

The car crosses the dam. The road drops again. I reach the stretch of road right next to the water, downhill of the Barn. I refuse to look up at it. I drive cautiously. The mist is thicker here, the wheels of my car crushing the fresh twigs blown down overnight. My mind is full of scattered thoughts. I don't even know where to look. Joe never told me exactly where he was working. Or maybe he did and I hadn't listened properly. I feel the guilt of my inattention to his chatter sink into the pit of my belly, like a piece of meat that's gone off.

I remember our first house, before Duncan and Joe and I moved into the Barn. It was on a hill in Matlock – I always did like a view. It had a narrow front garden, an iron gate and black and red tiles leading to the front door. Inside were high ceilings and plastered cornices thick with too many layers of paint. In the centre of the sitting room hung a cheap paper globe light, the kind you get in student digs, and the carpet was strewn with toys, messy with kids' stuff, exactly how I liked it.

I think of a day when I was sat on the sofa, squashed and hollow under my hips. It was the kind of sofa you can't easily get out of. The TV was on, flashing cartoon images. Bright primary colours jarred one against the other until my eyes flinched and my ears burnt from the unnaturally loud laughter. Joe was snuggled on my lap, his cheeks flushed from crying. Both his hands held my thumb tight against his chest. I loved the fact that he wouldn't let go, that he had to be close, that he needed me. It didn't last, it wasn't like that later. I remember the tune I sang to him then. I sing it now as I slowly drive the car:

> I had a little nut tree, nothing would it bear,
> But a silver nutmeg, and a golden pear.

Gold and silver – the two things that fascinated Joe as he grew older.

The mist swells above the water. Tenuous strands unravel like a skein of carded wool. A curl of apprehension creeps across my skin. It's proper fog now. The days often start with fog down here in the bottom of the valley, but today is worse than normal. It stretches across the road, obscuring the way. My lips move silently, a mantra to bolster my courage, and the words are a physical memory teasing against my lips:

> The King of Spain's daughter, came to visit me,
> All on account of my little nut tree.

The skeletal shapes of trees drift in and out of sight. Visibility drops down to zero, only to open up again: a tantalising glimpse of reflections in the water, a brief shimmer of leaves suspended over the bank. I am distracted again, clinging to the sensation of Joe sleeping on my lap. All I want to do is close my eyes and remember.

The car swerves and I clench my hands around the steering wheel. I'm awake, fully in control of my driving again. A wash of white rolls against the windscreen.

I should go home; the fog has grown too thick. I have no idea what I'm looking for. This was such a bad idea and there's no point in stopping the car and getting out, not in this. I lean closer to the windscreen to see better. I hear but cannot see the lumbering movement of cows. It can't be far to the main road. I can take a short cut there and drive home the other side of the water.

I pick up speed, pushing back against my seat. The fog is too dense. I close the window, still singing to myself quietly to help myself stay awake. My car headlights pick out the very droplets of moisture in the air.

An arc of light spans the width of the road.

It's another set of headlamps. Too fast. Too bright. My eyes are blinded.

I hear the screech of brakes, the squeal of tyres and I pull on the steering wheel. My foot slams on the brake pedal. The car lurches to one side. My body is thrown forwards. I brace my arms, grip the steering wheel and still my head almost hits the glass.

The car comes to a juddering halt.

The seat belt strap burns against my shoulder. I lift my body, holding my arms straight against the wheel. I sit there, frozen to my seat. My heart thundering against my ribs.

In front of me, the other car lies slewed across the road. It's half-buried in the fog. I can't make out the driver. Only that they're sitting too, in the exact same pose. A man, I think, though I'm not sure. His head is turned towards me and we stare at one another.

The face is obscured. A blank silhouette. The clothes, the hair, are colourless, achromatic, like a paper cut-out folded into place. I can't blink, my eyes fixed open, a taste of blood upon my lips. All I see are the eyes blazing from his face. A fierce yellow, like a fox caught unawares in the night. It's like another of my nightmares.

Slowly, my hands peel from the steering wheel. I reach out to snap the lock down on the car door. The clunk jars me from my fixation and I grasp the gear stick, fumbling to push it into reverse then back into first, readying myself. I hear the gears of the other car crunch in reply. It moves back, straightening as it does. Then it stops, poised to drive, waiting again, but for what?

I hold still, as if to even breathe would provoke the other driver into action.

His car engine revs. It roars into life. It's speeding towards me, head-on. The mist is sucked away between us, a silver bonnet bursting into view. At the last minute, the car swerves to one side, scraping within an inch of my own and the hedge. It accelerates with a rumbling snarl. I twist round, breath held tight. I see the red glow of its rear fog lights and a cloud of black fumes unfurling in the mist.

The car is gone.

My hands push back from the steering wheel, my arms once again rigid. I can't believe that he did that. Whoever it was.

He almost drove right into me. Deliberately.

CHAPTER 33

CLAIRE – BEFORE

Something moves by the hedge at the end of the garden. A shape, blurred by the water droplets smothering the window. I step up to the glass and hold myself still. It's a man. He's standing in front of the hedge that marks the first of our fields at the foot of the garden – this side of the hedge.

He's maybe a few years older than me, with a wiry, seen-it-all, don't-mess-with-me kind of look. He wears a wax jacket and black knee-high country boots, the uniform around here, and one of those country hats with a wide brim. Water pools on the edge of his hat and drips onto his coat. His legs are slightly apart and both of his hands are in his pockets, elbows out, giving him an oddly aggressive stance. Through the alternating rain and sleet, he doesn't move at all. He just stands, watching and waiting.

I think of the phone call before Becky's. The one where no one answered. The crackling on the line had freaked me out a little, but it could have been the rain. The weather here often affects the telephone line. There's always a reason behind anything that seems a bit freakish. He's just a man, isn't he? On *our* property, where he doesn't belong.

I run to the utility room and shove my feet into a pair of green-buckled wellies. I grab my coat and pull at the back door, pushing my arms into the sleeves as I run across the lawn. He can see me running towards him, but he doesn't move.

I stop a few feet from the hedge. My breath comes in short, sharp gulps and the sleet is cold against my face.

'What are you doing on my land? Who are you?'

My land – not our land or Duncan's land, *my* land – because it sounds more assertive.

'Mrs Henderson, is it?'

'Who are you?'

He relaxes his stance and holds out one hand.

'Hello, there. My name is Ray Turner.'

I refuse to take his hand.

'I repeat, Mr Turner, what are you doing on my land? Did you try to ring me earlier?'

He contemplates me, ignoring my last question.

'I'm a friend of your son's, Mrs Henderson. I represent a few people who'd love to have permission to search your fields with metal detectors.'

'Why didn't you come to the door?'

'I'm sorry, Mrs Henderson. I was about to approach the front door, but you saw me first.'

He smiles, but it's unconvincing. The apology feels like anything but.

'And who are these people you represent?'

'A group of us, metal detecting enthusiasts. It's a hobby. We search the odd field here and there for anything of historical interest. Whatever we find is split fifty-fifty with the landowner.'

He makes it sound so casual and perfectly legit. Except when I remember Joe's anxiety, I feel uneasy.

'What makes you think it's worth your time searching in these fields?'

I'm not sure I should have put it quite like that. It's too suggestive that I know something. He brings one hand to the brim of his hat, wiping it clear of water.

'Nothing in particular. We work across the area, as and when we have the time and opportunity. Joe said he thought you wouldn't mind.'

Now I know he's lying. Joe would never have said that. I make a brief pretence of thinking about it, then deftly shake my head.

'No,' I say. My voice is overly forceful. 'Thank you very much, but no, we're not interested.'

I step away from him.

'It would be to your advantage, Mrs Henderson. And to your husband.'

I don't like the reference to my husband. As if this man is subtly implying it's Duncan's decision, not mine. His tone has turned deeper and more precise. It makes me feel worse, as if to say no to him will have consequences.

I turn back, eyes glittering.

'I don't like you being on my land without permission – most people would come to the front door, not stand at the bottom of my garden.'

'I'm sorry, Mrs Henderson, but I was only walking across the field – my car's parked down there by the reservoir.'

He gives a nod towards the road that runs alongside the water at the bottom of the hill. There is, indeed, a car parked in a passing place by the shore. He makes it sound so reasonable.

'That's our land too, and it's private, as you've just indicated you know. There's no public right of way.'

That's not strictly how it is – the road itself belongs to the estate, not us – but the bit about public access is still true. We had to make sure it was in the deeds that we could access our own property. I push my chin out.

'Then I must apologise,' he says. 'I really didn't intend to cause offence.'

There's a pause as I try to figure out my reply.

He must have taken it as the end of our conversation. He's hoisted himself over the five-bar gate and now he's striding across the field. Presumably to return to his car. Except he could have chosen to make his way along the lane, avoiding the repeated trespass of our land. He moves with a deliberate slow stride, turning to take one more look over his shoulder towards the Barn. I feel my jaw tighten. He's not looking at me. I follow his gaze.

Standing by the back door is Joe. He's barefoot, wearing jeans and an old T-shirt as if he's not long got out of bed. His arms are wrapped tightly around his body.

Joe's eyes are looking right through me.

He looks as though he's just seen a ghost.

CHAPTER 34

CLAIRE – BEFORE

Joe's in the kitchen when I get back inside. I'm surprised – I thought he might already have scarpered back to his room. It reminds me of when he was little and wanted to stay close. He looks unhappy. I place my boots against the wall in the utility room and, still wearing my coat, move across to fill the kettle at the sink. Water pools on the tiles at my feet.

'Do you want a cuppa, Joe?'

He doesn't reply.

He looks dazed. Like his brain is momentarily stranded. I'm determined to behave normally. The coin itself doesn't matter, I realise that now. But Joe does. I flick on the kettle and busy myself with a couple of mugs and the tea caddy. I cut two slices of bread and push them into the toaster, then search around for a tin of baked beans and some eggs. Food, that's always been my first response. Feed him and then perhaps he'll talk to me.

Joe slides onto a bar stool at the kitchen island and waits, exactly as he did when he was a child. One hand is picking at the skin at the base of the other hand's thumb and he still doesn't speak.

A few minutes later, I push a plateful of scrambled eggs and beans on toast under his nose and fish out a knife and fork.

'Eat, my love.'

He doesn't complain about the phrase *my love*. He eats. I join him at the island, nursing my cup of tea. After a moment, I speak.

'Do you know him, Joe?'

He looks at me briefly but doesn't reply.

'Is he one of your metal detecting friends?'

I'm sure *friend* is entirely the wrong choice of word.

He shakes his head. His grip on the fork tightens and he stabs a too big piece of toast and levers it into his mouth.

'Not freakin' likely,' he says, speaking with his mouth full.

'But you *do* know him – he said he knew you. He wanted to bring some of his mates to work on the field. He said he'd split anything they found fifty-fifty.'

Joe's eyes dart up to mine and he lets his fork drop loudly to his plate. Only half of his food is eaten.

'You said no, didn't you?'

'Course I did.'

I take a deep breath.

'Joe, is there anything you want me to do? Anyone we should ring? If you think these guys could get nasty, then we could talk to Martin.'

Duncan's best friend, DCI Martin White. He'd be discreet. What are police contacts for if not to be discreet?

'No!' Joe shakes his head vigorously. 'No, that's the last thing you should do. I . . . I need to figure this out myself.'

I reach out to touch his arm and he flinches like he always does. Or at least has done since he hit puberty.

'Joe, it's not worth it – nothing's worth it. If you think there's anything dodgy about these people, then you should let your father and me deal with this. We should contact the authorities and be done with it.'

'No, you can't do that, Mum. You promised me, remember? We agreed . . .'

He stands up, eyeing his plate as if the food has suddenly turned to poison.

I stand too, the rigid bulk of the kitchen island between us.

'It's okay, Joe, I won't say a thing to Martin, or anyone else outside of this family. I know I promised you. But we could at least try and speak to your father about it.'

He pushes back from the kitchen island, his face closed to me.

'No!' he says. 'No way! Definitely not him!'

His hands are shaking as he shoves his plate backwards and he runs from the room.

I clean the kitchen with a methodical efficiency, loading the dishwasher, rinsing the few items left by the sink, sweeping the floor with one of those fleece mops that can't scratch the expensive porcelain tiles. It's only more misdirected energy.

I thought things would improve after Joe turned eighteen. I've had it planned for so long. I'd promised myself when he left school and started work, I could go . . . *we* could go. It was not just his end date but mine too. That was on the basis that Joe had a job, that he was settled and happy. He's got a smattering of GCSEs: English, maths. His best subject was computer science. But he failed his A levels. I could have cried, but I did my best not to let him see how disappointed I was – for him, not me. The world out there passes judgement on you based on exam results and it's cruel, wrong. Not all kids fit into that mould of performance. Certainly not Joe. It's so hard on him. What was he to do now? There's been talk of an apprenticeship in horticulture, but Joe isn't interested. The summer has passed since he left school – autumn too – and he's been so obsessed with the metal detecting – always at night – that he's refused to do anything in the day except sleep.

So I've hung on. I'd not found the right house to rent, anyway. Now it's the middle of winter, well into the new year, and still he's not sorted. I'm beginning to feel angry – like he made me a promise. He didn't, of course, it was me that made myself a promise, but damn it, he needs to grow up, get real. *Bloody hell, Joe, this isn't fair anymore*, I think, as I scrub and scrub at a stupid spot on the floor that's been there for over a year. And why am I bothering to clean anyway, since I've no intention of staying here a day longer than necessary once I get those keys? What do I care if the house is clean when I go? How pathetic is that!

I've found the right place, signed the papers and paid the money. There's no going back. I keep saying this in my head, over and over again, as if I need convincing. It's a question of timing, that's all. I know I'll have to wait until the very last moment to tell Joe my plans or things will implode. You can see from the state of him today, he's not himself.

It's clear he knew that man I spoke to in the field. I rewind what Joe said – that we have to keep the other metal detectors out of our fields, that he has to find whatever might be there first. What he said about night hawkers. I didn't like Ray Turner. I wonder if that's even his real name. He had a look about him like he didn't care about the rules, or us. How far would someone like him go to get what he wants? No, I won't think like this, paranoid like Joe. It's only a coin, one stupid coin. Except it isn't just a coin to me. And it's not people digging in our field for coins that scares me but digging about by the reservoir. If the coin has come to light, then what else has come away, too?

My mind shuts down. I can't think about *that*, either.

My hopes of a career in veterinary research never happened. And looking after Joe has taken its toll. I can't go on like this, I tell myself, living half a life, never having that chance to start again, to be me. If I don't do this now, leave whilst I still have a chance of picking up my career, it will be too late. I'm not getting any younger.

I'll tell Joe tomorrow, right after I've got the keys. I'll help him to pack, load us both up and leave a note for Duncan. I've already written it – it's in the top drawer of my bedside cabinet, ready to go. That's how it should all pan out.

I stand up and stretch my back. It's odd to think that leaving is now a reality. Change. Change is a scary thing. For me as well as Joe.

I move to the fridge, pulling out a bottle of milk. I reach out to make a cup of tea. The kettle whines, the light on the base snaps off and I pour hot water over the teabag in my mug. I watch the water changing colour, the scent of it filling my nostrils. Camomile tea. It makes me think of summer lawns and floaty dresses, women wearing hats with ribbons trailing down their backs, and children playing on the swings, squealing with delight as the sunshine warms their skin.

These little routines, the little flights of fancy, they hold me by a narrow thread.

CHAPTER 35

CLAIRE – AFTER

Outside my car, the fog folds back into place, pressing against the windscreen. The car that almost drove into me is long gone and I let my breath release.

A wind blows across the water and the white fog lifts.

I see the solid tarmac of the road ahead and press down on the accelerator. My car doesn't move. I press again, right to the floor; the car still doesn't move. Again and again I try, panic filling me. The engine chugs angrily but won't bite. It must be flooded with fuel.

I give a whimper – *not now! Please, not now*. But the car won't budge.

I have to wait. I know I have to wait to let the engine clear.

I step out and breathe the air, filling my lungs, willing my thumping heart to slow. The road is empty. The mist has retreated. The car, the driver, whoever it was, has gone. It's alright, I'm okay.

Idiot, I think.

I can't think who would be driving along the bottom of this valley at first light. Someone taking the scenic route home from a night shift, or more likely, someone who's been out in the countryside all night, poachers, night hawkers, even. I shake my head. Joe's paranoia is getting to me. It was just someone, anyone. It doesn't matter anyway, because they're gone.

A narrow shaft of dawn sunlight breaks through the cloud. It warms the air. There's the heavy beat of wings in the distance, the hue and gaggle of geese jostling in flight. A line of them emerges from the mist, round heads, thick necks, a row of stubby orange beaks calling as they fly one behind the other. Their cries bring me back to normality.

> *I had a little nut tree, nothing would it bear,*
> *But a silver nutmeg, and a golden pear.*

In front of me, leaning out over the water, is a tree. It must have been completely hidden in the fog. It's smaller than the others – an oak tree, thick and stunted by the weather. The roots buckle beneath my feet like old rope left unfurled on the walls of a harbour.

Last year's dead leaves and dried acorns lie scattered on the ground, crunching beneath my feet. I gaze at their distinctive shape, so synonymous with English culture. I think of a man's painted face, skin, hair, even his beard stained with green. Only the whites of his eyes are different, blazing out. A twist of fresh leaves and acorns perch upon his head. I let the image fade like the mist upon the water and take another step.

Something is tied to the tree trunk.

It's a bunch of flowers. A limp, oversized sunflower head nods under the weight of its own seeds. Chrysanthemums cluster beneath, the thin multitude of their narrow petals blackened and dead. There are carnations too, their stems knotted and broken, heads folded down – sad, pathetic things with their petals brown and fading.

I reach out like a curious child. The petals separate between my fingers. They flutter useless to the ground. The florist's ribbon might once have been pink and shiny, but now it's tattered and grey. There are more dead flowers, in wet cones of cellophane and paper, drooping in piles at the foot of the tree. And a smell. A damp, fetid, rotting kind of smell that seems serenely familiar.

I stumble backwards. I fling my hands out to catch my balance and turn to face the reservoir. The first sunlight has spread across the water. There's a swell below the surface. A fish gulps for air and dives down again. There's another and another, a whole shoal of them visible in the water. I am mesmerised by their coiling silver bodies. They writhe one way and the next, mouths wide open, eyes unblinking and blank and I see more and more, bodies slipping this way and that as their tails slither in the murk. I watch and they slip from sight only to rise again, one after the other, like bubbles from some large object trapped underneath.

I've seen them before, in my nightmares. Only this is real. I think of stories of frenzied animal behaviour, portents of a world gone mad. The ten plagues of Egypt: blood and boils and thunder and hail and pestilence and marauding wild animals. Even the death of the firstborn, sent to punish the wrong.

I step away, mouth open in horror. I open the car door and almost fall onto my seat. My eyes are dry and gritty. I feel the tiredness from my early start and my stomach yowls with hunger. I swing my legs under the dashboard and try the engine again.

This time, it jumps into life. I slam the door shut. My clumsy fingers wrench the gears into first. The car judders forwards and I pick up speed. Behind me, the oak tree grows smaller, fading into the distance. The branches sway, and the dead flowers lift and nod their heads. The central span of the reservoir glimmers smooth and grey and one last streak of white sighs across the water.

CHAPTER 36

DUNCAN – AFTER

Duncan had stayed out too long. He'd driven home the worse for wear and he was lucky that the police hadn't stopped him – if they had, they'd have found him well over the limit.

What were you thinking of, Duncan? said the voice in his head. Martin would have lynched him and there were only so many favours a mate could do. The investigation was still ongoing at the Barn but, fortunately, it was too early in the morning for any of them to have arrived yet.

Duncan's car passed under the cherry trees, fog swirling through the branches. It had risen from the valley below, creeping up the lane, the drive, to settle over the Barn. He was scarcely aware of how he'd got home. Guilt, shame, fury . . . Claire's face kept looming in front of his eyes. He was supposed to be the cool scientific professional, but look at him now, an angry drunken wreck.

He parked with a slurry of gravel on the drive and sat in

his car, letting the engine idle with the heating on to keep warm. The world was a ghostly white, the Barn shrouded like a giant piece of furniture put to rest. Here in the quiet of first light, the building had taken on a different mood. The tall stone walls, the blackened windows, the cool designer chic that jarred with the landscape. Why hadn't Duncan realised it was like that before? Hadn't Claire said? He gazed at the carefully restored bricks leaching evaporated salts like dried-out tears.

He leaned back in his seat and closed his eyes, willing the nausea to go away. Then he pulled open the glove compartment and rummaged for his phone. He held it in his hands, trying to think of what he would say. He pressed the button and the screen sprang to life. He tapped on the first icon and began to type:

I'm sorry. I'm so, so sorry.

How easy it was to say the words, whether or not he meant them. Did he mean them? He pressed Send.

I shouldn't have done that, he wrote next. *I miss you.*

He waited but there was no reply.

You know I can't stop thinking about you.

He could tell she'd seen the message from the little green tick that had popped up alongside the box.

I'm at home. He wrote. *Do you want to come here?*

Again, he pressed Send, his fingers sliding out of control.

The car had steamed up. He reached forwards to wipe the inside of the front windscreen and looked down again at his phone. No answer.

She'd come, he was sure of it. It didn't matter what time it was, it was her little thrill, sex at odd hours of the night. And it had been long enough, hadn't it, her making him wait?

He leaned back in his seat, imagining them bursting through the big front door to stumble clumsily down onto the tiles, laughing as they fought with sleeves and legs, fumbling to undo zips and knickers until finally he . . .

His mind was befuddled, too spent from his long night. He needed to sober up. He got out of the car. As the engine died, the drive was swathed in a haggard gloom. He looked up at the Barn, the great bulk of it twice the height of the lower wing where the kitchen was, where the farmer and his family would have once lived.

He tried to imagine it as it had been then, a thriving workplace. The men caring for their stock, the flow of animals and supplies, the barn piled high with hay. It would have been a man's world, their shouts and calls bouncing off the walls. At this time of the morning, there might have been a brazier inside the doorway, keeping out the cold – they'd found one when they were clearing the site. He could imagine a father and his sons, readying for work, their voices filling the void above, the men gathered around a makeshift table as their womenfolk still slept next door. The whole place would have been seeped in the sickly, sweet smell of hay, laced with the pungent stench of manure.

It brought his thoughts to Joe. His son. How things might have been if they'd lived a generation or two earlier. Working the land. It would have suited Joe. The two of them in partnership in a way they'd never been before. Would he have had other sons? Grandchildren, even? A whole brood of children helping on the farm, each with their allotted jobs according to their sex and age. As people did in those days.

It would have suited Claire too, wouldn't it? A life on the land. She'd never been one for coffee mornings and the high-level grooming of the beauty salons of Derby. She'd always been interested in livestock, the problems of different genetic lines. She'd talked about getting a few sheep to graze the fields, chickens to give them fresh eggs, but Duncan had said no. He didn't have the time. She didn't have the time. Their lives were complicated enough. His head drooped. No, he couldn't go there.

But that hadn't stopped Duncan doing what *he* wanted to do, flouting his marriage. After he'd first slept with another woman, he couldn't meet Claire's eyes when he got home. He was sure it was obvious from his face, the timbre of his voice, or some other gesture revealing his betrayal. He'd been conscious of the very smell of feminine perfume still clinging to his clothes. Claire had carried on as normal, talking about her day, asking about his as if nothing out of the ordinary had happened.

It was that easy. It became a habit, like a beer after work, or a coffee first thing in the morning. Whether anyone else had cottoned on, it didn't matter – no one ever said a thing. Apart from Becky, his family lived miles away in Yorkshire. Claire's family, what was left of them, had moved to Australia. Their friends from uni were scattered across the country. Claire saw more of Becky than Duncan and he didn't think Becky knew.

It wasn't long before Duncan came up with the story of the gym. Not exactly original. But it was true. He'd joined up so he could shower before he came home. And it gave him the excuse he needed to spend more time elsewhere, a meal here, a trip to the pub there, time to talk and share more than just sex.

Unlike Claire. She'd been so immersed in her own feelings,

she'd never had time for his. He'd enjoyed punishing Claire for her indifference. Poor Claire, so caught up with her own preoccupations. Until . . .

He checked his phone again, the light from the screen spilling onto his hand.

Hello? he typed. *Are you there?*

Another pause, then finally a reply.

A gif popped up – one middle finger turned backwards, pushed into the air.

Duncan scowled. She always conceded something in the end. *Yeah, fuck you,* he thought in silent reply, wistfully, his lips pulling down even further.

He got back into the car and chucked the phone into the glove compartment. He couldn't face going into the house. What was the point? The drive would soon fill up with vehicles, invading his home again. Maybe a workout was what he needed, if he could get his limbs to function properly. He could always shower at the gym.

He looped the car round and back through the trees, fresh twigs and leaves filling the road in front of him. One of the two halves of the gate had swung shut – he hadn't remembered that – fog drifting through the bars. He had to get out to wedge it open so he could drive past. A gentle rain had started up, dousing his head and coat. He was damp by the time he clambered back in the car.

As he drove through the gates and pulled smoothly onto the lane, behind him a figure stepped out. Duncan caught sight of it in the rear-view mirror. Or thought he did. A figure wearing earphones and holding what looked like a stick in one hand.

Duncan squinted, the car already moving round the bend.

He could have sworn that was Joe. The height of him, the earphones and metal detector, the oddly bent shape of his youthful posture. Another wave of nausea caught in his throat. As the road straightened, he slowed the car, peering through the trees.

The figure had never been real. It was just a sapling ash tree, cut down by the wind. He could see it now. The slim trunk had split, bending over so that one skinny limb dragged against the ground. Its few branches were filled with last year's keys.

Dry and brittle, they shuddered in the wind.

CHAPTER 37

CLAIRE – BEFORE

I really don't want to go out. I don't want to go out tonight and I don't want to leave Joe, and I certainly don't want to spend an evening with my lovely husband.

It's the launch of a photography exhibition celebrating the county's industrial history. A collaboration between the Mill Arts Collective on the edge of Belston and Derbyshire's New Business Network. The idea of being paraded on Duncan's arm and being polite to the hoi polloi of the county's business community is enough to make me sick. Let alone tonight, when Joe is clearly upset and I'm on the verge of leaving.

I'm not sure Duncan's looking forward to it that much, either. It's part of an unwritten contract between us – that in public at least we appear to be a functioning husband and wife. He'll schmoose the financial advisors and local councillors and I'll stand there trying not to guess which female in the room he likes best.

'Are you ready?' he's shouting up from the hall below.

'I'm on my way,' I call back.

I shrug into my jacket, smoothing the short folds of it over my dress. I turn half around to check my back. I've lost a bit of weight, I think, and I scrub up well when I want to. I pull the neckline up, not that it makes much difference. I grab my heels, holding them in my hands as I head downstairs. The polished wooden treads are lethal in a pair of heels.

Joe's in the kitchen, cooking himself filled pasta for tea.

'We won't be late,' I say, putting on my shoes.

He nods, unspeaking. It's supposed to be him saying he won't be late, not me.

Duncan's sat in the car. He doesn't even look at me as I climb inside. I glance wistfully back at the house, the light emanating from the kitchen, the shape of Joe moving about the room. At least he's feeding himself. That has to be a good sign.

The exhibition is in an old converted mill on the outskirts of Belston. We park and join the guests already gathering at the entrance. The whole place has been recently renovated, painted a trendy blistering white, except where the odd bit of original stonework has been left tastefully bare. There are high ceilings, steel beams and architectural tension wires that span the rooms over our heads like the strings of a kite. There are several floors cut away so that there's an open area right up to the roof. It's the sort of thing Duncan loves.

On the ground floor there's a shop and a vegan café – very Belston – both already busy with custom. We start there, Duncan carving a path through the crowd towards Tim and a group of medics they both know from the hospital.

'Hi, Tim,' I say.

'Claire!' His eyes are warm and he looks surprised. 'You look . . . gorgeous!'

I nod and smile and murmur a few words, but it's soon Duncan holding fort.

'Would you like a glass of wine?' A man offers a tall flute of something sparkling. He's not a waiter, and he looks vaguely familiar.

'Might as well,' I say.

'It's Claire, isn't it?'

I throw him a quizzical glance.

'You don't remember me, do you?' He looks disappointed but not unkind. 'We were at uni together. I studied biochemistry and you started dating Duncan before I could get in there first.'

I stare at him until recognition hits.

'Good grief – is that . . .?

'Harry, as in Prince,' he says, laughing. 'You *do* remember.' He looks pleased.

There's no Mountbatten-Windsor red hair. It's brown with flecks of grey, sitting in soft swathes that sweep back from his head. Duncan gives him a cursory glance – he hated losing his hair in his thirties – then goes back to his conversation. Harry has a smile that's warm and unthreatening, interested but at a safe distance. I feel a trickle of heat, a brief reminder of how it used to be when I was unattached. Maybe this is how it feels for Duncan.

'How lovely to see you again! I thought you'd gone to London after we graduated.'

'Well, yes, I did – my girlfriend at the time got a job in Southwark. But I'm in Nottingham again now.'

'Oh, and . . . I'm sorry, I can't remember her name?'

'Lucy – she and I split up after a couple of years. I married someone else and worked in the US for a while, but I'm single again, as it happens.'

I'm not sure quite what to say. *I'm sorry?* That's sounds like she died. He doesn't elaborate on whether he's divorced or separated or . . . I feel a wariness creep over me. Why should I feel like that – I'm married myself, aren't I? Not for long.

'Do you have kids?' I say.

'Two, one of each. Nat's almost nineteen, and Liam is sixteen next month.'

'I have just the one. Joe. He's just left school.'

I realise that I've used the word 'I', not 'we'. Practising, I suppose. I sneak a quick peek at his face, hoping he hasn't noticed the significance of my grammar.

'It's a difficult time when they leave school, launching themselves into adult life. We had no end of trouble with Nat until she settled down to a course on film and photography. She's brought me here, as it happens – though I think she's disappeared upstairs. Looks like your husband is preoccupied too.'

He glances over to Duncan who has drifted towards the bar. Harry smiles at me, a warm, unthreatening, crinkly kind of smile.

'Shall we take a look at the exhibition? You can tell me what the pair of you have been up to all these years.'

We fall in together, browsing the ground floor. It gives us a chance to talk about impersonal stuff, rediscovering a common ground. We progress to the first floor, where there's a display of conventional photography and more experimental mixed media. There are scenes of rural Derbyshire, the moors and hills pitched against satanic mills and chimneys. Someone has printed landscapes and building silhouettes alternating on giant white sheets. They've been deliberately ripped and torn then suspended from the beams above our heads. They float in the draught like the frayed remnants of Buddhist prayer flags on a mountain. It has an oddly soothing effect. Or maybe it's the prosecco I've been drinking and the mellow conversation, neutralising my ragged mood.

Eventually, we head up to another floor. I'm actually enjoying myself now and I think, why should I have to go back to Duncan? Harry is full of hapless stories from his travels and uni and Duncan is still engrossed in conversation below. I wave to him, more to impress on Harry that all is well between us. Duncan frowns and turns away. I feel oddly hurt. I thought I'd got over all that now.

When I return my attention to Harry, he's scanning my face keenly. I hold his eyes. Again, practising? I drop my eyes and scoop up the last drop of wine at the bottom of my glass.

'Would you like another one?' he says.

'Maybe later,' I reply.

I'm unsure if I trust myself to drink any more. And I'm not sure I trust myself not to talk to Duncan later, to say something I might regret, let alone if I keep drinking. He won't be pleased that I wandered off, yet he's completely ignored me in favour of his friends. But then what did I expect?

'We haven't done the top floor yet,' I say, smiling brightly.

I like the black-and-white prints up there the best. There are shots taken at odd angles, trees sloping downwards from the top left-hand corner and the view of a farmyard taken from between a sheep's feet. I laugh at that one.

'The photographer must have got down and dirty for that one!'

I regret the words as soon as they're spoken. Harry laughs with me and my embarrassment is instantly gone.

'Fancy a cup of coffee?' he asks. 'I think I can see Nat down there – I'm sure she'd love to meet you.'

He leans over the gallery landing and gives her a wave. She waves back energetically, an exuberant young woman with her hair braided into rainbow dreadlocks.

'Sure,' I say.

We turn back to the stairs.

'Thanks for the company,' I say. 'I wasn't sure if I'd like this or not, but you've made it so interesting and it's been lovely to catch up.'

The café smells vibrant with coffee and cinnamon. There's no sign of Duncan. Harry's daughter is sat at a table leafing through a copy of the exhibition catalogue. Harry goes off to join the queue and I sit with Nat. I like her; she's got a bit of spark about her. She's into spoken word poetry as well as film-making and she tells me about the recent publication of her first collection. She's obviously thrilled to bits. I congratulate her and then she points to one of the pages of the catalogue.

'Have you seen this?'

It's a double spread of old-fashioned black-and-white photographs.

'I think we missed that display.' I squint at the pictures. 'It says it's on the top floor.'

She bends the pages of the brochure back, flattening it against the table. She points again.

'I've had this idea for a short film about the early history

202

of Belston Reservoir. There's a photograph here from the end of the First World War.'

She pushes the catalogue towards me so that we can both see.

'There was a church flooded in the making of the reservoir,' she says. 'It was dedicated to St Bertram.'

'Who's St Bertram?' I ask, feeding her enthusiasm; I'm used to that.

'He was the King of Mercia, around the time of the eighth century. He thought he had a calling for the Church and travelled to Ireland, but instead he fell in love with an Irish princess and brought her back to England.'

One of her braids falls over her shoulder and her hand smooths the page again with its photographs. She taps on one of them. It shows what appears to be an island in the middle of the water, a church marooned in the centre, as if it had been built that way.

'That's the church. This is from when it reappeared above the water in 1918. It was a particularly dry summer that year and the reservoir level receded dramatically.'

I look with her. There's the familiar loop of shoreline, the shape of the hills against the sky exactly as they are now, and a group of onlookers standing on a spit of dry land facing towards the church.

'Looks like it drew a crowd.'

'Oh, it did. Must have been a curiosity seeing the church rise above the water like that.' She returns to her story. 'Bertram married his princess but rejected his life of royal luxury. They took to a hovel in the forest and had a baby, a little boy. Then when Bertram went hunting one day, he came back to find his wife and newborn child had been killed by wolves.'

'Oh no,' I say, 'that's awful!'

'I know. He did the whole Christian hermit thing after that, dedicating his life to the poor in the forest, converting pagans into Christians, etcetera. You can find his grave at the church in Ilam, not far from here. But it's this church that interests me. I love the whole idea that it reappears in dry weather. Or did do.'

'Did?'

'It got demolished shortly afterwards. In the summer of 1918. When it reappeared like that, it drew such a crowd the authorities were worried for their safety. So they had the whole building and its steeple dismantled stone by stone whilst it could still be accessed. The stones were reused in the buildings around the area and I believe the old bell was rehung in the church of St Agatha's in Derby.'

'You know a lot about it.' I smile, still looking at the picture.

The arms of the people are pointing to the island, grey waters choppy about its shore. I don't tell her that I live nearby. It occurs to me that we should have brought Joe with us – he would have enjoyed meeting Nat. Though he'd probably have said no.

'The film is for my degree; it'll be narrated by poetry—'

'Is Nat boring you with her stories about churches?'

It's Harry. Back with a tray of coffee and flapjacks.

'Not at all.'

'Hello!'

Duncan has appeared behind me. He places a hand on my shoulder – I itch to push it away, especially here in front of Harry. I can't remember when Duncan last touched me like that, let alone in public. Duncan holds out his other hand to Harry.

'Harry? We've not seen you in years!'

Duncan's hand squeezes my shoulder. A warning. He presses too hard and even after his hand has gone, I can feel the pressure points of each finger. I wish now that I'd kept drinking. He's angry.

'Lovely to see you again,' continues Duncan. 'But if you don't mind, I'm going to whisk my wife away. Darling, there's someone I'd like you to meet.'

Eek, *Darling*. Who are you kidding, Duncan? Yet, before I know it, I've stood up and Duncan's holding my arm firmly as if to lead me away. He doesn't say anything but his grip is like fire. I want to shake my arm free but Harry is watching us. I feel my cheeks burn, like I'm the errant partner here – not *him*. He took his time. I grit my teeth and lift my chin.

'Goodbye, Harry,' I say, smiling. 'So lovely to see you again. Keep in touch, hmm?'

What possible right has Duncan to be angry? As we move away, he drops his hand. Now I feel worse. He's reining it in, of course he is. We're in public.

He'll be saving it for later.

CHAPTER 38

CLAIRE – BEFORE

The drive home is quiet. I replay the evening at the exhibition, meeting Harry, his daughter, that story about the church and whatever I can think of to distract me from the man who is my husband sitting next to me behind the wheel.

The country lanes are dowsed in silver shadows and the car slides to a halt outside the Barn with a deceptive calm. It's gone ten o'clock and Duncan doesn't say a word as he unlocks the door to let us in. He strides off towards the kitchen. I see him scoop up a pack of beers from the pantry and stalk down the long corridor to his beloved media room.

I shrug out of my jacket and shoes, placing my heels on the bottom tread of the stairs to take up later. I eye Duncan's disappearing figure warily. Finally, I can rub my arm. I see that Arthur is asleep on his bed in the kitchen, one ear cocked to acknowledge our return home. I look up the stairs. Joe is either catching up on his sleep, or preoccupied with his laptop and that coin. Either way, there's not much chance of him coming down to keep me company. The house feels like a mausoleum.

I'm grateful, though. Whatever is going through Duncan's mind, I've been spared another argument. For now. His face was cold and hard as we drove home. I recognise that face. He's gone to brood, to work himself up to it, to watch another of his horror movies, suppressing his anger as he drinks and ogles another poor woman running for her life as some slasher monster slices and dices his victims. I hate that kind of horror movie with a passion.

My head is bursting with too many thoughts. It feels like someone is trying to bury a screwdriver in my skull. I retreat to my usual spot on the sofa at the far end of the kitchen, curling up against the cushions with a rug. It's too early to go to bed. I pick up a book and lie on my side, but I can't decide which way to face. I turn over onto my back, then roll over onto my other side, tossing and turning, battling with both blanket and book, unable to get comfortable. I don't want to be comfortable.

Tonight, the moon is bright. My eyes are drawn to the trees clustered down by the water. I think of them all related one to another, spawned of the same seed. Beneath the ground their roots reach out, communicating unseen with their neighbours. I think about how long they've been growing there, decades, a century, or far, far longer, watching us humans, judging us humans and all the damage that we do. All of them constantly whispering about us, the living and the dead.

I sit up and reach for the TV remote. The all-night news is on, filled with scenes of an apocalyptic landslide in India. Crowds of men and women have gathered at the site, calling and wailing until they organise themselves into a human chain, their hands outstretched to help those who can still be reached. The camera pans across from above, showing a river of languid, swirling mud. The remnants of buildings float, splintered like matchsticks. It's as near a scene of hell as I can picture, the hands, the screams, the sickly movement of the mud, slow and thick and relentless. Not hell, I think, but purgatory – the victims who are not quite dead trying to swim, arms floundering, legs sinking, mouths opening and closing only to gag on the clagging brown sludge. I can't watch.

I turn over to another channel. This time it's a crime drama. There's a woman screaming off-camera and a man flings himself into a darkened room. The window is wide open, net curtains sucked out by the wind. The camera pans from the outside of the building in. He passes through a bedroom into the en suite. Blood lies slick across the floor and one arm hangs limp over the side of the bath. The music pounds like something out of *Psycho*. It's been done so many times before, but it works, doesn't it? The thrill of someone else's terror, the frisson of their last moments, the satisfaction of their horrifyingly violent death. Cathartic. Safe. Not me.

I flick through more channels and it's all the same: pain and death and drama and conflict, shouting, screaming, music so loud my headache will surely worsen . . . Why am I watching this stuff?

I switch off the TV and slide further back onto the sofa.

I don't want to think about Harry and his daughter anymore, or Duncan's dog-in-the-manger attitude to my spending time with them. It's not very likely that I'll ever see Harry again. He didn't offer me any contact details and I didn't ask.

Instead, my mind turns to that man in the field, Ray Turner. He still bothers me. Joe must think he's got wind of what he's found. The puppetrider, it's such a distinctive name for a coin. And the image of the skeletal half-figure clattering on his horse is hard to ignore. That Joe should find that coin after all these years seems prophetic.

I jump up and pace the room. I need to talk to Duncan, to tell him about the coin. But I daren't. We've never talked about it in all these years, a damning secret buried between us. If I did say anything, Joe would never forgive me. I've betrayed him once already, haven't I? It's just a coin, I think. Maybe not even the *same* coin. I twist my head from side to side. No, this is my guilty conscience coming back to torment me.

The kitchen is cold, the underfloor heating having long since switched itself off. Duncan always did like the house cold, another petty dispute between us. I pull the rug around my shoulders and move across to a small standing desk, pushed against the wall by the fridge. I need to know more about the puppetrider. How many are out there and what one coin is worth. I retrieve my laptop from under the bills and lift up the screen. I turn it on and type in the words:

How rare is a puppetrider?

Nothing much useful turns up – there's a load more coin-listing sites and images. But not a lot specifically about puppetriders other than what I've read before. I can see that coin values vary from a few pounds to hundreds or even thousands, depending on the metal content and rarity. I tap my fingers restlessly against the desk. Maybe I'm not searching hard enough. I lift my head to check the long corridor – there's no sign of Duncan. I return my gaze to the screen.

I swap to viewing images instead of text and open up one picture that shows me both sides of the coin at the same time. It's such a distinctive pattern. I could never mistake it. It must have meant something. I find a chat site where people talk wistfully about finding one. I swap back and forth between the two pages to find them speculating on who the rider on the back of the coin is. A sun god, a roman warrior, or perhaps a pre-Celtic representation of Death itself.

One commentator goes on about a folk tale about a young man who's lost. He enters a cave, lit up by a host of candles. They're set in the sandy floor and pushed into the tiny alcoves in the rock, all of them flickering in the dark. As his eyes adjust to the gloom, he notices that the various candles have different heights. Then he sees an old man standing in the shadows.

'Do you like my candles?' says the old man.

'Yes,' says the other, 'but why are there so many?'

'Each one is the soul of a living person. Those that are taller are babies and children, those that are short are old like me, or have some other reason why their life won't be long.'

The young man looks at all the tiny flames illuminating the cave. He swallows and the inevitable question comes.

'Which one is mine?'

'Are you sure you want to know?' says the old man.

'Yes!' comes the reply.

'That one.'

The old man lifts a bony finger and points to the smallest. The young man gasps.

'B . . . but that can't be mine,' he says. 'I'm only twenty-one years old!'

The old man shrugs. The young man thinks.

'How about this one? Whose is that?' he says.

He points to a stubby candle directly behind the old man. The old man turns to look and in that split second, the young man snatches up a new candle and jams it onto what's left of his. The flame is snuffed out. The young man falls dead. Death, says the narrator, cannot be cheated.

When you're young, you don't believe you'll ever die. It's one of those things you know is inevitable, unthinkable, but a long, long way away.

I toggle through more search results. There's reference to the ancient custom of placing a coin on each eye of the dead, or in the corpse's mouth, of giving a coin to the ferryman in payment for one's passage to the underworld. Or is it two coins – for the journey there and back again? My eyes are dragged back to the photos of the puppetrider. No wonder Joe's been obsessed with this coin. It has such a wild and pagan look.

It feels all wrong, knowing the coin is a payment for death. I, we, had no idea. It was intended as a discreet marker. I feel the horrific irony of it engulf me.

It must have slowly wriggled from its hiding place in the cement, or broken loose and fallen into the water. Then been washed out by stray currents through the tunnels of the old workings. Out into the wild. I picture it ebbing and flowing in the silt until it had finally lodged itself somewhere on the shore, our shore, right at the bottom of our fields.

What else lies nearby waiting to be found? Bones, tiny finger bones, like white pearls in the mud?

Duncan promised me it would be safe.

That no one would ever find her . . .

CHAPTER 39

CLAIRE – AFTER

I am angry with myself. For what happened earlier this morning and the time before, when I went in the other direction as far as the cattle grid and convinced myself I was driving to the police station. It seemed so real. And yet I had this kind of paralysis, sitting there at the wheel, imagining it all. Was that almost-crash in the fog also my imagination? I bite my lip, I *am* going mad. I can't go on like this. Not sleeping, not eating, living in self-imposed isolation.

There *are* people in the village. I think back to the man I met. The village is occupied after all, he'd said as much. And someone has to be responsible for the removal of all my posters. Unless I've imagined that too. No, that was real, he was real. Maybe I could speak to him, ask him what's going on. I don't understand why anyone would take them down like that. If I've upset anyone with my posters, I'm keen to explain myself. Besides, maybe one of them knows something about Joe.

I decide to walk to the village. I'm not driving this time. It'll do me good, a bit of exercise. The rain has gone, but the hanging basket by the back door has blown off its hook and scattered compost over the pathway. I can't face picking it up, gathering the pieces and having to go back inside again to clean up. So I leave it, rolling awkwardly back and forth like a severed head.

I turn left at the bottom of the track. The wind rips through the trees with the fury of a vengeful god thrusting his hand across the canopy. It buffets me from behind, pushing me down the lane. Almost like it wants me to go there. My steps are brisk and purposeful. The lane winds down into the valley and I stop at the first house.

This one's a little bigger than the others. It has a front door with a small window on each side. On the doorstep is a pair of worn-out leather boots; I don't remember seeing them before. The shoelaces are encrusted with mud with a peep of dirty yellow. I go to the door, one hand raised to knock, yet something makes me hesitate. There's an unexpected suck of air and the door is open. An old woman stands in front of me.

'Hello,' she says.

Her hair is like a wraith of white smoke about her head. Her face has a startled look with thin, painted eyebrows and eyes that blink a busy hazel brown. She looks strong, resilient, but her skin is thin and sallow. One hand grips the doorknob as if she needs it for support, and her veins are pronounced and blue-blooded with age.

'You'll be the new one up top o' the hill,' she says.

'Yes,' I reply, not sure what else to add.

Word has spread. I guess you'd expect that in a place as small as this.

'You'd better come in.'

She pushes the door wide open and lets me pass. I get a whiff of freshly baked bread. I catch a glimpse of a room with black beams and dried herbs hanging down from cast-iron hooks, then we pass into a front sitting room.

There's a sofa against the wall with white lace cloths draped on the back. An armchair has been placed directly under the window and the old woman perches on it as I sink into the sofa. Her face is shadowed by the morning light, so I can't quite see her facial expressions. I wriggle in my seat, metal springs digging into my legs beneath the fabric. The room's not as big as I thought it was when I first sat down – she's too close.

I'm not sure where to start. I unfold one of the posters and lay it out flat on my lap.

'This is Joe,' I say. 'He's my son. He's gone missing.'

I offer her the poster. She sits unmoving.

'I put these posters up, along the valley, but I don't understand – someone has taken them all down.'

''E looks a lovely boy,' she says, her tone level and appeasing.

She's ignored my question. I feel my frustration rise.

'He's eighteen. It's important; he's not well. He hasn't come home for . . .' I frown, a wave of tiredness sweeping over me. 'Several weeks.'

'Gone missing has 'e?' says the old woman. 'Are you sure about that?'

'Yes.'

There's uncertainty in my voice. I don't understand what she means – it's like she's suggesting that Joe *wants* to be missing.

I lean back, angry with her, myself. I'm already regretting being here.

'They grow up so fast, don't they?' she says, watching me.

She stands up awkwardly, each foot shuffling after the other. She walks over to the fireplace, lifting a birdlike hand to pick up a photograph frame. She looks down at the picture. It shows a man in an old-fashioned suit and two boys – both teenagers. It must be her family, a long time ago.

'I 'ad boys,' she says. 'A mother stays close to her boys. But they grow up eventually, find a wife and move on; if yer lucky.' She turns back to me. 'It's 'ard, letting go.'

I don't want to let him go. I want to *find* him. What's she going on about?

Her hazel eyes are sharply focused. I notice the irises, like the shoelaces outside, are flecked with yellow.

'I'm only trying to find him. I don't mean to upset anyone with my posters.'

'Posters?' says the old woman, as if she hadn't heard what I said before.

I nod eagerly.

'I put them up a couple of days ago and someone's taken them all down?'

I phrase it as a clear question, but she still doesn't give me an answer.

'Have you seen him? Has anyone else in the village said they've seen him?'

I hold out the poster with Joe's photograph, waggling it in my hand, willing her to take it. But she stands unmoving. I

215

think of the man by the Hall gates. The one who scrunched up my poster. What's wrong with these people? I don't get why no one seems to want to help me.

My eyes flit across the furniture in the room, the photograph on the shelf. I'd assumed this house was empty, that the whole village was empty, but evidently that was a mistake. I slide my eyes away, embarrassed, remembering the way I simply walked into one of the cottages before.

I note the wooden radio on the shelf in the corner, the sunburst mahogany mirror hanging by a chain over the fireplace, the red-and-white gingham tablecloth on the table half-folded back against the wall. It makes me think of my grandparents' front parlour, the kind of room kept only for Sundays and unexpected visitors.

Am I an unexpected visitor? Unwanted, for sure.

'A lad like that, well . . .' The old woman shrugs. 'I'm sorry, I know it's 'ard. Where do *you* think he is?'

We're getting nowhere. She's asking *me* questions and dammit, I don't want to appear rude, but this is clearly a waste of time.

I stand up.

'Thank you,' I say. 'I'm sorry to have disturbed you. If you hear anything, anything at all, please get in touch.'

I press the poster down on the table and turn to leave, still irritated that she hasn't taken it from my hand.

She follows me to the front door and I turn round to take one more look. Her skin is sunken against her face, paper thin. I can see right through to the bones beneath.

'Goodbye,' she says, those yellow-brown eyes slowly blinking. Her voice is crackled and painful now, like a bad radio transmission fading in and out. 'Maybe don't knock on

216

the neighbours' houses just yet – people are quiet around here, don't like to be disturbed – d'yer understand?'

I nod, mortified.

'Good,' she says. 'I really do wish you luck with your son. We've all been there.' Then she appears to hesitate. 'Have you thought of searching the Hall?'

I'm startled. It's like she knows. Joe's been found there once before.

'I . . . I don't want to intrude,' I say.

She peers at me with a quizzical look, and something else. Sympathy or pity.

'It's okay,' she says. 'If you go now, in daylight, you'll be okay. The place isn't lived in.'

But her words seem contradictory, as if there *is* someone living in the hall. Or something. *If you go now, in daylight, you'll be okay.* I'm not sure I know what she means by that.

'Maybe it will help,' she says.

CHAPTER 40

DUNCAN – AFTER

Duncan hated Claire when she left him. Not hated *it*, hated *her*. There was a difference. It was a visceral feeling, deep in his gullet. Born of a consuming sense of betrayal. As if he'd even had the right to feel that way. He'd betrayed her, not the other way around, that was how everyone else would see it. They didn't know the truth of it. Life is never black and white.

He was in the media room. He'd come home after work and withdrawn to his usual favourite spot. It was womblike down there, with the blackout blinds down and the lights turned low. The TV was on the sports channel, the screen a luminous green. The tiny figures of footballers in red and white shirts ran across the grass accompanied by four-way shadows from the floodlights overhead.

The volume on the TV exploded with rhythmic bursts of chanting. The commentator jabbered like an overexcited hyena. Colours flashed before Duncan's eyes and the camera zoomed in and out, taking care to pick out the bright lettering of the advertising boards lining the stadium. Then it swung to a trio of young women on the front row. They were wearing tightly fitted kit. They all had identical swathes of long layered hair and big, shining teeth and T-shirts emblazoned with a finance company logo. Duncan's eyes lingered in spite of himself. It was all about the advertising, he thought, never about the sport.

He let the colours and noise wash over him, reaching out to pick up his can of lager from the storage cavity in his seat. The light from the TV flashed up against the walls, across the handful of oversized cinematic armchairs, casting shadows in every corner. It seemed only to emphasise the emptiness of the room. This had been his space, the one room that he'd spec'd out for himself, at the far end of the house where it was quiet. Claire had never liked it. There'd been a certain satisfaction in that.

'If we're going to go for that all-out modern luxury thing, we need a swimming pool,' she'd said. 'We could put it in the cellar.'

She'd always fancied a swimming pool.

'But we've already planned to have a billiards table in the cellar,' he'd said. 'A pool isn't at all practical. It's far more hassle than it's worth – no one's going to use a pool enough to warrant the expense.'

'I'd use it,' she replied, 'and it'll add value to the house – great if we move on.'

She could be obstinate when she wanted. But then so could he.

'We're not going to move on. This is it, our home for life. I want us to have the things we've always dreamed of.'

219

His dreams, he'd meant, not hers. He acknowledged that. But then it had been him bankrolling all this, hadn't it?

'You can join a health club,' he added. 'We don't need a pool. Think of the noise from the extractor units, the steam and the vapour. It creates all sorts of problems. I've seen too many people put those things in and never use them. Joe would love to have his friends round and lounge about watching films, or spend time chilling out playing billiards. It's something we can do together, too. It'll soften the blow of the location.'

What teen wanted to be stuck out in the countryside, unable to drive, reliant on lifts from his parents or the intermittent buses? That's all it took to win an argument, referencing Joe's needs. Claire had always caved in to that. So the swimming pool idea was ditched, and the billiards table in the basement and the media room at the far end of the house won out. Not that Joe had ever wanted to use either.

Duncan crumpled the empty lager can in his fist. He stared at the sharp angles and the lustre of its surfaces, the warped lines of its new shape. The metal was so thin, so fragile, so easy to crush, one last drop of liquid spilling out onto his hand.

He'd known that Claire knew about his affairs. For some time. But it got worse after Christmas. He wasn't sure why. Those last few weeks had been fraught with tension in the house, the two of them manoeuvring along the corridors and up and down the stairs only when the other was somewhere else. Joe had kept to his room, appearing downstairs only to get food from the kitchen. He had the look of someone walking through a minefield, as if one word, one step in the wrong direction would trigger an explosion. Even their dog, Arthur, had mooched about with his tail between his legs, fully aware that the humans in the house were all upset.

When it came, when it happened, Duncan had never expected it. That Claire would leave him that way. He should have been relieved. She'd made it easy for him, hadn't she? That was one way of looking at it.

He sank back into his chair, reaching for the phone tucked into his pocket. He pressed the screen to bring it back to life and scanned his messages. There was nothing. His mouth set into a straight line and he tapped out a message.

Are you there? he wrote.

He waited. No reply.

Come on now, this is getting stupid.

He waited again. Still no reply. He stared at the screen, willing for her to respond. Then gave a snort of disgust. He pushed the phone back into his pocket and pressed the button on the remote. The noise from the TV grew louder.

CHAPTER 41

CLAIRE – BEFORE

It's D-day. Fuck Duncan day. I wake with a nervous energy that has me wriggling down into the warmth of my bed and an actual smile on my face. Not that it stays there for very long, but I feel the excitement quivering in my bones and an urgent need to get up and throw everything in the car and just go.

But of course, there's a lot to be done before I can do that. Joe is still asleep, Duncan's already at work. I grab a quick coffee then drive into Belston to get the key. I drive at speed but slow down as the road approaches the reservoir. It's so cold, the road glitters with ice, and the water is glacial and unmoving.

Something catches my eye – a metal object poking from the water. It's pitched awkwardly to one side, draped in strands of frosted green. It's a strangely shrouded thing of beauty and I don't like it. It makes me think of broken glass from a mirror, or clocks that strike thirteen, or three knocks heard at your door at midnight – bad luck waiting on your doorstep. I speed up again.

The woman behind the desk at the estate agents is smooth and efficient. It only takes a few minutes.

'Good luck!' she says, her words spoken with kindness.

She knows. Maybe she's been there, done it herself.

They say more than a third of marriages end in divorce. I'm not the only one to have gone through this. *Buck up, Claire. It's a new dawn . . .*

I drive home with my heart all a flutter. It reminds me of a conversation I once had with Joe. I'd tried to ask him once, how it felt, when he had a high.

'I don't understand,' I said, standing next to him in the kitchen. 'Explain it to me.'

He was almost sixteen at the time, his jaw squaring up, his neck filling out, his voice deeper than I'd expected. It was one of those rare moments he was willing to articulate, which probably had to do with the state that he was in. Hyper – not with drugs, but with energy and emotion.

'I . . . I don't know. It's like a buzzing in my head, my brain too busy to stand still.'

His hands were moving up and down as if he were doing semaphore.

'I have to *do* something. I have to *feel* something. I have all this energy with nowhere to go.'

Now he was bouncing from foot to foot.

'I feel like Superman! Like I can do anything! Don't you ever feel like that?'

He looked at me, almost pleading me to understand.

I shook my head. *No*, I thought, except that wasn't entirely true. When I was younger, hadn't I felt the same way? At

Christmas when I was a kid, or when I'd heard I'd won my place at uni. Or when I discovered I was pregnant.

I haven't felt like that since, not in a long time.

It scared me, watching him doing this bizarre little dance. Then his arms spread wide and he reached for a bottle of lemonade on the worktop.

'It's like this!' he said.

He swept the bottle into both hands and shook it.

'No, Joe, don't!' I cried.

I tried to snatch it back, but he swung himself out of reach and kept on shaking. I could hear the bubbles fizz, then it exploded all across the kitchen. We both ducked. Liquid surrounded us everywhere, swimming around our feet and running down the cupboard doors. It was all over our clothes, pooling on the kitchen island, bubbling up like acid. The bottle lay spinning on the floor and more liquid dripped from between his fingers. He was actually smiling, laughing. I was so angry – all that pointless mess!

Then I started to laugh too.

He *had* managed to get the message across. In a strangely visceral, memorable kind of way. We stood there, both of us dripping wet and laughing. I knew exactly what he meant after that. And all I could think of was how very much I loved him. Whatever he did.

It's still only mid-morning when I get back. I'm in the bedroom, packing the rest of my things, working myself up to waking Joe and having *that* conversation. We need to start on his stuff now. The mobile rings.

'Hi, Claire.'

It's Duncan. His voice is businesslike and assertive.

'Hi,' I say.

Fuck you, I think. It's going to be my favourite phrase of the day.

'I take it Joe's still at home?'

'Yes.'

There's a pause. I don't feel like encouraging this conversation.

'Good. I won't be back for tea. Martin and I are going for a drink and maybe a curry afterwards. Thought we'd go to that new place near the station in Derby. They've got an offer on at the moment.'

Really? I think, my mouth twisting into a sneer. The more elaborate his story, the more I don't believe it. What does he take me for? I'm surprised he's even bothering to ring me; I know what he's about to say.

'So, I'll be out late. Don't wait up for me.'

I tuck the phone under my chin and smooth the jumper that lies folded on my bed, then lift it into the suitcase that yawns wide open on the duvet.

'Sure,' I say.

Whatever.

He hangs up. Good, I think. That gives me more time, the rest of the day *and* the evening.

I've made soup for lunch. Parsnip and sweet potato soup. I take some up to Joe. He's finally up and bent over his laptop doing God knows what. I catch sight of something on his screen that looks a bit like building schematics, or maybe it's one of those computer games where the players have to hunt the enemy through an underground labyrinth. I put the soup on the desk beside him and sit on his bed.

I contemplate his back. I've been avoiding this all morning. Now the moment has come, I'm lost for words. How do I even start this conversation?

'Joe . . .'

At least he seems okay today, more himself. I thought perhaps he might still be freaked out by whatever upset him about that man. Ray Turner.

'Joe, I . . .'

He turns round, eyes bright and sparkly.

'Mum, can you go, please, I'm right in the middle of talking to someone.'

Talking to someone? He means online, I realise. He's jumping between screens, multitasking. I bite my lip.

'Okay, Joe, but I want to talk to you as soon as you're done. I'll have my lunch but can you come down when you're finished. We need to sit down together, hmm?'

'Sure,' he murmurs, but he's already turned away from me back to his screen.

I get up and leave, frustration eating into my fragile confidence.

The soup has that woody, spicy smell that fills the kitchen with memories of fireworks and blankets on the patio. I perch on a stool at the worktop in the kitchen with a steaming hot bowl. I've kicked off my slippers and my bare toes are curled against the metal supports of the stool. I butter a slice of bread and dunk it in the soup. The corner disintegrates in my mouth and warm liquid trails a slow heat into my stomach.

There's a pile of washing-up in the sink – I'm leaving it for Duncan. It's a small thing, but satisfying.

I think of that phone call with him. I know he's lying. But do I want to find out more? Today?

It taunts me, the thought that he's seeing *her* again, this evening. I'm sure of it, his voice had that crisp distance he puts on when he's lying. The story dressed up with cool professionalism. Duncan the vet, Duncan the superhero, Duncan the bloody cheat.

When I try to put a face on the body, it fills me with rage, the very idea that it's someone I know, someone from his work. Madelaine, Frances, Sally, Imogen, Paula . . . each face pops into my head only to be dismissed. I can't believe it of any of them. Apart from Paula, I've known them all for years. Familiar faces as the practice grew, names that popped up at mealtimes, their working lives a part of mine through Duncan. But it's more than that. I think of the times I've visited the surgery and chatted to the girls, laughed with them, sympathised with them, the nights out we've had at Christmas or when one of them has had a birthday. They've always included me in their celebrations. Oh God, how long has it been going on? Maybe it's Paula. She's new, she's got that glamorous red hair . . . Did he know her before she joined the practice? Has it always been just one woman, all this time? Which one – which bloody one?

I can't let myself think of it. It doesn't matter who she is. Not really. What would I do with the knowledge, anyway? I can hardly storm round and slap her face, beat her up in some back alley, or secretly pay to have someone kill her. Don't be stupid, I think. That kind of stuff only happens in the movies. My heart skips a beat and I can't go there.

No good will ever come of thinking about it, winding myself up with jealousy, tormenting myself with my own inadequacies by comparison.

I can't change *him*. I can only change *me*. The time has

come. I have a new life waiting for me. But it's no good, I can't get it out of my head.

I twist off my seat and pull out a bottle of wine from the built-in wine rack under the kitchen island – an expensive red that Duncan will notice has gone missing. I fumble with the cork and pour myself a generous glass. I'm not really a drinker but I need it. One more day. I can talk to Joe tomorrow and make the move then. I look around the room, to the hall and the big sitting room beyond. It was meant to be our new start, this Barn. I take a swig of wine.

I could delay things for just one more day, couldn't I? To find out.

What harm could it do?

CHAPTER 42

CLAIRE – AFTER

I turn out of the gate of the old woman's cottage. Back onto the lane that runs through the village. I'd always thought it was empty, both village and Hall, ever since we first got here. I look at the houses with new eyes now. Maybe this holiday cottage thing is a recent development, but that old woman looks like she's always been here.

The story was that the original family who owned the whole village had relocated to London. Sometime in the 1950s. Family finances or post-wartime taxes, or more likely it was the allure of a more glamorous life and paid work in the capital. No one really knew. Only one elderly gentleman had carried on living at the Hall, apparently senile, until the 1990s, when eventually he'd been moved into a care home and died.

Whilst he was still living in the Hall, however, the estate had been neglected. Until an agent had been employed. This much younger man turned up from London every once in a while, upsetting the tenants. People still remember these things and the stories about the agent were never good – that he'd shouted at everyone and imposed ridiculous rules on the tenants. Acting like *he* owned the estate not his fragile boss. There was even a rumour that he'd been fiddling the accounts, hiving off a percentage by charging too much rent and taking the funds intended for repairs and maintenance. One by one, people stopped renting the houses, until the village fell empty. The village, it seemed, had never got over it.

In the old man's last years at the Hall, he was cared for by a trio of aging servants. They carried on living in the house after he left until they, too, passed away, one by one. Duncan had told me once that the three of them haunted the house, still caring for their long-departed master. Lights were seen at odd hours of the night, flickering past a window. Or maybe that was just another story to encourage people to stay away.

I wasn't sure who currently owned the estate, some male descendent of a cousin, or something like that. He'd never visited the house either. When he tried to sell up, all the buildings were in such a poor state of repair, damp and unin-habitable, and he set the prices so high, with restrictions on development, that no one would buy them. So the village and the Hall stayed empty.

My pace slows. I peer at the houses, hoping I might see Joe moving in one of the rooms. There are no cars again. If anyone is using one of these houses for a holiday, there's no evidence of it now. And who would want to when you see the condition of them. I'm not sure it can be right about that holiday cottage thing. The man I met hadn't actually said so. It was just another idea I'd got in my head.

As I pass through the village, each building shelters behind hanging wooden shutters, gates and pathways obscured by nettles and overgrown shrubs. It's a place cast under a spell, frozen in time, the empty cottages like the leftover scraps of broken chains and cracked beads in a once well-loved jewellery box. Joe had loved it. More than once, when he was younger, we found him down here. For a while, it was his playground, his secret hideout, like a favourite shed or a treehouse at the bottom of the garden. Only bigger.

I can't see him. There's no sign he might have been here. No open doors. Climbers drape like lace across the walls: ivy and Virginia creeper, clematis and hydrangea, suckers reaching for the roofs, strangling the cast-iron guttering. The leaves glitter with the rain that came earlier, fluttering in gentle waves, and the net curtains, shredded with age, float at blank and lifeless windows.

It crushes me, all this neglect, despite the beauty. The silence reaches between the houses like a snake sliding into water.

No, I don't think Joe's here. There's not a single sign of life. And besides, as he grew older, it was the Hall that drew him, not the cottages. I'm not sure why. It's always creeped me out, but maybe that was exactly the appeal.

I pass a track that leads to my right, then stop outside the entrance to the Hall. Here, the neglected topiaries pose like overgrown poodles and long-forgotten rhododendrons ripen with slow-growing buds. The two halves of the tall gate hang absurdly from their bolts and the drive is pitted with potholes brimming with rainwater. Not a ripple stirs their surface, sky and branches reflected from above.

I lift my head and look each way. There's nothing, no one

231

to challenge me as I step through the rusting gates. The drive swings to the left. There's a hint of dark solidity through the trees, the Hall shrouded in green shadows that fill the gaps between tall pillars of chestnut, pine and ash. In front of me, a squirrel leaps across the drive. There are loads of them around here, feral creatures that scatter like sycamore seeds across the road. This one prods at the dead leaves and stops to stare at me, tweaking its tail in disapproval. I walk on undeterred. It gives another shake of its tail and springs into the nearest tree, spiralling up the trunk with the quick, lithe movements of a circus acrobat. Pausing at the top, it watches me again, body poised, tail quivering at the tip.

Now I see the Hall. It's a V-shaped building enclosing a weed-infested forecourt. The brick walls are the same colour as the cottages in the village and in the centre a wide semicircle of stone steps leads to a set of double doors. One of them is ajar. It's as if the owner can't even be bothered to secure the place, but then there are so many other ways to get in.

Here and there, the roof has fallen down, and on either side, the great wings of the building flutter with multiple stone mullioned windows so that the whole thing towers over its lawns and terraces like a bare-headed vulture poised upon its nest.

The gravel crunches loud beneath my feet. My eyes jump from ground to walls in spite of myself, searching the openings with an uneasy sense of guilt. I look for a face behind a window, a hand upon the glass, the brief movement of drapes falling back, even though I know there will be none. Unless it's Joe. In my head, at any moment, someone might leap from the front door and chase me indignantly from their sight.

But no, the windows are motionless. There's no obvious

sign of Joe. Not yet. The old woman from the cottage said it would be okay if I did this now. But I begin to question what I might find if I came back later.

I climb the steps and give the open door a push.

CHAPTER 43

CLAIRE – BEFORE

I kill a bit of time with more packing and an online food shop. The weather is getting worse and if I'm going to delay things a day, I might as well get a food order to come tomorrow so I have some fresh basics to take with us. I'm wondering what excuse I can find to ring Martin. I turn my wrist to look at my watch. Theoretically, the two of them will be in the pub by now. Except I am damn sure that Duncan was lying.

I play out a scenario in my head. I could try telling Martin about the man in our field.

There was this strange guy in our field today – wanted to use a metal detector. Joe's really worried about him. I said I'd get you to ask around.

Nope, can't do that – first, I promised Joe I wouldn't say anything and secondly, when I say it like that it sounds so ridiculous – the man was asking permission, after all. He's not committed any crime or made any threats. Perfectly reasonable when you think about it.

I tap my fingers on the table. It's Duncan's birthday next month.

Hey, Martin, I'm organising a surprise birthday party for Duncan. He's not there with you by any chance, is he? Only I don't want him to know – was hoping you might suggest a few names for me.

That one's a bit better. Though I'm really no good at this sort of thing.

I pick up my phone before I lose my nerve and dial the number. He answers straight away.

'Hey, Martin, it's Claire. How are you?'

I can hear noise in the background, the distinctive combination of voices, music and the clunk of glasses. Damn – perhaps Duncan was actually telling the truth.

'Hi, Claire,' says Martin. 'I'm fine, thank you.'

'Sounds like you're in the pub!' I give a laugh. 'Sorry to disturb you.'

'Not at all, Claire. A few drinks with the lads, you know. Are you after Duncan?'

Oh Lord, Duncan really was telling the truth. I feel a fool now, like Martin knows I'm checking up on my errant husband. I imagine the pair of them laughing with each other about it over a pint: Duncan moaning about his wife, Martin telling him that half the force are dodging their wives. He's direct with his question too – typical policeman.

'Actually, no – he's not there with you, is he? It's . . . it's a bit delicate.'

I've got his interest now.

'No, he's not with me – this is just work. We're not due to

235

meet up for a drink until next week. I did try to ring him earlier, as it happens, but they told me he was about to start an emergency operation. He'll be working late tonight, I think, did he not tell you? Might have been a bit of a rush. What's up, Claire?'

Phew – I've got my answer. How easy was that? Now I have to wriggle out of this call without him realising what I was really after. Unless, that is, Martin is fully appraised of Duncan's affairs and corroborating. It's possible, I suppose, but no, I don't believe that.

'Well, you know it's Duncan's birthday in a few weeks?' I speed up before he can think too long about the plausibility of my question. 'I was trying to come up with something different this year, you know, as a gift. And I was thinking maybe a balloon experience. You and Zoe went on one, didn't you? I wondered if you could recommend someone.'

'That sounds a great idea. We used Carsington Balloon Flights – they were excellent. We saw the most spectacular views at sunset. It can be a bit unpredictable date-wise, though. They have to cancel if the weather's not suitable.'

'I was expecting that – and I'm not worried about dates; it doesn't have to be on his birthday as such. Want us to make a day of it – you know, a nice pub lunch, a walk and then this as a surprise. Give him something to really remember.'

I bite my lip. Martin will know soon enough that I've left Duncan, and he'll look back on this conversation and twig.

'I think he'd love it. I can text you the number, if you like?'

'Brilliant!' I force myself to smile. 'Cheers, Martin.'

And then as a final thought, 'You won't say anything, will you?'

'Course not, Claire. Have a good night.'

'Bye.'

I hang up. I feel elated. I've just lied to the police. Ha ha, very funny, Claire. I have a brief fantasy about Martin and a pair of handcuffs. Jeez, I'm blushing now. I've never remotely fancied Martin. Never mind the fact that he's married. My lips twist into a sneer. There's no way I'd ever go for a man who's married. I know too well what that means. But then fucking Duncan's best mate could have its attractions. Imagine Duncan's face . . .

I put the phone down on the worktop and pick up a stray spoon. I fidget with it in my hands. I shouldn't care – about who Duncan is sleeping with. It won't make any difference when I am leaving him anyway. But hearing him lie to me on the phone earlier, so casually, so easily, so . . . My hand clenches around the spoon until my knuckles turn yellow then white. I must be a masochist to want to know, but I do.

I let my hand relax. The spoon drops onto the worktop with a clang. I pick it up and let it drop again. Again, and again. The sound is satisfying. Then I grasp it between finger and thumb. It bends at the neck. I push harder and the metal bends some more. I push until it's a twisted thing, like the broken head of a doll washed up against the sewage grate under the kerb of a street. It's like something out of one of Duncan's horror movies, its jaw slewed to one side, peering through the bars.

Laughing at me.

CHAPTER 44

CLAIRE – BEFORE

I ring the surgery next. The voice that picks up is warm and friendly. I feel the tension in me retreat – Imogen is happily married. There's no way it could be her. I hate the fact that I could have even suspected it was her.

'Is that Imogen?'

'Hi, Claire. If you're after Duncan, he's in the midst of surgery. We've had an RTA and the poor animal's a mess. He'll be in there for at least another hour. Did you need anything?'

'No, it's fine, nothing urgent. I was just wondering when he would be home for tea.'

Oh, the joys of wifely deception. I know Imogen's not lying, even if it were her, since Martin's already told me the same story. It can't be that all three of them are in cahoots. But I need to know roughly what time Duncan will leave the surgery.

'I would guess another two hours, allowing time for speaking to the owner and updating the records after.'

'That's great. Don't disturb him, I'll catch him when he gets home. Have a good evening, Imogen, when you finally get away.'

'Thanks, Claire, you too.'

I hang up.

Now I bite my lip. What if Imogen mentions my call to Duncan? He'll think it odd. I rub my head. I know it's unlikely, but I'm really no good at this. Deception, lies. I hate that Duncan has reduced me to this.

A couple of hours later, I park on the side road, behind the garages that belong to a row of terraced houses next to the surgery. It's on a slope and there's a gap in the buildings through which I get a good view of the staff car park.

It's bitterly cold and I'm grateful to be inside as the wind buffets the side of the car and sleet slides drunkenly against the windows. Most of the cars have gone. I wait until only two are left, one of them Duncan's, parked in his usual spot not far from the stockroom door.

There he is. The door out to the car park slams backwards in the wind and Duncan emerges in a thigh-length woollen coat and neatly arranged scarf. Behind him is Sally, the receptionist, her pale blonde hair bright against her faux fur-clad shoulders.

Sally?

Why would Sally have stayed late for a road traffic accident?

He stops a moment and she bumps into him. He catches her with his arms to steady her and they both pull a little closer. She pulls away. I catch my breath.

God in heaven above! It can't be *her*?

But he nods and they make their way to separate cars.

That's when the penny drops. Because I know Sally lives in a flat-share just around the corner – she doesn't need a car to get to work. So what's this business about two cars except if they have plans to go somewhere, separately but together?

My heart thunders beneath my ribs. Sally – oh God, it *is* Sally. But she's so *nice*. She's always been so sweet on the phone or when I go in. And she's young. Far too young, still in her early twenties, let alone . . . I feel my stomach do a gut-wrenching somersault. The bastard!

The two cars turn onto the main road. Duncan goes first and Sally follows. I start the engine and wrench the gears into first. I pull out from behind the garages, moments later slipping into the slow-moving traffic a few vehicles behind. I still can't take it in. How could Sally even conceive of sleeping with my husband? She's beautiful, vital, full of life. She could have any young man, why on earth would she go for her married boss? I feel my throat contract. Perhaps that's the very attraction.

It's not hard to follow them, despite the darkening night – her car is a distinctive red-and-white Mini and she's driving it right behind him.

He takes the road out of Belston, the one that goes to Derby. My car almost catches up, so I slow down, dawdling behind with several cars and a big truck between us. After a few miles Duncan brakes. He turns off at the cattle grid which leads to the southern road alongside the reservoir. It's the one that ultimately passes the bottom of the old village and along to the dam. It's not the usual way home; it takes much longer. She ignores the turning and drives on. I follow her.

Disappointment sinks like a weight in my stomach as I realise it's not her. Of course not. He wouldn't be so crass as to sleep with Sally. I've got it all wrong. Relief floods through me and guilt too, that I could even for a moment have thought it was her. Maybe Sally parks her car in the staff car park because it's conveniently close. You have to pay for daytime on-street parking in that part of town. Of course she parks her car at work; it's probably there semi-permanently. And he's gone home after all, hasn't he? Albeit taking the scenic route.

But then, at the garage on the crossroads about a mile further down, Sally pulls in, parks up and goes into the shop on the forecourt. I see her head bobbing down the aisle and then she pays for something at the till. A minute later, she's in her car again. She fusses with her hair, pulling it into a loose but charming ponytail. It makes her look bright and young. She sets the car in motion and loops back onto the road, the way we've just been. I follow again, two or three cars behind, wide-eyed and furious as the realisation floods me. *Has she just bought what I think she's bought? Condoms?*

At the cattle grid, she too turns up, bumping along the road beside the water.

I can't follow her down there – it's too quiet, she'd see me. So I drive on and pull onto the next layby to wait. I know the road doesn't go anywhere. After wending its way around the full length of the reservoir and back again, it pops out just a few yards from this layby. I wait and wait, but nobody comes out.

I rev the engine and pull out onto the road, turning around so that I, too, can pass over the cattle grid. It seems highly unlikely that either one of them has gone this way to the Barn. Which leaves only the abandoned village or the old Hall. The sleet is back, falling a little thicker now, white against the

241

evening sky. A wet slush lines the verges and gathers in the nook of my slowly batting windscreen wipers. The darkness enfolds me and a red snowflake light is showing on the dashboard to warn me of the icy conditions. My hands are damp with sweat.

I take the road that leaves the side of the reservoir and enters the village. Trees loom across the lane. My headlamps pick up the growing layer of white gathering loosely on the tarmac. It's so fresh there are only two other sets of tyre marks – Duncan's and then Sally. At the entrance to the old Hall, both sets of tracks turn in through the gates. I halt the car. Wet clings to the elaborate iron frame and the gates are wide open, half-cocked on their hinges like the folded wings of a white butterfly. The engine of my car thrums. Steam from the exhaust pipe blows up against the rear window.

I try to find legitimate reasons why they might have come here. But there's not one. I feel a surge of anger as the realisation spreads. He's brought her here, to the heart of our valley, so close to the reservoir that was always *our* place. I feel the blood rushing to my neck, my cheeks. I feel disgust, pain, betrayal – a deepening sense of the surreal.

The tyre marks are already melting, but I can see they travel up the drive, where they disappear into the deep shadows of the trees.

I'm unwilling to take the car down there. If they've parked outside the house, they'll hear my engine. A confrontation is not what I'm after. Not yet. I reverse out of the entrance, backing onto the lane, where I park out of sight by one of the empty cottages. I close the car door as quietly as I can and pull my coat tight around me. I pick my way along the verge before clambering through a gap in the fencing by the

242

side wall to head under the trees and walk unseen but parallel to the Hall driveway.

When I get to the end of the drive, there are no cars outside the house.

That leaves only the stables.

CHAPTER 45

CLAIRE – BEFORE

The stable complex lies to the side and rear of the Hall. It's a quadrangle of buildings adjoining the servants' quarters. One huge archway leads into a cobbled courtyard. I duck out of sight into a doorway that I know leads into the tack room where a ladder goes up into the roof. The rungs bend queasily beneath my feet. My hands grip the sides of the ladder, wary that it might suddenly give way. A burning need to know for sure drives me on.

My mobile phone sits in my pocket. I've turned it to silent, but I have a vague idea of photographing them, evidence for my day in court, should I need it. Or maybe I'll sell it to the local paper: *Veterinary superstar caught in flagrante delicto in old abandoned Hall.* Duncan would have a fit. I'm not sure the *Belston Times* is up to *in flagrante delicto*.

I clamber along the floorboards to crouch at a small round window under the top gable. It looks out across the internal courtyard. The panes of glass are intact but loose, smothered in dirt and cobwebs and the cold whistles through the gaps in the old wooden frame. The courtyard is lit only by an unearthly shade of white where the artificial light from two sets of headlamps splays out across the cobbles. Both vehicles are clearly visible, parked in the middle of the yard, their engines off, one behind the other. Duncan's car is lit up from within.

The courtyard is silent, the brick walls too tall to see the trees outside. The small, high windows and grey painted carriage doors, what's left of them, seem to me to mimic the monochrome mood of the night. Weeds grow in swathes of grey between the cobbles and the wet snow half settles in between – not enough to give any depth, but enough to whiten the ground. Through the open doors of each building and the cracks in the brickwork on either side of me, the stables reek of centuries of urine-soaked slabs. I think of all the insects that must be living within, burrowed in the wooden stable dividers, cocooned against the walls, hiding between the floor-boards under my knees. My hands pull away and I feel the hairs on my skin contract. I try to hold my breath so I don't panic or give myself away. I won't let this whole thing get to me, I won't.

Duncan has wound his window down, leaving a small gap for ventilation. It's a habit of his, whatever the weather. The driver's seat has been lowered and I see his long body lying back. He's waiting.

Sally is still in her car. She's taken her coat off and is fiddling with something in her handbag. Now she's getting out of her car. She must have been sat in there for a while. I wonder why. Her car sits a few metres from his and the door, when it slams to, echoes against the walls. A flurry of pigeons sweeps up from the roof tiles and her face lifts towards the sky. I pull back from the window, fearful that she will see me, but it's too small and too high up, and with her evident preoccupation, it seems unlikely that I'll be discovered.

I reach forwards again to look. Duncan's front passenger door is flung open and she slides onto the seat.

'You took your time,' Duncan says, sitting up.

Thanks to the unique acoustics of the quadrangle, I can hear his voice despite the distance.

'I know you like to wait,' she says.

There's an edge to her voice, like something else is going on. Is she angry? No, it must be raw anticipation. Revving that engine, Duncan? She closes the car door and I don't hear what either of them says next.

Then Sally crosses her arms and pulls her top over her head. She flings it onto the back seat and Duncan leans back again to watch. Her hair had been dragged loose from its binding and it falls down around her shoulders. Keeping her bra on, she wriggles in her seat. I see her drop something in the car well between them and with her skirt riding up over her hips, she climbs onto his lap.

I can't watch. I close my eyes and taste the bile in my throat. How long has this been going on? I think back, before the conversation with those women at the supermarket. The times when Sally rang to say Duncan was working late, the times I called by and she'd smile an apology from behind the desk – *He's in theatre, Mrs Henderson*. The times I sat at home thinking of the other women that he's had, imagining unknown faces flirting with him at the gym, the bars and clubs he went drinking at. The anonymous texts on his phone.

I adjust my position. It's painful here on my knees by the window. If I'm going to take a photograph, I need to look. I scrabble for the phone in my pocket, my hands shaking as I check that the flash is off. I'm not sure if it will even work in this poor light, but I can't risk a flash being seen.

Now she's taking her bra off, slowly as a tease. One shoulder strap after another until each breast hangs loose before him. I can see that Duncan wants to touch, but her eyes hold him fixed against his seat. He's letting her have control. He's never done that with me. Her hands fold around his neck and she presses her body closer. I juggle the phone, taking as many pictures as I can, fumbling with the settings to get a better picture. Adrenalin has kicked in. And anger. Pure raging anger.

Outside, the night is deepening. The sleet has changed back into rain and it slices down against the car windows. I zoom in with the camera. The water rattles on the car roof, trickling through the gap in the window. I see Duncan's face, the way his eyes have rolled back, the sigh that hovers on his slightly parted lips. Sally's fingers have moved out of sight and I can't look at what happens next.

I pull back. The rain is filling the gaps and dips between the stones outside, driving against the glass in front of me. I take a peek and Sally's arms have reached for the headrest behind Duncan's head, bracing herself. Their rhythm grows and outside, the skies have darkened almost to a solid pitch-black.

Only the small internal light of the car pools above their heads.

The courtyard fills with the sound of the rain drumming on the gleaming slate roofs and my face, here inside this cramped but dry roof space, is wet.

247

How could he? How could she?

Sally. Of all the scenarios that played out in my head, I never thought it would be Sally. How could I be sat here, watching my husband fuck his best friend Martin's only daughter?

CHAPTER 46

DUNCAN – AFTER

Duncan had arrived early to work. As he came into the surgery, Sally was already there, sat behind the reception desk. He appreciated the sight of her, with her snugly fitted polo shirt and the carefully groomed curls resting on her shoulders. She'd always looked after herself, unlike Claire.

They were alone in the building and it was still an hour before opening time. It was his turn to check the animals on the ward and he didn't even pause to say hello. He was still smarting from her refusal to come to him when he was too drunk to know better. Never mind her complete radio silence since.

He marched across the waiting area to his consulting room and slammed the door shut behind him.

Sally followed, as he'd hoped she would.

He kept his back to her. The PC had sprung into life and he was shrugging out of his jacket, watching the screen as he heard the door close again behind her. He swung round in anticipation. But she was gone. She'd simply put an envelope on his desk and left.

Duncan stared at the envelope. It wasn't hard to guess the contents. He ripped the envelope open, scanned the page and launched himself from the room.

'Are you serious?'

He stood legs apart, flapping the letter in his hand, knowing that he towered over her, even when she was standing.

'You're resigning? Is this over that prat of a man who had his own healthy dog killed?' His lips curled.

'It's not about that.' Sally hugged herself and made to step out from behind the desk.

Duncan had a sudden thought. Frances. That day when she'd overheard him arranging a date. Hadn't she implied she was going to tell Sally? About his new running partner. But he hadn't thought she'd meant it, for the same reason she hadn't told Claire about Sally, she'd liked them both too much. Caught in a dilemma, she'd had no wish to hurt either of them, whatever her feelings about the relationship.

'Then what *is* it about?'

Then it occurred to him. Perhaps Sally had found someone else. Closer to her age. His eyes narrowed.

'You don't know?' Sally lifted her head, her body still turned away from him. 'Ever since Claire's been gone, you've been a complete bastard! And I know you've started seeing someone else!'

She flinched as he moved forwards and stepped smartly around the desk.

'Don't you touch me!' she cried. 'And don't think that you can change my mind with . . . *that*.'

She pulled herself out of reach.

'It's over, Duncan. You . . . me . . . my job here. I can't believe you're seeing someone else, already. I . . . I thought that after . . . after a bit of time, you and I would be together properly. I can't believe how I could have been so mistaken about you. How I've been fool enough to hang around for so long! You treat people like . . .'

She sucked in her breath, as if the effort of speaking the words almost suffocated her.

'But you weren't bothered about how we treated Claire,' said Duncan.

The statement hung in the air between them.

'That was different, you know that. She stopped loving you a long time ago.' Sally ground the words between her teeth. 'And now I understand why! You don't care about people, not anymore. I'm not even sure you care about the animals! You did once. When I first came here, you charged around the surgery, fixing everyone – animals, staff – but now it's become something else. A technical challenge, another ring of the till, a step closer in your *ambitions*.' She pushed out her chin. 'And you don't have any respect for me.'

She swung her body away and then back again.

'No wonder Claire gave up on you. I hate how you were with Garfield. I know the man's repugnant, but you took it too far. Ever since Claire, you take everything too far. And I won't stand by whilst you start seeing someone else. It might be a run here or a drink there, but I know how it starts. I've been there, remember? I don't want to be with you anymore. It's clear you don't want to be with me. Not properly.' Her mouth tightened, as if determined not to give way to any sentiment of love. 'And I can't continue to work here, either.

I've given you one month's notice, as per my contract, then I'm gone!'

'So, you're going to jack all this in for the sake of a nasty old man!'

'Haven't you heard a single thing that I've just said? No. I don't like what he did, any more than you, it was hideous! But you can't manhandle an old man and threaten him the way that you did, don't you see? Are you so obsessed with what's going on in your own head that you don't care about other people anymore? Or even what they think? Are you going to do the same to the next girl as you've done to Claire and me?'

Duncan didn't reply.

'You don't care about me,' she said. 'You never did! You don't care about any of us! It's all about consumption with you. The posh house, the nice things, sex . . .' She almost spat the last word.

'You like those things too!' said Duncan.

'Yes – I do. But they're not as important as the way you treat people. You've lost sight of that, Duncan. Sure, you can press my buttons, and I can press yours, but it's just sex, Duncan – with you, it's just *sex*!'

Duncan visibly flinched.

'I thought your feelings about Claire and Joe were completely understandable. Your relationship with Claire was . . . complicated, I know that. But . . .' Sally caught her breath. 'I can't do this, Duncan. I don't want to be a part of *this* anymore. What we did was all wrong, I see that now. In so many ways. I need to move on with my life, to be with someone who actually cares about me. Who's worth me. I want a family. A proper family – I don't mean loads of kids and the whole country dream thing, I know that's what *you* think. I mean people around me who love me.'

Her voice faded away, as if the word *love* was too hard a thing to say. She clutched her hands to her chest in an oddly youthful gesture, her ribs rising and falling as she sought to calm herself.

'Is this Frances telling you I'm too old for you? Has your dad found out?'

Duncan knew that Martin would murder him if he found out.

'Dad's got nothing to do with this. He doesn't even know.'

Duncan heaved a sigh of relief.

'You're just trying to deflect this from yourself,' she said. 'You need to take a long, hard look at yourself, Duncan Henderson. Not everyone . . .' She gave a sort of half-smothered hiccup and stopped speaking.

Her next words were quieter, slower.

'I thought I understood you. But I don't think I ever really understood you, Duncan. I just wanted to.'

She lifted her head and looked directly into his eyes.

'I can't stay here. I can't work for you anymore. I'll work my notice, give you time to find someone else. But you and me – we're through.'

CHAPTER 47

CLAIRE – AFTER

The gloom falls like a blanket over my head. The air inside the Hall is stagnant, redolent with the scent of decaying wood. Slowly, my eyes adjust. There's a fireplace and panelled walls and a staircase cascading from above. White streaks of daylight stream down from the open roof and bird shit stains the banisters. It's in a far worse state than I remembered. How quickly nature has reclaimed its own.

The sunshine glitters through the windows, the dancing pattern of leaves trapped in the cracked and broken glass. It's not hard to imagine those three ghostly servants drifting down the corridors. I give a shiver. I'm intruding on someone else's space, unknown figures from the past frowning at my trespass, painted eyes swivelling to follow my shape. I shrug the feeling off. There are no paintings, no furniture, no objects at all, only dead leaves crunching under my feet.

I take the corridor to my left. As I pass between familiar

rooms, drips of water fall from over my head and the chill air whistles around my legs. I swing my head round. Somewhere behind me I'm sure I heard a door bashing to and fro. It's just the wind, playing with an empty house, albeit bigger than some, with doors and windows and rooms like any other. But the scale of the place has always been overwhelming.

I don't like it here. I have never liked it in here.

In the drawing room, I step up to the fireplace. There are markings in the stone lintel, a series of wheel-like shapes with overlapping circles. They are witch marks, the same witch marks as in my cottage, symbols to ward off evil spirits. Didn't the estate agent say something about them being a feature of the area? I suppose it makes sense, given the age of the place and the beliefs that people had then. Although the current building is younger, the whole estate must have been originally medieval, or at least dating back to the sixteenth or seventeenth centuries. And the lintel might have been reused from whatever was here before. Except these markings . . .

I let my fingers trace the shapes – they look more recent. I have a sudden thought that this place may have been visited by local pagans, used for some secret ceremony. Like the stone circle up at Stanton Moor. But no, now I am giving way to the same superstitious nonsense as those who condemn paganism, unaware of what it's really about.

Duncan brought me here once. It was the first time I ever saw it, long before Joe arrived. We were in our second year as students.

When I'd first met Duncan, he'd been much fitter than I and keen to push me further. Every weekend had seen some kind of physical activity: walking, climbing, sailing, cycling – the Peak District was known for all that. Duncan had the lean body of a cyclist with not an inch of spare flesh. I liked the fact he spurred me on. Left to my own devices, I'd have headed for the galleries of Manchester or Leeds, or the grand rooms and sweeping gardens of Chatsworth House, followed by the gift shops and a cream tea. I wasn't a naturally physical type. He left me out of breath and heaving.

As a compromise, he brought me here. We'd already sneaked into the valley several times by then. On that particular day, we were exploring further. We hid our bikes in the shrubbery and entered through that open front door. It was his idea of another romantic adventure. I knew what he had in mind and the anticipation had us both excited. He took my hand and led me down a corridor.

'Let's try down here,' he said.

'Are you sure? I mean, what if someone's here?'

'Are you kidding? Look at the place!'

He laughed and tugged my hand harder.

We peered at the grandeur of the rooms, spaces that must once have been decorated to impress. The plasterwork was ornate but sodden and crumbling. The wallpaper, elaborate but peeling. Sunlight streamed through freshly wet windows, throwing rain shadows across the floor. The odd fragility of the light flashed through diamond-leaded shapes, lending each room a delicate translucency, as if the whole building had been shrouded in a grey sequinned veil. I soon forgot my reticence. I was fascinated. It seemed to me the Hall was a corpse bride, hiding in her woods.

We took another corridor, down the other wing. The rooms were smaller, each one leading to the next, each one more functional than the last. There was no fancy plasterwork or wallpaper here, only horizontal bands of grey and blue paint that flaked to dust beneath our hands. There were shelves and cupboards and rooms with stone windows, deep enough to keep the sun out and the cold in. We stumbled on the kitchen, a huge room with a solid black range filling one wall. Cast-iron ovens and giant griddles were driven into the brickwork like the cave homes etched into an Italian mountain. There were hooks and spikes of every dimension, enough to satisfy any medieval torturer.

More rooms led off at the far end and we passed through those, too. Duncan was determined to see it all. Each room was smaller and darker than the one that came before. Pantries for dry goods, larders for meat and dairy, all with wooden planks suspended against the wall. Then we came to a room with a single large stone table drilled with holes. A second door led from the back and beneath the table was a narrow channel etched into the floor. Drainage, I presumed. More stone shelves lined the walls and I tried to think of them stinking with fresh cheese, or running red with the juices of a freshly butchered animal, its legs and feet pointing stiffly in the air, a meat cleaver buried in the middle of its chest cavity.

'How about on there?' Duncan said, grinning as he pointed to the stone table.

'You've got to be kidding!' I retorted.

'I dare you!' he said.

He pushed me up against the table; I felt it behind my legs. It was like ice. His arms reached around my waist and he hoisted me up onto the surface.

'Mmm . . .' he said. 'It's the perfect height.'

I giggled, half in fear and half in anticipation.

'Should have brought my white cloak and sacrificial knife!' he said.

He leaned over me, pushing my legs apart and reaching up beneath my T-shirt.

I tugged at Duncan's hand. Suddenly, I didn't like it. There was a heavy stench to the place, like in a butcher's shop, and the light had almost gone. The cold stole over me and somehow it didn't feel very funny anymore.

Then I heard the bell.

'What was that?' I felt breathless and alarmed.

And another. The old-fashioned delicate kind, tinkling softly from the far side of that second door.

'I don't know,' said Duncan. His hand drifted across my skin.

I heard the bell again, a distinct but ethereal sound.

'There must be someone here!' I whispered.

I pushed Duncan away, ducking from under him and almost slipping on the rounded groove of the channel under my shoes. Duncan caught my arms, setting me back on my feet.

'Maybe. You alright?'

His voice had gone quiet too. He wasn't looking at me anymore. And I didn't answer. I was looking where he was looking, at the door at the far end of the room. I was too intent on listening for another ring of that bell.

Duncan took my hand.

'I think we'd better look,' he said, his voice reticent and hoarse.

We approached the door. I held his hand like a small child at school. Duncan pushed open the door and we entered the room. It was a small sitting room, much more appealing than the kitchens. We heard the sound again and I looked up. On the wall high up to our left was a row of servants' bells. Each one sat in line beside the next, bigger, smaller, their coils neatly labelled in faded Gothic script, their wires disappearing into the ceiling. The clappers were still shaking.

They rang again, a series of chimes, each one a different pitch and tone, jangling on their spiral leads. It was a light, pretty sound, but one I listened to in dread. I looked at Duncan and his face was frozen in fear. It was more than I could bear.

I tugged my hand free from Duncan's, and ran.

CHAPTER 48

CLAIRE – AFTER

He'd laughed at me. When he reached the drive where I was waiting for him, he roared with laughter.

'You surely don't believe in ghosts, do you?'

'How was that even possible?' I cried.

'The wind and the old wires can play tricks on you,' he said. I stared at him.

'Did you plan that? Was that *you*? How . . .'

He laughed again and pulled me close, planting a big kiss on my lips before I could say a single word more.

We ran through the dark undergrowth of the shrubbery, squealing and shrieking like pigs in a slaughterhouse, found our bikes and raced each other back along the lane.

But Duncan never did explain exactly how that trick of his had worked and I was left wondering what had really happened.

*   *   *

I don't go into the kitchen wing. I can't imagine Joe would stay in there. It's too cold and uninviting. Instead, I stick to the other corridor, the family's living quarters, checking every room on the ground floor, listening for any sound of Joe. It still spooks me out remembering what happened that day with Duncan all those years ago, along with all this emptiness and decay.

I try to think of voices talking in a room, the clink of teacups and the hiss and crackle of a warm fire. In spite of myself, I picture the butlers' bells jumping into life on the wall in the kitchen and long skirts rustling up the stairs – the house as it would have been, a home for a rich, contented family, music playing in the distance, children racing down the corridors, a newborn baby sleeping in its cot . . .

I feel sick. The images of that past life shimmer in my head. I push on, but all I want to do now is run down those front steps and get out, exactly as I did before.

I'm such a fool, letting this place get to me.

I force myself to calm down. It was a prank – nothing but a prank. To this day, I don't know how he did it. But Duncan enjoyed my reaction.

Instead, I climb the stairs one by one, to what's left of the upper floor. There's a room up there where I found Joe once. He'd been about twelve years old. He'd made himself a little nest, with blankets and even a fire in the grate. I gave him a sound telling off; it worried me that he could have set fire to the place or fallen through the rotting floor. Thankfully, he'd been more careful than I gave him credit for. Duncan mentioned the word 'ghosts' and Joe promised me fervently he'd never come back. I guess he doesn't believe all that stuff now.

The door to 'Joe's' room is shut. I knock, feeling more than a little foolish, then push slowly on the door and enter.

'Joe?'

He's not there. Damn and double damn, I really thought . . .

But he *has* been there, or someone has – there's a blanket neatly folded in the corner of the room, though it's not one I recognise, and the place is surprisingly clean and tidy. He doesn't keep his own room at home that tidy. Maybe it was someone else, but I can't imagine who that might be. It's not like there's a gang of teenagers living nearby.

I lick my lips. Perhaps it was Callum and his mates.

There are candles on the floor, solidified wax spilling out across the floorboards and an empty can of baked beans. I search for any signs of drug use – needles, foils and stub ends – but there's nothing. From what I remember of Callum's flat, I don't think he'd leave this place so tidy. It's such a relief. Joe's always denied using drugs and I believe him. His brain couldn't cope with being out of control. But his friends are another matter.

I poke the ash in the fireplace with a stick. It's cold and sparse; there's no sense of warmth at all. If Joe had been here last night or the night before, he didn't light a fire.

I push back on my heels and scan the room. I'd been hopeful after the old woman suggested I come here. She'd looked as if she knew something. I pluck a crisp packet from the hearth, turning it over to check the use-by date: two months ago. The disappointment is almost crushing. If that was Joe's, it predates when he went missing. I spin round, taking in the damp walls, the old wallpaper and crumbling plaster. Then I swear I hear something.

My head pulls up. I'm frozen to the spot. I can't see out

into the corridor because the door opens the wrong way. This is the last room right at the end of the building and I feel an unnerving sense of being trapped.

I lean forwards, straining to hear. Along the corridor, the wind whistles beneath the doors and the dead leaves skitter in the draught. There's the chink, chink of water dripping through the gaps in the roof and outside, in the grounds, I hear the creak and groan of the trees. The gaps between the branches open and close like the gills of a fish, giving brief glimpses of the distant silver water.

I slip through the door, easing round to peer warily along the corridor. I walk past more doors, faster now. I feel the rush of air behind me, like ice-cold fingers drifting down my back. I spin round to look the way I've come. I thought I heard a mewling, from the very room I've just left. It sounded like a cat trapped behind the door. My heart skips and I almost go back to check. Except it can't be – I know there's nothing in that room.

My feet stumble backwards, unwilling to turn around and look away from the source of that noise. My hand reaches out to the wall and tangles with the spiders' webs hanging from the ceiling. They drape between the old light fitments and the walls and cornices above, with tight bundles of eggs swathed in white. Dead flies dangle suspended from the strands, wrapped like tiny Egyptian mummies. I think of the eggs breaking open, all those miniature spiders spilling out across the floor, waves of them rolling over my feet and rising up my legs, a million spider bodies crawling up my skin . . .

There it comes again, a keening of the wind from the far end of the corridor, there where I've just been, like a baby's cry drifting from within.

I hold myself still. Then turn and break into a run.

I clatter down the stairs, disregarding the rotting wood. I run out through the front door and sprint across the gravel. Towards the shelter of the trees. This time, there's no Duncan to reassure me.

I run in earnest, water from the puddles splashing up my legs. I trip once, crashing onto my hands and knees. I lever myself up, grit pressed painfully against the soft under-skin of my hands. I brush them off, but one of my hands is bleeding. I hold my hands in tight fists and run faster, until I'm through the gates and out onto the lane, into the village.

I swing left and right, unsure which way to go. I feel stupid, standing there, red-faced and panting. What if someone could see me, that old woman even, terrified by my own breathing? I hate this place. The faded beauty of the Hall and village speaks only of heartache and neglect.

For a moment I regret deciding to rent a house here in this valley, so near to this village. I should have gone as far away as I could, taking Joe away from here, from the Barn, the fields, the metal detectors, night hawkers – whoever they are – from Duncan . . . Except Joe isn't here. Of course he's not here. He didn't come with me.

This is all my fault – what on earth possessed me to leave without him?

I feel a stabbing pain right between my eyes. It's as if my head is trying to deceive me, protect me. I clench the blood seeping from my hand and plunge up the road, my lungs heaving up and down. Stumbling towards the top lane and that small ramshackle cottage on the brow of the hill.

CHAPTER 49

CLAIRE – BEFORE

I lie on the bed with no sense of time. I have no reason to move or linger. I listen to the wind and the rain that buffets the window. The rain grows louder until the noise of it fills my head, as if the world outside has been crying for me all this time, so that I don't have to.

It's very late when Duncan comes home. Earlier, I nudged open Joe's bedroom door to see him sprawled safely comatose, fully dressed on the bed, his laptop screen blank beside him. Arthur gives a distant, welcoming *woof* and I lie frozen under the covers listening to the sound of my husband moving about in the kitchen.

It's one thing to imagine his betrayal, the doubts and questions churning in my head. But quite another to actually see it.

I reach out to grasp my phone. He's betrayed not only me, but also his best friend. What would Martin say if he knew? Martin's one of the good guys. But I bet he's seen some dirty stuff. You don't rise that far in the police force without seeing the worst side of humanity and learning how to deal with it. I reckon if he really wanted to, Martin could play it pretty rough himself. He adores his daughter; he'd do anything for her. Isn't that how she ended up getting the job at the surgery, Martin asking for a favour from his best mate, finding her a job that kept her close to home, where Martin could keep an eye on her? He sure as hell wouldn't be giving Duncan his blessing, whether or not Duncan is married.

I almost ring Becky instead, never mind how late it is, but I can't bring myself to tell her. It couldn't be worse.

No, it couldn't be better! Think, Claire, think! Whilst this is all a secret, I've got him over a barrel. How would Duncan feel if this leaked out? Oh, Duncan, I've got you good and proper now. What if I tell Martin exactly what you've been up to?

I veer from rage, to shame, to pure elation. Foolish, foolish Duncan.

So, I lie here awake, pondering what to do, almost enjoying the moment, despite my pain. I hear the kettle coming to the boil downstairs and the clunk of the fridge door. After about ten minutes, Duncan leaves the kitchen and the door to the media room at the far end of the house slams shut.

I lie awake all night. By the time morning comes, I'm burning with rage.

Anger – watch me, Duncan, I can really do anger.

And this is an anger held in for too many years.

CHAPTER 50

DUNCAN – AFTER

It was eleven o'clock at night. Duncan walked down the corridor to the kitchen, if walking was what you could call it, and pushed an empty bottle of vodka into the recycling bin. He could scarcely feel his legs beneath him and his brain felt detached from its stem. In a pleasantly, muzzy, good way. But Sally's face still intruded on his thoughts – her defiance, her rejection of him. Numbness was all that he wanted to feel right now.

Outside, beyond the kitchen sink window, the light was unusually bright.

He blinked. There were floodlights splayed across the drive. Vehicles were parked higgledy-piggledy one behind another, rain dripping from their bumpers and slapping against the windscreens. There were even vans on the grass under the cherry trees, smeared with mud. Duncan ground his teeth; they were wrecking his lawn. Surely, at this time of night, the drive should be empty?

They had wrapped things up – the police side of things, at least. That's what Martin had said. The archaeologists from the university had taken over and they were usually all gone by five o'clock. Yet the police food van was back, lit up in a haze of steam, and two generators grumbled at full throttle.

Duncan peered blearily through the window at men and women in plastic overalls moving up and down the slope like workers on an anthill. Parked behind his Lexus SUV were two more vans, plastered with the insignia of Derbyshire Forensics. Duncan hadn't been aware of all this down in the media room.

The doorbell rang. Duncan groaned as he turned his head. He walked into the hall. He grappled with the door and it swung back, a beautifully crafted smooth plane of contemporary pale oak. There was a small but satisfied smile on his face as he watched the door move. He slid slightly to lean against the door.

'I need a word.'

It was Martin, his features schooled and unreadable. A woman in uniform stood behind him, her black hair impeccably pinned under her hat.

'I'm sorry it's so late,' said Martin. His eyes took in Duncan's state. 'I have an update for you and we really felt you should know before the press get hold of it.'

Duncan looked at Martin, holding his gaze a second too long. The wind roared through the doorway, rattling the blinds on either side of the door.

'You'd better come in,' he said.

They followed him through to the sitting room.

Here, the glare of the floodlights was particularly intrusive, stretching out across the carpet through the floor-to-ceiling glass. Duncan flicked a switch on the wall. Then regretted it

268

and flicked another. The room filled with discreet swathes of ambient colour. He let his hands drop to his hips.

'Would you like to sit down?' It was Martin speaking, like this was *his* house.

'No, thank you,' said Duncan. 'What is it?'

Martin gave a sigh. 'I think you should sit down, Duncan,' he said.

Martin stood in front of him, legs apart, watching Duncan's face. He frowned, reaching out a hand to Duncan's elbow and manoeuvring him on to a seat. Martin and the policewoman sat opposite. The woman pulled the hat from her head, her eyes sliding towards her colleague.

There was a pause. It vaguely sank into Duncan's brain that his friend was finding it difficult to speak the next words.

'We've made a mistake.' Martin leaned forwards. 'The bodies we found, we thought they were historic. And most of them are. Like I said, we believe they're the remains of burials relocated from St Bertram's Church. But now I'm led to understand that there may be one that's much more recent.'

A silence fell between them.

'How recent?' Duncan struggled to sit upright, clutching the arms of his chair.

His brain had kicked into gear but he wasn't sure that he wanted it to.

'We don't know exactly – not yet. The material needs to be examined in greater detail at the lab. That may take a few days.'

Material . . . Duncan ran his tongue across his lips.

'What material?' he said.

Another hesitation. As if Martin was weighing up how much he could say.

'Fabric. Remnants of clothing.'

Duncan shifted his balance, trying to remember exactly what they'd all been wearing.

'But the whole thing is so badly damaged . . . I'm sorry, Duncan.'

Duncan. Duncan felt his body stiffen, his brain painfully alert. There was something about the way Martin had said his name. An image flashed up in his head.

The whole thing is so badly damaged . . .

There was another grinding pause.

'Who?' he said.

Martin didn't reply.

'*Who*?' Duncan asked again, energy pushed into that one word. 'Come on, man, you must have some idea, or you wouldn't be looking at me like that. You wouldn't be here. What's going on?'

There was still no reply. Duncan held his breath. He realised then that Martin was struggling with this just as much as he.

'I'm really very sorry, Duncan. At this point, until our test results come back, we can't confirm an identity. That's as much as I can tell you.'

Duncan felt his eyes sliding shut. They both knew they were skirting the facts. He'd already known, hadn't he? He knew this day would come, sooner or later.

'Male or female?' he said, his voice quieter. 'You must at least know that.'

His voice was vibrant with emotion.

'A man,' Martin said. 'But you mustn't infer anything from this.'

Then Martin gave a sigh.

'Possibly a teenager.'

270

CHAPTER 51

CLAIRE – BEFORE

I don't have to sneak off anymore in fear of what he might do. I am so in control of this now.

A headache hammers at my head and my eyes are dry and crusty. I've been awake all night, telling myself to keep it under control. I have a phone full of evidence. I can negotiate whatever I want. But divorce is somehow not enough. Today, I am going to leave, but how can I do that without first confronting Duncan?

I pull my dressing gown around me and descend the stairs. Dawn has started to ignite the horizon and the Barn is filled with a barren solitude, the first sliver of orange-red light sliding across the floor. I don't think Duncan went to bed at all; at least, I didn't hear him come upstairs. His car – oh God, his car – is still parked outside, sullied by the memories of him and Sally last night.

I bet it stinks in there, I think maliciously.

I glance towards the media room – the door is firmly shut. I've been working myself up to this all night. I march down the corridor and thrust open the door.

He's there. Slumped on one of the big cinema chairs. One hand hangs over the side of his chair and the other is folded over his chest. There are several empty cans of lager piled up on the floor and the big screen is flashing a blur of frozen figures against a solid black background. He must have crashed out mid-film.

I give his leg an unrestrained, vicious kick. He starts awake and looks at me.

'Zombies not good enough to hold your attention, today?' I say.

He doesn't even seem to have noticed that I kicked him, too far gone in his sleep, or drunk. But then very little of what I do gets his attention.

'Claire, what is it now?' he says.

'I saw you last night.'

He sits up a little and rubs his eyes.

'You saw me . . . do what, Claire?'

'I mean, I saw *you*.'

Plural, that is.

'You and *Sally*. In the stables. Well, let's say not the stables exactly, but your car in the stables. Our only son is out of his mind with worry and you're shagging your girlfriend, right on our doorstep!'

'What do you mean—'

But I scarcely draw enough breath for him to interrupt.

'What if *he'd* seen you, not me? You know he wanders off around there sometimes. Well, you know what, it doesn't matter anymore. I simply don't care.' *Liar*. 'You're not a father to our son, you're not a husband to me. All those clients of yours who think you're so clever and virtuous, what would they say if they knew you were shagging the hired help? What will the staff say? The good folk of Belston? And Martin, eh? What about him? What's he going to say, when he hears you've been shagging his *daughter*!'

Duncan tries to pull himself out of his chair, lunging towards me, but in the semi-darkness, he trips over a change in the floor level. I back up and run for the door. It slams against the wall, so hard the handle bashes into the plaster. I feel a sharp flash of fear. I dart along the corridor, but he's right behind me. He's still drunk, I realise, his breath stinking of alcohol as he grabs my arm and pulls me round.

'And what about you, Claire? The perfect wife and mother!'

His fingers tighten around my arms and his voice curls with disdain. He pulls me towards him then shoves me back against the wall. My head hits hard and my eyes fire off white sparks behind my eyelids.

'There's two of us in this marriage,' he says, his pupils wide and black. 'Or at least there were supposed to be, but you just couldn't hack it, could you?'

'Hack it? I've stuck it out over twenty years. Ever . . . ever since . . .' I give a muffled spit of a sob. 'It's been one woman after another, and now *her*. Your own receptionist. Your best friend's daughter. Feeling your age, Duncan? Trying to recreate your youth? Can't you even relate to a grown woman anymore? Or have you fancied her ever since she was a little girl? *Uncle* Duncan, was it?'

It's a nasty, cheap shot but nonetheless satisfying.

'That's beneath even you, Claire,' he says. 'Absolutely

273

nothing happened until Sally was a full-grown woman. I didn't even notice her until she came back from uni.'

Oh God, I think. *How long has this been going on for?* That was over three years ago. I thought it had been a sequence of unrelated strangers up until now. Is this why he offered Martin's newly graduated daughter a job at the surgery? I feel sick, revulsion overwhelming me at the very idea of how long this has been going on, right under my nose.

'You have to sack her,' I say, my voice shaking with rage. 'I won't have her working at the surgery for one more day!'

He laughs at me then.

'Why on earth would I do that? Sally's very good at her job, thank you very much.'

'I won't tolerate it. What wife would put up with that?'

'Jealous, Claire? At least she wants me. Hitting middle age, Claire, and feeling it, are we? You're as dry as a bone in more ways than one!'

I gasp. He lets go of my arms, as if he can't bear to touch me.

'And Joe,' he says, bitterness dripping off his tongue. 'It's always Joe. You're obsessed with him. There's no room in your life for anyone else! Why should I live out my life in the cold? Why should I even continue to support you? Either of you. I'd be better off never seeing either one of you again!'

We both know why he's still with me – who else would go chasing after our son, and what about the mortgage? He loves this barn, far more than either of us, but it's funded up to the hilt, along with his growing business. Get divorced and the house will have to be sold, simply to pay me off. Let alone the business. He can't afford a divorce. But I can. I push back with my hands.

'It's not like you can have children anymore, is it?' he adds with a snarl, holding me firm.

He doesn't mean he wants more children. He's said that because he knows how much it pains me. He went off and had the snip without even telling me, ten years ago.

'You bastard!'

I twist under his grip, arms hitting up from underneath his. I refuse to be cowed.

'I hate you, I—'

Something catches my attention. I cast my eyes over his head towards the hall. My eyes widen. It's Joe. His gaze is fixed on Duncan.

'Joe . . .'

Joe spins on his heels and runs from sight.

Horror fills my mind. He must have heard every word. He won't understand, he'll take it all literally, he'll . . . Duncan sees the change in my expression. He turns round. But he's too furious or drunk to back down.

'Go on, boy, run! That's all you're good for,' he shouts. His words are slurred.

'No, Duncan. Don't say that. Please . . .'

His words have finally shocked me into submission. This isn't Duncan. Not the real Duncan, the man I fell in love with. It can't be. It's the alcohol speaking. Suddenly, I'm unsure. I remember him as he was before, dynamic, eager, full of unexpected gestures. Do I really understand him? Why he drinks, why he shouts, why he rejects me like he does. I've never wanted it to come to this. Me leaving him. Our lives were never meant to be like this. He's just pushed me too far.

I drop my voice, clenching my fists in one last attempt to hold it all in and reach him.

275

'Don't hurt him like that, Duncan. I've stayed for Joe, it's true. But I stayed for you too. Don't you see?'

I feel the heat of his body against mine and I let my eyes soften in one last plea for a reconciliation.

'Don't you care for either of us at all?' My voice drops away.

He turns back to me to look me in the eye. And lets me go.

'No, Claire, I don't. Not anymore.'

CHAPTER 52

CLAIRE – BEFORE

I take the stairs to Joe's room two at a time. I almost fall against the opening of his door, to see him gathering his coat, the metal detector battery pack and what looks like the printout of a map.

'What are you doing, Joe?'

He looks at me briefly but doesn't say a word. His eyes are like those of a frightened rabbit, startled and confused by the world. Expecting the worst. He blinks then struggles with his jacket, as ever all arms and legs. He hastily folds the map and stuffs it into one of his pockets.

'Talk to me, Joe, please. You're not going out, are you? You can't go out in this!'

The light outside has turned a dark furry grey. Large flakes of snow are falling like ash from a volcano, furtive and silent. The ground is already turning white.

I block the doorway.

'Joe, your father's drunk. He's angry and upset. He didn't mean it!'

'He hates me!' Joe speaks to me then, words pushed through his lips like stones spat from fruit. 'He thinks I'm worthless, useless, that I can't do a thing!'

'No, Joe. No, he doesn't think that. He just says stuff he doesn't mean when he's upset. People do that.'

I speak the words, but I don't even believe them myself. Duncan hates us both – he made that very clear. *Oh, Joe, Joe*, I think, *please believe me.*

But his eyes don't meet mine and he pushes past me, launching down the stairs. I look across the room. Those schematics I saw before are on the screen of his PC. I take a step towards them, trying to see what they are. The name 'Belston Reservoir' registers before I turn and chase after Joe, catching up with him in the utility room by the back door.

There's no sign of Duncan. Gone back to his stinking man cave, I think, or throwing up in the downstairs loo. Joe shoves his feet into his trainers and grabs his metal detector. Arthur leaps to his feet, pattering across the tiles towards him. There's a blast of cold air rushing through the kitchen from the open back door.

'Joe, where are you doing?' I lower my voice, sterner, fiercer.

He doesn't reply. He's fixing the battery pack on his detector.

'Joe, please, don't do this now. I need you at home, I—'

White streaks of snow are swirling through the open door.

'Gotta go,' he says.

He's moved outside. Arthur trots up to him uncertainly, but Joe shoos him away.

'No, Arthur. Stay!'

His voice is unusually sharp and he's holding up one hand.

Arthur sits down and stands up, then sits down again, giving a soft whine. There's a puzzled expression on his face. I throw my head back across my shoulder, but there's still no sign of Duncan. I don't want another confrontation like last time and I'm torn.

It's too late. Joe has run out onto the drive.

I plunge from the back door after him, barefoot on the gravel.

'Joe!' I scream.

He's already reached the top gate and I'm only halfway across the gravel. The grit stabs like thorns under my feet and the cold is numbing on my flesh.

'Joe, no! Wait! Come back! *Joe!*'

My voice disappears unanswered on the wind.

CHAPTER 53

CLAIRE – AFTER

I take Arthur for a walk. It's a new day but my nerves are still shot to pieces from my visit to the Hall and I can't face walking through the village. So I take the car and drive down to the water instead. The paths have been flooded on and off, but this morning they are clear and the valley is bright with frost with a beauty that's crisp and innocent.

Behind me, Arthur snuffles along the shore. I hear his soft breath and the water supping at our feet, and the sad, guttering cry of a cormorant. Arthur picks up speed, racing in and out of the water despite his gammy leg. Like a small child on the beach, he's excited to feel the waves against his feet yet too wary to plunge right in. It's not just the cold, he's always been a funny dog that way, curious yet nervous too when we're out and about. I think that's why he and Joe connected. Duncan said it was because Arthur had had a bad start in life. I don't know the details, he never told me, but

I know that he came to us healthy, albeit an unusually quiet and subdued puppy.

I look out towards the distance. On the far shore, a stray heron drags itself into flight. Its looped silver neck and skinny legs hang from its body like a stork making off with a baby. The huge wings beat up and down and it slowly gains height. Then it crash-lands into a tree. The wings fold, its legs and neck too, until it disappears into the foliage. All that can be seen is its bright yellow bill, long and shaped like a butcher's knife. And black eyes, glittering as they scan for prey in the water.

When Joe was little, we'd hike the trails of the Peak District, Joe strapped to a carrier on Duncan's back. There's nothing better than climbing to the top of windswept crags overlooking vast horizons. Derbyshire is full of dramatic landscapes, from the epic wall of rock that is Stanage Edge, to the stepping stones of Dovedale, names that conjured sleeping giants and prehistoric monsters – Thorpe Cloud, Mam Tor – the mother hill or shivering mountain.

When he was older, Joe's favourite place was Stanton Moor. It's a gritstone plateau overlooking half the county. From a distance, it's like a stone goblet held up to catch the rain. At the top, there's a series of sandstone pillars punctuating a wide sea of purple heather. Joe would climb them until we decided that was probably not a very good idea, that if he wasn't careful, he would damage them. Surprisingly, he was okay with that. He cared about nature – mineral or animal.

Joe particularly liked the stone circle. It stands at the far end of the plateau, sheltering under a copse of silver birches. It's known as the Nine Ladies, turned to stone for dancing on a Sunday. This was a place trapped in time, where people came to celebrate the old beliefs, in defiance of modern science, Church or State. The wind blows on loose strips of bark hanging from the tree trunks, tangling with the tattered ribbons of pagan tributes fluttering from their branches. Paganism has always been alive and well, here in the heart of Derbyshire.

I've never quite understood what 'pagan' meant. But I know it has nothing to do with the cliché stories of films and books, wild sacrificial dances and plots to raise the Devil or the dead. There are people I know who are really funny about pagans, as if they're all in league with the bastions of hell.

We had friends once who invited us to celebrate the winter solstice. They'd hired a tiny one-roomed eighteenth-century village hall about twenty minutes' drive from our barn. It was a typical Derbyshire gritstone building, with stone mullioned windows and square leaded casements. Candles had been placed in every nook and cranny, with more crammed onto the mantelpiece. The fire was lit and the flames flickered against polished floorboards and whitewashed walls. The whole building had been decked out with flowers and winter greenery as if for a wedding.

It was an evening I will never forget, faces glowing with the warmth of innocence and wonder, an eloquent celebration of nature and her union with man. There were songs and good wishes, shared food: the friendship of strangers bonded by a common belief. It was a far cry from the cliché spooks and spells of the cheap tourist shops in Matlock Bath dedicated to witchcraft: *hoodoo, voodoo, tat and tell* as Duncan used to call it.

He's never been very patient with the superstitious type, those people who leaned towards the mystic and unfathomable, who thought that spirits lived on in the shape of animals and plants. One of the guests had a wand. A magic wand, he claimed, made of ash. The wood supposedly had special protective properties. He told us how St Patrick himself had banished snakes from Ireland with a stick of ash. 'St Patrick?' said Duncan, speaking to me under his breath. 'What's a Christian saint got to do with paganism?' He laughed at them then and I didn't like it. But Duncan is no more patient with formal religion, the outdated language and patriarchy of the Church. He hates the rules and rituals of faith.

'It's a con,' he said. 'The lot of it. Doesn't matter which faith or church. They're money-making machines. Look at all that land and property they hang onto.'

'It's more than that,' I said. 'It's history and faith. Think of the Reformation and their desire to bring the Bible to the masses – they rebelled against the Church's wealth.'

He wasn't having it.

'What about those weird sects?' he said. 'No, it's not just the weird sects, it's all of them, in their different ways, selling forgiveness and confession. Like the pardoners in the Middle Ages. They want to count pennies, not souls.'

Pardoners – he meant as in *The Pardoner's Tale*, Chaucer's story of hypocrisy and greed, a tale of three thieves who separately plot to murder each other behind their backs. They only succeeded in fulfilling their own prophecy of finding Death.

'That's not quite fair,' I said. 'I think for those who find comfort in these things . . .'

I shrugged. The pardoner was meant as a character of irony, not faith.

There was no arguing with Duncan; he was so adamant

he was right. The power of science and logic over blind mysticism, that's how he saw it. I was annoyed with him that night. I wanted to absorb the pagan welcome and relax and enjoy myself, not judge those who'd been kind enough to invite us. I think we all of us need a little magic in our lives.

Then we found the witch marks in the Barn. One of the builders pointed them out. Concentric circles and daisy wheels etched into the old beams. Like the ones at my rented cottage and the Hall. Once we'd found the first one, they kept turning up everywhere. Then we discovered something else buried behind a wall. It looked like a piece of cloth, an old heart-shaped scrap of leather wrapped around an object. Duncan slowly unfolded each half and inside was a bottle. It was made of brown stoneware with a bearded man carved on its neck. It might have held liquid once, judging by the stains. Inside rattled a collection of iron pins, human hair and something else – I wasn't sure what it was. Only later did we find out. Whole human fingernails.

It was a witch bottle, apparently, created either to cast or defend against a spell. It had been carefully hidden all those years, probably to protect the Barn. And we'd uncovered it, removed it. Released the Barn from its spell. Who knows what that meant. What we'd done.

No one listened to me when I said we should have left it there, buried in the wall.

CHAPTER 54

CLAIRE – BEFORE

He's gone. Gone from the house without even taking Arthur. He always takes Arthur. And those schematics – I feel horror like a pool of blood in my mouth. I think I know where Joe has gone.

I burst into the kitchen calling for Duncan. Arthur's on his feet, whining. He doesn't understand. He stands in the doorway wanting to run after Joe, but he can see my distress. He backs away from the door, tail between his legs, and whines some more. He looks like the small, frightened puppy he once was when he first came to live with us.

Duncan exits the cloakroom. He hears and sees me straight away and he stands upright, taller, straighter, like he's suddenly sobering up.

'What's wrong?' he says.

He *has* been sick. Maybe he feels better now, not that I feel one iota of sympathy for him. I don't reply. It's all too much and to my shame, tears are welling on my face.

'Crying, Claire? Bit too late for that!'

There he is. Old Duncan. He's back again.

'You fool!' I yell at him 'He's gone to the tunnels! What have you done? He must have heard every word and now he thinks you hate him, that you despise him.'

'Good!' says Duncan. 'Perhaps that'll be his wake-up call to sort himself out and get a job! What do you mean, gone to the tunnels?'

He frowns at me. His brain still isn't quite there.

'He's been searching for a hoard. Thinks he's found one. This is Joe, our *son*, Duncan. If he's gone in there, you have to go after him!'

I don't ask him if he cares. He's already answered that one. He does care, doesn't he? I think of that moment when he let Joe take the axe when he was little. He must do, he's Joe's father. In his clumsy, patriarchal, stupidly blind kind of way.

'I don't know why on earth you think he's gone there. And I can't go after him now, I should be at work.' Staccato words, monosyllabic. Then, after an imperceptible pause, he says, 'If he's gone off metal detecting again, he'll be back once he's calmed down.'

He's the voice of masculine reason. Rational Duncan, crazy Claire. We've played that game before.

'No, you don't understand,' I say, lowering my voice. 'We need to call Martin and the police.' I'm almost out of breath.

'I think that's an overreaction, Claire, and it won't help.' Duncan still isn't taking me seriously. 'He won't go anywhere near those tunnels, why would he? And he's eighteen now. He's gone off so many times, the police won't take a blind bit of interest. Martin has helped us out enough. Joe has to grow up. He's upset, sure, but he'll come back.'

'You don't understand! He's left Arthur behind. He wouldn't do that if he was just metal detecting like he normally does. Those tunnels are lethal if you don't know what you're doing!'

I have an image of Joe out there on his own, wading through rising water with no Arthur to keep him warm and safe or bring him home. Knowing Arthur is with him is the one thing that's always kept my anxiety at bay.

'Joe has no reason to go in those tunnels. He doesn't know anything about them. He's gone off like he always does. You know he has to let off steam. He'll dig around for a bit then go into town to one of his mates and crash out somewhere. Try his phone after an hour or so. Send him a text. You know he'll be back when he's ready, especially in this weather. And you can give him a bollocking then.' There's a bitterness to his tone.

I swallow. The knot in my stomach tightens.

I take a deep breath. This is Joe – I can't let how I feel about Duncan and my plans to leave cloud my judgement. Suddenly, I know that I have to tell Duncan about the puppetrider coin, even though I promised Joe I would not.

I press my eyes shut and debate it briefly in my head. Courage, I need all my courage now. We've not spoken of this for more than twenty-two years. But it's always been there between us.

'He found it.' The words slip out and the air snatches from my throat. 'The coin we used to mark the grave.' I feel a cold sweat blister on my skin. I wait for Duncan to take it in.

There's silence. A long silence. And then it sinks in.

'I know he knows about the tunnels,' I say, 'because I saw

a plan of them on his computer. He thinks there is a hoard, coins washing down from the old works. I think he's gone to find it, to prove himself to *you*. He'll find her, Duncan, never mind the danger.'

Duncan stares at me.

'You can't let that happen,' I say. 'You can't let him go down there.'

His face is shuttered and pale.

'I'll find him, Claire. I'll stop him. I promise you, whatever it takes.'

His voice is so perfectly calm and reasonable. And yet there's something else. In the cold timbre of his voice.

I feel my brief courage slide into fear.

CHAPTER 55

DUNCAN – AFTER

The generators grumbled across the driveway, a physical throbbing that went right through Duncan's body. Martin was completely still, watching his friend in silence.

'You think it's Joe,' Duncan said.

It was a statement, not a question.

Martin gave a sigh. 'What I'm telling you now, you understand, Duncan, is unconfirmed. But all the indications are that it probably is; and the clothing fits the description you gave us at the time. But it's been more than six, seven weeks and nature has taken its course, so . . . This all needs to be verified.'

Duncan was a vet; he knew what happened after death.

'Duncan . . .' Martin leaned forwards, frustrated that he couldn't sit alongside his friend and put an arm around his shoulder. 'I . . . I don't know what to say. Except to say how very sorry I am. We all are. I wish this was different. No parent ever wishes to hear these words.'

'Thank you.' Duncan shifted on his seat. His face was impenetrable. 'I just don't understand how . . . Why has it taken so long to find him? That's not a criticism, you understand. I just need to get it in my head.'

Martin nodded.

'Of course,' he said. 'The body was lodged in the mud along the shore. But we don't think it was there long, or it would have been found earlier. We've been using sonar, as you know, to sweep the whole reservoir, but nothing turned up. Then the flooding happened, along the far bank. One of the engineers suggested diverting water through the old works tunnels and our theory – it's only a theory at the moment – is that's where he was, stuck in one of the tunnels behind a wall of concrete, until the water washed him out. I don't know how he got in the tunnels in the first place. Maybe he got dragged down into the main spillway. We'll find out more over the next few days.'

Martin looked as if he thought he'd said enough. Duncan dropped his gaze, once again distracted by his thoughts.

'There's something I need to ask you, Duncan.'

Martin looked reluctant to speak further.

'What?'

'Do you know a Ray Turner?'

'Never heard of him. Why?'

'Not sure yet, but I've been told he's been seen hanging around your property. He has a reputation shall we say, for taking more of an interest in archaeological sites than he should. It's probably nothing, but do me a favour – if you see him, give us a bell?'

'Okay.' Duncan nodded. He wasn't listening.

'We'll leave you now, but as soon as I have any further news for you, I will of course let you know.

'Thank you,' said Duncan and he stood up.

Martin and the policewoman stood too.

'I'm so, so sorry,' she said, holding out her hand.

Duncan acknowledged her words, feeling the warmth of her grip against his but not responding. They left.

Duncan returned to the sitting room, moving to the window that faced the shore. Outside, the bottom of the hillside was a hive of activity. He'd known this was going to happen, sooner or later. But he still felt numb, a void where there should have been something else. What – grief, pain, relief?

Denial? Or guilt.

CHAPTER 56

CLAIRE – BEFORE

I watch Duncan leave the house. I can't go with him. All my nerves are screaming at me to go with him, but I can't. Of all the things that I have had to do to protect my son, this is the one thing I can't face. Besides, I tell myself, what if I've got this all wrong and he's not gone into the tunnels and he turns up at home again? I need to be here, that's what I tell myself. Duncan agreed. He didn't want me to go with him.

Coward, Claire.

Duncan has gone, the car grinding slowly over the gravel.

It's like Groundhog Day. As if it's just another day with Duncan at work and me at home and Joe out metal detecting. Except it's not. I clear the kitchen and faff about in the house. Another plate slips between my hands and goes crashing to the floor. Two broken plates in one week. I look at it with tears in my eyes, but I can't cry because there are no tears left to cry. I gather up the bits and hoover the floor and keep looking at the phone, hoping Duncan will ring. Even, praise be, Joe. I try both of their phones again, but there's no answer.

Arthur butts against my knee, slowly wagging his tail. He wants a walk.

'No,' I say.

He looks at me in a puzzled, hurt sort of way. I reach down and give him a brief hug then push him away. I haven't got the patience to be nice to him, not today. I ignore his soft moans, the whining and then the determined thumping of his tail.

'No, Arthur,' I say again, too loud, too forceful. And then, more kindly, 'We can't go out, I'm sorry, mate. Maybe later, hmm?'

Arthur looks at me like he's very disappointed. In that headteacher, 'we don't like it when you make bad choices' kind of way. He goes back to his bed, spiralling around restlessly until he finds the exact preferred spot and lowers himself onto the cushion with his head and body facing away from me. Very eloquent.

Outside, it snows. It stopped for a while and then set up again. Not very seriously at first, like a child playing with bubbles. But as the time wears on, the snowflakes have got bigger and fatter, wetter, until they stick to the glass window and thick snow accumulates on the ground outside. When I was little, I used to tell Joe it was the snow monster, snuggling her young. He'd look back at me with his big round eyes, waiting for the story.

'She has to find somewhere to rest, to lay her great body down and give her little ones a drink. Sometimes, she's so tired, she can't move for days. But she never means any harm. Eventually she goes, taking her babies with her.'

Babies – I couldn't say that word very well. Joe is my only child – there was no way Duncan had ever intended to let me have another. I was the monster here, crushing the love from those around me. Wasn't that what Duncan meant? I'd brought this all on myself, by loving Joe too much and not loving Duncan enough, by carrying my – no, our – guilt too long. There's a pain in my stomach, as if my innards are twisting round and around . . . I need Joe to come back, to not know what's in those tunnels. I need to leave Duncan because I can't do this anymore.

'See?' I say. 'It's not a great day for a walk, is it, Arthur?'

He doesn't even prick up one ear.

I distract myself with packing Joe's stuff. I've given up on the plan I had to let Joe do it for himself. I don't even care if Duncan comes back and sees me. The weather is agitating me further. We could get snowed in; it wouldn't be the first time. We could get trapped. When he gets back, I could lose vital hours waiting for Joe to get his stuff together. I'm not staying here another night. As soon as Duncan returns with Joe, we're gone. So I do the packing for Joe, after all. To distract me.

I lug suitcases and boxes down from the space over the garage, filling them with Joe's clothes and books and equipment, even his laptop; he'd be lost without his laptop. Arthur eventually trots up the stairs to see what I'm up to. He sits on the carpet, unhelpfully blocking the doorway, his head alternating between resting on his feet and looking towards the stairs and the back door visible at the end of the utility room. The time grinds slowly on.

I hear horse's hooves from the other side of the house. Someone riding on the lane. I perk up. That's odd, I think, at this time of day, when it's almost dark. At any time of the day, in fact, since we're isolated up here. Not many people come riding or walking past our house.

I peer through the window. The landscape is transformed, white snow covering the fields and hills and hedgerows. But I can't see anyone on the lane. Instead, I see a group of three magpies. They stand bright and eager in the middle of the drive as if revelling in the snow. Their blue and black feathers shimmer like peacocks and their heads bob up and down, twisting dead leaves pointlessly from under the growing snow.

One for sorrow, two for joy,
Three for a girl . . .

There's a horse. I see it now in the distance further down the lane. It's riding away from me. The animal's speed has picked up, a fast, rising trot. It's almost dusk. The light has taken on an eerie glow, the kind of light when it's hard to know exactly what you're seeing. Perhaps the rider had taken a wrong turn, caught out by the weather and the fast-advancing night. Judging from that speed, he or she must be eager to get home.

Except now the pace has slowed again, almost to a stop.

I see him or her swinging the horse round, getting their bearings, peering through the gloom and holding the reins tight. Then the arms relax. The rider turns his head first one way and then the next before once more spurring on the horse.

The sound of ironclad hooves is dull against the snowy tarmac, quieter as it fades into the distance.

The magpies are still there, determined to find something under the snow.

. . .four for a boy.

I feel the knot at the pit of my stomach tighten again.

Where are they? Why hasn't Duncan rung me? What's happened?

CHAPTER 57

DUNCAN – AFTER

The wind blowing off the water was cold despite the spring sunshine. Duncan sank onto his haunches, looking out across the reservoir. The ducks had taken shelter in the reeds and the breeze had whipped up waves so that curls of white chased across the surface.

He wanted to run. To feel the regular pounding of his feet against the path, the blood pumping through his veins, his brain in neutral – just him, his body and the wind. But he'd come without the right kit, using his lunchbreak to escape the confines of the surgery for a short while.

Frances was right. It had been too soon to go back to work. He'd gone back after barely three weeks, but it had been the only way Duncan could deal with it – the way he always dealt with things he didn't want to face. Claire had her own way of dealing with things, but for Duncan it was by immersing himself in work. That and the booze and the one-night stands and the sex, anything to keep his mind from . . . Sally had put up with a lot. She'd been quite right to dump him.

Claire, too. He couldn't deny that. He turned his head away as he remembered the contents of her letter.

He stood up, listening to the rasp of his own breath. The bending of his body must have pulled on the jacket collar so that he suddenly felt half strangled. He reached to tug it free, plucking loose the top button of his coat.

He'd been eighteen when he went to uni. What do you know when you're eighteen, with your hormones raging through your body? There were all those girls everywhere, tall and round, long-haired, short-haired, clever and sporty, so many of them eager to experience life. Just like him. Oh God, those first few weeks of the new term, he'd been like a kid in a sweetshop, until he met Claire, and why not?

He pushed his hand over his head. There was a thin thermal cap tucked into his pocket and he put it on, a small defence against the cold. It wasn't that cold. This spring had been inordinately mild and wet, but today, with the wind coming off the water, it felt cold.

After he met Claire, it all stopped. The girls, the dates, even to some extent the drinking. What student doesn't go a bit mad at first, drinking? Claire had been special. He gave a sigh. *The one*. That's what he'd thought then. It had been intoxicating.

He'd been the same age as Joe. Joe, who to his knowledge had never had a girlfriend; nor even perhaps a boyfriend, at least as far as Duncan knew. He was shy, painfully shy. And awkward.

Duncan had never known how to talk about these things to his son. When Joe had reached sixteen, Claire had talked Duncan into taking him to the supermarket. Joe had trailed behind his father as they picked up bread and milk and all the usual things, until Duncan steered him down the aisle with the medicines and personal care products, to the shelves lined up with discreet boxes of condoms.

'You can pick one out,' he told his son.

Joe had gone a fiery beetroot red. He didn't reply. He seemed to take the line that if he ignored his father, the most painful of topics would go away.

It had the effect of making Duncan even more forceful.

'Well, go on, lad! You might not need them now, but one day you'll be grateful to have a few of those by your bed. Better with than without, eh?'

He was trying to make a joke of it. Joe still didn't say anything, let alone choose a box. Duncan was starting to feel embarrassed himself now.

'Oh, for heaven's sake!'

He plucked one off the shelf. The package was tastefully decorated with a falling blue feather. He dropped it in the basket and at the till, Joe studiously looked the other way.

'There,' Duncan said later, when they were back in the car.

He'd leaned over and ferreted around in the shopping bag, then tossed the pack onto Joe's lap.

'Don't panic. Just because you're sixteen now, doesn't mean you have to rush out there and get laid. It's just in case, hmm?' He softened his voice. He didn't want to sound harsh; he wanted his son to be safe.

Joe looked at him, holding the packet in his hands as if it were a pack of sanitary towels, not condoms. He rolled his eyes, like the very idea was disgusting, and Duncan frowned.

'You do know what to do with it, Joe? They have shown you in school, haven't they?'

He had an image of a rubber-clad banana. He almost gave a laugh, except Joe looked so serious. His son nodded reluctantly.

'Good – you do need to use them, Joe. Otherwise . . . well, you know.'

Enough said. His parental duty to explain contraception and safe sex, *done*.

Duncan shifted on his feet, letting the sound of the water lapping in the reservoir soothe him. He knew he was no good at talking. To Joe or his wife. The knowledge of his failure only served to frustrate him even more. It was different for Martin – he'd always been close to his kids. Their small house had hosted big family gatherings – Sally often spoke of them with a warmth lighting up her face. Her dad, her mum, her older brothers and sister, the babies that had already arrived, cousins . . . Duncan envied her all that and yet he'd never wanted it for himself or Claire.

Had he?

He thought of the Barn. It had been his gift to Claire, a way of reaching out. Something tangible, the envy of all their friends. It had cost a fortune, after all. Let alone all the work that had gone into it. He'd got that wrong too. There had been times when he'd caught an expression on her face or thought he'd heard a sneer beneath her words – she'd hated it, hadn't she? Joe too had seemed happier elsewhere than in the house. Always going AWOL. He pulled the woollen hat from his head, suddenly irritated by the thing, one hand rubbing the bare skin at the top of his skull that always made him feel self-conscious. Joe had loved the valley. Claire too. He'd got that right at least, surely.

He couldn't face going back to work. Or the Barn. His brain ached from a morning of complicated surgery and his emotions were strung out. He'd been working so hard at not letting himself think of these things. Joe and Claire and the past. His failures and regrets. He knew it made him appear cold and unfeeling. He was anything but.

His mind veered to all those police vehicles on his drive. Martin and his crew digging on his land in earnest now and investigating the tunnels. It was only a matter of time before they found her. Evangeline. No, he didn't want to remember.

Animals were so much easier to understand. To manage. Though really not much different to humans. Each animal that passed under his care was unique, as filled with emotion, appetite and the potential for violence as any human. If their buttons were pressed the wrong way.

He looked out across the water, tracking a movement beneath the surface, the ripples in the current catching in the sunlight. If humans had a soul, then so did animals, birds and fish – even the insects that thrummed above the water – that was his belief. Humans were no different to any other living thing. No better or worse. Maybe a good deal worse. We all have the same plumbing, he thought, it was just a question of scale.

He would go back to work in a bit. He had to. Carry on. Then later he'd go to a bar, drink, dance, chat up whichever girls were there, staying out as long as he could. Long enough to forget again. He pushed the hat into his pocket. He was good at his job and if he was good at only one thing, then he would do his very best to make it count. Whilst he could.

It wasn't the money, or the respect. Or even the satisfaction of being in charge. He folded his fingers into his palms – no, it was more than any of that. He loved the animals he cared for. Sally was right. Perhaps he had lost sight of that. He'd loved Joe too. Claire had seemed to think he didn't. That wasn't true. Joe had been different for sure, not what either of them had hoped, but he was clever, passionate, intense, difficult – oh God, so difficult . . . Duncan felt his hands clench into two fists. Every day had been filled with so much anger.

A buzzard swooped overhead, its shrieking cry loud against the hills.

He wasn't going to brood about Joe. Or Claire. It would only drag him down. What's done was done. Mistakes were to be learned from, not wallowed in. He was paying the price now.

He walked again, along the path that led away from the lake. His fingers found a stick of unused chewing gum tucked deep into his trouser pocket. He flicked the paper wrapping open with his thumb and unfolded the silver foil with one smooth movement. He pushed the gum under his tongue, tucking the rubbish back into his pocket.

The air was ripe with pine and cedar. He could hear the buzzard still, the sound like bees in summer, or the cars on the street outside the surgery, an ever-present background noise to which he no longer listened. Memories were like that. Yet even with the bird out of sight, he could see the small shadow that skipped across the waves of the reservoir, a dancing glimpse of black and silver flashing through the trees. It reminded him of the larger shadow that followed him in the skies above.

Another sound stirred his consciousness. Between the lake and him. He stopped walking and searched the foliage. There was a shifting pattern of shade, something dark against a tree, branches swinging the wrong way. A deer.

It was almost completely camouflaged, its coat and antlers blending into the bark of the tree. Movement separated it from the background, together with the weight of its head lowering to the ground. It hadn't cast its antlers, but it wouldn't be long. From the size of them, the beast was young, no longer a fawn but not yet a full-grown adult. The creature's eyes stared, its nostrils wide and soft. Its warm breath misted in the air and one foot lifted after another, stepping forwards and then back, as if it were uncertain of its way.

Duncan didn't move, his breath held trapped in his throat. Beside the deer, a few newly fledged leaves quivered on the ends of their twigs. He watched the creature's body turn to one side. Then he understood. On its left haunch was a gaping wound.

The deer tossed its head, eyes flaring black. For a second, Duncan was reminded of *that* day. Joe's eyes wide and dark. Confusion and disbelief. Terror. Flies already crawled across the thick flaps of the animal's ragged skin. The blood flowed afresh and red stained the animal's hindquarters, dripping to the ground below. Its hooves paced the forest floor as if to run and yet it stayed, trapped by its own fear and confusion.

It wasn't fear that Duncan saw in the deer's body language, it was pain. He knew that look. Raw, piercing, unadulterated pain. Duncan's eyelids lowered briefly and his jaw moved slowly, chewing on the gum. That small movement was enough.

With a backwards trot, the creature turned.

It gave a single toss of its wretched, reproachful head, and fled.

CHAPTER 58

CLAIRE – AFTER

Someone is knocking on the front door. Hammering with their fist. My mind is groggy with sleep and I think I hear Arthur barking in the kitchen, scrabbling at the door to get out.

Pain shoots up my body as cramp sears through my legs. The arches of my feet are twisted like water being squeezed from a rope. I roll from the bed onto my heels, hobbling across the room as if my bones are all in the wrong place. I rip open the curtains, peering down at the front path in an attempt to see who it is.

Something moves just out of sight beneath the guttering.

I grasp the edge of the window sill, dragging myself upright as I push down on the soles of my feet. The pain ricochets across my limbs until the muscles snap into place and I feel the bliss of relief. I stand properly and look more keenly from the window.

It feels like I've hardly slept. The mist is back again and I screw my eyes up tight, frustration and despair clouding my sight. There's that hammering again, sharp and loud and demanding.

I can't see anyone on the doorstep. And Arthur has gone quiet.

I check the second window, the one that faces out the back. A moment later, I catch a movement by the hedge. I track along the perimeter of the garden, first left and then right. There he is, a shape taller than the hedge, motionless beneath the trees. My pulse surges. Is that . . .? My hands splay, I press my face cold against the window pane and I cry out.

'Joe!'

My voice blooms against the glass. He can't hear me. Not from here.

I run from the room, bursting open the front door. It swings against the wall with a flutter of old plaster. I take a hasty step backwards from the stone porch. I must be going mad. He's not there by the hedge, he's here, right in front of me.

Not Joe. But the man I met in the village.

He wears the same jacket as before, riding boots and equestrian breeches. He's standing with his legs apart and one hand behind his back. He looks like something out of a Victorian melodrama, dated, rigid and intimidating. On the lane, tethered to the gate and pulling on the reins, is a handsome thoroughbred horse.

'Hello, Mrs Henderson,' says the man.

I hear Arthur whining from behind the kitchen door. The man casts a glance into the cottage behind me, frowning as if he can see into my decrepit kitchen with its sink full of dirty crockery and the old range piled up with saucepans from yesterday's tea. I think of the witch markings on the beam above the fireplace. Aren't they meant to protect me from strangers?

'I . . . I . . .' My hand lifts to my throat.

'Your hanging basket has fallen in the wind.'

His other hand is holding what's left of my basket. I flash a look at his face; he must have been in the garden round the back. The plants are withered and black, the wickerwork unravelling from its frame. I catch sight of something briefly slithering between his fingers, like a worm pushing back into the soil where it belongs.

I don't want to take the basket from him. Instead, I nod and gesture to the pathway. He puts it down reluctantly, as if disappointed he couldn't tempt me with it.

'I was thinking about that poster you gave me,' he says.

He produces one, fresh and flat and white, like it's only just been printed – but I saw him crush the one I gave him, didn't I? My eyes dart to his face. Has it been him taking down my posters?

'Didn't you say that this was your son, Joe?'

'I . . . yes.' I'm all breathy and stupid and feminine. 'Have you seen him?'

'I found this,' he says.

With his free hand, he reaches for a pocket inside his jacket and pulls out a phone.

It's Joe's phone! The cover is unmistakable, black with a white Chinese dragon sprawled across the casing. I snatch it from him, still hugging my doorstep.

'Where did you get that?'

I'm appalled and amazed at the same time.

'Ah, well, found it in the village, on the lane. Thought you'd be pleased to see it.'

I stare at it – I am pleased, it's something tangible that is Joe's. And evidence he's not been far, all this time. I'm so happy. But then my brain kicks into gear. His phone should be with him, so he can use it to ring me. Or answer my call. Is this why he hasn't picked up? How long has the phone been there on the lane? My emotions plunge. I won't be able to talk to him now, wherever he is. And what does it mean, that he's lost his phone?

306

I grip it between my fingers. It feels wet. I look down and there's water dripping from between the tiny gaps in the casing.

'I found this too.'

He produces something else, smaller, pressing it into my other hand. It burns into my flesh. I open my fingers, staring at it. It's a coin. The coin that Joe found. The puppetrider.

I pull my eyes up to his face. The man's expression is quizzical, as if he's expecting me to know what to do.

'You can ring him,' he says.

I look uncertainly at him, full of doubt and hope and scepticism at the same time.

'How . . . how can I ring him?' I say.

'With the phone, of course.'

He gestures to Joe's phone, sitting in my hand, as if his statement is perfectly logical. He makes me feel like Duncan used to make me feel, like an ignorant child.

'I don't understand.'

My grip tightens on the phone. He looks at me as if deciding what he needs to say to convince me.

'I saw him only yesterday,' he says. 'I know he wants to speak to you.'

'You saw him? When? Where? Is he okay?'

My head is roaring. I look at the man as if he's something from outer space.

'You can ask him yourself.'

My gaze returns to the phone. The man scowls as if I'm so stupid, I don't know how to operate it. He takes it from me impatiently, our fingers touching briefly. It's like an electric shock. I watch him punch in the numbers – what numbers? He presses Dial and passes the phone back to me, nodding encouragingly.

307

The tone rings out in my ear. Then stops. There's a crackling, buzzing, a fizzing like it was with the TV.

'Hello?' I say, disbelief making my voice tremble.

The static gets louder. I give the phone a shake, looking back at the man on my doorstep. How is this possible? After so much worrying, suddenly it's as easy as that – one phone call?

I give a moan. This isn't real. I'm still in my bed and it's another of those nightmares, my brain trying to unravel the truth. My hands reach up to my head, but they are shaking violently. The pain isn't just in my legs and feet, it's everywhere, ricocheting from one side of my body to the other. I fold my knees into my chest, hugging myself as if that will stop the shaking.

The phone is back in my hand. I can feel the coin in the other, too. I think I hear something over the sound of the fizzing. I'm vaguely aware that it must be my fault, all that noise and disturbance, because I can't stop my hands from shaking.

'Hello?' I say again. 'Who's there?'

'Hello?'

A voice comes back at me, distant and tinny through all that noise.

'Who is this?' I say. 'I can't hear you properly.' I speak louder. 'Hello?'

'Hello?' comes the reply.

The line pops and crackles some more.

'Who's speaking?'

Dear God, *I think.* I know that voice! Surely . . . it can't be . . . can it?

'Joe? Is that you?'

CHAPTER 59

CLAIRE – AFTER

I'm not dreaming, am I? This is real, it feels like it's real. That man is playing with me. Or I must be going mad. It's all gone wrong. Since coming to the cottage, I can't tell truth from fantasy. I open my hand and the puppetrider coin is clutched between my fingers. It's real, that coin is real.

But my mind is still a blur. I can see the fingers of my other hand curled around the phone and the fingernails are growing, like long strands of Virginia creeper winding about the phone. I feel sick. I *am* mad, but they keep on growing, one strand overlapping the next with five-pronged dark green leaves sprouting into life. They grow and wither and grow and wither, until the leaves are almost as big as my hand. They're not five-pronged anymore but three, then two. I've seen this before – where have I seen this before?

My eyes move to my other hand and the coin. Then I know.

They are puppetrider hands – the thick, claw-like fist of the rider, opening and closing, opening and closing . . .

It's coming back to me, something on the edge of my mind. Joe, what happened to Joe . . . And the tunnels beneath the dam. I don't care any longer if I am still dreaming or this *is* real. I want it to be real. My hands shake even more, but I hold the phone back up to my ear.

'Hello? Mum?' The voice gets louder in my head. *'It's me! I'm here! I've found something! Do you want to know what?'*

The line goes dead.

CHAPTER 60

CLAIRE – AFTER

I slip through the trees, moving like the night mist that glides at my feet. The vegetation is damp with dew, water touching my hands, my clothes – I am only partially aware of the pain in my body, my arms and legs, the muscles exhausted from running. It feels like I am floating. Like one of those nightmares where anything is possible despite all physical limitations. I won't stop until I get to the dam.

I have already passed through the village, the houses and their outbuildings skulking like black demons in the dark. I couldn't bear to look at them, wondering who lives inside each one. They must have been still asleep, for no lights shone from the windows. As my eyes gravitated to the sky, only then did it occur to me that amongst all those trees there were no streetlamps, no telephone poles, no pylons, or overhead wires. Not even a stray satellite dish. The whole village is devoid of any contact with the outside world. It's always been like that, the place ruled by the eccentricities of an old family seeking to defy time.

Since the first day I got here, the whole valley has felt like that, cut off from the rest of the world, left behind like an island in a flood. Inhabited, it seems, only by those who don't care anymore, or too set in their ways to bother with the real world to catch up with the rest of us. I almost smile but don't, for hasn't the same been happening to me? There's been a distancing from reality ever since I got here, stuck in the valley where I've been seduced by its beauty, the self-imposed isolation, close to but hidden from my old life. From Duncan, Becky . . . even, I can acknowledge it now, Joe. From everything that's caused my pain.

I pass through the woodlands by the shore, along the path that leads to the dam. Finally, I step onto it, a slender bridge of concrete only three metres wide but almost a hundred metres long. It's the one place I have been avoiding, even more than the Barn. The highest point of the route around the reservoir.

On one side is the flat glacial lake. On the other, a solid wall plunges down to a maelstrom of foaming yellow water. I stand beside the rails, catching my breath. My chest is heaving up and down, aching. *Not too close*, I think, my head spinning as I peer down to the churning depths below.

With my right hand, I twist the length of my ring finger. The pale band of skin where once my wedding ring belonged feels naked and exposed. I've never liked rings. We argued about it, Duncan and I. He said he wouldn't wear one and I said that if I had to, then he should too. To me, a wedding ring is a mark of ownership and control, like the rings that track wild birds or tie animals to their stalls. I picture it with gladness, dropping from my finger as my withered flesh shrinks, swaying slowly into the murk below.

I reach into my pocket, for the coin that Joe found. The puppetrider.

Five for silver, six for gold.

Precious metals. In themselves they mean so little, just another lump of rock, but honed and crafted into a thing of beauty and given as a token of love, they mean so much.

This sense of loss that haunts me isn't about Duncan. Nor even Joe. It's something else, steeped in tears. Something I've been hiding from myself for far too long. Now that I'm here, I'm afraid. The past cannot be undone. If I could do it all again, it would, *could* be no different.

I walk to the centre of the dam. From here, you can see the whole expanse of the reservoir. It pans out before my eyes, a smooth plane of water that skates along the foot of the valley, gouged out by ancient glacial forces. Dawn is inching over the hills. This early in the morning, as always, the water is obscured by fog. Behind the banks, small shallow pools of water lie hidden under a thin layer of pollen and white petals fallen from the hawthorn trees above. My eyes sting. The night chill and my running has turned my cheeks pink. My breath floats in the air and my chest aches with each staggered lungful.

Beneath me, in the concrete wall, is a row of circular openings, each one covered with a thick iron grille. More water spews from within, brown and muddy. The constant flow holds me, line upon line of gushing water, sweeping down to join the turmoil below. It's coming back – the whole rhyme this time – all of it rushing to my head:

> One for sorrow, two for joy,
> Three for a girl, four for a boy,
> Five for silver, six for gold,
> Seven for a secret, never to be told.

CHAPTER 61

DUNCAN – 22 YEARS BEFORE

The tunnels of the old workings that led to the reservoir dam hadn't been in use for many years. Duncan had known they had to plan it carefully. Flooded for most of the time, he'd had to track the timings and work out when it was safe to enter the tunnels and how long they had before they had to get out.

He and Claire had watched from the dam, waiting for the water gushing from the channels in the wall to ebb away. The heat of summer had lowered the water levels and that had worked in their favour. There was a sough, an opening cut into a bank in the grounds of the Hall, near a collection of crumbling utility buildings. Duncan had known about it from his time exploring the grounds as a student and it had been his suggestion to access the tunnels from there. Some of the passages went right under the Hall, ventilation shafts popping up within the building, cooling the pantries and storage rooms of the kitchens above. The Hall, the old works, the reservoir itself, they were all connected.

Claire and he had driven from the dam to the sough, parking at the end of a track by what was left of the buildings. Moonlight and darkness defined the woods around them like a pen-and-ink drawing, all black-and-white lines, trees reaching for the night sky or tilted over, still growing where the storms had left them.

Duncan cut the engine. The lights and noise were gone. An old tractor stood inside the broken walls, its tyres slashed and deflated. Its rusted metal arms branched out from either side to throw shadows like some supersized alien spider. They both got out of the car. A shallow mist clung to the ground, glowing milky white in the moonlight. Their combined breath floated out in the cold air and something stirred beneath a tree. Claire had turned her head, scanning the undergrowth. A pair of eyes blinked and was gone.

'I don't think I can do this,' she'd said.

'Yes, you can,' Duncan replied.

He zipped his jacket up to his cheek and reached into the boot.

The opening had been blocked by a mesh grille, but time had long since worked it loose. They'd pulled it free, Claire and Duncan, the two of them working together, armed with a single torch. Duncan had carried Evangeline's body through the dark guided only by the small dancing circle of light held in Claire's shaking hands. Duncan knew the way; he'd found the schematics online and already done a recce, leaving what was needed there.

They'd followed the twists and turns, wading through water

that rose up to their knees, until they reached a short passageway that lifted clear of the highest water level and ended with a metal door.

'Here,' Duncan had said.

Claire had agreed.

He dug out the hole, carefully setting aside each brick until a ledge big enough had been opened up in the wall. Together, they laid Evangeline's body on the flat, rough surface and gazed at her awhile. Then Duncan bricked her up. The wet cement gleamed dully in the darkness and Claire was crying by then. She gave him the coin. She had this idea that it was a mark of respect. They might have killed her, sought to hide her where she would never be found, but it was important to Claire to lay Evangeline to rest with dignity.

Duncan slipped the coin end on into the fresh cement and quietly finished the job.

When he was done, they walked back the way they'd come, pushing the grille back to how it should have been. They drove home through the woods and carried on with their lives as if Evangeline had never been.

Neither of them ever referred to her after that. It was that one thing they never spoke of. One small seed of guilt and fear and shame, undermining their marriage, poisoning their lives. Slowly pushing them apart.

It had been *her* decision, not his. He'd given her every opportunity to change her mind. He'd helped her, supported her, had done what was necessary, but ultimately this had been what Claire had wanted.

CHAPTER 62

DUNCAN – AFTER

Duncan leaned forwards on his chair. The only light in his consulting room came from his computer screen. It was night. He hadn't been able to sleep. Nor had he been able to stay in the Barn a moment longer, rattling in its empty, sterile rooms.

He swung out of his chair and made his way to the animal ward, flicking the switch so that only the night lights came on. A few animals stirred on his arrival, barking, whining, shifting in their beds to watch their visitor as he walked in front of the cages. He knelt in front of one, a cat with both its back legs in bright blue bandages. She lifted her head backwards to acknowledge his presence. He opened the door, reaching in to stroke her head, that special spot between her ears where the friendship gland was. She purred, her eyes slow and blinking.

He kept thinking about Joe. Little Joe being given a tour

318

of the veterinary ward, the day before the new surgery was due to open. Joe wide-eyed and squealing as Duncan swung him up into his arms to show him the skeleton charts on the wall. Joe holding Arthur that first day he was brought home as a young pup. Arthur's giant puppy paws, his round-eyed puppy face, his wriggling nervousness as Joe scooped him up in to his arms. Joe grinning as he buried his nose into Arthur's velvet puppy-soft fur. Arthur had had such a bad start in life and yet he'd taken to Joe right from the start. It had been a good decision, bringing Arthur home, on so many counts, watching Joe find his confidence with Arthur.

He thought of Garfield and Betsy. The way the dog's shoulders had slumped in pain the day that Garfield brought her in. He thought of the faces staring from the back window of the bus as he shouted at Garfield, and the student who'd tried to intervene. They'd got it all wrong, hadn't they? That wasn't him, *normal* him.

He remembered Frances taking him to task, threatening to tell Martin about his daughter. To tell Sally too, about his new romantic interest. She *had* told Sally, hadn't she? Perhaps she'd been right to. He saw Sally – that secret smile she'd had only for him as he walked through reception each morning. That same smile hovering over his, pink and flushed and parted, the pair of them entangled on the bed. The look of horror on her face as Duncan confronted the old man at the bus stop. Her set expression as she'd placed her resignation letter on his desk. He thought of the envelope even now scrunched up in the wastepaper basket.

She didn't mean it. She'd come back. Maybe tomorrow he'd find her sat behind her desk as if nothing had ever been said. Or maybe next week, after she'd had time to think about it.

But then again, maybe she really did mean it. He had only himself to blame.

Then he thought of Claire. Her face day in, day out as he went to and from work. Joe watching them both across the kitchen. And the faces he didn't want to remember. The same faces twisted in disbelief. A frantic fist banging against the window, lips opening to scream. A face, with its eyes wide open, blank and unmoving.

Evangeline's body, limp and bent and folded in his hand.

He pushed away from the cage, shutting the door, switching the lights off so that the ward was dowsed only in the dim green glow from the emergency exit. He returned to his office. He grabbed his coat and strode urgently out to the car.

CHAPTER 63

CLAIRE – AFTER

The fog over the water has rolled back. Enough at least for me to see the shoreline at the bottom of the land by the Barn. And the tree – the one with the dead flowers. I can see which one it is from the stunted shape of it. It's different to all the others.

I think back to those nodding dried-out blooms on the tree, all those cellophaned bouquets. Someone must have died there. My eyes rise up the slope, towards the Barn that not so long ago was my home. I have avoided going anywhere near it since I left, except for that one night I drove along in the fog. There are tents low down in the field, almost completely hidden by the trees, and another one at the top near the house. Why didn't I see those before?

The fog, of course – I couldn't see a thing that morning in the fog – and the Barn is perched in a fold of the hills where things aren't visible from elsewhere. I can see blue-and-white tape too, weaving a zigzag line up the slope, some of it torn free and waving in the wind like a gymnast's ribbon.

Police tape.

My head swings back to the tree. The flowers, those dead and dying flowers.

My eyes widen. Those flowers torment me. I squeeze my eyes tightly shut and remember.

CHAPTER 64

CLAIRE – AFTER

Memory saturates my thoughts like watercolour on wet paper. Blossoming, staining, pushing where I don't want it to go. I remember being in the kitchen as I waited for Duncan and Joe. That day six, seven weeks ago. Has it been that long?

I remember how I'd been hugging another mug of tea when my mobile rang. I hadn't been able to eat or drink but somehow the act of holding a warm mug had kept me connected to normality.

I remember hoping and praying that Joe hadn't gone into the tunnels, after all. Then the phone had suddenly played out its familiar tune and I'd snatched it up, shoulders hunched, fingers digging into the leather case of my phone.

'Hello?'

'*Mum?*'

Oh! Jesus, Mother of Mercy, it was him!

'Joe! Joe, is that you?'

I'd juggled the mug with the phone before letting the mug drop onto the kitchen island, liquid pooling across the surface.

'Oh God, where have you been? Why haven't you called me? Where are you, Joe?'

The words tripped over my tongue and my chest had tightened with anticipation.

'It's me! I'm here! I've found something!' he said. 'Do you want to know what?'

I'd felt the shock of his words in the clawed movement of my hand. I didn't want this to happen, I didn't want him to say those words – what he'd found.

'This is the real deal, Mum. You'll never believe what I've uncovered!'

Excitement made him almost incomprehensible down the phone.

I bit down on my tongue. Hope, I felt hope. He sounded happy, he couldn't have . . . It was okay after all and I needed to *listen* to him.

If I'd listened to him then, I think now, *and before – would that have changed everything?*

'What, my love. What have you found?'

'That coin, the puppetrider. I thought there were more. But now . . .'

'That's lovely, Joe, but where are you?'

'No, you don't understand, Mum—'

'Joe, for goodness' sake, *where are you*?'

'I'm outside – on the road. I'm back!'

I slammed the phone down on the worktop and rushed to the front door. I flung it open as best I could, given the weight of it.

I ran out and down the drive and called out to him.

'Joe! Joe!'

Snowflakes filled the sky – thick, broad snowflakes obscuring everything yet lighting up the late afternoon. The cold caught in my throat, my breath dancing in the air. He was there – I could see him, a dark figure walking up the lane just below the entrance to our property.

The cold had frozen everything, branches, twigs – even the last few individual leaves were weighted down, held fast in suspended frigid slumber. The stones on the wall by the entrance to the drive were covered in white and the snow sank beneath my feet.

Arthur barked in joy. He'd been waiting all day, too. He slipped past my legs to go bounding and galumphing ahead of me. A sudden gust of wind shook a pile of new snow from the trees over my head. I felt the cool air whisper across my skin and I saw Joe, his long hair flying out behind his shoulders, running to greet his beloved dog.

From the other direction on the lane a lorry came hurtling round the bend. I vaguely registered a supermarket logo. The lorry lurched one way and then the next. In a rush, perhaps, to beat the weather. Too silent in the thick snow. Too fast on the road. Way too fast.

The dog barked again.

I flew onto the lane.

There was a screech of tyres and a single piercing scream from Joe. I smelt diesel and something else – the acrid stench of burning rubber foul on my tongue. Then everything went quiet. It was so quick, so fast, yet that one second drawing out so slowly.

I heard nothing. No one.

325

Everything was muffled by the snow, melting on my skin.

Just the soft, delicate touch of snowflakes landing on my outstretched fingertips.

CHAPTER 65

DUNCAN – AFTER

Duncan drove out of town, in the dark and the quiet, taking the twists and turns in the road too fast before braking and indicating and rumbling onto the road that led to the reservoir.

He took a deep breath and slowed down.

He drove along the flat of the valley, the water only inches from his side, He drove towards the cross that still hung suspended above the water. It was even taller than before.

He carried on driving until he saw the tree with its dead flowers.

He brought the car to a stop right in the middle of the road.

It was here that he'd almost crashed into a car only a few days ago, in the fog, when he was too drunk to know better. Too stupid, more like. Remembering. He still wasn't sure it had actually happened. Here, where he'd sat in his seat transfixed by the driver's face. He could have sworn that it was Claire he'd seen then.

He twisted round and reversed a few feet, then pulled off the road onto the verge. He cut the engine and the headlamps were extinguished. The darkness pooled around him until his eyes adjusted and the shapes began to clarify. Thick, solid hedges and tall grass, nettles and brambles reaching out to grasp at unwary animals, and the skittish movement of last year's leaves dancing on the road.

He got out of the car, stumbling the few yards to the tree, as if he were still half-drunk. Then he pulled himself upright and looked out across the water.

The density of woodland framed the far side of the shore. The lack of streetlights had meant that the valley had always been dark at night, with or without the moon, the natural bowl of the reservoir making it perfect for stargazing. He tilted his head up and down again. There were the seven stars of the Plough lined up across the sky and the three bright stars of Orion's Belt reflected in the water. Venus, goddess of love, was the brightest star in the sky.

Tonight, though, the water was black. It felt deceptive, oppressive, vindictive almost, calling him, and Claire, to account.

CHAPTER 66

DUNCAN – AFTER

Duncan stood by the tree with the dead flowers for a long time, waiting for the dawn to break. Cool fingers of damp prickled on his skin, the water drifting in and out of view as the mist breathed across the reservoir.

For the first time in a long time, he let his mind go back. It had all started with Garfield and his dogs.

With Arthur.

Arthur had been less than six months old when he'd come to live with Duncan's family. Five years ago. He'd been an oversized but too thin, loopy, big-footed puppy whimpering at Garfield's leash.

'There!' Garfield had said. 'Glad to be shot of 'im. He makes that much of a mess.'

A large puddle of urine had appeared between the puppy's rear paws.

'He 'as no idea how to behave, the stupid mutt. I bought him to guard me 'ouse and all 'e does is mewl like a cat. That's not a proper dog. Can't be doing w' it no more.'

Garfield gave another tug on the leash, dragging the poor pup across the floor.

'There's no need for that,' said Duncan, his voice sharp and angry.

He could barely contain himself, but he'd had to keep his anger under control for fear of Garfield taking offence at the last minute and refusing to hand over the dog.

'Cost me five hundred pounds! That's almost a whole month's pension!'

Garfield looked up from under his heavy eyebrows, his yellow teeth chewing an imaginary piece of wood. His hand reached down between his legs and he scratched himself. He might have been about to spit on the floor, but then he seemed to think better of it.

'Free treatment, right?' Garfield looked smug. 'That's what yer said. For Betsy, me other dog. For life.'

'Aye. On condition you always bring her to me, here at this surgery.'

Garfield held his gaze, scowling. Then he nodded. He handed over the leash. He shuffled out of the room without even looking back at the dog. No attempt to say goodbye. Already, Garfield's shoulders were slumped, his head down, doing his weak, poor old man act again. For the benefit of the other folk in the waiting room.

Duncan hated that people took on a puppy without realising what was involved. Especially a dog that was going to grow into a big animal – you could tell from the size of their feet, even if you weren't familiar with the breed.

Garfield had been particularly obstinate. He was a wily old fellow. He claimed he loved both his dogs, the puppy and his other full-grown dog, Betsy. He knew Duncan couldn't report him for animal abuse, or force him to hand over his dogs without definite proof. So Duncan had made a proposal – that he would take the two dogs himself and give them both a home. No reports, no recriminations. Sorted.

But Garfield wasn't having it. Maybe one dog but not both. It had taken several weeks to persuade Garfield to agree to a revised solution: Duncan could adopt the puppy and Garfield would keep Betsy on condition he brought her in to the surgery for regular check-ups. Duncan phrased it as 'free veterinary care for life'. Garfield finally said yes.

Duncan gave a sigh of relief. It was one of those win-win situations, he told himself. Garfield got rid of an unwanted dog and gained a financial benefit, and Duncan got to rescue Arthur *and* keep an eye on Betsy.

A win-win. Sort of.

Those first few days, Arthur cowered behind the sofa in the kitchen. Then his four big feet pattered cautiously on the hard surfaces of the Barn, sniffing and snuffling as he familiarised himself with new smells. It took him a while, but he seemed to know that his new owners were different.

Once out of Garfield's hands, he thrived. By the end of that first year, he was skidding as he raced around the corners, black ears folded by his cheeks, head moving from side to side in a constant state of excited curiosity. The dog was an absolute softie. Duncan, Claire and Joe were all besotted with him.

But it was Joe who Arthur particularly took a liking to.

He'd sidle up to Joe's legs at the dinner table, tail sweeping on the floor. Or flop down beside him the moment Joe entered the kitchen. He whimpered if Joe left the house without him, and at night, the two of them lay together in Joe's bed, the young teenage boy under the duvet, the dog on top.

'Shhh!' Claire had said, opening the bedroom door a crack.

Duncan peered through the gap. There was Joe, settled for once in his bed, one arm curved around the dog's body, Arthur with his wet nose nestled right under the boy's neck.

'Look at them,' she said. 'It's a miracle!'

Duncan loved that his son and Arthur had bonded so well. It was what they both needed. The utter faith that someone loved you unconditionally. Duncan acknowledged that it must appear as if he'd failed Joe in that respect. He and Claire had each struggled in their different ways with the reality of what life with Joe was like.

Duncan thought back to Garfield. It was hard to live with the knowledge that Betsy was still at the old man's mercy. Each time Garfield brought her in, you could see the poor animal was miserable, her big eyes round and reproachful. Duncan felt his guilt about that even now – he had colluded with her situation, hadn't he? It made him despise Garfield even more.

Duncan shifted his weight, pushing himself away from the tree.

He thought of that day he and Claire had argued. She'd seen him and Sally at the stables the night before. Duncan had been drinking later as he watched a film after he'd got back. Then early that next morning Claire had picked a massive row. Not surprising, really. He'd deserved every moment of it. Joe had heard. Joe had always heard. Duncan and Claire had got so used to playing out their private conflict in the Barn, they'd forgotten that Joe lived there, too. Duncan had said things in the heat of the moment he never should have.

Joe had run off. Like he always did. When Claire told Duncan about the coin, Duncan had gone too, heading for the sough in the grounds of the Hall in the conviction that was where Joe had gone. He knew more than anyone how dangerous those tunnels could be. It wasn't about Evangeline – the likelihood that Joe would find her burial place in the wall was about as likely as finding a needle in a haystack, especially now that the marker, the coin, was gone. The police search was far more of a realistic concern now. But then . . .? He knew Claire had been fraught with worry that maybe Evangeline's skeleton, what was left of her, had been disturbed, too. Duncan had never believed that.

No, it was the danger of those tunnels that was the real issue, Claire had known that too. Joe not being aware of when the water came and went, risking an exploration inside in search of some mythical hoard. *Damn you, Joe*, Duncan thought, always setting hares running with his stupid, hopeless treasure hunting.

A snow storm had descended on the valley, a true blast of winter, the road around the reservoir filling up with snow. Duncan had spent hours checking out the sough and the dam and the woods and all the other entrances to the tunnels that he knew of, when the call came through.

It was Claire.

'Duncan? It's Arthur! He's been run over!'

CHAPTER 67

CLAIRE – AFTER

'Duncan! Are you there? Did you hear me? Arthur's been run over!'

My memory is getting stronger, mimicking the pockets of clear air that drift between the layers of fog. Still it teases me. Frustrates me, and yet I remember making that particular call like it was today.

It comes flooding back: the crackling on the line, the interference from the weather, the urgency of reaching Duncan as soon as possible if we were to have any chance of saving Arthur. His knowledge and expertise by then was far greater than mine.

'Slow down, Claire. What state is he in?'

'He's conscious but badly hurt. At least one of his back legs is broken. He's taken a hit on the chest, I think, and there's internal bleeding. Please, Duncan, can you come now? Joe's fine, he's here with me. As fast as you can!'

'I'm on my way.'

The snow was bad, but with his sleek, shiny new four-by-four, within twenty minutes he was at the Barn.

He burst through the front door. Joe and I were crouched on the floor in the hallway, soothing Arthur's head. I was holding back the tears, and Joe was pale and silent. There was blood and shit and a strong smell of urine. Our eyes met – Duncan and I both knew enough about animal road traffic victims to know exactly what to expect.

He fell to his knees, examining the dog. Arthur's ears were flat against his skull and his eyes were rolled back. His breath came in short, sharp, staggered rasps.

'I need to get him to the surgery,' Duncan said. 'There's not much I can do here without the right equipment.'

He turned to Joe.

'Can you fetch the old blanket? It's in the garage by the camping gear. Lay it flat in the boot of your mum's car. We'll carry him between us.'

My car, not his. Because it was an estate. Because it was older and didn't matter. Typical Duncan.

'Is he going to be alright?' I looked at Duncan with eyes that were too bright.

I was itching to do something, but I knew I had to let Duncan do his job.

'I don't know, Claire. In all honesty, I don't know. It depends how much internal damage he has.' Duncan kept his voice unemotional.

How else could he be, if he was to be of any use to Arthur? It was what Duncan was, always in an emergency, the consummate cool-headed professional. You have to be.

He eyed the pile of expensive white cotton bath towels. Was that a fleeting curl of disapproval? But I knew I'd done the right thing. I'd used several to prop up the dog's body to stop his chest from being compressed. Arthur was panting now, not in a good way. A strange gurgling came from deep within his lungs. Duncan's and my concern increased, but neither one of us was going to voice it, not in front of Joe. We had that much sense, at least.

'How did it happen?' he asked.

'Joe had just come back,' I said. 'Arthur was so excited, he ran out onto the lane. There was a delivery lorry going too fast. My online food shop. It didn't stop . . .' My voice petered away. If only I'd never ordered that food to be delivered when I had.

'It's all my fault,' said Joe. He was already back.

He shook the thick snowflakes from his arms and held out the blanket.

'He was thrown to the side of the road,' said Joe. 'The driver drove right off, the fucking wanker! He didn't even do his delivery.'

He sounded so much like his father then.

'I meant put the blanket in the car, Joe, not here,' Duncan snapped.

Joe didn't move. He stared at his father for a moment, eyes shuttered. I felt for him, but now was not the time. Without a word, Joe swung round, grabbed the car keys from the rack and dashed outside.

'Right, Claire, help me get Arthur onto this towel.'

Duncan adjusted his position, unfolding a towel and gesturing me to position myself at the dog's head. He slipped his hands under Arthur's body and counted.

'One, two, three . . . lift.'

Arthur gave a strangled howl of pain, then lay back against

336

the towel. His legs were stiff and oddly angled. More blood seeped from beneath his body and stained the towel bright red. I closed my eyes, willing myself not to react.

Joe had returned from the car. His legs leaned inwards like a young deer and his face was furrowed with anxiety.

'Right, Joe, grab that end. Claire, you take the other. We're going to carry him outside and lay him on the blanket.'

Duncan snapped on the outside lights and we shuffled awkwardly. Through the door and across the snowy drive. We set the dog down in the boot of the car. The snow had whitened everything and the trees were muted and still. The outside world was quite impervious to our drama. I pulled the blanket around Arthur, covering him with more towels, fussing in spite of myself.

'That'll do,' said Duncan. 'We don't have long.'

'I'll drive.' I took the keys from Joe.

'No! I'll drive,' said Duncan. 'I know what I'm doing in these conditions and I need you to ring Sally. Tell her to prep for surgery.'

I felt an irresistible burst of pure hatred.

'You can't expect me to speak to her!'

'Not now, Claire.'

Duncan was cool and measured. He glanced quickly towards Joe.

'You have to sack her!'

Duncan ignored me, reaching out to snatch the keys. He folded himself into the car.

'For fuck's sake, Duncan, did you hear me?'

'Do you want an argument about this now, Claire? Or are we going to get Arthur to the surgery?'

He turned the key in the ignition and the engine jumped

into life. Joe had climbed into the rear, apparently oblivious. He was leaning over the seat to check Arthur in the boot. I didn't know what to do, all my hatred and resentment of Duncan, of *her*, was flooding back. I clenched my hands and reluctantly slid onto the front seat. Duncan swivelled round to address Joe.

'You don't need to come.'

Joe didn't reply.

'Joe! I'd rather you stayed at home.'

'There's no way I'm leaving him,' said Joe.

Duncan grunted. Joe's face was closed and mutinous. Duncan turned back to the wheel, glancing at the rear mirror.

'Okay. Then sit down, Joe. And put your seat belt on.'

'I'm not speaking to her,' I said, my voice tight with anger.

I was filled with so many emotions, but that he should expect me to address even one word to her after what I'd seen the night before . . .

'Don't be ridiculous, Claire. Now is not the time to have a paddy about Sally.'

The car moved forwards, crunching over fresh snow. I was only vaguely aware of how Joe's eyes slid between Duncan and me before lowering his head.

'A *paddy*? Seriously, you call my objection to Sally a *paddy*?' I twisted round to glare directly at Duncan, but he refused to look at me.

'I don't care what you call it, you need to ring the surgery. I can't do it if I'm driving, can I? She'll be the only one there. I called in to tell everyone else to go home early with the snow. You need to tell her to prep the operating room and phone Frances.'

'You promised me only this morning!'

'No, I did not! I distinctly remember *not* responding to your ridiculous demands. Sally's perfectly good at her job, completely professional. I have no intention of sacking her.'

'But you're quite happy to screw her! That's not exactly professional, is it?'

By now the car was speeding down the hill and I'd long forgotten about Joe sitting in the back. Snowflakes trapped in the two beams of the headlamps hung like listless snow-white fairies.

'She likes it, which is more than I can say for you!'

I gasped. The gloves were off. I wanted to hit him then, truly I did. It was all that I could do not to lash out. The wheels screeched as Duncan braked at the junction. They skidded as he swung the car left onto the road beside the reservoir. I had to clutch the armrest on the passenger door, my heart in my mouth. My head swung to look outside.

On the one side, snowflakes had filled the crevices of the hedgerow. On the other, they were melting into the surface of the lake. Daylight had almost gone, but the valley was eerily bright, transformed by its white covering.

'I wouldn't touch you with a barge pole after what you've done!' I spat the words. 'You sit there driving my car and expect me to speak to her like nothing's happened?'

'This is about Arthur, not you or me or Sally.'

'This is about *us*. Don't you care at all?'

To my shame and humiliation, my voice had broken. No, he didn't care, didn't I know that already? I pushed my back against the seat, arms rigid, fingers bent against the dashboard as a rush of energy filled my head.

'Shut up!' he said. 'It's hard enough driving in this. You're distracting me!'

'Fuck you, Duncan! I'm leaving you. I've already found a place and I'm going. Joe, too. I want a divorce!'

The words came out without me thinking about it. My eyes flashed towards Duncan, inadvertently catching the rear-view mirror. I saw Joe, his expression startled like a wild animal. I felt my instant regret. The car swerved again until Duncan brought it back under control. He accelerated along the straight section of the road.

The wipers batted back and forth, snowflakes slapping against the windscreen too fast to be swept away.

'Fuck you, Claire!' said Duncan through gritted teeth.

His eyes were shuttered. He didn't want to hear it – even now, given what I'd just said, he was refusing to listen to me.

'Don't you speak to me like that! Don't you . . .'

'Stop it, both of you!'

Joe leaned forwards between the two front seats.

'Arthur's dying and all the two of you can do is fight! You always fight. You *should* get divorced! Why don't you both go to hell . . .'

He shoved his father's shoulder in anger.

Duncan's hands slid off the steering wheel. The car veered to the right. The front wheels must have hit a patch of unseen ice. One minute we were driving along the road at full speed and the next we were hurtling into the air.

The car flew out across the water.

CHAPTER 68

DUNCAN – AFTER

The second the car impacted on the surface of the reservoir, pillars of water exploded into the air. They smashed down again all around them. The car bounced and bobbed on the surface. Then water began to shoot through the joints.

The pressure of the liquid outside meant the doors wouldn't budge. Duncan's window had been partially open, like it always was, enough to demist the windscreen. As the car careered towards the reservoir, he'd at least had the good sense to hit the down button before the electrics cut out.

But now the distribution of weight and air tipped the car at the front. All sight and sound faded to the periphery of Duncan's senses. Water filled the space around his knees, his thighs, his waist. His hearing reduced to a buzz. He was only vaguely aware of voices. Claire, Joe, and the dog. Water fogged his eyes. His limbs felt like dead weights as he tried to haul himself through the opening, then turn and reach for the others.

One vital minute to save all their lives.

It wasn't enough.

He plunged into the icy water, the roar of the current erupting onto his ears, his lungs seizing from the extreme cold. He blinked furiously as he clung to the car. It was drifting down the shore. Hail – was that hail? – pounded down all around him. On the car roof. On the water. Snowflakes smothered his face, his eyes, stones of ice pummelling his skin. He screamed for Claire to follow, but she wouldn't leave Joe.

Joe first! Joe first! she cried.

But Joe was trapped in the back, the driver's headrest in the way. He couldn't get through the gap. Time was running out, water sweeping into the car, the level rising rapidly.

The trapped air had reduced to a narrow bubble right beneath the roof. Duncan saw their heads being forced back. Water poured down his throat. Coughing and spluttering, he fought to open the rear door. He swung his elbow into the glass, trying to smash the rear window. Pain ricocheted through his shoulder. Every blow was useless. He could see Claire gasping for air then diving underwater, struggling to pull Joe between the seats.

Then the car tipped the other way.

It was over in seconds. Water had filled the car completely, dragging it under. A few gulps of air ballooned up to the surface and then there was nothing. The groaning car, the surging waves, their voices . . . gone.

Only the continuous sound of hailstones hitting the water.

He dived again. But the water was so churned up he could see nothing. He dived again and again. Until his limbs were frozen numb and his lungs almost burst for lack of air. Until a gut instinct for self-preservation kicked in.

With barely enough energy to breathe, he clawed and dragged his way up the reservoir bank and collapsed, his body shuddering violently. Defeated.

Snow and hail at the same time. It was surely a meteorological impossibility. It was as if nature had rallied to celebrate an obscenity.

His entire family wiped out in a few moments.

CHAPTER 69

CLAIRE – AFTER

The snow is sliding down the windows. The water roars at my side. I feel the sickening pitch and roll of the car floating on the surface, white sheaths shooting through the cracks in the door, soaking my frozen flesh. My fingers wrap around the door handle, pulling and tugging and pushing, but it won't move. I see yellow eyes peering through the density of water on the other side of the glass. I hear the creak of the roof of the car bending from the weight of all that water – buckling, cracking, pouring over my head . . .

I can't bear to think of it. My nightmares coming to life. It wasn't real, was it? None of it was real. It can't have been real, that's what I tell myself as I stand there on the dam. I survived. I'm here. I still don't remember what happened next. It's too painful and it drives me to distraction. Joe's face, Joe's voice. Duncan – he left us to die, didn't he?

No, I know he tried to get us out. Joe, me. But it had to be Joe first.

Joe's still missing, isn't he?

Horror fills my gut, a wrenching pain that twists my body in half. No, not Joe. He's alive. I know he is. He's missing. Like he often is. I just have to find him.

But the truth hits me then. The police tape flapping in the wind, the flowers on the tree, there where the car entered the water. They have found his body.

All this time I've been in denial. Joe is dead.

CHAPTER 70

CLAIRE – AFTER

Evangeline is buried here, underneath the dam. The original tunnels to the old waterworks beneath the reservoir lead right here, under my feet.

Duncan took her corpse and buried it where no one would ever find her. We did it together in the end. I couldn't make him do it on his own.

Evangeline.

Our daughter.

She was so small. A baby. No bigger than the size of Duncan's hand. I remember her body curled within his fingers like a flower fairy sleeping in a leaf. Except she had no hair, no clothes, and her body was naked, her skin golden and translucent like butter melting in the sun.

I can't move. My legs are anchored to the ground by an emotion I cannot name. My eyes burn, my ears roar. Joe.

Evangeline. The memories swamp me.

My little girl.

I never held her. They wouldn't let me. The moment she was born they took her away. They'd scooped her up into one of those kidney-shaped stainless-steel bowls, as if she were so much detritus to be disposed of. Not a person, not a living, breathing human person, just an unwanted medical problem.

Except she was never unwanted.

I couldn't look, not then. I'd been told what to expect. Well, some of it. Not the too many fingers and toes. That was a shock. But they had told me about the brain, how it hadn't divided. She had a hole in her stomach too, which meant she could never eat or process her food, even with all the technical knowledge that they had. And her heart was a mess. It had been one of those things that nature had got wrong, the genetics all jumbled up.

My body had gone into overdrive trying to keep her alive. I was so ill, throwing up every hour, every moment of the day. I'd been exhausted, far worse than was normal in the first trimester. And it was all for nothing, for a child who could never survive outside my body.

There was a choice.

Not much of a choice, the consultant made that clear.

Let her go now, or later.

Abortion – it was a word I'd never thought to bring into my life.

I feel my fingers clench around Joe's coin, *her* coin, the puppetrider, fingernails digging into my skin. I force myself to open my hand and look at it. One small coin, one tiny coin. A treasure so small, yet worth so much.

She'd been our first child, Duncan's and mine. An accident in our last year at uni. Accident – I hate that word too. No child is an accident. But her condition was. An unbelievably cruel quirk of fate, a biological anomaly that meant she would never live, in any state, no matter what we did, no matter how much I . . . we willed it.

It was still a full labour, I was distraught. After she was born, I called them back, the staff who tried to take her away. I'd clambered from the bed, but the drip connected to my arm kept me tethered. They were already almost out of earshot, or not listening, believing, perhaps, that what they did was for the best. *Don't let the moment linger*, I'd heard one of them whisper as they left the room.

I called to Duncan to go after them. I'd thought I didn't have the courage to look at her; they *had* asked me, but I'd said no. At sixteen weeks, she was no bigger than a small pear. I'd caught a brief glimpse of her shape but turned my head away, too fearful of what I might see. I've regretted that ever since. It's haunted me, that failure to even look upon my newborn daughter in those first and last moments. But I wouldn't leave her to be thrown in to some furnace, disposed of in such an impersonal, functional way.

We can deal with it, they'd said. *There are procedures. You don't want to go to the crematorium, she won't be the only one; there will be other babies and it'll only distress you further.*

I'd felt suspicion rise over me. They'd asked me if I was willing to let her be used for research. I'd said no. The very idea appalled me. She wasn't just another body part, a liver or a kidney, or a sample of cancerous flesh. I couldn't let my child be dissected or held in a jar. Or dumped and burnt with all those others. I sent Duncan running from the room and eventually he brought her back. In a simple plastic container with an opaque lid, no bigger than the size of a tissue box.

We signed the forms and took her home, against all advice. Legally, they couldn't stop us. I don't know what they thought we were going to do with her, but surely it would be more dignified, more respectful and loving than what they had planned.

I still couldn't look at her, or even hold her. But I did give her a name.

Evangeline Margery Henderson.

In the end, Duncan said it had to be done now, not later, that already her body was decomposing. He'd do it, he said, I didn't have to come with him. At the last minute, I tugged on his arm.

'Please,' I said. 'I want to see.'

He took her out, holding her so carefully on a white muslin cloth in the cusp of his hand. I gazed upon her in silence. When he turned away, I tugged again.

'I'll come with you,' I said.

He'd found the perfect spot, deep within the reservoir dam, in a long-abandoned channel, where it would be dry and safe, where no one could disturb her and no animal could ever get to her . . . I couldn't bear to think of that.

'The old tunnels,' he said. 'The old waterworks beneath the dam. I know how to get in there. No one will ever know.'

I nodded.

The reservoir was the place that meant the most to us, where Duncan and I had spent so much of our time together as students. Where Evangeline had most likely been conceived.

We went together. We carved out a dry ledge well away from the main channels and tucked her box into it. Duncan bricked the whole thing in and I gave him the coin. The puppetrider.

'Place it next to her,' I said, folding his fingers around the coin. 'Let her take it with her, to wherever, whatever that might be.'

I don't know what I believed. Death is something we each of us choose not to think about. Until we must. He did as I bid.

My mother had given the coin to me when I was a child. She'd said her mother had given it to her, that it had been found in the water, the river near the house where generations of the family had once lived. She'd kept it all those years, waiting to pass it on. She said that it was the most precious thing she had, apart from us children.

She'd spoken with love in her heart.

So *I* passed it on. I gave it to *my* daughter.

Duncan used the coin as a marker for her grave, cementing it between the bricks end on. There was this unspoken pact between us after that. That we would never speak of her again. We both of us wanted to move on.

Is that a sin? Wanting to forget and move on? To *live*?

CHAPTER 71

CLAIRE – AFTER

To the east, the night sky fades to pink and a haze of vacillating colour radiates across the horizon. Dawn and dusk are the two times of the day when the landscape in this valley shimmers, like the spring and autumn equinox, on the cusp of one state and another. This is when the mists thrive, when both sun and moon are present in the sky, bending the fragile light, allowing the creatures of both worlds to meet.

As I stand on the dam, I think of myself like that, straddling one world and the next, alone in my head with all the memory and pain trapped within. I never dreamed for one moment that I would ever have an abortion. You don't. This hadn't been an unwanted child; unplanned, yes, but never unwanted.

I remember the anti-abortion leaflets at the student union, pictures of aborted foetuses, lurid headlines of moral judgement, religious assumptions about the value of life from the moment of conception. Those few days between hearing the news and effecting the abortion were the worst days of my life. And no one *cared*. Or so it seemed to me. Duncan didn't want to talk about it and I couldn't share it with anyone else. We hadn't told our parents or family about the pregnancy and Duncan didn't want me to now. They'd only pass judgement, he said. Complicate matters. I knew he was right. And I couldn't share something so personal, so devastating with anyone else. I wasn't offered counselling or any other support. Just a medical result and a choice to be made. Sooner rather than later, they said.

I scoured the internet. I cried and cried and sat there tormented by the need to make a decision, thinking about all those arguments for and against, about when a baby can survive outside the womb. But Evangeline could never have survived outside the womb. The prognosis was so bad, it was highly unlikely we'd even get to term. There was no further discussion about this with the doctors, no debate. There was no need – the diagnosis was unequivocal. The consultant immediately assumed I would, should, of course, abort. They waited only for my signature on that wretched form. My signature. Not Duncan's.

Duncan. I couldn't forgive his indifference. His refusal to talk. It seared in my heart that he wouldn't let me talk about it. That he wouldn't share the burden of that decision. I loved him so much then. *Coward* – that's what I thought later, in my bitterness.

And that's how our unhappiness began. His betrayal. Everything that came later was just consequences.

On the maternity ward, I was hustled into a side room at the end of the corridor. It was clear that some of the midwives thought differently. That I had made a 'choice' that some of them abhorred. They scowled at my request for pain relief, as if I didn't deserve it. They told me not to leave the room or walk down the corridor. One of them even jabbed my arm so roughly with her needles that I whimpered every time. She didn't seem to notice. All this as my body was wracked with the pain of contractions that had no real purpose.

I took every drug I could lay my hands on and listened to music to distract myself from the cries of the newborn babies further down the ward. I guess if your work is all about bringing children into the world, you perhaps don't want to participate in the flip side of that. Abortion. I can understand that.

It *was* my choice. Not Duncan's, not the doctors', nor anyone else. My body, my responsibility, my decision. My failure, my fault. Ultimately, I was to blame, not God or science or fate, nor anyone else, that was how I felt. Then. I see it differently now. Oddly, it was an easy decision to make, however painful, because she was so profoundly affected.

'You'll go on to have another one.'

It was one of the older, more experienced midwives, sitting on the edge of my bed.

'There's no reason to worry this will happen again. Not at your age. I've seen so many other mums go on to have a thriving, healthy family. You're only twenty-three. You've got all the time in the world, luv. Every time it's a shake of the dice and the odds are so against this ever happening again.'

She meant well. I know she did. The doctors had said the same. But I hated that phrase, 'shake of the dice'. It was too casual, too random. Chance can go either way, for good or bad.

With time, I have come to understand that this was fate, a cruel quirk of fate. I had no control over her condition. I was not to blame; nor Duncan, either.

And I will always grieve for her. My daughter.

CHAPTER 72

DUNCAN – AFTER

We were married, Claire and I. It was a marriage hastily arranged after she fell pregnant, *before* we got the news. Before the abortion.

It had mattered to us both. Her, because she wanted that security for our child; me, because I thought it was the right thing to do. I like to think I'm a good man, but good men still make the wrong decisions. And I loved her. I loved her body and her mind. Her sharp intelligence and quirky sense of humour. I loved her fierce support of everything I did and her determination. We might not have married as quickly as we did, if she hadn't fallen pregnant, but I always thought that eventually, once I was established with my career, we *would* get married.

We didn't tell our families. They'd have wanted to know why, to make us wait and do the whole big wedding thing. We knew both our families couldn't really afford it. It was a madcap student wedding done on a shoestring – Claire wore a second-hand floaty summer dress, and I wore jeans and a dinner jacket. Martin tied a bunch of old cans to Claire's bicycle and Claire and I rode it home, Claire balanced on the handle bars, the both of us screeching with laughter, not caring who saw or heard us.

That evening we shared a bottle of champagne on the back doorstep of our student digs. We were penniless but happy then. Not after.

Summer turned to autumn and I began my new veterinary career. After five years at uni, I was champing at the bit. I joined a practice in Derby as a junior vet and Claire found a position as a research assistant. No one knew about the baby. It wasn't something either of us wanted to share.

Things had changed. After the abortion, she seemed to pull away from me. She wasn't carefree like before. In the days leading up to the abortion, she was so upset, I didn't know what to do or say – there *was* nothing I could say. I couldn't change the outcome. We had to get on with it, move on. I think when you see animals dying all the time, you come to realise life is cruel but you have to be practical. Save the next one. You do what you can, to the very extent that you can, but when there's nothing more that can be done, you have to let it go.

You can't live with it otherwise.

I think she thought I was indifferent. Or that I was even relieved. That I could get on with my career without worrying about being a parent. It didn't seem to occur to her that maybe I had lost a child, too. That I couldn't bear to talk about it over and over.

Nor did it occur to her that I was worried it might happen

again. I felt to blame, that it was my family's genes, not hers. I could see what Becky, my sister, was going through. She was having all sorts of problems with her son by then with his own medical condition. The doctors told me no, it had nothing to do with what had affected Alex, that although it was a genetic abnormality it wasn't one passed down through the family. But I still felt to blame, as if I had put Claire and our baby through all this.

Becky is a passionate defender of pro-life beliefs. We could never tell her, she'd never have understood, even though Evangeline's condition was profoundly different – survival under whatever circumstance just wasn't going to happen.

Everything I did after the abortion got spun the other way. My silence was indifference, my friendships disloyalty, my efforts to improve our lives arrogance and vanity. Claire accused me of being too immersed in my work. I accused her of being obsessed with making a home. She was nest-building, I guess, readying herself for another throw of the dice. As if somehow that would put things right. We bickered over money and location and everything else, punishing each other for each new offence. We stopped spending our weekends together on the hills. Sex was our only meeting point, a way to make up after an argument.

Eventually, she fell pregnant with Joe. It wasn't planned and I felt so guilty, putting her through that again. She was sick as a dog just like before and we spent nine months terrified something would go wrong. I know what they mean now about counting the baby's toes.

Joe was born healthy and beautiful. And a new set of problems began. Joe's problems. Every time I approached Claire, she pushed me away. She said I did the same. I think she was depressed, beyond the normal ups and downs of motherhood. But then hadn't she a right to be? And the shadow of Evangeline still haunted us. Claire couldn't forgive herself for what had happened, or me. How could she let me make *love* to her, she said, after Joe, when there was no longer any emotional connection between us?

It was all about her.

But there were two of us in this marriage, didn't she realise that?

CHAPTER 73

CLAIRE – AFTER

It was never the same again after Evangeline, even after Joe. Our marriage never had a chance. Joe was the accident – oh, God how I really, really hate that phrase. Joe was the only good thing that came from our marriage. But now Joe is dead.

I look down at the dam. I feel the sense of enclosure, the depth of water, the vast energy held in check by this great wall of concrete. Man-made. That's me, isn't it? This place is all about holding back, keeping things under control. There has to be a balance, I see that now, between letting go and holding in – too much or little of either is destructive.

Perhaps I should have had more sympathy for my husband. He held it all in and focused on the practical and I couldn't reach him. I remember how Frances came to the Barn for dinner once, not long after it was completed. She was so in awe of the place, all the careful attention to detail, the smooth lines and perfect symmetry.

'Duncan must love you very much,' she said, when she followed me into the kitchen. 'He talks of nothing else but how much he wants you to like the Barn, for you to be happy. If only all husbands were like that!'

I saw it as intrusive. How dare she bring me to task, as if he needed my approval for anything he did, as if he was trying to make it up to me. And then it dawned on me. She *knew* about Evangeline. He must have told her, despite everything he'd said about keeping it from our families. I was so angry.

But that wasn't what she meant. Frances didn't have an agenda. She meant to be kind – why didn't I see it before? I've been so overwhelmed by my own feelings, my own needs, all this time, that I didn't think of him. Everyone assumes it's the mother's loss, but it's the father's, too. I'd been so intent on wanting him to listen to me, that I hadn't thought to listen to *him*. Or that Duncan must have felt he was losing me as well as his child. Evangeline, and Joe too. I failed Duncan even more than I failed Joe.

By day, I have walked amongst people who carry on with their daily lives unknowing, uncaring of the grief that roots me to this place. By night, I have lain awake, immersed in my own fears, reliving every moment of the past as if that might change how things turned out. I have felt as if I could never leave this valley, here where my daughter lies beneath my feet and my son lay trapped in the water.

It seems prophetic to me now, that the puppetrider coin, which I set in place to watch over Evangeline, found Joe. And now it has found me again. I clutch the coin in my hand as if my life depends on it. Like an unlucky penny that won't go away.

I turn to face the reservoir, draped with its sweeping layer of white. The day breaks and the fog begins to stir, weakening its grip. It separates to reveal dark ripples that move with the belly of a current that should not be there. A black shape appears through the mist, the water swaying back and forth, like it's some ancient creature emerging from the deep, something prehistoric that's always been hidden from human view. An island. I've never seen an island here before.

I see green rock and stone blocks tumbling one over another. They're gleaming wet. They morph into walls, broken and dysfunctional, but with the definite shape of a building. Gaping holes frame the sky where once there must have been huge windows and above it all stands a church tower, almost complete, from which a narrow steeple points upwards. At its tip is the leaning, twisted metal cross. The one I have seen slowly rising all this time.

Sunlight is creeping down the hills and burning off the mist. The last few fragile strands slip through the gaps in the walls of the church and hang like giant cobwebs across the arched windows. The glass has long gone, but some wood remains, rafters and beams that hold up the tower. The rest of the building is barely stones and pillars that stake out the original shape of the church, rising from the earth like the empty husk of a whale. Green and wet, it steams gently as the day begins to heat.

I don't understand where this has come from. Perhaps it's like before, when the church emerged in a drought. But there is no drought. Quite the opposite. The water flow in the reservoir has been reversed, taking the excess water over the last few days from the surrounding flooded land. It makes no sense, revealing once more the old church. It's the church of St Bertram's, isn't it? Drowned all those years ago.

The one that Harry's daughter, Nat, told me had been demolished.

CHAPTER 74

CLAIRE – AFTER

Is that Duncan standing by the tree? The fog has lifted completely and in my confusion about my memories and the island I hadn't realised that was him. Why have I left it so long? I've been so near to him and yet so far. Is there still a chance for us? – I could believe that now. I've always loved him. I think he loves me too, despite what he said. If I can just let him.

No more memories, no more pain, no more grief and hurt and loss. I think of that story of the wife who held on despite all that the faerie queen could throw at her. What if I go to him and tell him I love him one more time?

I push away from the railing and run back across the dam. My shoes slap against unforgiving pavement. The sound bounces against the concave wall beneath like the lost cry of a child in an empty playground. My feet land on soft wood chippings and I race along the path into the woods. My eyes search for a glimpse of the dead flower tree and Duncan, and once more I see him in the distance.

The early morning light casts long shadows through the trees, shafts of shimmering gold between the black. My chest is burning. I have to stop to lean against a tree. I drag the chill air into my burning lungs and my fingers curl against the rough bark. Somewhere in the distance is the scream of a fox.

The path leads directly to the shore. I run and for the first time I am not afraid. The woods are filled with the vivid scent of wet moss and dry pine and I hear my own heartbeat thudding in my chest. I feel my upper body lift, my chest no longer in pain. My arms and legs are pumping with a strong purposeful rhythm as I dodge the trees and power across the uneven ground. I only stop when I reach the shore and the closest point to the island.

A last hub of mist lingers around the old tower. It fills the void where there should be only water. I am so close, I can see the individual strands of ivy, the green ferns that hang between the gaps in the stonework, the bold, intrusive shape of its staggered, bleeding walls.

The path has disappeared behind me. I've been following the hidden animal tracks, worn away over time. I am the same as them, the creatures of this woodland, pure instinct, blood and flesh made good. As I look out across the water, I feel more alive than I have ever been. I can't see Duncan. Where has he gone?

Instead, I see all around me creatures along the shore. Deer pushing through the undergrowth, a family of badgers on the bank. There are cows and sheep that flick their ears, and on the water, ducks and geese that swim out from the reeds and spin around to face me.

I don't feel threatened. A buzzard swoops low over the reservoir, its long shadow streaking past the island. Its cry is like a call to all the others.

She's here.

The sun warms my deadened skin. It's the first time I've felt warm in a long time, my fingers tingling. But it's the cold reservoir that holds my gaze. It's sparkling clear and I can see something through the water. A solid shape of gleaming metal, three windows still intact and a swell of fish that slip and slither in the murk – the remnants of my car.

The metal roof is crumpled and bent, the wheels torn and shredded. The doors and bonnet are scratched and dented as if the whole thing has been dragged by the intermittent currents this way and that. The car is draped with brown and green weeds like a beggar cloaked in rags. One of the rear doors has been wrenched open and on the back seat is a body.

I feel my blood chill. I don't want to look. I don't want to remember that last sight of my son. I don't want to see what's inside.

I feel a shadow cross my back. I turn round.

'Duncan?'

But it's not Duncan. It's someone else.

I stumble backwards. It's the man from the village, my landlord, the rider. I cast a look across to the island. It is so much closer now and I see people crowding on the bank. The old woman and a host of others I don't recognise, a strangely mismatched congregation standing in the old church openings. The wind tangles long threads of riverweed over their heads and the sun shines through the building, giving colour to their old and faded clothes. The woman from the village lifts one hand and smiles at me. My mouth opens as if to speak, but I can't bring myself to say the words.

And all the time my eyes are drawn back towards the car and the shape slumped over on the back seat.

I vaguely think about the crumpled mess that is my car. *My* car – Duncan chose *my* car so that his would stay squeaky clean. I hope he thinks about that, that he broods on it every single day.

'I don't think you'll be driving that again,' says the Puppetrider.

I follow his gaze. To the car and the body trapped within. It's not Joe. I feel the joy of it sweep through my body. He's alive! I've got this all wrong. I remember now, he got out, after me, after the car sank to the bottom of the reservoir, after the water pressure equalised and the door could finally be released.

My eyes swing back to the tree with its flowers. The blue-and-white ribbons that flutter in the breeze. No, I'm not sure. Doubt clouds my heart. My memory deceives me. My joy plummets. It took too long, Joe trapped on the back seat. He panicked, struggling with his seatbelt. Duncan didn't realise. And I couldn't help Joe. I couldn't get him out. I tried and tried, finally pushing my way through the gap, but by the time I got the belt loose and the door open, it was too late.

After. Somehow Joe's body must have floated away, drifting on the currents towards the spillway. It must have been sucked down into the tunnels until it wedged up against a wall, where it waited all those weeks. Lost. Missing. Until the old water-works were flooded again, the first time in a long time, and it was released.

Then it drifted once more until it found the muddy banks,

his body stuck, his limbs floating out like riverweed, blank, sightless eyes staring through the green murk of the water. Joining the rest of them, these people who stand around me, who were buried at the bottom of our garden.

All this time that I've been searching, inhabiting the cottage that should have been mine . . . hoping to find Joe . . . to understand my loss . . .

Haunting the valley.

That's finished, I know it now. I only have to go to that island to find him. It's not Joe's body resting on the back seat of that car. Nor anyone else's.

It's mine.

CHAPTER 75

DUNCAN – AFTER

Duncan stood by the tree on the road, overlooking the reservoir. The water was still swathed in drifting fog. It seemed to him to have been like that ever since the accident.

He'd placed the flowers there every week since that day. Carnations, chrysanthemums, alstroemeria and zinnia – flowers that last. For Claire. And sunflowers, big and bold and full of life. For Joe.

His hand reached out to the flowers, letting the petals drop between his fingers. Grey and dry, they fluttered down like shreds of burnt paper. Like an illicit love letter thrown then snatched too late from the fire.

Claire must have hated him in the end. Those last hours filled with a burning resentment over Sally. Their feelings had simmered, had done long before that, waiting to come to the boil, the atmosphere in the house like a volcano about to explode. And all the time, Joe had watched and waited with trepidation, not knowing what to say, what to do, or where to go. What did you expect a kid of that age to do, to feel?

Why had he, Duncan, slept with all those women? Why had he married Claire? Why had things panned out the way they had, that first summer after Claire and he had graduated from university? They had both suffered a cruel twist of fate. Life was a sequence of never-ending choices, a decision table, this way, that way, yes or no. But not all of it was under your control. And the arrows never pointed back the way you'd come. Time doesn't work like that.

Claire had said it was his fault, their combined misery. That she'd lost her career, her independence. She'd trusted him, loved him, and he'd let her down. But she had made her choices too. She should have accepted responsibility for that, not blamed it all on him.

After the accident, things with Sally had changed. His fault, not hers. He'd kept her distant, just like he had Claire. Sally's status had been unclear, he got that – the *other* woman. It was made worse by the fact Sally worked at the surgery and further complicated by her being Martin's daughter. Duncan had just lost his wife and son. It was not the time to stir things up and go public. Let alone trigger a confrontation with Martin.

Duncan had been like a wounded animal, snapping and biting at those who would help. He was confused, filled with guilt and self-loathing. Everyone had said it was a dreadful tragedy. But to Duncan, it had been the culmination of all of his infidelities, the bickering and tension, his deliberate withdrawal of affection for Claire, his failure to consider the impact of all that on Joe. It was even down to his choices on that day. If only they'd driven in his new car, with its winter tyres and traction. If only he hadn't asked Claire to ring Sally. If only he'd not been out of control, angry, worried about Arthur, driving too fast for the conditions. If only it hadn't snowed like that. Or the dog had never been run over in the first place. Or they'd never had the dog at all. If Garfield had been a better owner, if, if . . .

One split second when *before* was 'normal' and everything was okay.

And *after*, when everything was not.

After that day, he'd functioned but didn't feel. Ignoring his pain, seeking distraction where he could, just as he had before. Denial, anger, work, it was the only way he knew to cope. He was aware that he was alienating people. He didn't deserve their patience, their kindness or Sally's love. She was gone now and he knew she wouldn't change her mind. Would she tell Martin? Probably not.

Time – isn't that what everyone said? Time will heal. That's a load of bollocks, he thought. Time doesn't heal, ever.

The police had recovered the car within twenty-four hours, along with the body of his wife and Arthur, their pet dog. But not Joe. Somehow Joe's body had floated free of the car once one of the rear doors had drifted open. Duncan had had to live with the knowledge that he hadn't been able to save any of them.

The police search hadn't stopped; Martin had said they would find Joe eventually. That moment had come. He knew forensics would soon officially confirm that the body they'd found was Joe.

It was a good thing. The thought of his son's body lost in the reservoir had been agonising. Now Duncan could cremate his son and take his ashes to scatter alongside those of his wife and dog, from the dam.

Something small glittered at his feet, half submerged in the mud. Duncan reached down and picked it up. It was a coin.

Using his finger and thumb, he washed it briefly in the water. On one side was the head of an emperor, with an arrowhead poking from the eye socket. On the other was a half-skeleton rider on a horse. The Rider. The Puppetrider.

Duncan stared at it. Claire had said that Joe had found the coin. It must have fallen from his son's pocket into the water. There was no hoard. Never had been. Duncan had already made it clear to Ray Turner and his friends that he didn't want them anywhere near his land. Or Martin would intervene.

But Duncan knew what it was. That rider figure on the coin. Curiosity had prompted him to look it up after he'd placed it beside Evangeline. The Puppetrider was a strange pagan character. Academics were undecided as to whom or what he was. Something akin to Charon the ferryman, perhaps, the mythical figure who guides the dead to their proper place of rest. A collector of lost souls, or hunter, chasing down those newly departed not yet accepting of their fate. Helping them to move on.

Duncan contemplated the coin, letting his fingers feel the shape of the pattern embossed in the metal.

He closed his eyes. He squeezed them tight, still refusing to let himself cry. He didn't deserve that release. One day, maybe, given time. When he was finally ready to forgive himself. But he did forgive her.

Raising the coin to his lips, he kissed it. *For Joe*, he thought. He held the coin close and then kissed it again. *For Claire*.

Then he threw it far out across the water.

Acknowledgements

I feel I have grown to know Derbyshire a little better in the writing of this book. Living here and watching the way the countryside changes over the course of the seasons was a part of what inspired the ideas for this book. As were the tools of my oral storytelling trade, the way people communicate, empathise, each listener interpreting a story in their own way according to their own life experiences and mindset. It got me thinking about how perspectives differ, stories grow and mistakes are made that can suddenly spin out of control. And the damage that can do.

There are two interconnected folk tales that spawned the initial idea. One story tells of how a vicar confronts the pagan beliefs that linger in his village. He is asked by his parishioners to preach a sermon 'to the dead'. He indulges them, and on New Year's Eve is horrified to see his church filled with the newly dead, including those who will die in the coming year. One of which is him. That village was Derwent Village, itself drowned in the creation of Ladybower Reservoir, to the north of Derbyshire. Later, the village church was said to reappear when the water levels reduced, and its bells heard tolling in the water when the water levels were high. This, despite the fact the church was demolished after it was first revealed by a drought. I took those ideas and transposed them to a valley

371

near to where I live. Add to that the sad story of St Bertram (mentioned in the book), and the haze of wet weather that hangs over our own house on the hill in autumn and spring, and the ideas began to fuse.

Writing a second book under contract is a very different experience to writing your first one out of contract – less time, more intense, with deadlines and a formal editing process – I have found it exciting and inspiring to work with the team at Avon. My sincere thanks go to my editor Rachel Faulkner-Willcocks and to Tilda McDonald who took over towards the end as Rachel went on her maternity leave. It's been a delight to work with and involve the team in feedback right from the early stages of the book. I'd like to thank Claire Pickering, my copy editor; that last stage is like a final polish, very satisfying, and her eagle eyes spotted so much that I missed. My sincere thanks too, go to Sabah Khan, Molly Walker-Sharp, the HarperCollins Canada team and Emma Pallant (who narrated the audio book of *The Stranger in Our Home*, bringing it to life so wonderfully). And to everyone else who I haven't perhaps met but who have still been involved in the production and marketing of both *The Stranger in Our Home* and *The House of Secrets*. I couldn't ask for a more supportive, and kindly, environment to write in.

I also wanted to thank those bloggers, readers and fellow authors who supported *The Stranger in Our Home* when it first came out. There are too many to name each of you but I was overwhelmed by the support with tweets and reviews as the book was launched, and very appreciative of the time people took to read the book and comment on it. I have particularly enjoyed all those little messages and kind words that came my way from readers. They motivate me each day, thank you. For a new author, it has been brilliant and exciting and nerve-wracking all at the same time.

I have to mention and thank my friends and fellow #Doomsbury writers: Roz Watkins, Fran Dorricott, Louise Trevatt and Jo Jakeman. Our journeys each continue, and Lou's work with rescued dogs inspires. I hope a little bit of her love for dogs is in this book too. I'd like to thank Coleen Coxon and Gemma Allen for being early beta readers for *The House of Secrets* and for their ongoing generosity, kindness and support.

I also had invaluable advice from a couple of police contacts which has been very much appreciated. I promised not to name you but my thanks are nonetheless there.

Finally, my thanks go to my family – my husband Rob, and our boys: Ben, Jamie and Jasper. And to my parents, Ronald and Irene. Their interest and on-going support and patience has meant the world to me and kept me going through what was a difficult year. Not because of the writing, but those other things that we encounter in life. For me, that included breaking both my legs in the summer (and being unable to walk or drive for months), and then later, the very sad loss of my sister Anne. I am sure this has influenced *The House of Secrets*. As the first draft took shape, and later with editing, I experienced both grief and a sense of isolation, and the realisation that life, with all its troubles, is to some extent just what happens. It may be framed and moulded by our response but some things still remain outside our control.

At the front of this book, I have dedicated it to each of my much-loved boys, as per my original plan. But this book is also dedicated, with love always, to my sister, Anne.

Don't miss Sophie Draper's debut
psychological suspense

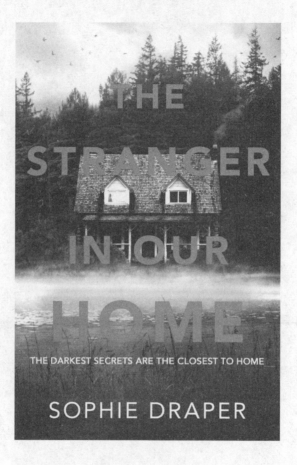

Available now